Blue Moon

(The Blue Crystal Trilogy)

Book One

Pat Spence

Blue Moon

For Steve and Amelia, my inspiration and muse…

Pat Spence

'All other things, to their destruction draw,
Only our love hath no decay...'
The Anniversarie. John Donne.

Love, all alike, no season knows, nor clyme,
Nor houres, dayes, moneths, which are the rags of time.
The Sunne Rising. John Donne.

Pat Spence

THE BEGINNING

30. The Blue Crystal
31. Attack II
32. The Lunari
33. Family

THE BEGINNING

Monday 25th March 2013 was an ordinary day, no different to any other.
But when I look back, I see now that this was the day things began to change.

I can also see that I couldn't and wouldn't have changed a thing. It was as if everything that happened was somehow pre-ordained, and I was simply playing my part in a story that was meant to be, that had started many thousands of years ago....

PART ONE: ATTRACTION

1. The Viewing

The estate agent glanced impatiently at her watch, and looked out of the window for the fifth time that minute. 'Time-wasters,' she muttered to herself pursing her lips with irritation, 'they probably won't show. Just like that lot the day before. And if they do, there's no way they'll want to buy this old heap'. A look of distaste passed across her carefully made-up face as she glanced around the room. The once ornate fireplace had long since lost its earlier splendour and was now dimpled and chipped. A large chandelier hung from the central ceiling rose, cracked and mottled, and pieces of the delicately decorated ceiling scattered the floor like old confetti, yellowed with age. Everywhere, the stench of damp and decay hung heavy, the windows too rotten to open and let in fresh air.

Outside, the grounds fell away into the distance, a mass of tangled vegetation and thick undergrowth. The once formal gardens were now desolate and unkempt, the flower beds ravaged by age and neglect, and the pathways choked by an advancing army of weeds and lichen. Above it all the Cedars of Lebanon towered, majestic and tall, looking sadly over the mayhem below.

The estate agent moved her manicured forefinger down the filthy glass, trying to see out a little better and get a glimpse of her missing clients.

Without warning, a loud bell sounded in the hallway, making her jump.

"What the...?" she muttered, "How did they get to the front door? I never saw them coming."

Baffled, she rushed out of the ballroom and into the vast hall. The huge brass bell echoed again in the cavernous walls.

"Alright, alright," she called, hurrying to open the huge, metal studded oak door, stiff with disuse. The door creaked open, its hinges rusty and unyielding, and the estate agent peered out, her eyes struggling to take in the brightness of the sunshine after the gloominess within. A man and a woman stood on the doorstep.

"Mr and Mrs de Lucis?" she asked falteringly.

"That's us. So sorry we're late," said the blonde woman before her, with a voice as soft as butter candy. "I hope we haven't kept you."

"No, not at all," said the estate agent, her eyes wide open in disbelief, taking in the sleek black car that stood outside and the swarthy chauffeur who lounged nonchalantly against the passenger door, "I didn't see you arrive, that's all."

"Can we come in?" said Mr de Lucis, with a smile, revealing perfect white teeth.

"O… of course," said the estate agent, stepping back, and allowing the couple to enter. She swung the heavy oak door back into place, feeling so unsettled she quite failed to register that it swung easily and noiselessly back into place, without a hint of rust or creakiness.

She turned to look at the couple, noticing how they seemed to light up the dark entrance hall. Tall, elegant and well dressed, each wore a pair of large sunglasses, giving them an air of mystery and more than a touch of Hollywood glamour. Mrs de Lucis wore a pale pink pencil skirt with matching jacket, showing off her slender figure to perfection. A string of pearls nestled at her neckline, and her blonde hair was pinned back in a chignon, giving emphasis to her high cheekbones, small straight nose and pale pink lips. To say she was beautiful was plainly an understatement.

Like his wife, Mr de Lucis was impossibly good looking. His face was strong and chiselled, framed by tousled, blonde hair, and there was no denying the athletic build beneath his expensive pale blue suit. To the estate agent, he was the closest thing to a Greek god she had ever encountered. They were probably in their early thirties, she guessed, staring enviously at their flawless pale skin. It was as smooth and white as alabaster. Simultaneously, they removed their sunglasses, revealing the most electric blue eyes she had ever seen.

She stared, fascinated, and for a moment struggled to find a word to describe them. Striking? That didn't do them justice. Stylish? They were more than that. Then she had it. Radiant! That was it. They were like two exquisite jewels, shining brightly.

"Are you alright?" enquired Mr de Lucis, in a caramel smooth voice that took her breath away.

"Yes, I'm fine," she said, gazing into his deep blue eyes and feeling a strange fluttering in her stomach, "I'm sorry, I didn't hear your car. I was a little surprised to see you, that's all."

"It has a very quiet engine," said Mrs de Lucis, in her smooth, silky voice. "One doesn't always hear it. Now, perhaps you could tell us about the house."

The estate agent snapped into professional mode. "Yes, of course. Please, follow me." She led the way into the ballroom, talking animatedly: "Hartswell Hall is a wonderful example of Victorian architecture. It was built by a wealthy merchant in 1851 for his wife, who sadly died before she could move in. It had many uses over the years, but was most recently owned by a recluse, who shut himself away from the world. It went on the market nearly two years ago, when he died. As you can see, it is in need of a little re-decoration." She laughed affectedly.

"More than a little," said Mr de Lucis, prodding one of the rotting window frames and revealing the black decay beneath.

"But nothing we can't handle," said his wife, running her fingers down the chipped stone fireplace, then removing a cobweb that hung from the chandelier, "Have you had many viewings?"

The estate agent stared. Was it her imagination, or did the chandelier suddenly look brighter, as if life had suddenly been breathed back into it? And didn't the carvings on the fireplace look somehow a little more defined? She shook her head and focused on the question.

"Viewings? Oh, yes," she said, seizing the opportunity, "There are plenty of people interested in this property. I wouldn't be surprised if it went to sealed bids. It has great potential."

"It certainly does," said Mrs de Lucis, her voice barely discernible, "I think it will suit our purposes admirably." She glanced at her husband. "We'd like to make an offer."

"You would?" asked the estate agent, in surprise, "Don't you want to look around?"

"That won't be necessary," replied Mr de Lucis, "We've seen enough."

It was enough for the estate agent. Scenting a deal in the making, she drew out a clipboard from her large shiny handbag and snapped into pecuniary mode.

Right," she said, "As you know, it's on the market for £1.5 million, but we do have other interested parties."

"£2 million," purred Mrs de Lucis, "That's what we're prepared to pay."

"For total exclusivity," added her husband, "No other viewings, no other offers considered. Do we have a deal?"

The estate agent could hardly believe her luck.

"£2 million? We most certainly do. I'll need to run it by the Executors, of course, but I don't anticipate a problem. Consider Hartswell Hall yours. Congratulations!"

She went to shake Mr de Lucis's smooth white hand, starting slightly as an electrical charge seemed to pass from his hand to hers. As she looked into his eyes, she noticed small flecks of grey that glinted like granite amidst the electric blue.

Behind her, Mrs de Lucis smiled agreeably.

Outside, the rust-bound hands of the three golden clocks that adorned the old Clock Tower began to move slowly and inexorably around their tarnished faces.

2. Meeting Theo

I wiggled my toes to the bottom of the bed, feeling cosy and warm. I tried to open my eyes, but the effort was just too much and I lay back on the pillow, luxuriating in its downy softness and trying desperately to get back into my dream. Somewhere in the distance I could hear my name being called, but the pull of sleep was just too great. I couldn't respond.

"Emily," the voice sounded, getting louder, "Wake up."

I felt someone shake my shoulders gently.

"What time is it?" I rubbed my eyes, trying to see the red digital figures on the alarm clock.

"Time for you to get up if you don't want to miss the bus," came my mother's voice.

There was an edge to her voice that said: 'If you don't respond now, I will get very annoyed,' and I sat upright, noticing with horror that it was already 7.30am.

"Mum, have you seen the time?" I shouted at her, "I've only got half an hour before the bus goes. Why didn't you wake me sooner?"

'Better get a move on, then, hadn't you?" she retorted, "Your breakfast is ready, all you have to do is eat it and put some clothes on."

I quickly pulled on a pair of old grey jeans, ripped at the knee, a black T-shirt and my new grey SuperDry jacket, a recent purchase on ebay. Converse trainers and a black leather rucksack completed the look. Yes, that worked. I might be late, but I still had an image to keep up.

Running into the bathroom, I splashed cold water on my face and took a good look in the mirror. Yuk. Dark circles under my eyes made me look ancient. I searched through the various pots and potions on the shelf until I found my mother's Instant-Action Anti-Fatigue Eye Gel. *'Refreshes skin, reduces puffiness, regenerates appearance. Proven formula. Instant results....'* Great, just what I needed. My mother swore by this. I applied it liberally and was instantly disappointed. If anything, it accentuated the dark circles, which now glistened brightly. Sighing impatiently, I attempted to wipe it off and applied eyeliner to my now greasy eyes, usually my best feature. Why did these disasters always occur when you were late? I quickly dragged a brush through my tangled blonde hair and tied it up in a high ponytail. That would have to do. One day I would find the time to have a proper beauty routine. Grabbing my rucksack, I ran to the top of the stairs, and letting my hand slide down the stair rail, took the steps two at a time, rushing into the breakfast room, breathless and flushed.

Granddad was already there, wearing his brown cardigan and eating his usual boiled egg and toast. Mum was in the kitchen, stacking up the dishwasher.

This was my family: Mum, blonde, pretty, a young-looking forty year old, who worked as a wages clerk for a local timber company, and Granddad, aged somewhere in his 70's. Mum had divorced my dad when I was just two and had never remarried despite various offers. He lived in America and worked in sound production, but I didn't have much to do with him. There'd been sporadic contact over the years, when he'd visited the UK on business, but when I was ten, he'd remarried and started a new family. After that, there'd never been room in his new life for me and, to be honest, it didn't much bother me. I'd been too young when he left to have established a relationship with him, and on the few occasions I had seen him there'd been such a distance and awkwardness between us I was always glad when the visit came to an end. Enforced trips to McDonalds and the cinema were hardly my idea of a laugh, and I dreaded the obligatory questions about school and family. Over the years, he'd sent me a few photos of my new step-siblings, twin girls and a boy, but they looked nothing like me. They were thick set and dark, and I could never relate to them as family. It would be quite interesting to meet them, I suppose, but there again, you don't miss what you've never had. So I didn't give them much thought and was actually quite relieved when dad stopped visiting. And, of course, we had Granddad. We'd lived with Granddad for fourteen years now, ever since my gran had died and the house had got too big for him. It was an arrangement that suited us all. Mum and I had exchanged our small, rented flat in the city for a nice house in a village, in the right catchment area for the best local schools. Granddad had company and we had security. Mum had a permanent baby-sitter and I had a surrogate father figure, albeit a granddad. Although, mum did get a bit miffed when people occasionally mistook him for her elderly husband, which was always a source of amusement for me. I mean, who in their right mind could think my mum and granddad were an item? He looked just like a granddad: snowy white hair, twinkly bright eyes and a kind, friendly face that was always smiling. There again, by implication those same people must have thought he was my dad, which is a bit embarrassing now I think about it, although it's hardly something I'd lose any sleep over. He was just my Granddad and he was there when I needed him. I didn't think much beyond that. His nose was permanently in a book, and when not reading, he'd be listening to jazz records - most of my formative years had been spent listening to Acker Bilk, Kenny Ball and his Jazz Men, Louis Armstrong, Dizzy Gillespie and other notable greats. He also had a predilection for wearing carpet slippers and brown cardigans, despite mum's best efforts to smarten him up. As you can see, not exactly the kind of husband you'd automatically place with a well-presented, fit-looking, forty year old woman.

"Morning Gramps," I shouted at him, making him jump, then grinning widely at him.

"Morning, Emily," he said, neatly cracking open his egg, "Ooh, good, a nice dippy yoke. Yours'll be hard. It's been standing there for ten minutes." He looked up. "What's wrong with your eyes?"

"Nothing. I shouldn't have watched the late film, that's all. It didn't finish till 1.30 this morning. Don't tell mum," I added quickly.

"Don't tell me what?" asked my mother, coming out of the breakfast room.

"That your Instant Action Anti-Fatigue Eye Gel is complete rubbish," I said, "I've just tried it. Doesn't work."

"You have to give it time. You know, that thing you don't have much of…" she answered.

"Then why is it called 'Instant-Action'?" I pointed out, "Honestly, I think most of these potions are a complete waste of time. And I bet it wasn't cheap."

"No, it wasn't," she answered sharply, "So don't waste it. Anyway, you don't need potions and lotions just yet. You're only seventeen. Make the most of your youthful skin while you can. You'll be on the anti-aging treadmill all too soon."

"Not me, I'm going to stay young and beautiful for ever," I told her, confidently.

She raised her eyes to the ceiling: "Yes, we all thought that when we were in our teens," she said, sagely.

Granddad gave me a knowing wink over the top of his spectacles. Then with intense concentration, he carried on mopping up the yoke that spilled out of his egg. He was right, mine was rock solid and so I quickly peeled it and put the whole egg in my mouth at once.

"Emily, that's disgusting," said my mother,

I pointed at my watch and raised my eyebrows, momentarily unable to speak. "Gotta go," I managed to splutter, grabbing my school bag from under the breakfast table with one hand and taking the piece of buttered toast Gramps held out for me with the other.

"If you got your car sorted out, you wouldn't need to set out so early on the bus," I heard my mum calling out behind me, "… and wipe that stuff off your eyes."

I let myself out of the front door and walked past my old mini, fondly known as Martha, standing sadly on the driveway. Its failed MOT meant I couldn't drive it and since I'd left my part time job at the local Garden Centre, I couldn't afford the new tyres, exhaust, spark plugs and various other items it required. I set off at a brisk walk, eating my toast rapidly.

I glanced at my watch. 7.55am. I would just make the bus if I hurried. Further up the road I saw Seth, my next door neighbour, walking with Tash, who lived just down the hill. Both attended Hartsdown College with me. Tash was my best friend in the whole world. We'd met when I'd just moved into the village and my mum had taken me to Tiny Tots, held in the village church on a Friday afternoon. We were both three years old and had bonded instantly. Since that point onwards, we'd been inseparable, right through infant school, juniors and now senior school. We'd laughed together, cried together, fallen out, made up and knew just about everything there was to know about each other. With Tash I shared my innermost secrets and trusted her as I would no other. Seth was, well, the boy next door. Funny, annoying, bit of a smartass, just your average boy, really. I'd known him since I was about five years old, when he moved in, and it seemed like he'd always been around. If truth be known, I suppose I'd always had a bit of a crush on him, but that was something I barely admitted to myself, let alone anyone else. Even Tash.

"Tash, Seth," I called, "wait for me."

They both turned and looked, shielding their eyes against the early morning sun.

"Hi, Em," shouted Tash, her long red hair glinting vividly in the sunshine.

She reminded me of a Pre-Raphaelite painting. You know, the one of Ophelia lying in the lake? Slim, pale and interesting, with big green eyes and hair to die for.

"Come on," called Seth, "run. The bus is coming. You can make it."

Seth on the other hand was olive-skinned and dark. Good looking, I think you'd say, with a permanent 'who-gives-a-damn' slouch, lazy manner and unruly black hair that flopped over his face. He sometimes rode into college on a moped, but generally preferred the bus as it took less effort, even if he did have to get up earlier.

They both started walking quickly up the hill and, panting with the exertion, I reached them just as they got to the bus stop.

"What's happened to your eyes?" asked Tash, peering at me. "They look odd."

"Nothing," I replied, "it's just this gel I put on. It's supposed to refresh you but it obviously hasn't."

"You can say that again," said Seth. "You look like you've gone ten rounds…"

"Just ignore him," advised Tash. "If you want to tighten your skin up, I've got this amazing beer face-pack you can use. I'll bring it in, if you like."

"Yeah, and you'll end up looking like this," said Seth, pulling back the skin on his face with his fingers, so his eyes and mouth stretched widely, and staggering around. "Drunk and tight."

"Stop it, Seth, that looks horrible."

Within seconds the bus pulled up and we piled inside along with the usual office workers, village school kids and other

Hartsdown students. Seth, Tash and I went to the back of the bus and, unusually for us, got the rear seat. This prized place was usually taken by the Meriton Mob, as we liked to call them, an unruly bunch of sixteen year olds from the next village. Normally, they'd have occupied all the rear seats and we'd have taken whatever was left. Today, the back of the bus was strangely empty.

"Where are the usual suspects?" I asked, sitting in the centre, with Tash and Seth either side of me.

"Geography field trip," said Seth, "They've gone to the Blythe Sewage Works. Had to start early at 7.45."

"Let's hope we lose a few of them," said Tash. "I can't think of a better place for Sarah. Or Imogen."

"Or Micky," I added. "Mind you, you couldn't really tell if he fell in. He already looks like the Creature from the Swamp. And his breath certainly smells like it. He'll probably feel quite at home there."

"Heard Micky had a bit of a thing for you," said Seth, looking at me and grinning.

"Don't even go there," I warned. "He's young, spotty and obnoxious. I'd rather wash out my mouth with hydrochloric acid than get anywhere near him!"

"That's not what he says about you," persisted Seth.

"Get lost, Seth."

"Hey, have you heard the latest about Hartswell Hall?" asked Tash, changing the subject, as the bus passed the private road leading up to the village's Victorian mansion, its impressive gate posts guarding its mysterious entrance like huge stone sentries.

The bus came to a halt at the stop just past the hall entrance and the school kids from the other end of the village clambered aboard. Seth, Tash and I peered through the side windows of the bus, trying to catch a glimpse of the old house, but it remained tantalisingly hidden behind the wild spring foliage that grew unchecked in its grounds.

"Go on, what's the story?' asked Seth.

There'd been a great deal of speculation about Hartswell Hall ever since it came on the market. First it was going to be a care home, then a property developer was going to turn it into trendy apartments, there was even a rumour that someone wanted run it as an animal sanctuary. For years, an old man had lived there as a recluse, allowing the house to fall into disrepair and the grounds to grow wild. As kids, we used to think it was haunted and would dare each other to run up the driveway and look through its small panelled windows, thick with grime, into its crumbling interior. Then the old man had died, adding a further element of scariness to the stories. A midnight raid on the property by a gang of local daredevils ended in terror, when they swore they'd seen something moving up on the first floor. They hadn't stuck around for long enough to find out what it was.

"I heard Dizzy Detroit wants to buy it," said Tash conspiratorially. "You know he used to live in Birmingham? Well, apparently, he wants to come back to this area and is looking for an old place to do up."

"Could be true, I suppose," said Seth.

"But how do you know?" I asked.

"The man in the corner shop told my mum," explained Tash. "He said, the other day a long, black limousine with darkened windows drove up the High Street and into Hartswell Hall entrance. Someone told him they saw Dizzy Detroit get out."

"Cool beanz," said Seth. "Imagine having a rock star in the village. That'd shake things up a bit...."

"Just what this village needs, shaking up a bit," I murmured, gazing back through the rear window, as the bus resumed its journey and the grounds of Hartswell Hall gradually disappeared from view.

Hartswell-on-the-Hill was a typical middle class village. True, it had history, as you could see from the High Street with its pretty black and white fronted cottages, quaint old pub and medieval stone church. But a combination of picture postcard appeal and a wide selection of large properties, dating from Victorian times to the present day, along with the addition of a new housing estate of luxury detached homes on the edge of the village, had given it an affluent, commuter-belt style. Someone once told me there were more consultants per square inch in Hartswell-on-the-Hill than any other neighbouring village, due to its vicinity to a nearby major hospital, but I don't know if that was true. One thing was certain – to live in Hartswell you needed money, as its expanding population of doctors, lawyers, accountants, businessmen and other upwardly thrusting young professionals testified. There was the obligatory council estate at the other end of the village – where Tash lived, and a number of smaller houses in some of the less desirable roads – such as the one where Seth and I lived, but for the main part, the houses were large, expensive and afforded only by birthright, inheritance or a big salary. All of which meant one thing. Desirable as Hartswell-on-the-Hill was from a real estate point of view, it was a fairly boring place to live. Especially if you were young. Other than the church youth group, a football pitch, sports centre, tennis courts and the local pub - okay if you were sporty or liked drinking - there was very little to do. An infrequent bus service into the neighbouring town meant you were back in the village by 10pm on a weekday, and 10.30pm on a Saturday night, which was hardly conducive to partying. For a few months, until it gave up the ghost, my old mini had been our passport to freedom, but now we were beholden once more on the bus service, or our parents, which was not an option we favoured, given our advanced years.

The bus pulled up outside Hartsdown High, the local red brick senior state school, with its assortment of add-on portacabin classrooms housing a growing population of fifteen hundred plus pupils, and the majority of passengers alighted. The campus also housed Hartsdown College, the post-16 educational facility, and it was to this more exclusive area that we headed.

We settled noisily into our tutor group, more interested in discussing the previous weekend than the forthcoming lessons, and very glad this was the last week before the Easter break. There was one piece of news to make these last few days a little more interesting. A new student was to join us, according to our tutor, Mrs Pritchard, and we waited expectantly while she took the register.

"She's taking English Literature, Art, History and Philosophy," said Mrs Pritchard, studying the file, "so any students enrolled on those courses, please help her to settle in."

"Same as us, apart from Philosophy," I said to Tash, who nodded back. We'd both attempted this mind-expanding subject, but after sitting through one tutorial had decided it was far too

24

mind-boggling and altogether strange for our liking. Instead, Tash had opted for Geography and I'd chosen Business Studies, both solid, down-to-earth subjects you could get your head around.

By 9.10, the new girl had failed to show, and Seth, Tash and I went down to our first class, double English Literature, wondering when she would arrive. There was an unmistakable buzz of excitement in the air, based on a sense of expectation that something new was about to happen, and as hard as we tried to concentrate on Shakespeare's use of language in Macbeth, it proved increasingly difficult to focus on Miss Widdicombe's monosyllabic voice. A general sense of disinterest settled over the class as we all tried and failed to follow the lesson.

"Where is she?" Tash mouthed to me, turning round from the row in front.

I shrugged my shoulders and started to mouth a reply when Miss Widdicombe zoomed in on me.

"Emily, would you like to explain the difference between Shakespeare's use of an iambic pentameter and trochaic rhythm as found in Macbeth, and give an example of each?" she asked pointedly.

"Er, trochaic rhythm is, er, where Shakespeare, er....." I floundered, and struggling to answer, looked down at my textbook for inspiration, my cheeks scarlet. I hated being picked on, especially when I didn't know the answer.

"Yes?" asked Miss Widdicombe, "Can anybody help Emily with this?"

The whole class looked at her blankly and she tutted in irritation, about to launch into yet another diatribe on our lack of appreciation of the subtleties of the English language, when her attention was distracted by a knock on the door. It opened almost immediately, revealing Mrs Pritchard followed by the long awaited new student. Suddenly we were all interested.

"Sorry to interrupt," said Mrs Pritchard quickly to Miss Widdicombe, "I have a new addition for you. Everyone, this is Violet de Lucis."

The new girl stepped out from behind Mrs Pritchard and there was a sharp intake of breath on the part of the whole class, followed by a stunned silence as we gazed at the vision before us. I don't think anyone knew quite what to say.

The new girl was unbelievably beautiful. Her long blonde burnished hair was straight out of a fairy story, tumbling gracefully over her shoulders. Her blue eyes were piercing and large, her nose small and elegant, and her lips pink and full. She wore a pale blue sweatshirt, faded skinny jeans and high-heeled black boots, and with her slim figure, looked more like a fashion model than a college student.

We stared at her and she stared back without smiling, her look neither hostile nor unfriendly, but simply sizing us up, selectively examining each one carefully. Then two things happened simultaneously. Somebody wolf whistled from the back of the classroom, breaking the tension and causing everyone to giggle, and at the same time her eyes met mine and I felt as if I'd been pierced with a laser beam. I'm not kidding, I felt like she was looking inside my head and turning me inside out. I stared back, locked into her gaze, feeling something I can only describe as a magnetic pull linking us together. For an instant, time stood still, the classroom faded away and there was only her and me, staring at each other. Then she smiled a dazzling, friendly smile and the moment was gone. The classroom came back into focus and I took a deep breath, feeling exhausted and energized at the same time. I looked around, expecting everyone to be watching me, but no one appeared to have noticed.

"Violet, why don't you sit next to Emily?" suggested Mrs Pritchard. "There's an empty desk there."

"Thank you," said Violet, in a voice as clear as crystal, and came to sit alongside me. She turned and smiled once again, although not with the previous intensity, and this time, I grinned back.

"We were just examining the difference between ...' began Miss Widdicombe.

"Shakespeare's use of trochaic rhythm and iambic pentameters?" said Violet, smiling confidently. "I know. I heard as I came in." She then proceeded to give a detailed explanation of each, backed up by examples from the play, and we all stared once again, mouths agog in disbelief.

"I was just about to say that," Seth called out, and we all laughed.

The rest of the lesson passed in a haze, as we all gawped at Violet, quite unsure what to make of her knowledge, her composure or her dazzling beauty. Miss Widdicombe might just as well have been teaching us Chinese as English, for all the notice we took of her and when the bell came for the end of the lesson, she gathered her books with an exasperated sigh and swept out of the room muttering something about the end of term not coming soon enough.

I turned to Violet and said: "It's break time, do you want to go to the café for a hot chocolate?"

"That would be nice," she started to say, before she was literally mobbed by the rest of the class, all asking questions at the same time.

"Where do you come from?" "Where are you living?" "Where do you get your skinny jeans from?" "What are you doing tonight?" The questions came thick and fast and Violet looked at me, shrugging her shoulders. She held up her hands for silence and, miraculously, everyone stopped talking.

"My family has come to live here from Egypt," she said in her crystal clear voice. "We had to leave with all the trouble that's going on. It was getting too dangerous to stay. We're going to be living in Hartswell-on-the-Hill, at Hartswell Hall, which we're turning into a luxury hotel. There's me, my mum and dad, and my older brother Theo, who will also be coming to college. He's already done A-levels, but he wants to do a refresher course. "

Thirteen female minds did the same equation at exactly the same time. She had an older brother. Coming to college. If he was anywhere half as gorgeous as his sister, he was going to be an absolute heartthrob.

"Now, if you don't mind, Emily and I are going to get a drink," she said, and linking arms with me, literally pulled me towards the door. "Sorry," she muttered under her breath, "I simply can't stand all the attention, it really freaks me out. Now which way do we go?"

I guided her down the stairs as if in a dream, realising too late that I'd left Tash behind. Never mind, I'd see her at lunchtime and we could talk about things then.

For the next twenty minutes, we sat in the café, sipping hot chocolate, talking and swapping stories. She exuded a natural warmth and radiance, and I felt totally at ease in her presence. As our body chemistries meshed, I felt re-energised and refreshed, glowing in her reflected glory, and I remember thinking that she was a better tonic than any pills or potions.

I told her about life in Hartswell-on-the-Hill, which didn't take long, about my family and friends, and about Hartsdown College. She told me of her life in Egypt, of the heat and the dust, the markets and bazaars, the colours and the spices, and the fabulous house that her family owned, with its outdoor pool, many rooms and servants.

"Servants," I repeated, "I can't imagine what it must be like to have servants waiting on you."

"Oh, you get used to it," Violet answered glibly. "Every house has them over there."

"Did you go to school?" I asked.

"No," she answered, "there was a school for foreigners, until it closed down. Then my mother arranged home schooling for us. It was okay, just a bit boring with only Theo for company. "

"What's Theo like?" I ventured to ask.

"Well, he looks like me, said Violet, "Taller, blond hair, blue eyes. Put it this way, he never has a problem attracting women. Not that he'll be interested in the girls here. It'll take a very special girl to catch Theo's eye."

My interest was aroused immediately, although I doubted very much he'd notice me. For a start, he was two years older than me and I guessed a lot more sophisticated. He was obviously very handsome and while I was passably pretty, I could never be described as beautiful, certainly not in Violet's league. Nonetheless, I was intrigued and couldn't wait to meet him or, as was more likely, admire him from afar.

"Have you moved in to Hartswell Hall?" I asked Violet. "It's just no-one's mentioned a family living there and turning it into a luxury hotel. Only this morning, I heard a rumour that a local rock star was interested in buying it."

"We're in the process of moving in," explained Violet. "The sale has just gone through and there's a lot of work to be done on the house and grounds before we can open it as a hotel."

"It sounds very exciting," I said. "I've only ever seen Hartswell Hall from the outside, but it looks like a fabulous place."

"You must come round and have a look...." Violet started to say, then hesitated. "Well, I'll have to check with my mother and father first. I'm not sure they want people seeing inside until all the work's done. It's a bit of a mess at the moment."

The bell for the next lesson sounded and any thoughts of looking round Hartswell Hall were put to one side, as we made our way to History, with the world's most boring teacher, Mr Greaves. I sat next to Tash, who muttered: "Enjoy break time with Blondie?" before studiously reading her History course book for the entire lesson, in a way that was most unlike her. At the end of the lesson, she gathered up her books and disappeared through the classroom door before I'd even realised she was gone. I saw her walking down the corridor with Seth, heading for the cafeteria, and was aware that there had been a major and unpleasant shift in our friendship. It didn't make me feel good, but I had no time to dwell on it, because Violet was there at my elbow, smiling her radiant smile and asking if I'd like to have an early lunch with her. Being in her company was like bathing in brilliant sunshine. It made me feel alive, relaxed and energised all at the same time, and I was soon engrossed in her stories of Egypt and a lifestyle I could only imagine.

That afternoon, we shared the same classes and she sat next to me on the bus going home. I vaguely noticed Tash sitting with Seth towards the back of the bus, but Violet pulled me into a seat at the front.

"Come on, let's sit here," she said. I sat where she indicated, feeling as if the situation was out of my control.

"Where's your brother?" I asked. "Wasn't he at college?"

"No, he couldn't come today," she answered. "He'll start tomorrow. You'll probably meet him."

When the bus stopped outside Hartswell Hall, Violet got up and, flashing me another of her radiant smiles, said, "My stop. I'll see you tomorrow. Bye."

I watched her walk up the drive way, a jacket thrown nonchalantly over her arm, her beautiful golden hair catching the afternoon sunshine. She seemed to shimmer, barely disturbing the air as she moved, and as the bus started up again, I felt strangely dreamlike and serene.

My stop was next and I was barely aware of Tash and Seth walking past me down the centre aisle. As he passed, Seth turned to me and said, "Are you getting off, Em? It's our stop. What's the matter with you?"

"Nothing," I murmured, "I'm right behind you," and followed them off the bus.

"Have you and Tash had a disagreement?" asked Seth, "It's not like you two to avoid each other."

"No, we're fine, aren't we Tash?" I spoke to Tash's back.

She turned and said in a flat voice, "Yeah, absolutely fine." And we carried on walking down the hill, the conversation stilted and awkward, despite Seth's best endeavours to keep things going.

The next day proved no different. Tash and I seemed to have little to say to one another and I found myself looking forward to seeing Violet with undue interest. As the bus approached her stop, I looked in vain for her golden hair, but she wasn't there and I felt disappointed.

Our first class was once again English Literature with Miss Widdicombe, but the desk next to mine remained empty and I began to wonder if I had imagined meeting her the day before. Then, at break time, as I walked into the locker area, I saw her mass of blonde hair. She was standing talking to a striking blond-haired boy, who had to be Theo, I reasoned, and for a few seconds, I stood watching them closely. No doubt about it, Theo was absolutely gorgeous. Just like his sister, he too could be a model. He was tall and well proportioned, wearing faded jeans and a white T-shirt, and exuded a grace and style that came straight from the pages of a fashion magazine. Even his hands, I noticed, were elegant and expressive, giving him a sophistication way beyond his years. I hovered uncertainly, unsure whether to approach them. They seemed to be deep in conversation and while I didn't want to interrupt them, I was conscious that break time would soon be over and I might not get another opportunity to meet him on my own. If I left it until lunchtime, he'd probably be surrounded by adoring girls and wouldn't notice me. At least now I would have his undivided attention. So, heart beating loudly and with a sudden rush of excitement, I walked over to them.

"Hello Violet," I said, excitedly, "I wondered where you were."

Too late, I became aware they were in the middle of an argument. They both stopped talking abruptly and you could have cut the atmosphere with a knife. Violet turned and looked at me with a look so cold it took my breath away.

"Sorry," I mumbled, backing away and feeling confused. Then the coldness disappeared and she gave me a dazzling smile.

"Emily," she said, in her crystal clear voice. "How nice to see you, I was just telling Theo that there was one girl he simply had to meet."

"Were you?" I said, going red with embarrassment. "Er, who's that?"

"You, of course," cried Violet, laughing at my awkwardness. "Theo, this is Emily. Emily, meet Theo."

The blond haired boy opposite Violet smiled at me.

"Very pleased to meet you, Emily," he said, in a voice similar to Violet's in its clearness and clarity, but with a depth and resonance that sounded like pure music. "Violet's been telling me all about you." He went to shake my hand.

I looked into the face of the most beautiful boy I had ever seen and was instantly captivated by the tousled blonde hair, the ivory skin, the even white teeth and the perfect features. Gazing into his eyes, I was lost in their intensity. It was like looking into the bluest sky and carrying on to infinity. I felt mesmerised, hypnotised and transfixed all at once. Time slowed to a standstill and became a series of freeze frames, enabling me to recall every facet of our meeting in immense detail. I remember the hustle and bustle of the locker area as students hurriedly got out their books ready for the next lesson, and someone nearby laughing abruptly, their voice sounding muffled and faint, as if they were far away. I remember feeling mild panic in case my handshake was too sweaty, as my nerves kicked in big time and adrenalin flooded my system, and then feeling relieved that my hand was actually quite dry. But more than anything else, I remember his hand touching mine and feeling the soft warmth of his skin, the firmness of his grip and the slight pressure from his nails as they touched the palm of my hand. It was one of those perfect moments and such was its intensity I felt I'd lived my whole life just to come to this point. But no sooner had our hands joined and I was experiencing the most wonderful sensation of well-being, than I felt what I can only describe as a bolt of electricity shoot from the centre of his palm into mine, white hot and burning, searing my skin with a scalding pain. I cried out immediately, registering the sensation and shock with disbelief, and then, as my reflexes took over, jerked my hand upwards out of his reach, forcing us apart. For a split second he stared at me, seemingly as shocked as I was, unable to speak and trying to comprehend what had just passed between us.

I looked down at my hand, expecting to see some kind of mark, a burn maybe, some evidence of the scorching pain I'd just felt, but there was nothing: no wound, no redness, no indication that anything out of the ordinary had just occurred.

"Sorry…." I gasped, feeling stupid and embarrassed, rubbing my palm with the index finger of my other hand.

Recovering quickly, he laughed awkwardly and said, unconvincingly, "Static electricity – that's what comes of wearing the wrong shoes on a nylon carpet. That was quite something, wasn't it?"

"It certainly was," I murmured faintly, glancing up at him again and feeling a little weak as I looked into his perfect face. But while his words offered a seemingly rational explanation, his eyes told a different story. There, I saw pure panic swirling amidst the deep, hypnotic blue, and he seemed to struggle to control himself. With a huge effort he broke his gaze and looked down at his watch, saying, almost too quickly, "Hey, look at the time. I must fly. I have a tutorial. Don't want to be late on my first day."

He darted away and reached the double doors at the end of the corridor in less than two seconds. I watched him go, wondering what on earth had just happened between us, willing him to turn round and look at me one last time. Just as he went through the doorway, he turned and our eyes locked once more. For a split second, we stared at each other, linked together by a gaze that spoke volumes, yet which I was totally unable to understand. Then, he was gone, the double doors swinging violently against an empty space, and I turned back to find Violet staring at me, but with quite a different look. This was one of suspicion and mistrust and, if I wasn't mistaken, fear.

I smiled at her weakly but she was clearly shaken by what she'd just witnessed and, making some excuse about needing to go to the school office, she picked up her bag and jacket and abruptly left the locker area. There was no doubt in my mind she was going after her brother.

For some minutes after she'd gone, I stood going over in my mind what had just happened, trying to rationalise it and failing totally. If I'd thought Violet had a powerful effect on me, it paled into insignificance compared to the connection I'd felt with her brother. This was like nothing I'd ever encountered before. It was all consuming, all-powerful and quite simply beyond my sphere of experience. Some deep inner instinct warned me it might also be dangerous, but this simply added to his attraction and, if I'm honest, gave me the greatest thrill of all.

Hearing the bell, I reluctantly went to my next lesson and tried to concentrate as best I could on double History. But I may just as well have been trying to get my head around time travel as the dissolution of the monasteries, my mind felt so unsettled.

At lunchtime, there was no sign of Violet or Theo and so I sat in the café with Tash and Seth.

"We're honoured," said Tash sarcastically. "Where's Blondie?"

"I don't know," I muttered. "Look Tash, what's the matter? Are you jealous of Violet, is that it?"

"What's there to be jealous of?" quipped Seth, "Perfect skin, gorgeous hair, looks like a fashion model. Can't see why Tash would be jealous of that…"

"It's not the way she looks," said Tash slowly, "it's something else… I can't put my finger on it. She's too perfect, somehow. There's just something that's not quite right about her. And look at the way she zoomed in on you. It was almost as if she chose you out of the rest of us." She faltered and started playing with her silver bracelet. "Look, I don't know why I'm saying this, but don't get taken in by all her golden charm. Just be careful, that's all.

What d'you know about her and her brother? Have you checked them out on Facebook, or googled them?"

"No, of course not. I've only just met them. Why should I?" I asked indignantly.

"Good thinking, Tash," said Seth, taking out his laptop. "Let's see what we can find out about them." He quickly opened his Facebook page and typed in Violet De Lucis. He pressed the search button.

"Nothing," he said. "Okay, let's try her brother." Again, there was nothing.

"So, they're not on Facebook," I said, "A lot of people aren't. And they have just come from Egypt, maybe it was safer not to be on Facebook."

"What about Twitter or Instagram or MSN?" suggested Tash.

Seth tried them all, every social networking site we could think of, but every time he drew a blank. There was nothing.

"Okay," said Seth, "let's try googling de Lucis. See what comes up about the family."

I kept quiet, feeling protective of Violet and her brother, but not sure why.

Once again, his search brought up nothing. There wasn't even a mention of the family.

"Try Hartswell Hall," suggested Tash.

This proved slightly more successful and a holding page appeared on the screen informing us that Hartswell Hall was undergoing a massive restoration programme and would be opening for business as an international conference venue mid-May. It said nothing about the new owners of Hartswell Hall.

"All very strange," said Seth. "You'd think there'd be something about the family, particularly the parents. After all, they are supposed to be international business people. I would have thought Google would throw up something. It's like they didn't exist before they came here."

"Maybe they're just very private people," I said, defensively. "Honestly, I think you're making a mystery where there is none."

"Seems to me you're being very defensive, Emily," said Tash. "I still think there's more to Violet than meets the eye. I don't like her and I don't trust her. Anyway, I have to go. I have some library books to take back."

She got up quickly, throwing her bag over her shoulder and leaving her lunch tray behind. Without looking back, she walked quickly out of the café.

"What was all that about?" I said, looking after her.

"If you ask me," said Seth, "it's a question of two's company, three's a crowd, and she's feeling a bit crowded out. How about I take Violet off your hands, Emily, and you can make up with Tash?"

"Thanks, Seth," I grinned at him, "but what makes you think a girl like Violet would be interested in someone like you?"

"Hey, there's more to me than meets the eye as well, you know," he cried. "I have hidden depths, too."

"Yeah, depths of depravity, more like, and you'd certainly be out of your depth with a girl like Violet," I informed him. "She has high standards. Don't even go there."

For some reason, the thought of Seth asking out Violet was not an idea I liked. He'd always been there for me, as a friend, and so far there'd never been a serious girlfriend to come between us. I didn't like the thought of that one bit. Besides, Violet was my friend and I didn't feel inclined to share her with anyone.

"I gotta go, too," said Seth, closing his laptop and putting it into his backpack. He stood up. "I've got rugby practice, and the way things are looking, I am going to get picked for the team this weekend. You watch, the girls'll be crowding round me."

"In your dreams," I called after him, as he left the table and slouched his way out of the canteen.

After he'd gone, I sat and thought how things had suddenly changed in the last couple of days. Tash was not happy about my friendship with Violet, whom she clearly saw as a threat, and I was more than a bit put out at the thought of Seth getting friendly with Violet. And what had Tash meant about Violet being too perfect and selecting me? I remembered back to the moment she'd first come into the classroom and how she stood at the front, looking at us all, as if searching for the right person. But surely it was just coincidence she'd sat in the empty desk next to mine? Oddly enough, I couldn't remember that desk ever being empty before, but as hard as I tried, I couldn't recall who usually sat there. And what did Tash mean by telling me to be careful? Surely she was just jealous that Violet was so attractive and had chosen to make friends with me? That was the thing when you were beautiful – you chose your friends, not the other way round. But why was there no mention of the family on Google? Surely there should have been something? Tash's words had unnerved me, and she didn't even know I'd met Theo yet. Now, that had been strange and I really didn't know how I was going to tell her what had happened. If she thought I needed to be careful of Violet, what would she think about Theo?

Which got me thinking about Theo. Beautiful, charismatic, handsome Theo. It took my breath away just remembering the look he'd given me, let alone the electric handshake. I'd never seen such blue eyes. They were the kind of eyes you'd look into and simply melt, the blue of a scorching summer's day, smouldering, sensual and hypnotic. And what about that handshake? I didn't buy his excuse of static electricity. I'd had static shocks before and they were nowhere near as intense as that. This was something more, there was some kind of connection between us and it had obviously surprised him as much as me, because after it had happened, he couldn't wait to get away from me. And then there was the look that Violet had given me. What was that all about? Was she jealous? Had she seen what had happened between us?

Although I tried to put these thoughts out of my mind for the rest of the day, I simply couldn't. And it wasn't just the thoughts. It was the physical sensation, too. Again and again I ran through the handshake in my mind and could still feel the shock flowing into my palm. It was as if life had suddenly taken on a fresh intensity, as if I was suddenly living for the first time and seeing the world as a wondrous, vivid, intense place, full of vibrant colours and sensual feelings. Something had awoken inside me, or to be correct, Theo had awoken something inside me, because it had taken his touch to unleash this heightened awareness. One thing I knew with absolute certainty. I had to see Theo again, I had to see him soon and I had to see him alone, to find out exactly what was going on between us.

3. **Out damned spot**

Sitting in her office, flicking through a pile of files, the estate agent noticed a couple of small brown circular marks on her hand. Always particular about beauty routines and especially manicures – she was most proud of her smooth hands and long red tapered nails – she stared in disbelief. If she was not mistaken, they were age spots.

She looked again and could have sworn they darkened as she looked at them. Surely they couldn't be age spots, not at 42? Age spots came when you were, well, late 50s or 60s surely? And there'd never been age spots in her family. Her mother had had beautiful, smooth white hands right up to her death the previous year.

She put the thought out of her mind and picked up the phone.

"Can you get me Mr Burrell of Bushell Burrell and Brown on the phone please?" she instructed her secretary, "I need to check where we're up to on the Oakfields Drive sale. It should have gone through last week. I can't think what's delaying things." Replacing the phone in its cradle, she muttered to herself, "Well, I can actually. Solicitors. It's always solicitors. They think they're so superior. But who does all the work? Who phones up everyone in the chain to make sure the sale goes smoothly? Estate agents, that's who. If it wasn't for us, nothing would ever get bought or sold."

She picked up a little hand held mirror on her desktop so she could watch herself as she spoke to Mr Burrell. Just a little quirk she'd developed that made her feel so much more professional. So much more confident and superior, a necessity when dealing with solicitors. Let's face it, you needed every small advantage you could find when dealing with them. The phone rang and she picked it up, hearing her secretary announce she had Mr Burrell on the phone for her.

"Mr Burrell," she began, in her firmest, most professional voice, admiring in the mirror her new shade of lipstick. 'Deadly Nightshade' really suited her so well. Added the perfect extra touch to her professional appearance. "I was wondering if you could explain to me exactly what the delay is on the Oakfields Drive sale. Really, it is too……"

But she got no further. With a shriek, she threw down the phone, staring aghast at the face that was reflected in her mirror. Surely this was not right? This had to be a joke. She rushed from her office to the small ladies' toilet at the rear of the building, locking the door carefully behind her, then forcing herself to look in the large mirror above the washbasin. What she saw made her gasp in horror.

Instead of the immaculately permed tresses her hairdresser had perfected only that morning, her hair hung about her face, wispy and lifeless. And instead of the Honey Blonde hair colour with white blonde lowlights she'd so fastidiously selected earlier that morning, it was matted and grey, with streaks of dirty white, like old cotton wool. But it wasn't the hair that caused her to gasp so much as her face. Gone was the carefully made-up, cleansed and toned skin of which she was so proud, to be replaced with sagging, bagging, ancient pouches that hung beneath her eyes and either side of her mouth, like an aging elephant. Her skin was now the colour of old parchment, dried and brittle. Her eyes once clear and bright were now red ringed and bloodshot, drooping downwards to match the general direction of the rest of her face. Feeling something in her mouth, she spat it out and was aghast to see two yellowing teeth fall into the basin, leaving her with a witch-like gap in the middle of her mouth. The remaining teeth were blackened and decayed. Her posture she noticed was stooped and low, and her clothes hung on her shrunken frame, now at least three sizes too big for her.

"My God, I'm an old hag," she said breathlessly to the mirror and her voice sounded rasping and cracked. "With every minute that passes, I'm getting older and older," she stopped abruptly, as she took in the ramifications of what lay ahead. "At this rate, I'll be dead by tonight....."

A knocking on the door brought her back to her senses and she panicked as she heard her name being called out. No one must see her like this, of that she was certain. The knocking and shouting sounded again and she looked around for a means of escape. There was none. No small back window, no other means of getting out. She was trapped and about to be discovered.

Once again, she heard her name being called and then felt someone gently rocking her shoulder. With a jolt, she sat upright, and uttered a small cry. Oh joy of joys, she was in her own bed and it was her husband who'd been calling out her name. The hideous hag experience had been nothing but a bad dream.

"You were dead to the world," her husband informed her with relish, words which made her shudder with revulsion.

"I was having the most dreadful nightmare," she told him, holding her head in her hands and feeling quite weak. "I dreamed I'd turned into an old hag." She looked up. "Quick pass me that hand mirror," she instructed him.

He gave her the small gilt mirror from the dressing table and she held it up to her face, examining herself closely. She gave a sigh of relief. If anything, her face looked younger. Her eyes were bright, her skin taut and her complexion fresh. She smiled at her reflection and noticed, with satisfaction, that even the miniscule wrinkles at the corner of her eyes had completely disappeared.

"You're looking beautiful, dear," said her husband, "I don't know which rejuvenating potion you've been using recently, but it's having marvellous results. You could easily pass for a 20-year old. Here, I've brought you a cup of jasmine tea. You'll just have time to drink it."

She went to take the cup of tea from him, but before she could grasp the handle and savour the hot, steaming liquid, she let out a scream of terror.

On the back of her hand were three brown age spots....

4. **Missing Theo**

Wednesday morning, I woke early at 6am and could not get back to sleep. Although I'd met Theo for less than a couple of minutes, I couldn't get him out of my mind. Those few minutes had turned my world upside down and I knew instinctively that nothing would ever be the same again. Something had happened between us, some deep connection and I was totally unsure what would happen next. I hoped and prayed that he would come and find me at college, declare his undying love and sweep me off my feet. That was my ideal. Or at worst send me smouldering glances across the corridor, too overcome by the depth of his feelings to articulate how he really felt. I chose not to consider that nothing might happen, that was simply too unbearable to contemplate.

Just thinking of the possibilities, I felt a sense of excitement building within me, tinged with trepidation and anxiety. It was a delicious pain that I didn't want to stop. I felt drawn to him, like a moth to a flame, and although a little voice inside told me to be careful, that I could get very badly burned in the process, I chose to ignore it. If Theo was interested in me, I was powerless to resist. The attraction between us was just too great and I felt as if every moment of my life had been leading to this point.

I tossed and turned until the alarm went off at 7am, then surprised my mum and Granddad by being first at the breakfast table.

"What's this?" said Gramps, walking into the kitchen and seeing me sitting at the table sipping a steaming mug of black coffee. "Up before us? Something's afoot. It's not an exam day, so it's got to be a boy."

"Of course it isn't," I replied indignantly, "just woke up early, that's all, and thought I'd get an early start."

"Morning!" said my mother, walking in. "You're up early, Emily. What's the matter? Is anything wrong at school?"

"Honestly, can't a person get up early without being given the Spanish Inquisition?" I protested. "There's nothing wrong."

"Fine," said my mother, knowing when to back off, "would you like some toast?"

"No, I'm not really hungry," I said, staring into my coffee cup, wondering what the day ahead would bring.

"Lovesick," said Gramps, and I caught him giving my mum a wink.

'I am so not," I responded, a little too quickly. "Okay, give me some toast."

I waited impatiently while my mother loaded up the toaster, feeling suddenly edgy and irritable.

"Got any plans for the Easter holidays, Emily?" asked my mother, buttering the toast far too slowly for my liking. "Don't forget, I'll be working most of the time, so I won't be around."

The Easter holidays. How could I have forgotten? Just three days left of the spring term, just three days to get it together with Theo. And what if I didn't? The thought of spending two weeks at home, on my own, not seeing him, sent me into a blind panic. But if something did happen between us, then we had two whole weeks away from school to really get to know one another. I fast forwarded mentally and saw myself being invited to Hartswell Hall, walking up the long driveway to find Theo waiting for me at the door, smiling and gorgeous. I saw us exploring the old house together, looking at the renovations, taking long walks in the splendid grounds, hand in hand. I saw us laughing, talking, telling each other our life stories, kissing…

"D'you want jam on this, Emily?" my mother's voice broke into my thoughts and I came crashing back down to earth.

"Yeah, whatever." This preoccupation with the mundane was getting very tedious. "I'll probably hang out with Tash over the hols," I informed my mother. "Don't worry about me. And I have a college assignment to write for English Lit. Anyway, Granddad will be at home if I need anything, won't you, Gramps?"

"Always here, at your beck and call," Gramps smiled at me, his watery blue eyes twinkling in his old, lined face.

I smiled back at him and giving him a kiss on his forehead, I picked up the toast in one hand, school bag in the other and made for the door.

"Gotta dash," I said, stuffing the toast in my mouth. "See you later…"

"Bye," called my mother, as I ran from the kitchen. I felt suddenly claustrophobic and needed some fresh air. I needed to get to school. I needed to see Theo.

But disappointment awaited me at school. Neither Theo nor Violet was there. At the start of each lesson, I waited for Violet to walk through the door, but she never showed. At break, I rushed to the locker area, hoping to see either Violet or Theo, but neither appeared. At lunchtime, I scoured the café, hoping for a glimpse of them, but there was nothing. They clearly had not come into school and I felt desperate, wondering where they were and what they were doing. Something must have happened to stop them, I reasoned. You didn't enrol at college and then simply fail to show up. What if there'd been an accident? What if they'd been hurt? Dare I go up to Hartswell Hall to find out if they were okay? Did I know them well enough? What if everything was fine and there was a good explanation? I'd look pretty stupid. Get a grip, I told myself, determined to rein in my thoughts and think rationally. But try as I might, I couldn't get the thought out of my head that their absence had something to do with me and my strange meeting with Theo.

"Emily, what is the matter with you today?" asked Tash irritably. "You've haven't heard a word I've been saying."

"Sorry, Tash," I mumbled, "not feeling myself today."

We both sat at a table in the cafeteria, picking at our lunch, and not relishing the thought that we had another History tutorial coming up.

"I just said I've brought you that face pack I mentioned. The one that makes your skin look amazing." She took a small plastic pot out of her bag and slid it over the table to me.

"Oh, okay, great," I said unenthusiastically, picking it up and reading the label, "*'Beer Bio-phase Pick-Me-Up Facial. Revives the parts other facials cannot reach.'* You have to be joking, Tash."

"No, it's really good stuff," she protested, "makes your skin feel fantastic, really smooth. Just smells a bit beery, that's all."

"Alright, cool, I'll give it a go, if it'll keep you happy."

I peered over her shoulder as a crowd of students came into the café.

"Who are you looking for?" she demanded, "Every time someone walks through the door, you look up expectantly. Oh, I get it. It's Violet, isn't it?"

"No," I answered, half truthfully.

"Well, who then?"

I hesitated, wondering how much to tell Tash, knowing she wasn't going to like it. She'd already warned me off Violet. If I told her about Theo, she was going to like it even less.

"I'm not looking for anyone, I'm just worried about the English assignment, that's all," I lied.

"Are you?" asked Tash, looking surprised. "What are you doing for it?"

We had to write a thousand word essay on 'Love Poetry' by the poet or poets of our choice.

"The love poems of John Donne," I said. "You know, the Metaphysical Poet? What are you doing?"

"Shakespeare's Love Sonnets," she answered, adding in a dramatic voice: "Shall I compare thee to a summer's day, Thou art more lovely and more temperate. Rough winds do shake the darling buds of May, And summer's lease hath all too short a date…"

"What's this? Reciting love poetry to each other?" said Seth, sliding into an empty space beside us, "I am seriously worried about you two."

"Get lost, Seth." Tash threw her screwed up paper napkin at him, and thankfully, amidst all the laughter, I realised she'd forgotten about Violet.

At home that night, I could barely conceal my disappointment, and found myself getting short tempered with my mother and granddad.

"Sorry, Gramps," I said to him, sliding in next to him on the old blue sofa in the lounge. I'd snapped at him unnecessarily over dinner, just because he'd asked me twice if I wanted more vegetables. "It's not you. It's me. You were right this morning. It is about a boy."

"I thought so," he said, putting down his book and sitting back thoughtfully. "Name?"

"Theo," I said. "He's just started college."

"And what's the problem?"

"I don't know. He didn't show today."

"Have you fallen out?"

'No, not really. I don't know." I could hardly tell him we didn't know each other well enough to fall out.

"Well, I'm sure he'll be in tomorrow. And I'm sure everything will be fine." He gave me a smile, put his arm around my shoulders and gave me a squeeze.

I smiled back, but somehow couldn't share his optimism, and went to bed feeling very unsure about everything.

The next day, Granddad proved to be right. Well, in part. Violet and Theo did show. But everything was very decidedly not fine.

It started in the first lesson. Although there was an empty desk next to mine, Violet chose to sit next to another girl and I could barely contain my jealousy. Then at break time, before I could get to her, she'd disappeared. I didn't see her again until lunchtime, as we had different timetables, and then I saw her sitting with Theo in the canteen with a crowd from the Upper Sixth. I hovered in the canteen doorway, not knowing what to do. Should I go over and speak to them? Would they be glad to see me? If Theo had been alone, I wouldn't have hesitated, but in front of all the others I simply didn't know if I had the courage. In the end, I collected my lunch from the serving hatch and sat at an adjoining table, close enough for them to see me and come over if they wished. They obviously didn't. I heard them laughing and joking, and every time I heard Theo's voice it was like a knife going through my heart. At one point, I turned sideways to look at the group at the next table and for a brief moment, caught Theo's eye. No sooner did he see me looking at him, than he looked away immediately and began openly flirting with Georgia Thomson, an attractive brunette with very obvious attractions. Leaning over, he brushed away a strand of hair from her face in a gesture of intimacy that made me feel sick.

They all started laughing and I felt my throat constrict. Pushing aside my tray, I ran out of the canteen, desperate to get away. I hurried to the nearest washroom, feeling as if my heart would break. Tears ran down my face and I felt hot and faint. What had I been thinking of? Why on earth would a boy like that be interested in me? He'd never go out with a girl like me. He must have thought me very gauche and unsophisticated, especially given his background, and there were so many gorgeous girls in the year above. He was obviously interested in Georgia Thomson. I'd made a complete fool of myself. And I'd lost Violet's friendship into the bargain.

Never had I felt quite so wretched, and willed the end of the day to come, which it inevitably did, but all too slow for my liking. If I thought things were bad, however, they were soon to take a turn for the worse, as I found out the next day.

It happened late morning, just after netball practice. For three quarters of an hour, I played for all I was worth, assuming my usual position of Goal Attack and managing to put all thoughts of Theo completely out of my head. Welcoming the physical exertion as a means of banishing my mental torment, I was on top form. The sun shone down on the netball court and as its warming rays touched my body, I felt energised and invigorated. I leapt, I ran, I had total control of the ball, weaving my way in and out of my opponents and time after time reaching the goal circle with ease. When it came to taking aim and getting my ball into the net, I was unstoppable, achieving no less than an embarrassing twenty goals for my team. I'd always been a passable netball player, although never quite good enough to make the college team, but today I was in a different league and afterwards the girls crowded round me full of praise for my performance.

"Play like that every time, Morgan, and you're in the team," called Amanda Weston, the netball team captain. "Very impressive."

"Whatever you're on, I'd like some," said Tash. "You played like someone possessed."

I smiled, enjoying all the praise and wondering where my newfound energy had come from. And then I saw him. Theo was standing in the shadows at the corner of the sports block, by the entrance to the changing rooms, and he was watching me. I felt the blood drain from my face, as the demons of the last couple of days came rushing back. As soon as he realised I'd seen him, he dropped further back into the shadows, but it was too late. Fuelled by my success on the netball court, I was determined to confront him and marched over to where he stood.

"Hi Theo."

"Hi Emily. You played well."

"Thank you."

My resolve began to waiver as I looked into his blue eyes. He had the beginnings of very tiny smile lines at the corner of his eyes, I noticed, giving him a maturity I hadn't seen in other boys. Shards of sunlight crept through the shadows and shone on his face, giving his perfect ivory skin a translucence I hadn't noticed before. He seemed to shimmer.

"Have you been watching long?" I asked him.

"Long enough."

He stared at me with such a look of tenderness and longing, it took my breath away and I truthfully didn't know what to do. This was not what I'd expected. I wanted to throw my arms around him, to be as close to him as I possibly could, and it really felt as if some invisible force was pulling us closer together. I struggled to find the right words, but none came, and feeling foolish and inadequate, I settled for the trivial.

"You've got a money spider crawling up your jacket," I spoke nervously, my voice higher than normal, and went to brush away the small spider that was climbing up the lapel of his jacket.

Then it all seemed to happen in slow motion. He jumped back, recoiling from my touch, his eyes flashing and his face set.

"Don't touch me," he commanded. "Stay away from me. For your own sake, stay away. This can never work."

"What d'you mean?" I faltered, staring at him in disbelief.

He gave me one last look, and his eyes were filled with such utter desolation that I simply stood and watched as he backed further into the shadows. Then giving a sigh that seemed to rend him in two, he turned and ran as fast as he could around the corner of the building.

I stared at the empty space where he'd stood, not comprehending what had just happened. How could someone look at you with such longing, but not want you near them? Why did he say not to touch him? And what did he mean 'for your own sake stay away'? It just didn't make sense. Yet again, something had happened between us and he'd run away. I looked around, aware the world had suddenly gone dark, and realised that the bright sunshine had been replaced by black, threatening clouds. Already, I could feel spots of heavy rain on my skin.

"Come on girls, every one in," shouted the Games Teacher, Mrs Wilde. "Looks like there's a storm coming. Quick as you can now."

Suddenly, the energy I'd experienced on the netball court was gone and I felt drained. I changed into my sweatshirt and jeans as quickly as possible, amazed that no one had seemed to notice my encounter with Theo. Thankfully, that meant no awkward questions and I hurried to my Art lesson without speaking to anyone. Outside, a storm raged, the rain falling fast and furious, flashes of lightning rending the inky black sky and loud cracks of thunder crashing right above us, causing some girls to cry out in terror. I barely noticed. Throughout the afternoon, my energy levels dipped lower and lower, to the point where I could barely concentrate.

"Are you okay?" asked Tash, as we walked out of the Art class at the end of the afternoon.

"Not really," I answered, "I think I must be going down with something. I feel so tired."

"It's all that running around on the netball court," she grinned. "I always said sport was no good for you. You've worn yourself out. You need to go home and have a good sleep."

"That's about all I feel like doing," I admitted. "I feel terrible."

I was barely able to drag myself onto the school bus, and I don't know how I managed to walk down the hill and get home.

My limbs felt like lead and every step seemed to take a huge amount of effort. The air hung oppressively and even breathing seemed difficult. At last I reached home and, feeling totally washed out, informed Granddad that I was going to bed.

"I think I'm going down with flu," I told him. "My body aches and I just want to sleep."

"I'll bring you up a Lemsip," he said, taking control. "We're having chicken broth for tea, that'll sort you out. You'll soon feel good as new."

When my mother came home from work, she felt my forehead.

"You don't have a temperature," she said, "but you are very pale. It's probably better if you don't go into college tomorrow."

I willingly acquiesced with that. College was the last place I wanted to be. I didn't care if I never went back. I just wanted to be as far away as possible from Theo. How could someone I'd met only twice have such a devastating effect on me? Was my mysterious illness somehow a manifestation of my inner turmoil? Was it psychosomatic? Perhaps psychologically I was protecting myself from further hurt by finding the perfect excuse not to go into college. That night, I had muddled dreams, all featuring Theo, of course.

I found myself standing on the bank of a huge, swollen river with a fast moving current that pulled the frothing waters, spewing and angry, down towards a waterfall. On the opposite bank, which was green and lush and bathed in sunlight, stood Theo. My side of the river, in contrast, was dark and cold and in shadow. However loudly I called his name, he didn't seem to hear me. The sound of my voice was drowned out by the fast moving water. In vain I called, but my words were carried away downstream. I realised the only way I could reach him was to brave the strong current and swim across the river. Fully clothed, I flung myself in and tried to battle the angry water, but my limbs were heavy and slow and refused to work properly, and I realised I was never going to make it to the opposite bank. With horror, I realised I was being dragged downstream by the strong current, towards the impending waterfall, and I screamed Theo's name even louder. Again he simply didn't hear, and I saw him slowly walking away into the sunshine. Closer and closer loomed the waterfall. I could hardly breathe and the water was filling up my lungs. Then suddenly my body reached the lip of rock and I was falling, falling...

I woke up to find my mother leaning over me, stroking my face.

"Emily, Emily, wake up. You're having a nightmare."

I stared up at her face and burst into tears. She held me in her arms, cradling me and rocking me, as if I were a small child. "It's alright, you're safe," she crooned, "It was just a bad dream."

A cup of warm milk and two paracetemol tablets later and I slipped easily back into sleep, this time a black, dreamless sleep that covered me like a warm, dark blanket. I woke in the morning feeling better but still tired, and at my mother's insistence, spent the day at home, watching TV, reading books and listening to music. All in all, not a bad day and I felt very relieved to be away from Hartsdown College, or more accurately, away from Theo and Violet. Tash came round after college and for a while, it was like old times, laughing and joking together, playing our favourite Coldplay album, and generally just hanging out.

My newly found equilibrium couldn't last, of course, and as the Easter holidays progressed, I found myself slipping into a depression. One day merged into the next and I still felt tired and drawn. With a heavy heart I attempted to write my English Literature assignment, not relishing the thought of reading John Donne's love poetry. I started to read 'The Good Morrow' and his words leapt out from the page at me, each phrase poignant and sad in view of recent events:

'If ever any beauty I did see,
Which I desir'd and got, t'was but a dreame of thee.'

I put down the book and stared mournfully out of my bedroom window at the fields beyond and sighed. Oh Theo! What had happened between us? Would the world ever be the same again? How I wished he and Violet had never come to Hartswell-on-the-Hill and I had never met him. I felt as if my peace of mind had gone forever. So, this is what love was all about. Pain, loneliness and longing. He'd made it plain that nothing would ever happen between us, for reasons of his own, but in so doing he'd destroyed my cosy little world. I read on, and the more I read, the sadder I became, especially when I stumbled upon the words of 'The Broken Heart':

'Ah, what a trifle is a heart,
If once into loves hands it come!'

I devoured the poem, relishing its intensity, understanding for the first time in my life the poet's emotion. This man had truly loved and lost because he understood only too well what I was going through:

'My ragges of heart can like, wish, and adore,
But after one such love, can love no more.'

I couldn't deny it. Although I'd met Theo only twice, there had been a deep connection between us, and I'd fallen for him completely and totally. But no matter how much I was in love with him, the situation was hopeless. He didn't want to know. Despite the fact I'd obviously had a big effect on him, something was preventing him taking things further, and I felt frustrated, angry and confused. None of it made any sense. Unless he had a girlfriend already, of course. I simply hadn't thought of that. Maybe he was seeing someone else and that's why he couldn't see me. Now I added jealousy to my list and felt even more depressed. I sat in my bedroom, playing The Lumineers' 'Stubborn Love', feeling bereft and alone, the words having fresh meaning every time I heard them.

Tash phoned and texted me a couple of times, suggesting we meet up, but I was unenthusiastic. There was an unspoken barrier between us, and things just weren't the same. I longed to tell her about Theo, but what was there to say? That I'd met Violet's brother, that he'd given me some kind of static shock when I shook his hand and I fancied him like mad, but he wasn't interested? It all looked pretty pathetic when you considered the facts. And apart from that, Tash clearly disliked Violet, and had even warned me away from her. So, I kept my distance, not wanting to share my thoughts with her, and pleading illness in my defence. In truth, I still felt depleted and tired, and my low spirits were doing nothing to help my energy levels. I had no appetite and my clothes had started to hang on me. My hair was lank, my skin looked sallow and I even thought about using Tash's beer facial, but couldn't be bothered.

All through the Easter holidays, I moped and fretted, until even my good-natured Granddad started to get fed up with me.

"Why don't you go out?" he suggested, seeing me sitting forlornly at the breakfast table, "Get some fresh air. You're just moping around and that's not good for anyone. Why don't you go shopping with Tash? Or see a film?"

"I'll go out for a walk," I said, " I think Tash is busy today."

I set off up the hill and found myself propelled towards Hartswell Hall. Once there, I paused, peering up the long driveway, trying to see the house and wondering if I dared go up and have a look. Just being here made me feel closer to Theo, although I don't know what I would have done if he'd suddenly appeared. That would have been most embarrassing. Without thinking, I allowed myself to walk a few steps up the driveway, then a few more, admiring the topiary designs that had been created in the privet hedges along the way. Someone had been at work, I noted, but there was still a long way to go, and beyond the topiary it was wild and overgrown.

As I rounded the next corner, Hartswell Hall was there before me, majestic and mysterious, looking now almost completely renovated and restored. I was amazed. How had they managed to achieve so much in such a short space of time? And where were the workmen and the scaffolding? Surely it should have taken months to get to this state of repair, yet Violet said her family was in the process of moving in. I stood open mouthed, taking in the detail. The stonework had been thoroughly cleaned, uncovering the original Cotswold honey colour lost beneath years of grime, and the bas-relief ornamentation had been meticulously restored, revealing leaves, fruit, stags and open-mouthed gargoyles. New wooden window panes were freshly painted in cream, highlighting the small leaded panes of glass that twinkled in the sunshine, and the huge oak front door had been sanded down to reveal the natural wood in all its splendour, providing an impressive entrance.

My feet crunched on the freshly laid gravel approach and I stopped, aware that I had come too far and could be seen from any of the windows on this side of the house.

Too late, I turned to leave and found my way blocked by a ferocious looking man, with a large hooked nose, glaring black eyes and wild dark hair. I simply hadn't heard him walk up behind me.

"Can I help you?" he asked in a low, guttural East European accent.

"Er, no," I stuttered, "I was, er, just having a look. Sorry, I'll, er…"

"Get away from here. Hartswell Hall's not open yet." He towered over me menacingly and I took a step backwards. "Strangers are not welcome."

I looked up at his face, momentarily transfixed by his black flashing eyes and his sheer presence.

"Aquila, the car, please!" A woman's voice called out commandingly, from the front courtyard, and I turned to see a beautiful blonde woman, standing by a long, sleek, black car.

I stared open mouthed. She hadn't been there last time I looked. How did she get from the house to the car without me hearing her? I didn't think the car had been there, either. But there again, maybe I hadn't noticed it.

"Yes, madam," said the tall, dark man, slowly and almost sarcastically. Reluctantly he walked towards the car, but before he reached it, he turned and glared at me once again with slitted, glittering eyes. The next second, he was at the car and opening the rear passenger door for the blonde woman. She was about to get in, when she obviously thought better of it and turned towards me, addressing me, in a softly spoken, cultured voice.

"Hello, you must be Emily."

I was totally taken aback.

"Er, yes," I stuttered, 'How did you…?"

"Violet and Theo have told me all about you," she said, with a smile, "it was only a matter of time before you showed up. But I'm forgetting myself. I'm Mrs de Lucis." She held out her hand to me and smiled graciously.

I walked towards her, feeling rather a fool. I really shouldn't have come. This was totally embarrassing. It was only as I took her hand that I realised just how beautiful she was. Tall, slender and small boned, she was dressed in a 1950s style powder-blue suit, with a tight fitting pencil skirt and short tailored jacket with three quarter length sleeves. Her blonde hair was swept up and back, revealing perfect bone structure and the same ivory white skin as Theo and Violet. Large sunglasses concealed her eyes, which I guessed to be the same piercing blue, giving prominence to her glossy pink lips and perfect white teeth. Her hands were long and tapered, with beautifully manicured nails, and her skin felt cool and smooth to my touch. She smiled broadly as we shook hands and I felt instantly relaxed and at ease.

"It's a pleasure to meet you," she said, "I'm afraid I'm late for an appointment, and Theo's not around at the moment, so if you don't mind…."

"No, no, of course," I smiled back at her, won over by her friendliness and calm manner. "I was just looking…." I trailed off, unsure why I was there.

"Goodbye," she said, smiling as she got into the rear passenger compartment. Her chauffeur closed the door with a soft, low click and walked round to the driver's door. I watched as he got in, started the engine and reversed the car. The car shot forward suddenly, forcing me to jump to one side, and I briefly saw the man's face again as he drove passed me. His face was contorted with rage and he gave me a look of pure malevolence, which chilled me to the bone. Then the car was gone, disappearing down the driveway and out on to the High Street.

I looked back towards the hall, feeling more confused than ever, and glanced up towards the first storey windows. They glinted and winked at me, reflecting the light. And that was when I saw him. I most definitely saw Theo looking out of the window, watching me. Too late, he drew back, but I knew he'd seen me looking up at him. I stared up for a few seconds more, my heart beating wildly, but the window remained empty. Feeling hot and embarrassed, and wishing more than ever I'd never walked up the driveway, I turned and ran. I ran as fast as I could, and didn't stop until I got back home. Then I closed the door behind me, breathing heavily, only realising then how much my hands were shaking.

5. **Mist shroud**

That night, just before midnight, a thick, swirling mist settled over Hartswell-on-the- Hill. The temperature dropped suddenly, the air became damp and the mist crept along, shrouding the village in an oppressive white mantle that deadened all sound, creating a cold, eerie silence in which it was impossible to see or hear anything.

A mist in itself was not an unusual occurrence, as the fields surrounding the village were often prone to foggy patches, due to their low-lying marshy terrain. But this particular mist left the fields untouched, their tufty hillocks and sleeping cottonwool sheep clearly visible in the bright light of the nearly new moon. Instead, it affected only the higher ground, and more specifically, the village, where it grew ever thicker.

Most villagers slumbered in their beds, oblivious to the snaking, silent fingers of fog that stretched into every nook and cranny, and only a handful of people experienced the strange phenomenon. Burt Bennison, driving back from a late night Legion meeting, spoke of one minute driving along a well-lit road with perfect visibility and the next being faced with a solid bank of fog, as impenetrable as a brick wall, just as he reached the outer boundaries of the village. Unable to see more than a few inches, he had no choice but to leave his car by the gated entrance to a field and walk the last few hundred yards to his house.

Mrs Beaton, taking her dog, Benjie, for a late night walk, more to aid her insomnia than for the dog's benefit, saw the mist starting to creep in. She hurried home, anxious to escape the damp and cold before it affected her bronchitis. Late night revellers, Larry Swanson and Mick Jones, stepped out of The White Hart after a late night lock-in, barely able to stand, much the worse for wear after six pints of Black Sheep. The mist curled around them, sweeping and caressing them, as they staggered on their way. Somehow it seemed to propel them homewards, and each arrived home with no sense of having seen anything out of the ordinary, falling into a deep, dreamless sleep and waking the next day, with only dim memories of the night before.

Only Father James, enjoying a few moments of silent contemplation in the old village church, saw the mist with any real sense of alarm. Rising to his feet after his late night prayers, he saw the first tendrils of mist curling through a small side window that had mistakenly been left open. For a few seconds he watched, transfixed by the sinewy beauty of the swirling fronds, dancing through the open space like silent wraiths. Then coming to his senses, he hurled himself upon the window, closing it tight in one quick movement. Clutching his crucifix, he watched the mist grow ever heavier, pressing itself against the shut window, but unable to enter. Later, he was to ask himself why he had been so frightened, after all it was just a heavy mist, easily explained by atmospheric conditions. But at the time, instinct took over and all he knew was a deep sense of unease, a foreboding that all was not well and a feeling that he had to protect himself and his church from this strange, unnatural, creeping entity.

* * *

At two o'clock in the morning, when the mist was at its heaviest, the roads were empty and everyone in the village was sleeping, things began to happen at Hartswell Hall. A car, which had been waiting for hours at the nearby airport for a private plane to come in, collected its precious cargo and made its way, seemingly unaffected by the dense mist, up the High Street and towards the hall.

There, a welcoming committee waited on the front steps. Mrs de Lucis stood alongside a statuesque black woman, tall and straight-backed, like a Somali tribeswoman, dressed in a stunning blue gown. The car crunched on the gravel and came to a halt, just yards before them. Aquila, the chauffeur, got out of the car and opened the rear door to reveal a handsome blonde boy of twenty or so, wearing a crumpled brown linen suit, holding a silver casket engraved with ancient symbols. The boy carefully handed the casket to Aquila, before getting out of the car and shutting the door with a soft click. Seeing Mrs de Lucis, he smiled, then bounded up the steps to embrace her.

"Viyesha," he murmured, kissing her on the cheek.

"Joseph," she said softly. "Have you brought it?"

"Yes," he replied, "but it's been a dangerous journey and we need to get inside quickly. We don't know who is watching."

"Hopefully the mist has provided some protection," said Mrs de Lucis, looking out into the grounds. Addressing the tall, black woman, she added, "Thank you Pantera. You've done well tonight."

The black woman inclined her head slightly in acknowledgement but said nothing.

"Now, the casket, if you please," said Mrs de Lucis.

Joseph turned and beckoned to Aquila, who solemnly walked up the steps and handed him the silver casket. He took it, then presented it, with some ceremony, to Mrs de Lucis.

"At last," she said quietly, under her breath, more to herself than anyone else. She gripped the casket fervently with both hands and for a few seconds gazed at it with a rapt expression on her face. Then, recovering herself, she spoke quickly and urgently: "Come, everyone, we must go inside. Be quick."

She led the way into the house, and the others followed. Once he'd made sure the car was locked, Aquila gave a last, scowling look round the misty grounds, then went into the house, carefully closing the heavy oak door and locking it with a large antique key. Next, he pulled the great iron bolts into place.

Joseph let out a whistle of approval as he looked around the entrance hall, with its impressive main stairway.

"Wow, this is some place you've got here. What a find. You've done well," he grinned at her.

"Thank you Joseph. Yes, we rather like it here. I'm hoping we can stay for some time to come."

"So, what's my role to be in this latest charade?" asked Joseph, quizzically.

"You, my boy, are in charge of the gardens," answered Mrs de Lucis, "Regenerating, maintaining and nurturing them. For someone with your exceptional talents, it's the perfect job. Now, we have no time to lose. Follow me. Leon and the others are waiting."

Holding the silver casket tightly, she led the way up the splendid main stairway and along the corridor of the east wing, Joseph just behind her, Pantera and Aquila following. When she reached the stairs leading to the old servants' quarters, Mrs de Lucis turned and spoke: "Up here, Joseph. This is where our secret will be kept safe. We believe we've found the perfect place." She started to climb the dusty old staircase, parting the cobwebs where they hung down, and slowly the others followed her.

Outside, the mist swirled in great eddies and currents, seemingly thicker than ever around Hartswell Hall, providing the perfect camouflage. Had anyone been watching, they may just have seen a faint blue gleam emanating from the old Clock Tower. There again, it could just have been a trick of the light, as the glow of the outside coach lamps bounced back against the silvery mist, creating strange effects and patterns. Then, after another half hour, just as quickly as it had mysteriously arrived, the mist began to clear, dissipating into the night air within a matter of minutes. Once again, the Old Clock Tower was clearly visible through the darkness, the three clock faces shining brightly in the silvery moonlight. Inside, silent figures filed down the stairs leading from the old servants' quarters.

6. **Age destroys her**

Earlier the same evening, in a neighbouring village a couple of miles away, a very different drama had unfolded. It began at 10.30pm. Ambulance driver, Bob Manners, glanced at his watch, willing the last half hour of his shift to go as quickly as possible. It had been a very quiet evening. One suspected heart attack that had turned out to be a panic attack, all too typical of men of a certain age; one old man who'd fallen out of bed and couldn't be lifted back in; one bad nose bleed that had required some emergency packing. And that was it. Nothing stressful, nothing threatening, nothing nasty. Then with five minutes to go, and thoughts of steak and kidney pie with gravy and chips and a late night movie running through his mind, they'd had another call. A woman, mid-forties, with breathing difficulties, in a local village.

Heavy-hearted, he set off, blue light flashing, willing it not to be serious.

"We could still be back home within half an hour," he commented hopefully, to his co-driver, Reg.

"Don't count your chickens," said Reg, ominously.

Arriving at the address they'd been given, they gathered their equipment and went into the house. It was a new, detached house on a suburban road, surrounded by other new, detached houses. They were all very similar: red brick square boxes, surrounded by neat lawns and tended gardens, most with two cars on the driveway. Inside, it was all very predictable and suburban too, from the pretty Sanderson fabric curtains to the Amtico flooring and framed Vettriano prints on the walls.

They were met by a man in his early fifties, with wild eyes and a grey complexion, who appeared traumatised. Wringing his hands together continually, tears flowed down his cheeks and he struggled to speak coherently.

"Upstairs," he managed to say, choking on the words. "In the bedroom… found her ten minutes ago."

"Okay, sir, don't panic," Bob Manners went through the usual drill. "Just show us where she is and tell us what happened."

"What happened? What happened?" echoed the man, his voice rising hysterically, "I don't know what happened. How can this happen to anyone? I just don't understand it." He fell to the ground, sobbing, clutching his head.

"Right, let's go and have a look," Bob indicated to the other paramedic and together they went up the stairs. "Which room is she in?" he called back down to the prostrate man.

"First on the left," he sobbed, looking up at them with large, fearful eyes. "But there's nothing you can do. Nothing. You're too late."

The two paramedics entered the room indicated. They'd heard all this before. Let them be the judge. She might not be breathing, but there was still a chance they could resuscitate her.

What they saw stopped them both in their tracks.

"I thought the call was for a woman in her mid-forties," said Bob, staring at the scene before him. "This woman's got to be at least…"

"100?" the other paramedic finished the sentence off for him.

They both paused for a moment, taking in the horror of the situation.

On the bed lay a very old woman, her gnarled fingers curled like claws around a pink, flowery duvet, her thin white hair laying in wisps on the pillow, her mouth open as though trying to suck in air. It didn't take a professional to see that she was way beyond help. Her crêpey skin was yellowed and brittle, dried out like parchment, her face sunk and gaunt, revealing the bones beneath. The overall impression was of a skeleton barely covered with flesh, that life had departed some time ago.

Following procedure, Bob took her pulse, thinking how the old woman's fragile arm felt just like a brittle twig, and shone a light into her discoloured, bloodshot eyes. "Nothing we can do here," he said, shaking his head sadly. "Looks like a case for the Coroner, unless we can get her doctor to sign the Death Certificate. Let's go back downstairs and inform the gentleman. We must have misheard her age."

He went to draw the curtains, determined to give the old lady some last vestige of privacy. Pausing at the window, he stared hard at the large oak tree in the front garden, and more specifically, at a large branch that was momentarily illuminated by the headlights of a passing car. Sitting on the branch, if he was not mistaken, was an enormous bird, with a broad, hooked beak and gleaming feathers that shone in the dim light. A split second later, the car was gone and the tree branches were once more hidden from view.

"Did you see that?" Bob asked his companion, straining his eyes into the darkness.

"See what?" asked the other paramedic, joining him at the window.

"That huge bird, sitting in the tree. It had to be a buzzard, or a hawk, or even an eagle…."

"An eagle? You, my friend, need to go home and get some sleep," laughed his companion. "It was probably an owl at this time of night. Since when did we get eagles in this part of the world?" And he laughed again.

"You're probably right," said Bob, feeling stupid and unsure of what he'd just seen. It was dark outside, the moon still hidden behind clouds and it would be some time before its silver light lit up the sky. He drew the curtains as quickly as he could. "Come on, let's get this sorted out."

Together, they went back down the stairs, leaving the skeletal figure on the bed. Finding the sobbing man in the hallway, they him into the lounge.

"Sorry, sir," said Bob. "You were right. There's nothing we can do for the old dear. She's passed on. We'll call for a doctor and see if he'll issue a Death Certificate, if not we may have to go to the Coroner. But don't worry, she'll be handled with respect and dignity. Now, I think we must have got the wrong information. I take it she's your mother… or grandmother, even?"

"No," burst out the man, "She's not my mother or grandmother, although I know she looks like it." For a moment, he was overcome with grief and couldn't speak. Then he forced out the words that chilled the paramedics to the bone.

"She was my wife. Her youthful looks were everything to her. She prided herself on keeping young. It was her obsession. She was only 42, and until two weeks ago, she could easily pass for early 20s. Then it all started to go wrong."

The two paramedics exchanged worried glances. Either the man was clearly delusional or they'd just witnessed something that defied explanation.

"What do you mean?" asked Bob.

"A month ago, she looked amazing," explained the man, in a choked voice. "Her skin gleamed, her hair shone, her eyes were bright. She seemed to be reversing the aging process. Whatever she was taking, it was working a miracle. And her energy levels… well, she was unstoppable. Walking, dancing, singing, she could go on forever. Sometimes she put in a twelve-hour day at the estate agency where she worked, then came home, cooked a three-course meal and went out dancing all night. She was phenomenal." He paused. "Then the nightmares started."

Both paramedics leaned forward, simultaneously horrified and fascinated.

"Yes," prompted Bob.

She had a recurring nightmare about aging," continued the man, "and the more she had the dream, the more it came true. Age spots on her hands, wrinkles across her face, skin drying out. Over the last couple of weeks, I watched her age. I saw her hair turn white and start to fall out, her body begin to stoop, her face sink in. And then tonight it all happened so quickly. One minute she was drinking tea with me, the next she was on the bed gasping for breath." He looked at the two paramedics in complete desolation.

"She turned into a living skeleton before my eyes. And now she's dead. How is that possible?"

The paramedics glanced at one another, not knowing what to say. This was beyond their experience.

Outside, with a near silent flurry of feathers, a large bird rose into the air, its outstretched wings momentarily bathed in the sodium glare of the streets lights, before it disappeared into the night sky.

7. **Family conference**

The next day was beautiful. At Hartswell Hall, sunlight streamed in through the windows, pouring into every room and illuminating each shadowy corner as if making up for lost time and all the years it had been unable to penetrate the grimy, dirty panes of glass. The house itself seemed to breathe with new life, its walls vibrant, the furniture spotless and the furnishings pristine. The chandeliers glistened and sparkled in the early morning sun and everywhere a fresh energy filled the air.

Outside, the grounds teamed with new growth. Late spring bulbs that had been dormant for too long burst into life, daffodils and crocuses combining with bluebells, primroses and polyanthus to create a riot of colour, set against a lush green backdrop. Buds on the trees pushed forth small green leaves, shrubs were fuller and leafier, and the great main lawn leading down to the ha-ha was once again restored to its former glory, stretching like a soft, green carpet to the rear of the house.

Joseph walked through the grounds, smiling at the scenes unfolding around him.
"You've been neglected for far too long,' he murmured under his breath. "Well, the barren times are over. Winter is gone and you're in good hands, now."
As if in reply, birds sang from the trees and squirrels jumped from branch to branch. A vixen ran across the lawn, followed by six small, red fox cubs, and in the paddock beyond the rose garden, rabbits jumped and hopped in sheer delight.

Hearing a voice call his name, Joseph looked up and could just make out the figure of Mrs de Lucis, standing on the top step by the French windows to the rear of the ballroom.
"Joseph, we need you in the library. Can you come?"
He strode back along the pathways, now edged with bluebells and snowdrops, and reaching the house, followed Viyesha through the French windows into the drawing room. From there, they went via the main hall, into the library, where he found Theo and Violet seated on a shiny leather Chesterfield sofa and Mr de Lucis sitting

opposite them. Pantera and Aquila stood to one side, both looking ill at ease. Mrs de Lucis sat down next to her husband and indicated for Joseph to sit.

"What's this about?" asked Joseph, curiously, looking around.

"Family conference," said Aquila, in his rasping voice. "A small matter of security that needs sorting out. Sit down."

"I see you haven't lost any of your legendary charm," said Joseph, grinning and sitting in the nearest chair. "What's ruffled your feathers, Aquila?"

The chauffeur glowered at him and Mrs de Lucis spoke.

'Aquila's right. We do have a small issue to sort out, but I don't believe it's a problem." She addressed Theo. "It's about your friend, Emily, Theo, as I think you know."

"Yes," said Theo, tersely, looking down at the carpet.

"Don't you mean *my* friend Emily?" asked Violet, indignantly.

"I didn't think…." began Theo, but was silenced by his father.

"I think we all know what the issue is," said Mr de Lucis, standing up. "A school friendship is one thing, Violet, but this has the potential to get out of control, wouldn't you say, Theo?"

Theo studied the carpet for a moment longer, before looking up at his father.

"Look, I know she showed up here yesterday, but I didn't invite her. In fact, I've gone out of my way to push her away." He looked pleadingly at his mother. "I am not putting things in jeopardy, believe me."

"But there is an attraction between you. You can't deny it," cried Violet. "I've seen how she reacts to you. And how you react to her."

"This 'attraction' needs nipping in the bud," said Aquila menacingly. Pantera glanced at him anxiously.

"No, Aquila," she said quietly, "We don't want that. Leave the girl alone."

Theo stared angrily. "What are you saying, Aquila? I've told you. Emily isn't a problem. I can handle it."

"The question is, Theo," said Mr de Lucis, talking slowly, "can *she* handle it?

Just how serious is this attraction? And could it get out of hand?"

"We don't want to risk everything we've worked for, everything we believe in…." added Violet. "The stakes are too high."

"Honestly!" said Joseph, looking round at everyone incredulously. "We've only just got here, and already there's a problem. Can't you just tell this girl to take a running jump?" He looked questioningly at Theo.

"Theo," said Mrs de Lucis softly, looking into Theo's eyes, "I need to know. Is she the one? The one you've been waiting for all these years?"

"I …. I don't know." Theo's voice was barely a whisper. "I think she may be."

The room was silent as everyone took in the significance of his words. Aquila stared at him with an intensity that was bordering on ferociousness; Pantera placed her hand on his arm, restraining him from further outburst.

"Do you know what you're saying, Theo?" asked Mr de Lucis.

"Yes, I do," cried Theo, defensively, "and I do understand the implications. And you have to believe me, I would do nothing to put us all in danger." His voice dropped low again. "But if she is the one, I can't let her go again."

Mrs de Lucis sat back and pressed the palms of her hands together thoughtfully. The others all watched her. "The way I see it," she said, at last, "is that we must proceed very carefully. There is too much at stake to squander on a mistaken infatuation. I suggest, Theo, you get to know Emily a little better. In a few days, invite her to Hartswell Hall, so we can all meet her. Take things slowly… Then we will decide on the best course of action."

"You put at risk all that is dear to us…" began Aquila, but Mrs de Lucis put up her hand.

"My word is final on this for the present," she said in a firm voice, and turning to her husband, she asked, "Leon, my love, are you in agreement with me?"

"Yes," he said, then added ominously, "it's essential we keep any potential threat close at hand. That way, we can deal with things quickly should the danger become too great."

He addressed Theo, "You must take great care, Theo. Our existence may depend upon your actions."

"Yes," said Theo, "I understand. Now, is there anything else, or can I go?"

"You can go," said Mrs de Lucis, giving her husband a worried glance.

Theo got up, his face taut and strained. As he walked towards the door, Aquila made a sudden movement towards him, pinning him against one of the old oak bookshelves.

"Nothing can get in the way of the Blue Moon Ball," he spat out venomously, his face close to Theo's, his voice little more than a whisper. "Do you understand?"

Theo stared at him, then roughly pushed him aside and walked out of the door without looking back.

"Be vigilant, everyone," said Mrs de Lucis in a calming voice, looking round the room. "Keep a close eye on Theo, we can't afford to alienate him. Especially you, Aquila."

Aquila snorted derisively and swept out of the room, followed by Pantera.

Joseph and Violet went after them, leaving only Mr and Mrs de Lucis behind. She stared thoughtfully out of the window, the sunbeams playing on her blonde hair, making it shine like a golden halo, and giving her white skin the translucency of fine porcelain. Her husband came to stand next to her.

"Aquila informs me the local 'situation' has come to an end," she murmured, under her breath.

"And can't be traced to us in any way?" he asked.

"Absolutely not," she replied. "It was most regrettable and not as we intended. But it reinforces the fact we are dealing with a force that has powers beyond even our comprehension, and that we must never underestimate its capabilities. To believe we control it could be our undoing." She turned and smiled sadly at her husband, who bent to kiss her cheek.

"The pathway gets ever harder, my love," she whispered to him.

"But the prize is worth it, Viyesha," he reminded her. "You must never forget that."

PART TWO: DESIRE

8. A Change of Heart

The first day of the summer term was sunny and warm. I woke up with the 7am alarm, drew back the curtains and let the bright rays of sunshine fall on my face. The sunrise was amazing; red, yellow, purple and golden hues streaked across the sky like a crazy Impressionist painting. I stared for a moment enrapt, bowled over by the beauty of nature. Things might not be great for me, but you couldn't deny the sheer magnificence of the morning sky. I pulled on my new skinny blue jeans and pale blue sweatshirt, relieved on the one hand to be going back to my regular routine, seeing my friends and getting back to normal, nervous on the other about seeing Violet and Theo, and wondering how they'd be with me, what to say to them, if indeed they deemed me worth talking to.

I must have been quiet at breakfast because my Granddad gently put his hand over mine and said comfortingly, "Never mind, Emmie, if he's not interested in you, he's not worth bothering with. Concentrate on your studies and your friends. Someone else will come along who doesn't play games, you wait and see."

I smiled at him sadly. The problem was I didn't want anyone else. I only wanted Theo. How could anyone else compare to him? Those deep cornflower blue eyes, that flawless skin, the tousled hair, the perfect looks. I pulled myself up short. What was I doing? They were his physical attributes. I knew nothing about him at all. We'd scarcely spoken more than a few words. Talk about shallow. Since when had I gone on looks alone? I'd always said personality was more important, the ability to laugh and share a joke. I had no idea if Theo even had a sense of humour. He might be a prize idiot for all I knew. And yet, I knew, instinctively, that he and I would be a perfect match. I felt with every particle of my being that we would be good together, would share the same sense of humour, belonged together.

"Stop it," I told myself. "He's not interested. Get over him. It never even got started, so there's nothing to even get over."

Still that niggling voice in my head refused to be silent, reminding me that he had been watching me from the upstairs window at the hall, had even told his mother about me. I had made an impact, I knew. I just couldn't work out why it was so problematic for him. What was it he'd said to me, that day by the tennis courts? "Stay away, for your own sake." What was that all about? It seemed a touch over-dramatic. I sighed. There was something here I couldn't fathom.

"I've just heard the most amazing story on the radio," said my mother, walking into the breakfast room and breaking into my thoughts.

"What's that?" I asked, blankly.

"A local woman has been found dead," she answered. "She was supposed to be 42, but when they found her, she looked as if she was over 100. Her husband said she'd been full of life and energy one moment, then suddenly started aging and died the next. The coroner said he'd never seen anything like it."

"Yuk. Sounds like something out of a horror movie," I said.

"Probably overdid the anti-aging products and they backfired," suggested Granddad.

"That's very funny, Granddad," I said, laughing. "You'd better watch it, mum, you might be next."

"Not funny," said my mother, pretending to be upset. "By the way, have you seen the time? It's ten to eight. If you don't go now, you'll miss the bus."

"Alright, I'm out of here," I said, grabbing my backpack and making for the door.

"Just for the record, Emily," she called after me, "You'll be old yourself one day."

"Not me," I called back to her.

I met up with Tash and Seth, walking up to the bus stop.

"Alright?" said Tash.

"Yeah, sorry haven't been around over the hols, I felt pretty bad. I think it was a virus," I glanced at her. She looked back, not smiling, which wasn't encouraging.

"You better now?" she asked.

"Yes, have you done your assignment on love poetry?" I ventured.

"Don't even mention it," she sighed.

"No don't," said Seth, "I don't want you two quoting love poetry at each other again."

"Seth!" we both exclaimed at the same time, and as we laughed, just like that, it seemed we were back to normal.

Tash sat next to me on the bus and I was hugely relieved when neither Violet nor Theo was waiting at the bus stop by the hall. With any luck they wouldn't be at college today and I wouldn't have to address the problem of what to do about them. They seemed to take days off with alarming regularity and I couldn't understand what they did or why the college allowed it.

"No Blondie," Tash said pointedly.

"No," I agreed, "I don't know what's going on there. It's all a bit strange."

"Told you I thought there was something about her that wasn't quite right, didn't I?" Tash laboured the point.

"Yes you did, but as I haven't seen anything of her, can we just drop it? Please? It's getting humungously boring."

"Okay. Consider the subject dropped."

"Did you hear that story on the radio, this morning?" Seth called over.

"What about the local woman who'd aged and died?" I asked.

"Yeah. Weird or what? How can that be possible? She was 42 but apparently looked over 100 when she died."

"I reckon she'd lied about her age," surmised Tash, "Probably was older than she said, then she got ill and suddenly started looking her age."

"My Granddad reckoned she used too many anti-aging products and they backfired," I said.

"Ha ha," laughed Seth, "Let that be a lesson, Tash, not to overdo it. You're always using some cream or other. You'll wake up one day all wizened and shrunken, looking like a mummy. That's what they reckon she looked like."

"Oh, totes hilaire, Seth. You are so not funny. Do you see me laughing?"

"No, heaven forbid you might get laughter lines," he taunted.

He ducked as Tash threw an exercise book at him.

I beamed. It was good to be back with my friends.

I felt as if life had resumed some degree of normality, and so it had until lunchtime, when events took a very unexpected turn. We'd had an uneventful morning. English Lit and Business Studies had gone past in a blur, and I felt slightly disembodied, the after-effects of the virus still with me. Violet did not appear and I allowed myself to relax a little. At lunchtime, I sat with Tash in the cafeteria, enjoying a pepperoni pizza and salad, both of us looking forward to Double Art in the afternoon and chatting about our Abstract Art project for the summer term.

"I was thinking about using light and dark and shadow," I said.

"I thought I might do something with broken glass and newspaper," said Tash, "you know, experiment with different textures. Oh no…" She broke off suddenly and focused on the opposite side of the café. " It's the terrible twins."

"What d'you mean?" I asked, turning round and following her gaze.

There, standing against the opposite wall, the sunshine framing them in a glow of bright light, stood Theo and Violet. My stomach lurched and my heart flipped. I felt the blood rush to my face and was conscious of going bright red. I turned back rapidly.

"What's with you?" asked Tash, incredulously, staring at me. "You're as red as a tomato."

"Nothing. Nothing," I muttered, looking down, desperately trying to calm down and stop blushing.

"Yeah, it looks like nothing," said Tash sarcastically. "OMG, they're coming over. Don't look."

It was too late, I'd already turned, and, like an idiot, I felt my hand rise up waving at them, as if someone was pulling my arm like a puppet on a string. Never had I felt more gauche and awkward, and totally not up to the situation.

"Hi, mind if we sit with you?" asked Violet, her crystal voice friendly and reassuring.

"No, not at all," I said, in total shock.

"Hi," said Theo, his beautiful smile lighting up his face, his eyes blue and dancing.

"I'm Theo," he said to Tash, going to shake her hand, "pleased to meet you."

"Likewise," said Tash, allowing her hand to be shaken, and gazing into his eyes.

I felt a stab of jealousy and watched for any sign of static electricity between them. Was he flirting with Tash? He couldn't be. It was me he was interested in. Tash appeared to be spell bound, overcome with the iridescent beauty before her.

"Do you have a name?" asked Theo.

"She's called Natasha," I said loudly, causing Theo to break his gaze with Tash and look at me. I saw with alarm that she continued to stare at him. "Tash for short, isn't it?" I almost shouted at her, forcing her to break her gaze.

"Yes, yes, it is," she said falteringly.

No. This was not going well. The last thing I wanted was for Tash to fall for Theo. If I couldn't have him, I most certainly didn't want her to succeed.

"How are you, Emily?" asked Theo, his voice tender and full of care. He looked into my eyes and I felt an involuntary shudder go down my spine.

"I'm good, thank you," I said primly, "How are you?"

No, this was far too formal.

"Yes, I'm good as well."

"Oh good," I looked at Violet in a panic, and unable to think of anything else to say, asked: "How are the renovations coming on? Is everything finished?"

"Yes, why do you ask?" she answered, which completely threw me. This was one totally weird situation.

"Just wondering," I said lamely, explaining to Tash, "they've been renovating Hartswell Hall. It looked fabulous when I saw it over Easter." I regretted the words as soon as they were out and couldn't bear to look in Theo's direction.

Tash snapped out of her spellbound dream and said in a spikey voice. "You were at Hartswell Hall over Easter? What about your virus?"

"Er, it was when I was feeling better. I went for a walk and ended up at the hall," I mumbled. "I didn't go in or anything. I just stood in the driveway and saw the renovations from the outside." This was now mega embarrassing. I'd just admitted to Theo that I'd been standing outside his house. Even if it hadn't been him at the window, he now knew for definite I was stalking him. Violet regarded me with amusement and I felt like an insect wiggling on the end of a pin.

"Look, I've got to go," I stood up quickly, banging into the table and knocking over a bottle of water. Thankfully, the top was still on. "I have to see Mrs Pritchard. She wants to talk about my essay. I'll see you all later."

I quickly picked up my backpack and walked out of the cafeteria as fast as I could, without a backward glance. I didn't want to see the expressions on their faces.

I saw Tash in Art, but she barely acknowledged me, and although she sat next to me on the bus home, our conversation was minimal and strained. I was glad to see Theo and Violet weren't on the bus. Judging by the gleaming black Jaguar that was parked outside the college gate, I guessed their horrible chauffeur had come to collect them.

Good. I didn't want any more embarrassing scenes. If I'd stood any chance with Theo, I'd most definitely blown it now. I'd behaved like an awkward adolescent, with absolutely no social graces. He was plainly light years out of my grasp. Too old, too sophisticated and all round too god-like for the likes of me. I slunk home, feeling pathetic and small. If this is what love was all about, you could keep it. It wasn't making me feel great at all, just a great mass of uncontrolled emotions. Never had I been so glad to see mum and Granddad. Sometimes, all you needed was the bosom of your family, I reasoned. Theo could go take a hike. I was way out of my depth with all this.

The next day, Tash was polite but distant, while Seth was irritatingly cheerful, trying to joke us back into familiarity. It wasn't working, and both Tash and I were relieved when we arrived at college and could go our different ways, her to Geography and me to Business Studies. At break time, I went to my locker, putting away the books I'd just used and getting out the textbooks I needed for my next few lessons. I was turning the key in my locker door, when I became aware of someone standing behind me. I didn't need to see who it was. I knew. I could feel his energy surrounding and caressing me, his presence strong and powerful. I turned slowly and looked into his eyes.

"Hi," said Theo gently.

"Hi," I said back, my legs feeling like jelly, my heart beating rapidly.

"Would you like to take a walk?" he asked.

I pinched the inside of my wrist, just to make sure I wasn't dreaming. A walk? With the god-like Theo? What was going on? Was he about to warn me off? Ask for Tash's details? Declare undying love?

"Yes, of course," I answered, trance-like. "Where do you want to go?"

"Follow me," he said, mysteriously, and I had no choice but to do as he said.

He led the way past the lockers, down the stairs and out of 'A' Block. Outside, he walked through the quadrangle and continued on towards the netball courts, close to the scene of our previous strange encounter. All the while, he didn't say a word. There was a small private area close to the Games Block, where the wall curved back, and it was here that he stopped and turned to face me.

"Emily, you must know how I feel about you."

"Well, not really," I admitted. "You've been sending out rather mixed signals."

"I suppose I have," he sighed, "it's just that..."

He looked into my eyes and I felt as if I was looking into eternity. Flecks of blue and steel grey granite flew towards me as I was drawn into his mesmerizing gaze. I experienced warmth, love, passion, pain, suffering and the utmost longing, all in a fraction of a second, and I found it hard to breathe.

"What?" I asked softly, "What is it...?"

He hesitated. "It's just that ... so much has happened... I just want to keep you safe..." He paused and seemed unable to continue. It was still making no sense to me.

"I know a lot has happened," I said, reassuringly, "You lost your home in Egypt, you've moved over here, you've had to start again..." I was trying desperately hard to understand him.

With a huge effort, he seemed to gather his thoughts and focus. "Yes, you're right, I'm feeling unsettled with all that's happened. The thing is..."

"Yes?" I whispered, leaning closer towards him.

"I really like you, you know that, don't you?"

"I guess so…"

"Emily, you know there's a huge attraction between us, don't tell me you haven't felt it…"

"I have felt it," I said softly, aware that my whole future lay in the balance with my choice of words. If I said the wrong thing, I knew instinctively I would lose him.

"I've never felt anything like it before," I admitted.

So far, we hadn't touched. There was an odd formality to what should be an intimate occasion and again I felt way out of my depth. I didn't have the experience to know what to do, and so I let him take the lead. He touched my face gently with his fingertips and I closed my eyes. A sensation of immense peace and what I can only describe as 'togetherness' filled my being. Was this love? Was it lust? I didn't think so. This seemed almost transcendental, a deep, intense spiritual fulfilment, allied with total confusion.

I opened my eyes and gazed into his beautiful face. Surely this was the moment when we kissed?

He backed away again, and a look of torture passed over his face.

"I don't want to hurt you, and I don't want to lose you… ever again," he said more to himself than to me.

"You won't," I said uncertainly. "Look, why don't we just take this slowly, see what happens?" I decided to take the lead, aware that this intensity, although delicious in its painfulness, was getting us nowhere. He stared at me and smiled, a glorious, radiant, sun-warming smile that transformed his face. "You're right, sorry, I'm getting heavy… Not used to feeling like this." Now he was the one who was uncertain.

Suddenly, his arms were around me and I was enveloped in an all-consuming embrace. It felt like a velvet cloak around me, safe, protective and warm, and I relaxed into it. Yet still, he didn't kiss me. He seemed so unsure of himself, so nervous, it gave me confidence.

"Why don't we just hang out together and see what happens?" I suggested, aware that lessons were about to start again, and I needed to get going.

"Okay," he said, laughing. "Let's hang out together. Starting with lunch. Let me buy you lunch today."

"Great," I smiled at him, and suddenly my world was transformed. In the space of a few seconds, I had a boyfriend. And not just any boy. It was Theo. Gorgeous, sophisticated, model-like Theo. I couldn't wait to see the looks of the other girls when we sat down to have lunch together.

He took my hand in his and we walked back together. I was floating on a cloud of euphoria and hardly heard a word my tutors uttered over the next two hours. My thoughts were filled with one thing only. Theo. His eyes, his smile, his skin, the feel of his arms around me.

Later, on the school bus I played my favourite Lumineers' song, 'Ho Hey', loudly on my iPod all the way home, mouthing the words over and over, and grinning from ear to ear. This song was meant for me. I was totally hooked.

9. **Surveillance I**

Just outside Hartsdown College, at number 27 Gillyflower Lane, which formed the eastern boundary of the school and college grounds, Mrs Henforth was enjoying her usual mid morning tipple.

She took the crystal decanter out of the sideboard and poured herself a generous schooner of Tio Pepe sherry. Raising the glass to a photograph of her late husband, which held pride of place on the crocheted mat on the top of the sideboard, she said: "Cheers, Harry, here's to you, darling. Just a little snifter to see me through the morning." She picked up an old pair of binoculars that lay on the coffee table and lovingly caressed them. Somehow, it seemed to bring her closer to Harry. She remembered all those happy days when they'd packed a picnic and taken off across the woods towards Hartswell-on-the-hill. Harry had liked nothing better than to sit in the bushes, watching the bird life, while she sat on the picnic blanket and read a book.

"Look," he would exclaim, excitedly, "A Tree Creeper" or "a Lesser Spotted Woodpecker", as some feathered wonder flew into view, and out would come the binoculars. "Yes, dear, that's lovely," she would say, on autopilot, lost in the intrigue of her latest whodunit novel. He'd spend ages oohing and aahing over each find, pulling out his battered old sketchbook and avidly sketching them as fast as he could. The book was full of his drawings: chaffinches, green finches, blue tits, long tailed tits, wrens, blackbirds, thrushes, robins and, best of all, a kestrel. She vividly remembered the day he'd seen the kestrel. It had sat on a branch so close to them you could see every feather of its mottled back and underbelly. Harry hadn't needed the binoculars it had been so close. That had been a very exciting day.

Now, she idly picked up the binoculars and put them to her eyes, twiddling the knobs to get the lenses into focused.

"Never could work these things," she said to herself crossly, "it's down to having an astigmatism, that's what it is."

She walked over to the front bay window and trained the binoculars on the trees opposite, turning the knob furiously in an attempt to focus the blurry mass of green that met her gaze.

"Ah, that's better," she exclaimed, "I can see a branch, and I can make out the leaves, and… oh…"

She gasped in surprise as a large beak and a pair of glittering black eyes came into view. She put down the binoculars and rubbed her eyes. Then she raised them again and took another look. There was no mistaking it. A huge bird sat in the tree opposite, looking at her malevolently, its black feathers ruffling in the breeze. A glance down its body revealed a long, sleek breast and two massive taloned claws.

"Oh my, Harry, I wish you were here to see this," she exclaimed. "What a beauty. If I didn't know better, I'd say it was an eagle. Let me find that bird book so's I can identify it."

She put down the binoculars, opened the sideboard door and rummaged around, looking for Harry's old Collins Book of Birds. A sudden movement caught her eye and she looked up, just as the bird took flight. For a brief second, it flew towards her front window and she saw clearly its cruel, hooked beak, its glinting, gleaming eyes and powerful, outstretched wings. Its gaze locked with hers and she shuddered involuntarily, as if someone had just walked over her grave. Then it was gone, skimming silently over her house and creating a momentary dark shadow as it flew across the sun.

10. **Getting close**

I was right. My relationship with Theo was the talk of the college. Groups of girls would whisper fervently as I approached, then fall silent as I walked past, staring at me with looks of envy, admiration and disgust. How could I, insignificant Emily Morgan, have possibly ensnared the best catch in the college? Theo stood head and shoulders above all the other boys, if not actually, then figuratively. He was, quite plainly, more handsome, more rugged and more athletic than any of his peers. He was charming, funny, intelligent and thoughtful. He was certainly more sophisticated than all the other boys put together, with a knowledge of the world they could only guess at. And yet, for all that, he was popular. Boys and girls alike seemed drawn to him, willing to be charmed by him, falling prey to his easy manners and social graces, like moths to a flame. It was an analogy I used all too frequently when I thought of Theo and made me realise my wings were already scorched and burnt. I knew I was getting in too deep, too quickly, but was powerless to do anything about it. I felt exhilarated, yet out of control; my feelings and emotions like alien beings that had taken me over. I welcomed this brave new world that had opened before me and wouldn't have changed a thing, yet part of me longed to go back to the tried and trusted world I knew, where my feelings could remain hidden and I had the comfort of my friends around me.

That was part of the problem. Tash and I had fallen out since I started seeing Theo. I would like to think it was just plain old jealously, but I didn't think it was. I trusted Tash's judgement implicitly, after all she was my oldest friend. She'd detected something about Theo and Violet that she didn't like and she felt mistrustful of them. It hurt her that I wouldn't listen to her doubts and warnings and I knew she worried about me, rather than being envious. But what could I do? I couldn't stay tied to Tash's apron strings forever. I felt instinctively that Theo was my future, and that had to come first. But I also felt the pain of our separation keenly, and wondered if we would ever get back that cosy intimacy we'd shared for so many years.

When she saw us together in the café that first lunchtime, holding hands and gazing at one another over the table, Tash had been quite unpleasant.

"So, how long has this been going on for?" she demanded, sitting on the seat next to me and throwing down her backpack on the table.

"It's just started…" I began to say, but she cut me short.

"Oh, save it. D'you think I'm an idiot? It's obviously been going on for a while, and you didn't have the guts or the decency to tell me. Well, it's obvious who comes first, isn't it? And it's not your friends."

"Tash, why are you being like this?" I failed to understand her animosity.

"It's okay," said Theo, diplomatically, "I understand. You feel let down and…"

She cut him short: "Let's get one thing straight, Blondie," she said nastily to Theo. "You don't understand how I feel and you never will. I don't feel let down. The problem is I don't trust you. We don't know anything about you, and you might have pulled the wool over Little Miss Naivety's eyes here, but you don't fool me. There's something about you and your sister that doesn't add up. And I am determined to find out what it is."

Theo attempted to placate her. "I don't know what you're talking about. I will never hurt Emily, she's too important to me."

Tash shot him a venomous look. "Save it, Blondie, I don't want to hear it. I'll be watching you and as soon as you put one foot out of place, you'll have me to answer to. D'you understand?" She spat the words into his face and I sat speechless, too shocked by her words to know what to say.

Again Theo smiled, but I sensed a chilliness beneath his outward demeanour.

"Like I said, I don't know what you're talking about, but I warn you, Tash, don't cross me or my family." He let go of my hand, folded his arms defensively and stared at her.

"Like I'm really scared," she mocked him. "Gotta go, some of us have work to do."

She looked at me dismissively and grabbed her backpack, swinging it violently over her shoulder. "See you around, Emmie."

With that parting shot, she tossed her long red hair over her shoulder and walked out of the café with her head held high.

Theo looked after her, a worried expression on his face.

"Sorry about that," I said softly. "I don't know what's the matter with her. She's not normally like that. I think either she's jealous, or more likely, worried about me."

"Yes, I'm sure that's it," said Theo, smiling, but there was no mistaking the coldness in his eyes.

We didn't fare much better with Seth. He wasn't as bad as Tash, but he certainly wasn't over-friendly. He eyed us holding hands with suspicion and before I had chance to speak to him, muttered something about rugby practice and having to go.

He accosted me later on that afternoon, as we walked to a tutorial together.

"So, what's going on Emmie?" he asked. "This is all very sudden with Theo, isn't it? You never mentioned anything to me or Tash."

"Well, I suppose it is very sudden, but it's not like I'm getting married to him. We're only dating, and it's only just begun. There's been nothing to tell." I failed to understand why my friends were making me feel so defensive. I had nothing to feel guilty about. This was their problem, not mine. If they didn't want to see me happy, they knew what they could do.

"Okay," said Seth, "just don't forget us, will you?"

"Of course not," I answered, feeling very perplexed with it all. "He'll probably get bored with me after a few dates."

Seth just looked at me and walked into the tutorial, silently finding his seat and sprawling in his chair. I sat down and once again failed to take in anything, so disturbed were my feelings and thoughts.

As I turned the key in my locker and took out my coat, ready to get the bus home, Theo was there once again.

"Hi, Emily," he planted a light kiss on my forehead. "I thought you might like a lift home…"

"Oh," I said, startled, "You mean, in your car…?

"No, on the front of my bicycle. Yes, of course in the car. What else would I mean?" he grinned at me.

"Okay," I laughed, trying to gather my thoughts. "Is Violet alright with this?"

"I don't have to get permission from Violet for everything I do," he pointed out.

"No, I know, I didn't mean that," I said awkwardly. Yet again, he was making me feel naïve and gauche. "I'm just not sure she approves of you seeing me."

"You leave Violet to me," he said sharply. "Now, do you have everything?"

"Yes," I answered, closing my locker door. I saw Seth at the end of the corridor and called after him. "Seth, can you tell Tash I'm not catching the bus? I'm getting a lift with Theo…"

I know he heard me, because he turned and looked at me. But he didn't respond, just turned on his heel, his expression unreadable, and walked away. I stared after him.

"Guess your friends don't think much of me, do they?" said Theo.

"Oh, they'll be fine," I said, trying to convince myself. "They just need a bit of time. Don't worry about them."

"I don't," said Theo, with arched eyebrows. "It's you I'm interested in, not them."

The way he looked at me made my stomach flip and goose bumps run down my spine. I shuddered, feeling completely weak in his presence. I would do anything for this boy. Even give up my friends.

"Come on," he said, taking my bag, and I followed him down the stairs, past the main hall, into the reception area, and out into the open air. As we walked through the college gates, I saw the gleaming black Jaguar and the unpleasant chauffeur lounging by the car door.

"Hi Aquila," said Theo, walking up to the car. "One more to take home today. This is Emily."

"Hi, Aquila," I muttered shyly from behind Theo's back, aware that this odious man didn't like me.

His black eyes glittered at me. "Yes, we've met," he said dismissively, asking Theo, "Do your mother and father know about this?"

Theo laughed shortly. "And what are they going to do about it? We're only giving Emily a lift home, what's your problem?"

"No problem," he answered through gritted teeth, and opened the door roughly, saying to me, "Get in, please."

I slid onto the smooth leather seats looking around me. This was the kind of luxury I could get used to. Theo sat next to me, placing his leg close to mine. My insides flipped again and I felt frozen to the spot, my body tensing in anticipation of things to come. Should he be doing this? Was it appropriate? Appropriate or not, it felt fantastic, and I grinned at him, feeling like the cat who's got the cream. He smiled back, his wonderful, sunny smile, and I knew, whatever happened, whoever disapproved, I didn't care. I just wanted to be with him. There was a slight commotion outside as Violet arrived and was ushered into the front seat by Aquila. She turned and looked at us angrily.

"Hi Emily, did you miss the bus?"

"Er, no…" I stuttered, "Theo said I could have a lift home." I glanced at Theo for support.

"It's okay, Vi, don't get in a sweat," he smiled sweetly at his sister. "Emily only lives down the road from the hall, it's no problem to drop her off."

"If you say so," said Violet, frostily and turned, staring very deliberately through the front window. "Can we have some music on, Aquila?" she asked, without even looking at the chauffeur, who by now was sitting in the driving seat, with the engine idling. "Elgar's Salut d'Amour would seem appropriate," she added sourly.

"Sure. Why not?" he said stonily, not looking back at her and pressed a button on the console. Beautiful music filled the cabin, and it would have been perfect had not the atmosphere been so chilly. I sat, feeling perplexed. What was with this weird family? I couldn't get their measure at all. Surely Violet wasn't jealous of me being with Theo? And why did the hook-nosed Aquila seem to dislike me so intensely? He looked at me as if I was a piece of meat on a plate, and I felt very uneasy in his presence. Frightened, even. If he was a servant, he had no business having opinions about me. Surely he was there to do his job? Something didn't add up, but I couldn't work out what it was. Then Theo took my hand in his and all my doubts and insecurities melted away. I felt safe and protected. The haunting melody of the violin filled the air and I sat back against the smooth, cool leather, losing myself in the experience. I'd come a long way in the last few days. From being a sad no-hoper without even the glimmer of a love life, I now had the most good-looking boy I'd ever met as my boyfriend, and I was being taken home in his chauffeur-driven car. Who'd have guessed at the beginning of the week that life could take such an upward turn? I squeezed Theo's hand and he squeezed it back, making me smile. I didn't need to look at him, I knew he was feeling as happy as I was. I purposefully didn't look in the driver's rear view mirror and risk seeing Aquila's scowling, angry face. Why spoil a perfect moment with his unpleasantness?

It hardly seemed to take two minutes before we'd arrived back in the village and I was giving Aquila directions, although I got the sense he already knew where I lived, for all the attention he gave me. The sleek black Jaguar pulled up outside my house, and Aquila unwillingly got out of the driver's seat and opened my door, looking at me coldly.

I swung my legs out and turned to say goodbye to Theo, but the seat was empty. Amazingly, he was already standing alongside Aquila, taking my hand and helping me to get out of the car.

"How did you get there so quickly…?" I started to say, but he put his finger to his lips conspiratorially.

"I'll walk you to your door," he said gallantly, picking up my backpack.

I turned to say thank you to Aquila, but he was back in the driver's seat and I was glad I didn't have the opportunity to speak to him. He was one nasty individual.

As we walked up the driveway, the front door opened and my mother and Granddad peered out, looking intrigued at the sleek black car outside the house and the stunning boy who stood next to me.

"Mum, Granddad, this is Theo," I introduced him proudly, and Theo stepped forward to shake their hands.

"Mrs Morgan, pleased to meet you…. Granddad… delighted……" He beamed at them and I knew my mother was instantly sold, judging by the slight flush that crept into her cheeks. Gramps was a little more reticent, taking Theo's hand with a curt "likewise", and obviously sizing up the beautiful creature that stood before him.

"Would you like to come in for a cup of tea, Theo?" asked my mother, "Perhaps your father would like to come too, and is that your sister in the car?"

"Yes, that's my sister," smiled Theo. "But that's not my father. Aquila is our chauffeur, and he most definitely doesn't take tea."

"Oh, your chauffeur… of course …" My mother looked visibly impressed and I stepped in to spare her or Theo further embarrassment.

"I don't think they can come in today, mum, they need to get back, don't you Theo?" I looked at him pointedly.

"I'm afraid so," said Theo, taking the hint. "Perhaps another time?"

"Of course, any time," said my mother, more than a little flustered, "any time at all, Theo…"

"Yes, pop," said Granddad. "It'll be good to have a chat with you…."

"Goodbye, Theo," I said, determined to put an end to this doorstep charade. Talk about embarrassing families. These two were impossible.

"Bye, Emily," said Theo, giving me a quick peck on the cheek. "I'll call you later. Lovely to meet you, Mrs Morgan …. Granddad…"

Once the front door was closed, the questions came.

"How long has this been going on for?" "How old is he?" "Is it serious?" "Where do they live?" "How rich are they to afford a chauffeur…?" My mother couldn't get her words out quick enough. Granddad stood by, watching, saying nothing.

I put my hands up. "Stop, Mum. Just stop. His family have bought Hartswell Hall, so yes they're wealthy. He's 19 and we haven't even had a date yet, so please don't worry. It's not serious. We're just getting to know each other."

"Sorry, Emmie, I can't help it," said my mother excitedly. "He's so gorgeous, and so charming. Almost too good to be true… Those blue eyes, and that skin… He's beautiful. And to think his family are renovating Hartswell Hall. How exciting."

My Granddad was a little more circumspect. "Good looks and wealth are all very well, Emmie, but you know as well as I do they're not important. I hope there's a bit more substance to him."

"Of course there is, Gramps," I said defensively, but in my head, a little voice still asked awkward questions. What did I know about Theo? Was there any more substance to him than good looks and money? Could I trust him? What did he want from me? And why was everybody so against this relationship?

I had to admit it, I didn't know the first thing about him. I didn't know where he came from or what his intentions were. I didn't understand why he'd selected me out of all the girls he could have dated. And I had no idea why he'd been so against me initially, then suddenly changed his mind. None of it made sense. My Granddad was right to be concerned. There were too many questions and not enough answers.

But there again, did I have the sense to heed his concern?

I didn't think so.

11. **The Hall Reborn**

Some of my questions were answered that weekend, when I received an invitation to visit Hartswell Hall and meet Theo's mother and father on Sunday afternoon. By this time, he'd already been to our house, visiting after college on Friday, to meet my mum and Granddad, which had been every bit as cringing and embarrassing as I knew it would be, but had to be endured, as a rite of passage. He handled my mother's flirting and Granddad's third degree with good grace, and was in every sense the perfect boyfriend. He spoke of his life in Egypt and how they'd had to leave in order to escape the unrest that had come with political reform, of his parents' diverse property interests and plans to turn Hartswell Hall into a luxury hotel and conference centre. He spoke of the private tuition he and Violet had received while in Egypt and their excitement at being able to attend college and meet other people of the same age. He even put up with my mother asking about his beautiful skin and beauty routine. Asking a boy about his beauty routine! How much more embarrassing could you get? But he took it all in his stride, answering candidly and politely, explaining that he followed a strict vegetarian diet and always avoided sunbathing.

"When you're living in such a hot country, it's more important to cover up than go out in the sun," he explained, "especially when you're as fair skinned as we are."

My mother hung on his every word and totally monopolised him. I could hardly get a word in edgeways, but a few smouldering glances from Theo while my mother re-filled the tea cups more than made up for the lack of words between us. I could almost feel the air crackling with electricity, such was the connection between us.

My Granddad asked more down to earth questions, like where they'd lived in Egypt, what was happening out there, what had happened to their Egyptian properties, and why they'd chosen Hartswell-on-the-Hill. He questioned Theo with all the thoroughness of a seasoned interviewer and I prayed he wouldn't start asking where they got their money from and how much they paid for Hartswell Hall. Some things needed to remain private. Thankfully, he desisted, eventually sitting back and beaming at us both. I breathed a huge sign of relief. It seemed Theo had passed the preliminary stages of the interview with flying colours, and we were free to get to know one another a little better.

Afterwards, Granddad said, "A very nice young man, Emmie. Polite, well turned out, articulate. Couldn't really fault him on anything. That's my only concern, really. A bit too perfect, a little too composed for someone of his years. It was as if he'd heard all my questions before and knew all the answers off by heart."

"Granddad," I exclaimed, "If being too perfect is Theo's only fault, I don't really think there's a problem. What do you think, mum?"

"I think he's gorgeous," she said wistfully, "and I think you're very lucky. I just hope he doesn't hurt you." She looked suddenly sad and I put my arm around her.

"What's the matter, mum?"

"Oh, it's nothing," she said, forcing a smile. "He reminds me of someone I used to know many years ago, that's all."

"D'you mean dad?" I asked, curiously.

"No," she laughed. "Just someone I fell for many years ago. He broke my heart at the time." She looked at me closely. "I hope Theo doesn't do the same to you."

"Mum, don't pour cold water on it before it's even begun," I remonstrated. "You obviously think he's going to dump me at the first opportunity. Thanks very much."

"Of course I don't, darling," she said, "I just don't want you to get hurt."

"Be glad for me, mum," I instructed her. "I have a boyfriend. A gorgeous, good-looking, lovely boyfriend. If it ends, it ends. But at least I'll have fun, and I'll be living, rather than hanging around here all the time."

"Okay, I take your point," she said, laughing, "Enjoy yourself, Emmie, just don't get too involved with him."

Her advice was good, I knew. But it was too late. I was already far more involved than she could ever know. And a great big alarm bell was ringing loudly in my head.

The day I was due to visit Hartswell Hall was bright and sunny, a perfect spring day. The sky was an unbroken blue, the breeze warm and gentle and the gardens a mass of colour, as late spring flowers came through, polyanthus competing with primroses and early bluebells to create a vibrant backdrop. I told Theo I'd walk over to Hartswell Hall and meet him there, and as I walked up the main driveway, my feet crunching on the new gravel under foot, I began to feel anxious and nervous. What if Aquila was there glowering at me? What if Violet was unfriendly? What if his parents didn't like me? I'd already met his mother and she seemed lovely, although impossibly glamorous. What if she thought I was too awkward and young for Theo? The closer I got to Hartswell Hall, the more exposed and inadequate I felt. It was one thing meeting your new boyfriend's parents, but when they lived in a place as imposing as this, and were so obviously rich, it was a whole different ball game. These people lived a totally different lifestyle to me. They had poise, finesse and beauty; they were people of the world, with a sophistication I could only dream about. I began to feel sick with nerves and nearly turned round and walked back down the driveway, so acute was my sense of dread the closer I got to the big oak front doorway. Then suddenly, the door was opening and Theo was standing there, looking fantastic in a white shirt and faded jeans, a huge smile on his face, radiating happiness. I relaxed. I was here because Theo had invited me and wanted me to meet his family. What could be so bad? He entwined his fingers in mine, looked into my eyes and kissed me on the cheek. Once again, his magic started to work and as his energy flowed into me, I felt instantly refreshed and strong, his glow and radiance transforming me from a gauche adolescence to a creature of confidence and style. I had no idea how he did this, only that he did. And I also knew that only he could make me feel this way.

"You look divine," he whispered in my ear. "Come on, they're waiting to meet you."

He led the way across the black and white tiled entrance floor, through another oak doorway and into a huge foyer, tastefully decorated in cream, lilac and maroon. Stunning works of modern art adorned the walls and a glittering silver sculpture of a woman held pride of place by the reception desk, contrasting with the bas-relief coats of arms set into the old stone walls. A dark plum carpet felt thick and luxurious under foot and a resplendent chandelier hung from the elevated ceiling, its crystalline elements sparkling and glinting in the sunlight that streamed through the main window.

"It's beautiful," I said, looking round in wonder. "So pretty and so tastefully done."

"Thank you, my dear, it's always nice to have your handiwork admired." A soft, shimmering voice sounded behind me and I turned to see the most exquisite, beautiful woman I had ever encountered standing in the doorway to one of the rooms that led off the foyer.

"Emily, this is my mother, Viyesha," said Theo proudly.

"Yes, we have met once before, have we not?" asked the beautiful vision.

"Er, yes," I stuttered, feeling inadequate and ill at ease, "when I came to have a look, a couple of weeks ago…"

Seeing my discomfort, his mother held out a slim, white, perfectly manicured hand.

"I am so pleased to meet you properly, Emily, I've waited a long time for this."

I went to shake her proffered hand and simply cannot put into words the sensation I experienced when our hands touched. Her hand was cool and smooth, her touch light yet strong, and I felt warm and happy, without a care in the world, as if I were bathing in a pool of amber nectar. I looked into her face. Her beauty was breath taking and I recalled the last time I'd seen her she was wearing large sunglasses. Now I was able to see everything. If Theo was beautiful, his mother was out of this world. I struggled to find the words to describe her. She radiated light, warmth and serenity. Her skin was alabaster smooth, with an even, ivory complexion. Her nose was small and perfect, her cheekbones high, and her lips full. Her blonde hair was swept up, giving prominence to her large blue eyes, which shimmered and twinkled, like beautiful sapphires. Her figure was amazing, as slender and well proportioned as a Vogue model, and she was wearing a long, clinging blue dress that emphasised her perfect curves. That was it. She was perfect, not a hair out of place, like an airbrushed face in a magazine. And yet, despite the perfection, she seemed kind and friendly. Looking into her eyes, it was like gazing in to a summer's day, full of golden sunshine. I couldn't help but be mesmerized by her, but at the same time, she made me feel at home and at one with the world. Now I could see where Violet got her amazing looks. I had truly never encountered anyone like this ever before. On her wrist was a silver bangle, decorated with blue gemstones, and round her neck a pendant bearing a large blue crystal, both emphasizing the blue of her eyes and creating an overall impression of luminous blue. I couldn't help myself, I stared, unable to take my eyes off her.

"It's all right, Emily, my mother always has this effect on people," said Theo, breaking the spell. "She can't help being so beautiful."

"I'm sorry," I gasped, suddenly aware of how rude I was being. "I'm very pleased to meet you, Mrs de Lucis."

"Let's not be formal. Call me Viyesha, please," said the vision before me.

"Okay... Viyesha....." I felt like I'd stumbled on to a film set, so unreal was the whole situation.

"Come and meet the family," Viyesha instructed, and led the way through one of the many doorways leading off the reception area. Theo gestured for me to go first, his hand brushing against mine, and as it did, I felt a spark of electricity flash between us, rendering me powerless and passive. I found myself in a large room, possibly a ballroom, beautifully finished in delicate shades of mauve and lilac, with enormous windows looking out onto the grounds. Sunshine streamed in, giving a warm glow to the room, and my eyes took in heavy purple velvet drapes, a large, ornate fireplace where logs burned brightly and a magnificent chandelier that gleamed and sparkled. A white grand piano stood to one side, its lid raised high, and fabulous pieces of modern art adorned the walls. It was contemporary, luxurious and quite simply, magnificent. Around the fireside were three sofas of immense proportions, each in a light purple fabric, and it was here that the family sat.

They all stood up as I entered the room and a tall man with tousled blonde hair stepped towards me, offering his hand.

"This is my husband, Leon," said Viyesha.

"Emily, pleased to meet you."

My hand was gripped in a powerful handshake and I knew instantly if I ever had a problem, Leon would take care of it. He emanated strength, power and position. I looked into his face and was met by the same intense blue eyes, slightly darker than Viyesha's and Theo's, flecks of grey combining with dark blue and black. I had the immediate impression that this was one man you did not want to cross.

"Hi, Leon," I said shyly, taking in the physique, the muscles and the handsome features. This truly was like being on a Hollywood film set. He reminded me of at least three leading men all rolled into one. I couldn't decide between Brad Pitt, Daniel Craig and my mum's heart throb, a young Robert Redford. He was an older version of Theo, as you'd expect, although he didn't seem old. He had Viyesha's youthfulness about him, the same smooth ivory skin, the chiselled features, the amazing blue eyes that sparkled and shone, making me feel important, wanted, valued… putting me at ease, yet drawing me in. I broke my gaze with him, afraid of being hypnotised by the intensity. Leon seemed to be studying me curiously, looking into my face as if searching for something and I felt an intimacy that was somehow premature, as if I was being pulled towards him.

"Hi Emily," said Violet, from behind her father. "How are you?"

I was glad of the diversion and pleased to see Violet looking friendly again.

"Hi Violet, I'm good," I answered. "I can't believe this place, it's magnificent."

"That's mainly down to my mother," she said, "And Joseph, of course. He's seen to the grounds."

On cue, the third person who was sitting around the fireside stepped forward to shake my hand and I found myself looking at a boy possibly in his early twenties, with the same alabaster skin, blonde hair and twinkling blue eyes, and the biggest smile I had ever seen. He was lovely.

"Hello, Emily, I've heard all about you. I'm Joseph, Theo's cousin." As our hands touched, I felt kindness, gentleness and friendliness, as if I could tell this boy anything and he would be my friend for life.

"Hi Joseph, I'm sorry, I didn't realise you were here, Theo didn't say…" I felt momentarily confused. Why hadn't Theo mentioned a cousin staying with them?

"It's okay, don't worry, I haven't been here long," Joseph grinned at me. "I've been overseeing the renovation of the grounds from a distance, a sort of remote landscaper."

"Well, from the little I've seen, you've done a fantastic job," I said. "I can't believe how you've transformed the gardens in such a brief time. When we were kids we used to play in the grounds. It was jungle-like, great for hide-and-seek and making dens. Now I imagine it looks how it did in Victorian times."

"Yes, I followed the old photographs and plans carefully," he explained. "We wanted authenticity, combined with every modern comfort and extravagance the hotel could offer."

"You've succeeded from what I've seen," I complimented them all, asking, "When will you open for business?"

"Soon," said Viyesha. "We have a private function to host first before we open our doors. But enough of that, will you take tea with us?"

She went to pull a bell rope that hung at the side of the fireplace and, as if by magic, a tall, elegant, dark-skinned woman wearing a royal blue robe appeared with an ornate silver tray, on which were placed a white china teapot, cups, saucers, milk, sugar and a plate of delicious looking biscuits.

"This is Pantera, our house-keeper," explained Viyesha.

Pantera didn't say a word. She just stared at me with a look that was so cold and hostile, it completely threw me. Placing the tray on a coffee table in front of the fireplace with barely concealed contempt, and ignoring me totally, she addressed Viyesha. "Will you be requiring anything else?"

"No, thank you, Pantera. That will be all."

Throwing me a further disdainful look with her black, glittering eyes, Pantera left the room. She moved with an arrogant, slow grace that was both beautiful and mesmerising, and I watched her go with fascination. She was like a sleek, black cat, mesmerising and deadly, and one thing was very clear. She did not like me one bit.

We took tea and, for a while, everything became more ordinary and manageable. Theo's parents asked me about college, university and career plans. They asked how long I'd lived in the village, about my mother and father and what I wanted to do with my life. I let them take the lead, answering their questions as politely as I could, exactly as Theo had done with my mother and Granddad.

After tea, Viyesha suggested that Violet play the piano, which was unexpected, as I'd no idea she was the slightest bit musical.

"Just one piece," she reluctantly agreed. "Chopin's Nocturne in E flat?"

"Perfect," said Viyesha, and for the next few minutes we listened, transfixed, while Violet played exquisitely, her hands moving effortlessly over the keys, filling the room with sublime cadences and trills. When she finished, there was silence for a moment, before we all applauded, Leon calling out: "Bravo, just as Chopin played it."

"How we imagine Chopin played it," corrected Viyesha.

"I don't know about that," I admitted, remembering my own half-hearted attempts to play piano when I was younger, "but it was beautiful, Violet. You are so talented."

"Thank you," she said, grinning. "Just don't tell anyone at college. I don't want to get roped in to any end of term productions. Now, I must get on. I have a Philosophy project to finish. *'Discuss the idea that free will is an illusion'.* Mr Harrison, you know? Apparently he's a stickler for deadlines…"

"Yeah, I've heard. Fortunately, not my subject," I said, "I wouldn't know where to start."

"Neither do I," said Violet, "which is why I must leave you. I'll see you at college."

"Okay, see you tomorrow," I said as she left the room, pleased that we seemed to be friends again.

"Theo, why don't you give Emily a tour of the hall," suggested Viyesha. "Show her the renovations."

"Great idea," said Theo, grabbing my hand. "Come on, I'll give you the grand tour."

"And when you've done that, I'll give you a tour of the grounds," said Joseph, beaming at me.

"Thanks, that'd be great, Joseph," I beamed back, liking him immensely.

"Have fun," said Viyesha, adding, "Do remember to stay away from the old servants' quarters."

"It's unsafe up there," explained Leon. "We have structural work to do. Wouldn't want you coming to any harm." He winked at me, which threw me somewhat. I felt every gesture, every word and every look had a nuance that I couldn't quite understand, that nothing was quite as it seemed and there was another subtle, underlying agenda that I couldn't fathom. Theo's family might be beautiful, but they were also mysterious. Perhaps it was their money or their film star looks that made me feel ill at ease, but I felt instinctively it was something else. Tash was right. Everything was just that little bit too perfect, as if their veneer of perfection was masking something else beneath the surface. I didn't feel threatened and I didn't feel frightened, but I knew I must be on my guard.

We toured the ground floor rooms first and I realised I'd never appreciated Hartswell Hall's vast scale. As I thought, the large room in which we'd taken tea had once been the ballroom and was now designated for conferences. Also leading off the main foyer was the old library, a glorious, olde worlde room, furnished in red, with a vast collection of books; the old billiards room, now a private dining area, gloriously finished in blue; and a light airy drawing room, furnished in yellow and cream, with a wonderful old carved fireplace. An inner courtyard had been transformed into a fabulous dining area by adding a large glass atrium, where exotic plants grew alongside wrought iron sculptures, and the blend of old and new worked perfectly. There was no denying, Viyesha had impeccable taste. My only concern was the speed with which it had been done. Surely it wasn't possible to achieve all this in such a short time span? I asked Theo, but he just smiled and said beguilingly, "Once my mother has set her mind to do something, nothing stands in her way."

After we'd toured downstairs, Theo led the way up the enormous carved central staircase. I remembered looking through the old rotten window frames as a child, peering in at the dark interior, thinking how scary and dirty it looked, and how one day soon it would start to fall down. Who would ever have thought it could be transformed into this light, luxurious country house hotel?

There were thirty bedrooms in the main house, with further 'overspill' rooms in the old stable block. Theo led me to the left of the main stairway, where a galleried landing led to fifteen stunning rooms, each more decadent and luxurious than the last, finished in beautiful fabrics and materials, and providing a level of luxury I'd only seen in magazines. We explored the rooms one by one, until we arrived at the hall's piece de resistance, the Bridal Chamber. It was a sumptuous room furnished in pink and red, and I glanced at the imposing four-poster bed, with its deep red brocade eiderdown and fresh white sheets, my colour rising when I thought of future possibilities. I quickly put such thoughts out of my head, realising how little I really knew Theo and how, so far, he'd been the perfect gentleman. As yet, we hadn't even kissed, just a quick peck on the cheek. That was all. I wasn't in any hurry for intimacy, things were moving fast enough as it was. But I was concerned how fragile Theo seemed to think I was, as if I would shatter into a million pieces unless he took great care of me. I'd never met a boy quite so attentive or chivalrous, and sometimes it seemed like we were embarking on an old-fashioned courtship. Certainly this whole 'meet the parents' scenario was like something from a bygone era. What had happened to simply hanging out, listening to music and watching DVD's together? I was pretty inexperienced in all this, but didn't the 'meet the parents' stage happen when things got a more serious? We'd only been seeing each other for a couple of weeks, and that had consisted mainly of holding hands and having lunch together in the college cafeteria. I was baffled by this strange boy and his perfect family.

There again, life had become a whole lot more interesting now he was around and I knew there was no going back. Theo only had to look into my eyes and touch my hand for every sinew of my being to become alive with an intensity I'd never experienced before. Whatever was going on, I was well and truly hooked.

As we left the Bridal Chamber, he turned to me.

"Thanks for coming to meet the family, Emily," he said quietly, "You have no idea what it means to me."

I looked up at him, his eyes full of tenderness and love.

"It's no big deal," I shrugged. "Just wanted to have a sneaky peek at the hall and see what you've been up to…" I grinned at him.

"And did you pick up some good tips on interior design?" he asked, smiling.

"A few. Now I want some tips on gardening."

He looked at me closely and for a moment, I thought he was about to kiss me. I savoured the anticipation with excitement. At last! But then the moment was gone and he turned away, saying briskly, "Let's go and find Joseph and see the gardens before the afternoon sun disappears. There are plenty more rooms, but I guess you've seen enough furnishings for one day."

Just like that, the intimacy was replaced by the commonplace, the tenderness by formality. We were back on neutral ground.

As Theo walked ahead, back towards the main stairway, we passed a narrow flight of stairs I hadn't noticed earlier. It appeared to lead to the upper floors and looked dark and mysterious, the bannister peeling and chipped, old plasterwork and dust littering the steps. Original gas lamps on the walls were festooned with dusty cobwebs, draped between them like spooky Halloween bunting.

"What's up here, Theo?" I called, peering up the dark stairway.

He turned abruptly, a flash of anxiety crossing his features. "You can't go up there, Emily. It's not safe."

"It's okay," I placated him, surprised at his tone of voice. "I wasn't about to. I'm guessing this leads to the old servants' quarters, yes?"

"Yes, it does, but the floorboards are rotten and your foot could go through. There's nothing to see up there. Just empty rooms."

"Okay, it's no big deal," I laughed, "Let's go and find Joseph. Lead on McDuff...."

As he turned away, I couldn't help but take one last look at the creepy old stairway, gazing up the steps into the inky blackness, convinced there was another reason why they were warning me off. A sudden cold draft wafted down the stairs onto my face, as if the house was sighing and I shivered involuntarily, the goose bumps rising on my flesh. Feeling suddenly afraid, I ran after Theo.

12. Danger in the Gardens

We let ourselves out of the huge oak front door, lifting the massive iron latch and stepping into the courtyard that would soon double as a car parking area. The afternoon was still warm and sunny, giving a sleepy, lazy feel to the grounds and the gravel crunched beneath our feet. As Joseph was nowhere to be seen, we walked round the outside of the hall until we were at the rear, where a swathe of vibrant green grass formed the centrepiece of the formal gardens. We walked up to the ha-ha, a concealed low-lying wall that formed the edge of the gardens and stood admiring the panoramic vista that opened before us. This was English countryside at its best, a patchwork of fields and farmland cascading away in front of our eyes, disappearing into the horizon.

"It's beautiful, Theo," I said, mesmerised by the view. "You are so lucky to live here."

"I know," he answered, "But it didn't always look like this. Joseph has worked magic on the grounds."

I turned to face the rear elevation, thinking how stunning the hall looked since it had been renovated.

"What's that over there?" I asked, noticing a strange tower positioned to right of the hall. "Come on, Theo, show me."

Without waiting for him to reply, I ran across the lawn, towards the tower.

"Emily, wait," called Theo, "I wasn't going that way. Wait for Joseph."

But I was ahead of him and took no notice, giving him no choice but to follow.

I ran round the side of the hall and there before me, forming the building's most easterly point, stood an intriguing hexagonal tower about five stories high, made of honeyed Cotswold stone. It was a true Rapunzel tower, complete with a turret room at the top and a black slate roof that sloped steeply downwards over three decorative gabled windows, giving it a gothic fairy-tale look. On the middle level, three of the six sides featured long, narrow, arched windows, while the alternate sides were each adorned with a beautiful ornate clock, finished in burnished gold. Beneath each clock face, strange symbols had been hewn into the stonework.

Theo caught up with me and grabbed my hand.

"Come on, Emily, let's find Joseph."

"No, wait, I want to have a look at this tower," I remonstrated, "It's amazing. What are those symbols?"

Before he could answer, there was a noise behind us.

"I see you've found our mysterious Clock Tower," said a voice, making me turn round sharply.

It was Joseph, the sun behind him lighting his tousled blond hair so that it shone like a halo, giving him an almost ethereal look.

"Hi Joseph," I said with a smile. "This is fantastic. I've never seen anything like it. "

"It's beautiful, isn't it?" he asked, looking up at the tower, "Quite a tricky renovation project. But I'm pleased with the results."

"What's it used for?" I asked, and noticed a glance between Theo and his cousin.

"It's just decorative, said Theo, dismissively, "an embellishment to the main hall."

"A typical Victorian extravagance," explained Joseph, "It has no use, other than looking nice."

"Can you get in?" I asked, noticing steps leading up to a small wooden door at ground floor level.

"Not via that door," said Joseph, "The wood's swollen and jammed into the doorframe. It needs replacing, my next job. There is another way via the old servants' staircase, but that's closed off at the moment."

Yet again, the old servants' staircase had been mentioned, rousing my curiosity. I was intrigued and longed to explore the upper regions of the house and take a look inside the gothic tower. As a child, I'd always loved exploring old castles and country houses, relishing stories of dungeons, priest holes, murders and ghosts. Now, childhood memories stirred and I felt a compulsion to see inside the tower.

"There's nothing in there," said Theo, reading my mind, "just a bare, empty room at the top and another smaller chamber on the floor beneath."

Once again, I detected a quick glance between them, so brief, I almost missed it. A mere flicker of the eyelids and a slight look askance. But it was there. And it was enough to arouse my suspicions. There was something they weren't telling me, and I wanted to know what it was.

"Come on," said Joseph, "I want to show you my new project."

There was nothing more I could do, so I followed Joseph around the outer wall of Hartswell Hall, Theo walking behind me. Almost like being escorted away, I thought, as if they're guiding me in a different direction. It was only later that I realised Theo had never answered my question about the strange symbols hewn into the stonework.

"Look, Emily, what do you make of this?" asked Joseph as we came to a small clearing, containing a low circular stone wall, covered in moss, encompassing a circle of grass, with the base of a statue at its centre. "This was where the old carriages used to turn around, rather like a Victorian roundabout. The statue in the middle was once a fountain. It must have looked amazing with the water cascading down, as horses and carriages drove around it. I'm going to get it all working again. And this pathway here," he pointed to a small, overgrown path leading into the undergrowth, "is an ancient walk-way to the village church. I'm going to clear it and open it up again."

"It's all so impressive," I said, "I can't believe how much you've done."

"Come and see the rest of the grounds," said Joseph, excitedly. We followed him around the side of the hall until, once again, we were standing at the front entrance, with the gravel beneath our feet.

For the next half hour, he showed us the gardens, revealing pathways cleared and statues cleaned; the lake dredged and parkland reinstated; floral borders and wonderful topiary shapes created; vistas and terraces reclaimed: and the kitchen gardens, planted with every kind of succulent fresh produce you could imagine. My gardening knowledge was next to zero and I didn't know the first thing about trees and plants, but I knew a beautiful garden when I saw it. Hartswell Hall grounds were truly magical. It seemed as if spring had suddenly burst upon the forgotten gardens and Joseph had brought the overgrown grounds back to life, creating order amidst the chaos in an incredibly short amount of time.

"You must have had an army of gardeners to achieve all this, Joseph," I said, "Where are they all?" I asked him, puzzled, seeing no staff at all as we walked round the grounds.

"Sunday," explained Joseph, "it's their day off. They need to have one day of rest from my tyrannical rule."

"Why don't you show Emily your Rose Garden?" suggested Theo, and Joseph led us towards an archway, specially created in the neatly clipped privet hedge. As we stepped through, I exclaimed in amazement as a sea of roses met my gaze. There were pinks, reds, yellows, oranges and whites, in every shade imaginable, and the scent was intoxicating.

"Joseph, this is beautiful," I said, taking in the sight before me.

He took out a pair of secateurs and cut off a stunning red rose. "For you Emily. A red rose. Symbol of youth and beauty."

"Why, thank you," I said, blushing at his sudden and unexpected gesture.

"It's my own hybrid," he said, "It's called Eternal Youth."

I put the rose to my nostrils and inhaled its sweet scent. "It smells divine," I said, "Thank you."

"Have we done now?" asked Theo sharply, and I had to smile at the jealousy in his tone. "It's time we went back."

"One more thing," said Joseph. "I want to show you my secret garden."

He led us to an old red brick wall, about two and a half metres high, partially hidden by a tangle of ivy climbing its surface. The bits of wall that could be seen revealed weathered, mottled bricks, with discoloured lime mortar coming away in chunks. Joseph pulled back a large piece of overhanging ivy, to reveal a wooden door, decorated with carvings. Joseph took a large, ornate key from his pocket and, with some effort, unlocked the door and pushed it open. We stepped inside to discover a wild, mysterious world waiting to be discovered. Trees, shrubs and bushes competed with one another for space, an overgrown pathway disappeared into the wilderness, and the crumbling stone arches of a forgotten folly rose through the confusion of greenery.

"I've just discovered the key," explained Joseph, "That's why nothing's been done here yet."

"This is amazing. Can we go exploring?" I asked.

"Of course," beamed Joseph, "Why don't we follow the old pathway and see how far it goes into the undergrowth."

"Don't you think we should be getting back?" said Theo, "It's getting late."

"There's plenty of time," said Joseph, starting down the pathway. Reluctantly, Theo followed, holding back branches to make it easier for me to follow.

We'd gone no more than twenty metres or so along the pathway when Joseph turned to us and said, "Damn, I've left the key in the lock. It's the only one and I don't want to lose it. I'd better go back and get it."

"I'll go," I offered, "I'm closest to the door. I won't be a minute."

I retraced my steps along the overgrown woodland path and retrieved the key. I tried to push the old door shut, but it caught on the uneven ground and refused to budge. I gave it a sharp shove, trying to force it, and as I did, I heard a muffled noise above me. Looking up, I saw the wall over the door lintel move precariously, tilting for a moment before falling. I had no time to think or shout. I saw the wall coming towards me and in the same split second, I was aware of Theo scooping me into his arms and carrying me out of danger. I heard the bricks crash to the ground, causing dust, mortar and soil to billow up in a cloud and for a brief moment all was still. Then I heard Theo saying urgently, "Emily, are you okay? Are you hurt?" He held me in his arms, and I could feel his heart beating against my shoulder.

"No, I'm fine," I said in a shocked voice. "What happened?"

"The wall over the door frame gave way," said Joseph, picking his way through the broken bricks and examining the large hole that had appeared above the door. "The movement of us opening and closing the door, combined with the dried out mortar, must have weakened the wall and caused it to collapse."

He looked at me. "Emily, I'm sorry. I would never, ever have placed you in danger. You know that, don't you?"

"Of course, Joseph," I answered shakily, "It was an accident. You weren't to know the wall was about to fall."

"No, you weren't, were you Joseph?" Theo spoke with an edge to his voice, and again I caught a look between them.

"I swear it, Theo, I didn't know the wall was unsafe. Why would I want to hurt Emily?"

"Why indeed?" said Theo coldly. "Come on Emily, let's get back to the house. Are you okay to walk?" He still held me in his arms and seemed reluctant to put me down.

"Theo, I had a near miss, but I'm fine," I assured him. "Please put me down."

He carefully placed me on the pathway and although my legs were a little wobbly, I felt okay to walk. It was only as I stepped over the broken bricks that I realised how close to injury I'd come. If Theo had not acted so quickly, I would have sustained a serious head wound and could even have been killed.

I turned, and saw Joseph, picking the red rose he'd given me, bruised and broken, out of the rubble.

"Joseph," I said gently, "I'm okay. It's not your fault."

He looked up and smiled weakly.

Theo firmly took my hand and led me over the broken bricks, through the old doorframe, now surrounded by a ragged edge of bricks.

"Come on, we're going back to the hall and I'm getting you a sweet tea or a brandy. I don't want you going into delayed shock." He looked straight ahead and I puzzled that his reaction seemed more of anger than concern, once he knew I was unhurt.

"Theo, don't walk so quickly. I'm okay. That's all the matters. Thanks to you, the wall didn't even touch me."

He turned and looked at me briefly. "Sorry, Emily. It's my job to keep you safe and I nearly failed."

"What do you mean, it's your job? You're not responsible for me. And I'd like to know how you managed to move so quickly. One minute you were over by Joseph, a good twenty metres or so down the pathway, the next you were saving me from a falling wall. How did you do it?"

"I wasn't that far away," he answered, "Memory plays funny tricks when accidents happen."

Maybe he was right, I wasn't sure. I was starting to feel a little weak and was glad when the hall came into view.

"Where's Joseph?" I asked, looking back.

"Sorting out the wall if he's got anything about him," said Theo angrily, pushing open the great oak front door.

As I looked back, a movement in the bushes caught my eye. A dark figure stood looking at us from some distance away, in the same direction as the secret garden. It was Aquila, the chauffeur. I could just make out his features: the hooked nose, the cruel, curling lips and the heavy, dark eyes. I only looked at him for a brief second, but his expression was so malevolent it made my blood run cold.

"Come on Emily," called Theo, causing me to turn. I looked back once again, but Aquila had gone and although I strained my eyes, I couldn't see him. It seemed improbable, but I couldn't help thinking that maybe he'd had something to do with the falling wall. Perhaps Joseph had been in on the arrangement, purposefully leaving the key in the lock? It seemed implausible and I couldn't believe Joseph would want to harm me. He seemed genuinely to like me. Aquila, on the other hand, plainly disliked me. But there again, disliking someone was a long way from trying to kill them. And what was his motive? He hardly knew me. And how did Theo manage to move so quickly? He was twenty metres down the pathway, and couldn't even see the door. I recalled Theo's words that it was his job to keep me safe and shook my head in disbelief. This was all too ridiculous to contemplate. I was letting my imagination run away with me. And yet, deep down, I knew that something wasn't right.

Perhaps I should have left at that point, walked away and never looked back. My instincts were telling me to run, to get as far away from Hartswell Hall and this strange family as fast as I could. But I didn't. I followed Theo into house and in doing so, closed my escape route forever.

13. Face on a Necklace I

Theo led me to a small room adjacent to the reception desk. It was a warm, welcoming room, with a bar and large square sofas positioned around low black glass coffee tables, where and guests could enjoy a pre or post dinner drink or a morning coffee. I sat on one of the sofas and Theo plumped up the cushions behind my back. My legs were feeling pretty shaky now the adrenalin had stopped pumping round my system and I felt glad to be sitting.

"Wait here," he commanded, "I'm going to get some sweet tea organised."

He heard him speaking to someone in reception, then he was back, sitting next to me and holding my hand.

"Pantera's seeing to it," he said, "You look very pale. You're not feeling faint are you?"

"No, I'm fine. It was just a shock, that's all."

I sat back amidst the huge cushions and forced myself to breathe slowly.

A couple of minutes later, Pantera walked in, bearing the same silver tray I'd seen previously. It contained one white teacup and saucer, with a small white teapot, a milk jug and sugar bowl. She looked at me with contempt, not a shred of concern in her dark eyes, and put the tray down on the coffee table with such force, the china rattled.

"Thanks, Pantera," said Theo, and she scowled back him.

"Anything else?" she said in deep, husky tones, barely moving her lips.

"No, that's all. Thank you."

She left us, darting one last malevolent look at me that made me feel even more insecure and shaky.

Theo poured the tea, adding milk and three generous spoonfuls of sugar. I wondered whether I dared drink it, or whether Pantera had added a generous touch of poison. It was clear the servants here had no respect for me and were making it quite clear I was unwelcome. Well, tough. They were the servants. I was the guest. It wasn't up to them who Theo brought into the house. They needed to know their place, I reasoned.

I sipped the tea and looked at Theo, whose eyes hadn't left my face. He looked white-faced and drained.

I smiled at him. "I'm okay. Please don't worry. Thanks to you, not a single hair on my head was touched." I put my hand on his arm, trying to reassure him. He seemed close to tears.

"If something happened to you, I would never forgive myself. Never," he said, with force. He leaned forward and kissed me gently on the lips. Near miss or not, I wasn't so traumatised, I couldn't react to the touch of his lips. I'd been waiting all day for this. It didn't last long and it wasn't what you'd call a romantic kiss. But it was electric. My stomach turned somersaults and I felt a surge of energy pulse across my body. I felt weak and energised at the same time, if that was possible. I opened my eyes wide, trying to understand the emotions that were stirring within me, feeling the faint imprint of his lips on mine, as if I'd been seared by hot metal. His deep blue eyes gazed into mine and I was lost, hypnotised by the intensity of the occasion, the strangeness of the day and my dice with death. Something unspoken had just passed between us and I knew there was no going back. Every fibre of my being needed this boy. I had never felt this way before, and was never more sure of anything in my life. He smiled at me and I knew that as long as I was with Theo I would be safe. He would never let anything happen to me.

As he sat back into the sofa, I noticed for the first time a silver chain around his neck, with a pendant attached to it. Previously, it had been hidden beneath his shirt. Now I could see it clearly.

"What's that round your neck, Theo?" I asked.

He instinctively put his hand to the chain and held it protectively.

"This? Oh, nothing, just a chain I wear." He was about to tuck it beneath the neck of his shirt.

"Can I see it?" I asked, and put my hand up to his.

"It's probably not a good idea," said Theo, trying to take my hand away.

"Let me see, please…?" I asked.

He relented and gently I took the pendant in my hand. I saw immediately it wasn't a pendant at all. It was a delicate and unusual piece of jewellery; a white cameo on a blue crystal background, showing a woman's head in three-quarter profile. It was almost feminine and certainly not what I would have expected a 19-year old boy to be wearing.

"It's beautiful," I started to say, then exclaimed in surprise, as I took a closer look, "Why Theo, it looks a little like me. Where did you get it from?"

"I've had it for a long time," he said, pulling the chain out of my hands and tucking it firmly beneath his shirt. "It's very old, an antique. I guess it does look a bit like you. What a coincidence, eh? Now, would you like some more tea?"

"No, thank you, I've had enough," I said, watching him closely. He was suddenly defensive and I wanted to know why. If it was an antique, the cameo couldn't possibly show my picture, it was far too old. But how odd it should look like me and what a strange choice of jewellery for Theo to be wearing.

Yet again, something didn't add up. There were too many questions surrounding Theo and his family. Nothing was as it seemed and I didn't know what I was getting into. This was not your average teenage relationship. There were issues here that went way deeper than hormones and physical attraction. As yet, I couldn't work out what was going on, but I would find out. My antennae were on high alert, and I was determined to uncover the secrets of this strange, beautiful family.

Had I known the truth I would later discover, I would have stopped there and then. But sometimes the truth is beyond your wildest imagination, and so far removed from your own sphere of existence, it is impossible to comprehend. So I blundered on, setting in motion a course of events from which there would be no return.

14. Face on a Necklace II

That evening, the de Lucis family assembled in the old library, where Viyesha addressed them in low, chilled tones. No one doubted the seriousness of the situation, nor the fury of the woman who stood before them.

"The situation is getting out of hand. We have only just arrived and already our safety is compromised. We are only ever as good as our weakest link, and Theo, you have introduced a weak link direct into the heart of the family."

She paused and walked over to the window, looking out at the evening sun setting blood red over Hartswell Hall grounds. On any other night the beauty and drama of the twilight sky would have calmed and grounded her. But not tonight. She took a deep breath and said, more to herself than the family behind her, "What was I thinking to allow a stranger in? I was momentarily distracted by innocence and love and the potential for something good to develop. But it is ultimately down to me that the threat now exists, and for that I must take full responsibility. I should have stopped things while I had the opportunity. Now, I fear, it may be too late."

"Mother…" Theo started to say, but his father, standing behind him, put a warning hand onto his shoulder, and indicated by a shake of his head that he should remain silent.

"Let me think this through," said Viyesha, walking again towards the window. She found the motion comforting, allowing the movement to give shape to her words.

"Theo and Joseph, I'll come to you in a moment. Aquila, you are my primary concern." She turned to face the lounging chauffeur, who sat sprawled on one of the leather Chesterfields, his legs angled towards her. His black eyes were slits, seeping anger and insolence, his lips curled in a sneer.

"Let me finish what I started…" he began to say in low, guttural tones, but Viyesha held up her hand.

"Enough," she hissed at him. "You have done enough damage. You were behind the falling wall. You were seen, you cannot deny it."

"Why should I deny the truth?" he spat his words out ferociously. "He…' he pointed angrily at Theo, "has put everything we hold precious in danger. Our very existence is now threatened. And it is up to me to clean up." He faced Theo. "Have you learned nothing over the years, you imbecile? I should deal with you also."

"Aquila, you go too far," hissed Viyesha. "I forbid it. If and when the time comes, I will deal with things in my way."

"If and when?" said a low voice to Viyesha's left. It was Pantera and she now stood up, tall and magnificent, angrily facing Viyesha. "Aquila is right. The threat is here now and must be removed as quickly as possible. The girl has seen too much, she has started to question. She will bring others. We must eliminate her as soon as possible."

"No," shouted Theo, "Mother, tell them, they cannot do this."

"Pantera, sit, please," said Viyesha, in a slow calm voice, waiting until Pantera sat once again, "Violence is simply not an option. You cannot use your usual methods, not in a civilised country. That, more than anything, would bring others here. Perhaps we were wrong to come to this place, but we had to settle somewhere and after everything that has happened to us, it seemed peaceful here. Safe. Just what we needed. And the alignment was right. There was nowhere else we could go."

"It was safe until he started bringing strangers in," said Aquila in his low, rasping voice.

"Silence," demanded Viyesha, "This is not helping. It was I who gave permission for the girl to visit. If you must put blame at anyone's door, lay it at mine. Although, Theo and Joseph," she turned to look at the cousins, who were sitting side by side on the other leather Chesterfield in the room, "what were you doing showing Emily the tower?"

Theo hung his head, "Sorry mother, she wanted to have a look. It's so magnificent, you can't miss it. She was only asking the questions other people will ask."

"It's true, Viyesha," said Joseph, "She didn't come to spy. She was just showing a healthy interest in the work I've done."

"So healthy, you felt you had to present her with a red rose," pointed out Theo. "What was all that about? I bring my girlfriend here and you come on to her?"

"I wasn't coming on to her," countered Joseph. "It was a spur of the moment gesture…"

"And it was you who suggested Emily go back for the key," said Theo, angrily. "Were you working with Aquila? Was it all part of the plot to get rid of her?"

"No," shouted Joseph, "She offered. I swear I knew nothing about it."

"Stop it, both of you," said Viyesha, holding up her hands. "Violet, what do you make of this girl? You know her as well as anybody here. Do you think she's a threat?"

Violet's eyes sparkled blue and a small triumphant smile appeared momentarily on her face at being consulted. She sat apart from the others and had observed the bickering with some amusement, waiting for her turn to speak. Now she chose her words carefully.

"I don't think Emily is so much the threat, as Theo," she smiled icily at her brother. "He seems unable to contain his emotions and stay in control. I find that more worrying than anything."

"You're only jealous, Violet, because you thought you'd found a new friend and she prefers to be with me, rather than you," Theo turned on his sister.

"Don't be ridiculous," she started to say, but Theo interrupted her.

"All that time when you only had me for company and longed for a female friend," he said, "when you'd gaze out of the window and curse being in Egypt, with the fear and the curfews and the paranoia. When you met Emily, you thought you'd found a soul mate, didn't you? A girl you could relate to, who was as pretty as you. It was only natural you'd be jealous when Emily took up with me."

"Mother, don't listen to him," pleaded Violet. "He's just trying to be hurtful."

"She's right, Theo," said Viyesha. "This doesn't help at all." She turned to her husband, who had remained silent throughout, observing all that had gone on, his face impassive . "Leon, help me. What do we do?"

Leon took a deep breath and looked around the room before he started to speak.

"Okay, first things first. No more violence." He addressed this primarily to Aquila, who uttered a snort of derision. "It goes against our principles to show violence towards a creature of youth and innocence. We have never overtly killed those who are weaker than ourselves. The girl herself poses no threat. It is others who threaten us and my fear is that they may use her to get to us. In which case, she is the one in immediate danger, not us."

"Wisely said, my love," uttered Viyesha. 'I knew you would see clearly. So what is our best course of action?"

"We have no choice," answered Leon. "We have to draw her in for her own protection. For the immediate future, we must watch over her carefully. Her safety may be paramount to our existence. So for now, we watch, we wait and we protect. But never doubt it," and now he addressed Aquila, "our existence takes priority, and if necessary, we will do anything to protect ourselves. Even disposing of an innocent, if the situation arises." Aquila's eyes glinted at the prospect.

Leon continued: "This girl has had an effect on every one. She has touched you all in one way or another, and that is something I have never seen before. She has unsettled and destabilised the family, which gives me cause for concern. Remember, division breeds weakness and leaves us open to attack. We must remain united at all costs."

"I'm not so sure she is an innocent," Theo spoke slowly, looking at Viyesha.

"What do you mean?" she asked anxiously.

"She saw my necklace," he answered, "She saw the face on the cameo and recognised it as herself."

"Could it be possible?" murmured Viyesha, "She certainly has a look about her. "

"I don't know, mother," he answered, and looking round the room, he added, "If she is who I think she is, it changes everything. You have to let me find out."

"What about you, Violet?" Viyesha addressed her daughter. "What did you see that made you befriend this girl? Tell me the truth."

Violet paused before replying: "She has a bright blue aura. I've never seen one so bright on a mortal being, it's as bright as ours."

There was a silence as everyone took in the implication of her words. The silence seemed to ripple and move outwards, like rings in a pool when a pebble has been thrown in, and the air itself seemed to quiver in anticipation.

Then Viyesha spoke: "Let us pray that it is she. With all my heart I hope she has returned to us, for all our sakes, but most of all for yours, Theo. You have waited too long for this."

15. Unusual powers

I saw Theo at college on Monday morning. As I closed my locker, he was standing there.

"Theo!" I exclaimed. "Don't creep up on me like that. You made me jump."

"Sorry," he grinned, "just wanted to make sure there were no after effects. You know, after your near miss yesterday."

"I'm fine," I said, putting my locker key into my jacket pocket and picking up my backpack. "I may look fragile, but I'm made of strong stuff. No after effects to report."

"Good, I'm glad you're feeling okay. I've told Joseph to get the wall sorted. I don't want a repeat of that happening. I'd never forgive myself if anything happened to you."

"But why should it, Theo? You're making it sound like my life is in danger. It does sound a bit over dramatic."

"Sorry, just being protective, that's all."

He smiled at me and I felt my insides melt, but before I could say anything a bell rang, followed by the sound of feet running and people talking

"I've got to go," I said to Theo. "History seminar. *Thomas Cromwell: Able administrator or agent provocateur?*" I grimaced, then reaching up, I pecked his cheek, saying, "Thanks for looking after me, Superman!"

I grinned at him, luxuriating in the energy flow that ran from his body to mine.

"All part of the service, ma'am," he said, mock saluting me. "Catch you later, probably lunchtime, I have a tutorial this morning that will likely run over."

"Okay, see you in the café for lunch."

He called after me as I hurried down the corridor, "Agent provocateur. He was always the spider in the web."

I glanced back. For a split second, I had the impression he spoke from experience. I smiled to myself and pushed the strange thought from my mind.

Now we were at college, I was glad to get back to normality following my unnerving afternoon at Hartswell Hall. To say I felt out of my depth was to put it mildly. I fancied Theo like mad and there was no denying there was a very strong connection between us, but it was all so strange and intense, and so different to anything I'd encountered before. Why couldn't I just fall for someone like me? Someone who lived in an ordinary house, with normal parents and no mystery surrounding them. Why had I fallen for someone with a millionaire lifestyle, who lived in a stately home, with servants at his beck and call, and parents who looked like film stars? And why did I get the impression that all was not as it seemed, that the house and the money and the beautiful looks were all smoke and mirrors? Something was not right about Theo's family and, although I was intrigued and determined to uncover their secret, all I really wanted right now was a healthy dose of normality.

On cue, Seth came lounging up the corridor towards me, his black hair falling across his face.

"Hi Emmie, how's it hanging?" he asked.

"It's hanging out of kilter, actually," I said, very glad to see him. I'd missed the bus that morning and my mum had driven me in, so I hadn't seen either Seth or Tash since the previous week.

"Don't tell me. You and lover boy have split up. I knew it wouldn't last."

"No, Theo and I are fine," I said. "It's just his family that's a bit strange." I felt disloyal talking about Theo's family, but my need to feel grounded outweighed my need for loyalty.

"Tell me about it at break time," suggested Seth, "and make sure you include Tash. She's been missing you. I think you should both make up."

"Okay," I agreed, "I miss her too, but she was pretty nasty about Theo."

"Probably jealous," said Seth, "I mean, he is the heartthrob of Hartsdown. After me, he's the one all the girls want to go out with."

"Delusional as ever, Seth. See you later."

"Yeah, see ya," and he slouched off down the corridor.

I felt better for our brief interchange, as if reality had come back into my life and I looked forward to seeing my friends at break time.

There was a slight atmosphere when I sat down with Tash and Seth in the café mid morning. Things had been very strained between us for the last two weeks, but

Tash was the first one to apologise, which made life easier.

"Sorry, Emmie, I've missed you," she said sadly. "It wasn't that I was jealous, truly, whatever Seth says." She shot him a 'button it or else' look and he adopted a 'who me?' look. I beamed at them both. It was good to see them.

"It's just I was worried about you. This whole Theo thing is very sudden and intense, and we don't really know anything about him."

"Far too good looking, if you ask me," said Seth, hanging over the table, his body almost too big for the chair he was sitting on. "No-one can be that handsome without having a seriously defective personality."

"Seth, shut up. As usual, you're talking rubbish," I said to him, playfully. "And yet, there is something in what you're saying."

Both my friends leaned closer over the table.

"What d'you mean?" ask Tash.

"Tell," said Seth.

So I told them of my strange visit to Hartswell Hall, about meeting Theo's impossibly beautiful family, how they'd renovated the old house in an unfeasibly short time span and how Joseph had totally transformed the grounds.

"Honestly," I said, "you should see the place. It's fantastic, like a palace, no expense spared. And how Joseph has managed to clear and tend the grounds in just a few weeks, I don't know. It's just not humanly possible."

Tash and Seth exchanged glances.

"Maybe that's it," said Tash, ominously, "They're not human."

I felt goosebumps all over my body and shuddered.

"What do you mean, Tash? If they're not human, what are they? D'you think they're aliens? That's a ridiculous thing to say. You've been watching too much Doctor Who."

"Tell us more, Emily," said Seth. "What happened while you were there? Did they make you feel welcome?"

"Yes, very welcome," I said. "His mother and father and his cousin, and even Violet, were absolutely charming to me. His mother seems to have this amazing knack of making you feel totally relaxed, even though she looks like something out of a fashion magazine. And his father conveys this immense protective strength, as if he'd do anything to keep you safe. And Joseph is just plain lovely, well, at least I thought he was...." I tailed off, wondering whether to tell them about the wall incident.

"Yes, carry on," instructed Tash. "Obviously Joseph did something that upset you."

And so I told them about looking round the grounds, how Joseph had suggested we look at the walled garden, and how I'd gone back for the key. I recounted how the wall had collapsed and it was only Theo's amazing reaction that had saved me.

"OMG," said Tash, "You really are in danger. Emily, you can't go back there. What if something else were to happen? Do you think they're trying to lure you in?"

"Thank goodness Theo is such a fast mover," exclaimed Seth, sarcastically. ""You said he was at least twenty metres down the path when the wall started to collapse?"

"I think so," I said.

"So how did he manage to get back to the wall and carry you out of danger so quickly? Does he have super human powers?"

"I don't know, Seth. Maybe he was closer than I realised."

"And how come the wall collapsed in the first place?" asked Tash.

"I'm not sure," I answered, "but I do have a theory, which is a bit unnerving. The servants seem to hate me. Aquila, the chauffeur, is the most evil character you could ever meet and looks daggers every time he sees me. Pantera, the house-keeper, barely acknowledges my presence and makes it quite clear she'd have more respect for a piece of dirt."

"Sounds bizarre," said Tash.

"Bizarre having servants in the first place," added Seth.

"The thing is," I continued, "after the wall collapsed, Theo and I were walking back to the house, when I saw Aquila hanging round the grounds. If looks could kill, I'd have withered on the spot."

"D'you think he had something to do with the wall collapsing?" asked Tash.

"I don't know," I said. "There's something very strange about the whole place. I get the feeling anything is possible there."

"I'll tell you something that is strange," said Seth, looking shiftily around for dramatic emphasis.

"What?" said Tash and I in unison, leaning forward.

"You remember the woman that died? The one who aged rapidly? Well, according to my mum, she was the estate agent who sold Hartswell Hall to the de Lucis family."

"Meaning what....?" asked Tash in a low voice.

"I don't know," said Seth in an equally low voice, "But remember, she went from looking like a 20-year old with awesome energy levels to a shrivelled old crone in just a few weeks. Apparently, she started turning to dust when she was at the Coroner's."

"So, maybe she had a premature aging condition," I suggested.

"Or..." said Seth, raising his eyebrows.

"Or what?" I asked.

"Think about how the family looks," said Seth, "You said they all have beautiful white alabaster skin and clear blue eyes?"

"Yes," I said, "their skin is amazing, it almost seems to glow. And they all have gorgeous blonde hair. Violet and her mother have perfect figures, Theo and his father and cousin have the most incredible physique."

"And they all have different powers..." continued Seth. "His mother makes you feel calm and relaxed, his father conveys tremendous strength and Theo is obviously faster than the speed of light ..."

"Joseph is green-fingered and makes things grow," added Tash.

"And Violet," said Seth, looking misty-eyed into the distance, "well, Violet is just perfect, let's face it. I wouldn't say no if she asked ..."

"Pigs and flying come to mind," I said to Seth. "Can we get back to the point please?"

"The point being," said Seth slowly, as spelling it out to us, "that these people are not normal."

"Er, yes, I think we've worked that one out," said Tash. "Tell us something we don't know."

"Have you ever seen them eating?" asked Seth.

"No, I haven't seen the family eating anything," I answered. "They only had cups of tea when I was there. Mind you, Theo and Violet are always in the café."

"Yes, and what do they eat?" demanded Seth.

"Now you mention it, not much," I admitted. "Just a salad here and there."

"Well, it's obvious, isn't it?" said Seth.

"Is it?" Tash and I said in unison.

Seth stared at us. "Come on, keep up, creatures who drain the life force out human beings… "

We both looked at him blankly.

"Vampires," he said triumphantly. "Speaking of which …"

He looked over to the cafeteria door behind us and we both turned round. Violet had just come into the café and stood, looking around. Seeing us, she started to walk towards our table.

"Act normal," said Seth as she approached, an instruction that was just about impossible, given what he'd just said.

"Hi Violet," I said brightly, as she sat down in a spare chair at the table. "How are you? Did you get your philosophy project finished?"

"Hi guys," she said in her clear voice, smiling at us, "yes, I did. Just handed it in." And looking at me, she asked, "How are you, Emily? Recovered from your little scrape yesterday?"

I was surprised that she was bringing it out in the open. If the family really were trying to do away with me, surely she would be keeping things quiet. I tried to avoid looking at Seth, who was doing fang impressions behind Violet.

"Yes, I'm fine," I said. "It was nothing. Luckily, Theo was on hand and I wasn't hurt in the slightest."

"Emily had a close call with a falling wall," Violet explained to Seth and Tash. "As I'm sure she's told you."

"Yeah, she might have mentioned it," said Seth, in an off-hand manner.

"Well, I thought you'd like to know that Joseph's had a look at the wall," she said. "Apparently, it's unsound all the way along. It was an accident waiting to happen and you happened to be in the wrong place at the wrong time. He's having the entire wall rebuilt. We certainly don't want an action replay when we start having paying guests."

"No, killing off your guests won't be good for business," said Seth, with a straight face, causing Violet to reply, "I can assure you, Seth, we have no intention of killing off any of our guests, paying or otherwise."

"Glad to hear it, Violet," he answered, and I was relieved to hear the bell go for lessons. I felt very uncomfortable seeing Violet after we'd just been discussing her family. And Seth's statement about vampires seemed completely ridiculous.

We walked out of the café and made our way upstairs for Double English Literature, Violet staying close to me and preventing further discussion.

Just as Miss Widdicombe entered the classroom, Seth turned to me from the row in front and mouthed 'vampires' to me once again, doing his ridiculous fang impression. I frowned at him and shook my head, glancing nervously across to Violet. I wasn't sure if she'd seen or not.

It was only later I realised I'd never mentioned the face on the necklace to my friends. For some reason, I didn't feel I could. There were things, for the moment, I would keep to myself. I owed Theo that at least.

At lunchtime, I sat with Theo, as had become my custom over the last week. He entwined his fingers in mine, sending shivers down my spine, and looked into my eyes. He didn't need to speak, I felt immediately overpowered by the intensity of his gaze and was powerless to resist him. He did things to me no one else was capable of, and all I wanted was to be close to him, to touch him, to feel him near me.

"How are you feeling today?" he asked.

"I'm absolutely fine," I answered. "Never better. Violet said the wall was unsound right along and that Joseph is rebuilding it."

"Yes, he is," said Theo. "You have to be so careful in these old houses, they can be death traps, and the last thing I want is for something to happen to you."

"Don't worry about me," I laughed, "I'm indestructible, as long as I have some kryptonite handy."

"Speaking of which," said Theo, his face absolutely serious, "I have something for you that I want you to wear."

"Yes?" I answered, not quite sure what was coming next. Surely, he wasn't buying clothes for me?

Theo pulled a small black velvet drawstring bag out of his pocket. I leaned forward, intrigued.

"What is it?" I asked.

He opened the top of the bag and emptied the contents into his palm. It was a necklace, a small blue crystal on a silver chain, similar to the one he wore, but smaller and without the cameo. As Theo held it in his hand, it caught the light, sparkling and shimmering, shining a spectrum of different colours.

"It's lovely, Theo," I said, totally taken aback, "but I can't possibly accept it. I don't want you to buy me gifts."

"For a start," said Theo, "I haven't bought it. It's something we've had in the family for years. And secondly, I'm not open to negotiation. I want you to have it."

"You mean accept a family heirloom?" I said, aghast. "I couldn't possibly. Do your mother and father know about this?"

"My mother and father have nothing to do with this," said Theo firmly. "This is my necklace and I shall do with it as I will."

"But who did it belong to?" I asked. "I'm assuming you inherited it?"

"Yes, from a distant relative," he said, a little evasively, "and I'd much prefer you to be wearing it, rather than leave it in a drawer where no-one can see it."

"I'm not sure, Theo, it doesn't seem right, somehow. I'd feel happier if your parents knew about this."

"Emily," he said urgently, "I said I wasn't open to negotiation and I'm not. I need you to accept this necklace."

"Need?" I asked.

"Yes, I need you to wear it. The blue crystal will keep you safe and if you're ever in danger, I'll know about it."

"Theo," I said incredulously, "this is starting to sound like a fairy story. A magic crystal that will keep me safe from danger...? Are you for real?"

"You don't know what's out there," he said enigmatically, "and I need to keep you safe."

"You keep talking about keeping me safe," I said, "it's starting to freak me out. What do you mean? I don't understand…"

"I don't expect you to understand. It's just there are things in my world that can be dangerous. Please don't ask me to explain, just wear the necklace."

"What things?" I asked. "Am I in danger? What do you mean 'your world'? You have to tell me, Theo. You can't just give me a beautiful necklace, come out with all these cryptic comments and expect me not to ask questions."

He looked at me blankly, not knowing what to say.

"I'll do a deal with you Theo," I said. "I'll wear the necklace as long as you tell me what's going on."

"Great," he said, sound relieved. "Let me put it on you."

I allowed him to stand behind me and bending my head forward, felt him doing up the clasp. The blue crystal swung down on top of my T-shirt, sparkling and gleaming. It was beautiful and I had truly never seen anything like it before. I tucked it inside my neckline, so that it wasn't on display for all to see.

"Okay, that's my side of it. Now it's your turn. Tell me ……..." I broke off, unable to continue speaking. As the crystal touched my skin, I experienced the most extraordinary sensation. It felt as if something very cold had touched my chest, but was generating an incredible heat within me. It wasn't unpleasant. On the contrary, as the warmth spread outwards from my chest, into other parts of my body, I felt the most wonderful peace come upon me. I've never taken drugs or alcohol, but this is how I imagined it would feel. Immense love flowed from me to Theo and to the rest of the world. I was at one with everything; energised, refreshed and reborn. I felt radiant, as if rays of light were shining forth from my fingertips and my body was emitting starbursts of energy. It was the most heavenly, beautiful, amazing feeling.

"Theo," I whispered, "it feels incredible. What is this crystal?"

He looked at me kindly. "Hush, don't ask any more questions. There are some things it's better you don't know. Keep the crystal hidden and never take it off. If ever you need me and I'm not around, hold the crystal tightly and mentally call my name. I'll know straightaway you're in trouble and I'll be there as quickly as I can."

I entwined my fingers with his, cocooned in a bubble of wellbeing, and looked into his deep blue eyes. Eternity stretched out before me, deep and clear and blue, and I knew I was lost. I was irrevocably linked with this boy and whatever he wanted, I would do. I was utterly and completely in love with him. Body, mind and soul were totally ensnared.

"What are you, Theo?" I asked faintly, afraid to speak and spoil the moment. "I have to know. You're not – a vampire, are you?" My words were so quiet I hardly made a sound. He looked at me and for a moment, I thought he was angry. Then he threw back his head and laughed, looking at me with amusement.

"Is that what you think I am? Oh Emily, you've let your imagination run riot. No, I can assure you I'm not a vampire."

"Oh," I said, feeling stupid, "it's just something Seth said…"

"This has come from Seth, has it?" Theo's voice sounded a little cold. "I think Seth would be better concentrating on his college work, rather than spreading ridiculous rumours."

"Oh, he hasn't," I stuttered. "He hasn't said it to anyone else, only me. I think it was probably more a joke than anything." I looked down at my hands. "Sorry, Theo, I know it sounds ridiculous. Please forget I ever said it."

He looked at me tenderly. "Okay, I'll forget it. One day, I will explain things to you. But not yet. For now, can we just be happy together?"

"Of course."

"And no more awkward questions?"

"No."

"Good." He glanced at his watch. " I have to go. I have a tutorial that I can't miss. See you later?"

He stood up and bent over the table to kiss my forehead.

"Yeah, see you later."

As I watched him leave the cafeteria, my fingers unwittingly went to the crystal lying just beneath my T-shirt. My fingers felt its outline and once more, feelings of peace and love filled my being.

That afternoon, I didn't travel back with Theo and Violet in their car. However good the crystal made me feel, I didn't relish the thought of seeing Aquila again, and I told Theo I needed to sit with Tash and discuss a new assignment we'd been given. It was almost true.

As we were sitting on the bus, Tash turned to me and asked, "Are you using a new foundation cream, Emily? Or was it that beer facial I gave you? Whatever it is, it looks good. Your skin has a real glow to it."

"No, I'm not wearing foundation," I replied. "And I still haven't got round to using the facial."

"Maybe it's because you're in love," said Tash, enviously. "Your pheromones are activated or something like that, making you look all bright-eyed and glowing."

My hand went to the crystal and I wondered whether to tell Tash about it. There again, we seemed to be back on an even keel and I didn't want to spoil anything. If she thought Theo was giving me expensive gifts, she might just get angry again. I decided to keep quiet about it for the present.

"Tash, you don't half talk a load of rubbish sometimes," I said with a grin. "You're nearly as bad as Seth wittering on about vampires. Theo thought it was completely ridiculous."

"What, you told him Seth thought they were vampires?"

"It sort of came out," I said, feeling silly.

"Oh, smart, Emily. Now they know we're suspicious of them. Why couldn't you keep your mouth shut?"

"It's okay," I said defensively, "he thought it was funny. It's not a problem."

"No?" said Tash, frowning, "He would try to fob you off, wouldn't he? I still think there's something not right about them. He might have pulled the wool over your eyes, but not us. Seth and I are going to keep a very close watch on them. And if we see anything strange or out of the ordinary…."

"What?" I asked, looking at her with amusement. "What are you going to do? Sprinkle them with holy water or call for Van Helsing? Come on, Tash, you don't know how ridiculous you sound."

Tash looked studiously out of the window. "Okay, I agree vampires sounds a bit far-fetched, but I still don't trust them. Especially after what you told us about your visit yesterday. Surely you haven't forgotten that already?"

"No, I haven't, I just think maybe I over-reacted a little. I don't think Theo would put me in any danger," I said.

"What's happened to you?" Tash asked, "You've changed your tune since this morning. Are you on happy pills or something? I still maintain, we don't know anything about them and we need to keep an eye on them."

"Okay, Sherlock," I acquiesced. "Let me know if you find anything out, and I'll do likewise. But if we don't get up now, we're going to miss our stop."

I felt dreamy and other-worldly, and when I got home, I took off the necklace and placed it in my pocket. Immediately, the drugged feeling lifted and although I didn't have quite the same sense of peace, I felt more in control again. I decided to keep the crystal in the breast pocket of my SuperDry jacket; close at hand should I need it, but not close enough to be under its spell.

Later that afternoon, after we'd had an early tea, I received a text from Theo:
'Hi Em, Missing u. Fancy going 4 a walk? Your favourite vampire.'

I texted back:
'Dear favourite vampire, Why walk when u can fly?"

He texted back straight away:
'U r muddling us with witches. Shall I come over?'
I answered:
'Yes. C u in a bit(e). Ha Ha.'·

At last. This felt more normal. This is what you were supposed to do. Hang out. Send silly text messages.

I went up to my room and changed into my faded blue jeans and new Hollister top. As I did so, the blue crystal necklace fell out of my pocket and onto the floor. I picked it up, staring into its many facets and thinking how pretty it looked. I wondered how old it was and what kind of crystal it was. Some crystals were supposed to have certain properties, which might explain why it had such an effect on me. My mum was in to all this sort of thing, attending a meditation circle, using Angel cards, dowsing with crystals, looking for orbs and so on. I'd grown up with it and while

I'd occasionally dabbled, I hadn't embraced it in the way my mother had. Granddad thought it was all a load of 'New Age baloney', to quote his exact words, but there again, he didn't believe in anything. 'When you're dead, you're dead', he would say, not wanting to contemplate the possibility of a great hereafter. He maintained all religions were simply a means of controlling the masses, and worship of gods had nothing more to it than agriculture and fertility. 'Food and fornication,' he said, 'the basic requisites for survival, that's why the old gods were revered and worshipped.' It was a very black and white viewpoint, with little room for discussion or manoeuvre, and was the complete antithesis to my mother's beliefs. I'd grown up amidst these two opposing camps and, as a consequence, had taken on a little from each, which meant I basically didn't know what I believed in. I found it easier not to think about such things, preferring to concentrate on the here and now. Books, films, music, make-up and technology were the mainstays of my world, and maybe I was shallow, but at least I wasn't deluded or bigoted.

The crystal glinted in my hand and I felt compelled to put it on. It would complement my blue Hollister T-shirt very well, I reasoned. As soon as I'd done up the clasp, I felt the same mellowness and peace flow through me, although not as powerfully as before. This time I felt more in control and, while I was still aware of the crystal's presence, it didn't seem to dominate me so much. I decided to leave it on.

"That's a pretty necklace, Emily," said my mother, as I came downstairs, "Where did you get that from?"

"Theo gave it to me," I answered.

"Did he?" she said, with a glint in her eye. "I'm getting to like that boy more and more." Taking a closer look, she asked, "D'you know what it is? Would you like to look in my crystal book?"

"There's no need, mum," I said. "Theo will be here in a moment. We can ask him."

Right on cue, the doorbell sounded, and I ran to answer the door.

There he was: beautiful, gorgeous, radiant Theo, standing on my doorstep.

"Hi, Theo," said my mum, in a flirtatious voice that was totally embarrassing, hanging over my shoulder, desperate to feed her eyes upon him.

"Hi, Mrs Morgan, how are you?"

"Come in, Theo," I said, smiling at him.

His eyes went immediately to the crystal round my neck and he looked relieved.

"I see you're wearing it. It looks good on you."

He stepped in the hallway and I closed the front door behind him.

"It's a beautiful necklace, Theo," said my mum, "and a very unusual crystal. I was going to look it up in my crystal book, but Emily says you can tell us what it is."

He looked momentarily reluctant, then gathering his thoughts, said: "It's a crystal called Celestite, the celestial crystal. Very powerful, creates feelings of inner peace and harmony, facilitates telepathic communication, brings balance and purity. It's very calming, but also sharpens the mind, it creates openness to new experience, and provides a channel to universal energies... Is that enough?"

We both stared at him, wide-eyed.

"Wow, no wonder I feel good when I wear it," I joked.

"You'll have to let me borrow it," said my mum, winking at me. "I could do with some universal energy."

"No," said Theo sharply. "Nobody else can wear it. Sorry. Emily is the only person..."

"It's alright, Theo," said my mum, seeing his discomfort, "I was only joking. Emily doesn't let me borrow anything of hers. It's quite safe."

"Okay," said Theo, relaxing slightly. "Sorry, Mrs Morgan, I didn't mean to jump down your throat. It's just..."

"I know, it's okay, I get it," said my mum. "The crystal's attuned to Emily's energy, you don't want a different energy field messing things up."

Sometimes my mum's new age crankiness does come in handy.

"Something like that," said Theo. "I've told Emily to wear it all the time and it will protect her."

My mother looked fit to burst that I should have found such a wonderful boyfriend who not only looked divine, but also shared her off-the-wall beliefs. In her eyes, he was perfection personified. And in my eyes, he came pretty close too, despite his slightly weird family.

"So, what are you two going to do this evening?" asked my mum.

"I thought we could take a walk," said Theo. "It's a lovely evening and it seems a shame to waste it inside. What d'you think, Emily?"

I would walk anywhere with him, whatever the weather.

"I think it's a great idea," I said, grabbing my jacket off the coat stand in the hallway.

"Be back by around half nine, will you?" said my mother, "It'll be getting dark by then."

"We will," said Theo, adding, "Don't worry, Mrs Morgan, I'll take good care of her."

My mother had started to look starry-eyed and love-struck, and I quickly got Theo out of the house before she embarrassed herself further.

"This old car has seen better days," he commented, as we walked past my sad old Mini, marooned on the driveway, its once cream paintwork concealed beneath layers of grime.

"Watch what you say about Martha," I cautioned him, with mock alarm.

"Martha?" he teased. "You're joking."

"No," I said defensively, "Martha was very useful until she fell into disrepair. She was my first car when I passed my driving test. She took us all over the place, 'til her age caught up with her."

"You should let Joseph take a look," he suggested. "He'd soon bring her back to life."

"He's not just green-fingered then?" I asked.

"No, Joseph's fantastic with anything mechanical. He'll have her roadworthy in no time."

"Brill," I beamed at him. "It'd be great to give her a new lease of life."

"Why don't we drive her over to the Hall and let him work his magic?" suggested Theo. "That is, supposing she's still driveable."

"Of course she's still driveable. She only failed her MOT. Although doesn't that make it illegal to drive her?"

"Technically, yes," said Theo, "but we're only going to the hall and I guarantee no-one will see us. Do you have the key? Let's see what this old girl's capable of."

I found the key at the bottom of my bag and we were soon sitting in Martha, Theo at the driving wheel. I had thought her battery would be flat, but amazingly she sprang to life as soon as Theo turned the ignition. He reversed her out of the driveway and on to the road.

"I have something I want to show you when we get to the hall," said Theo mysteriously, as we pulled on to the High Street.

"What that?" I asked, intrigued.

"It's something I've bought for Violet," he explained, "but I wanted you to take a look first, and then we can give it to her together."

"Okay," I said, a little surprised. It wasn't quite what I'd been expecting to hear.

"She's been a little out of sorts recently," said Theo. "I think us getting together might have had something to do with it. You should have seen her when she came home from college that first day. She couldn't stop talking about you, how she'd made a friend, how great you were, how good it was to have someone to talk to."

"Oh dear," I said. "I hadn't realised."

"What you have to understand," said Theo, "is that when we were in Egypt, she didn't have any friends. We did our schooling together and nobody else was around. Joseph was always visiting, and he and I would go off together, but Violet had no one. She was on her own. So for her to make a friend at her new college was a big deal to her. And then I came along and took you away from her. She still hasn't forgiven me."

He looked at me. "Don't worry, it's not your fault…"

"I had no idea, I was just trying to make her feel welcome."

Suddenly I felt awful. It had never been my plan for anyone to get hurt.

"If it's any consolation, Tash was just as jealous of her those first few days," I informed Theo. "She thought Violet had become my best friend. It's all a bit of a mess, isn't it?"

"Don't worry," he said, squeezing my hand, "Violet will come round, as will Tash. Deep down, Violet really likes you. And there's no reason why you can't be good friends with her and go out with me."

"I hope so," I said, feeling confused. The situation was more complicated than I'd realised, but at least it explained why Violet had been so cold towards me. And perhaps that was why the servants were so dismissive of me. They saw me as a threat to family unity. Loyalty to their family came first, and I was perceived as the interloper. Suddenly, our theory about vampires and strangeness appeared very far-fetched. I'd allowed myself to read far more into the situation than was actually there. I began to feel rather stupid.

"So, what you have bought for Violet that will make things better?" I asked Theo.

"Wait and see," he answered.

By this time, we'd arrived back at the hall and Theo parked Martha in the courtyard in front of the house. As we got out, right on cue, Joseph appeared.

"Nice wheels, Theo," he commented, drily.

Theo threw him the key.

"A little renovation project for you, Jo," he said. "This is Martha, Emily's car. Failed her MOT. Think you can do anything?"

"I should think so," he said, running his hand over Martha's bonnet.

I stared. Martha looked immediately brighter and cleaner.

"How did you do that, Joseph?" I asked, astounded.

"Do what?" he asked, looking puzzled.

"Make her glow like that?"

He grinned. "A trick of the light, that's all. Leave her with me, Emily, I'll soon have her as good as new."

"Thanks Joseph, I really appreciate this."

"Come on, Emily," called Theo, opening the hall's huge oak front door and holding it open for me. I followed him inside, turning to give Joseph and Martha a final look. If I wasn't mistaken, she was really beginning to gleam. Joseph beamed at me.

Inside, no one was about, which made me feel better. I certainly wasn't up to meeting Aquila or Pantera. The sounds of Clair de Lune wafted on the air from the ballroom. Violet was playing the piano.

"Come upstairs," Theo whispered, and I followed him up the enormous carved central stairway. He led the way along the corridor, stopping by one of the bedroom doors.

"It's in here," he said conspiratorially, turning the brass doorknob and opening the door. It was one of the rooms he'd shown me on my previous visit, a large airy room, beautifully decorated in shades of red and pink.

"Over here," said Theo, indicating the sofa, where a large cardboard box had been placed. Now I was intrigued.

He carefully opened the box and lifted out the most gorgeous grey kitten. It was tiny, no more than about seven or eight weeks old, a small fluffball of grey and white fur, that sat in the palm of his hand. He looked up at me.

"What d'you think?" he asked.

"It's beautiful, Theo," I said, totally taken aback. "What a lovely surprise. Violet will adore it. What is it? Girl or boy?"

"It's a boy," he answered, "I call him Grey Boy for the moment, but I'm sure Violet will give him a name."

"Can I hold him?" I asked, and Theo placed the small bundle of fur into my hands.

He was the prettiest little kitten I'd ever seen. A tiny little face looked up at me, with a small pink nose, long white whiskers and huge dark eyes. He made a plaintive little cry as he looked up at me and I held him close to my jacket, giving him warmth and comfort.

"Oh, Theo, what a brilliant idea," I said, thinking what a kind, thoughtful person he was. Who else would have thought of doing something like this?

"Can we give him to Violet now?"

"Stay here with Grey Boy and I'll go and get her," he said, walking to the door, then turning to me and saying, "Remember, he's from both of us."

He closed the door behind him and I looked at the tiny little creature before me, playfully trying to catch the toggles of my jacket. He was perfect, a friendly, playful little kitten that represented a gesture of friendship between myself, Theo and Violet.

"Let's hope you smooth things over, Grey Boy," I whispered into the soft fur on his head and he meowed again.

A few minutes later, the door opened and Theo appeared with Violet.

"Oh, hello, Emily," she said in surprise, "I didn't realise you were here. What's this about?"

She suddenly saw the little grey bundle in my hands and squealed.

"A kitten! Oh, he's so cute. Where did he come from? Can I hold him?"

"He's yours," said Theo. "A present from Emily and me. Go on, take him."

I placed Grey Boy in her arms and she cuddled him, looking up at us.

"He's gorgeous. Thank you. I wasn't expecting this."

The kitten mewed at her and tried to paw her hair hanging over her shoulder.

"Oh, look at him," she beamed at us, "isn't he just adorable?"

Theo and I glanced at each other and breathed a sigh of relief. The plan was working. Hopefully things were on the mend and we could look forward to a new era of friendship.

"Does he have a name?" asked Violet.

"Well, I just call him Grey Boy," said Theo, "but if you want to name him, it's up to you."

Violet looked at the kitten closely. "Grey Boy," she said and he meowed again. "He seems to answer to his name, doesn't he?" she asked. "Perhaps I'll just stick with Grey Boy. It's to the point. He's grey and he's a boy."

We all laughed and I felt the iciness that had been around us for the last couple of weeks begin to thaw.

"Come on, let's take him downstairs," said Violet. She cuddled the kitten close to her. "Thank you. He's beautiful."

She carried Grey Boy downstairs, across the reception area and into the old ballroom, where Viyesha and Leon sat on the huge purple sofas, warming themselves by the fireside. A bottle of wine stood on the coffee table and they drank from exquisitely ornate, old-fashioned wine glasses.

"Emily, I didn't realise you were here," said Viyesha, placing her glass on the table and rising from her seat. She looked stunning in a close-fitting cream shift dress, her hair pinned up, showing off ornate silver earrings and a matching silver necklace that bore a blue crystal similar to the one I was wearing. I was glad I'd tucked it beneath my T-shirt. I wasn't sure Theo had told his parents about it yet, and didn't want to place him in an awkward position.

"Will you join us for a glass of wine?" asked Leon, looking once again like a Hollywood film star, with his straw blonde hair, piercing blue eyes and pale blue linen jacket.

"No thanks, Leon," I said politely. "I should be going, really."

"Look, mother," said Violet, holding up the kitten, "See what Theo and Emily have got for me. Isn't he adorable?"

"He's gorgeous," said Viyesha. "Bring him here."

Violet carried the kitten over to her mother, and she gently stroked his head, while Grey Boy tried to catch her fingers with his paws and we all laughed.

Leon looked across at Theo. "Nice move, Theo," he said.

"Come and have a seat," said Viyesha, indicating for Theo and me to join her on the sofa.

For the next half hour, I enjoyed a pleasant family evening with the de Lucis family. Violet sat on the floor playing with the kitten, while Theo and I chatted with his parents. The servants were nowhere to be seen, which made matters easier, and the conversation bowled along, talking about Hartsdown College, their future plans for Hartswell Hall, life in the village and all manner of ordinary, everyday subjects. Viyesha, of course, had the gift of making me feel relaxed and at ease, and I found I was enjoying myself. I even allowed Leon to pour me a small glass of wine.

As I laughed with them, I thought how normal it all seemed and how ridiculous our vampire theories were. The de Lucis's were just different to me, that was all. They had a moneyed, cultured background I could only dream about, and that's what had created the problems in my mind. They were friendly and welcoming , and I really couldn't ask for more than that. Even their beauty seemed less overwhelming than last time. Theo looked across at me fondly and I suddenly realised how much I wanted to be part of this family. It was early days, but I was already starting to feel closer to them all.

At 9.15, I decided it was time to leave. Viyesha fondly kissed my cheek and for a brief moment I caught a scent of her perfume. It was such a delicate, floral fragrance that instantly brought a picture of warm summer days and happy times into my mind. I made a mental note to ask her what it was. Leon kissed my cheek and, once again, the feeling of immense strength and power flooded into my being. I felt safe just standing next to him.

"Emily, it's been delightful," said Viyesha, in her soft, well-spoken voice.

"We look forward to seeing you again," said Leon, twinkling at me and smiling.

"Thank you for a lovely evening, both of you," I said warmly, adding to Violet, who still sat playing with Grey Boy in front of the fire, "Bye, Violet, see you tomorrow."

"Bye, Emily," she answered. "Hang on, I'll come with you and see you out."

She scooped up Grey Boy into her arms and followed Theo and me across the ballroom and out into the reception area.

"You're going to love exploring this old house, aren't you, little one," she said, nuzzling her face into his soft face. "Thanks again, Emily, it was very kind of you and Theo."

I looked at Theo, an unspoken message going between us. Things were going to be all right.

"I'll walk you back," he said, gallantly. "It's getting dark and I don't want you wandering through the grounds on your own."

I gladly accepted his offer. Hartswell Hall grounds were one area where I didn't feel entirely safe, especially not at night, and even more so after the events of the other day. Once I reached the main road, I'd be fine.

As Theo opened the huge oak studded door at the entrance, things seemed to occur very quickly. One minute Violet was holding the kitten in her hand, standing waving goodbye, the next moment Aquila was driving into the courtyard in the sleek, black Jaguar. He was driving fast and swerved to go round Martha, who was still parked there. Startled by the sudden movement, Grey Boy leapt out of Violet's arms and within a split second had run into the pathway of the Jaguar. There was nothing Aquila could do. The wheels turned, the brakes screeched and the kitten disappeared under the car. Violet screamed, and Aquila, seeing that something

was wrong, brought the car to an immediate standstill. Theo darted
from my side, trying to save the kitten, but even for him, it had
been too fast. He reached under the car and brought out a lifeless,
bloodied, small grey body. It had been instant and the kitten had
obviously felt nothing, but the shock was palpable amongst us all.

"Grey Boy," sobbed Violet, grabbing his tiny body from Theo.
"Wake up, please wake up."

Her father gently took her arm and looked at the kitten.

"Violet, it's no good. He's gone. Give him to me." He took
the kitten in his hand and Viyesha led Violet, sobbing and shaking
into the house, murmuring words of comfort. I watched helplessly,
aware that there was nothing I could do, and that our gesture of
friendship had been instantly erased. Aquila scowled horribly and
stormed into the house after them, muttering, "How did I know she
had a kitten? And whose heap of junk is this parked here? If I
didn't have to swerve, it wouldn't have happened."

"It's best you go, Emily," said Leon, holding the tiny grey ball
of fur in one hand. "I'll deal with this. Theo, walk Emily home,
this has been a shock for all of us."

Theo took my hand, leading me silently across the courtyard.
As we walked down the main driveway, he put his arm round me,
drawing me close.

"Don't worry, Emily, Violet will be fine. Remember, we come
from a country where death and disease are commonplace. She's
seen worse than this. It's not as bad as it seems."

I looked up at him, tearfully, hardly trusting myself to speak.

"What a horrible end to a lovely evening. Poor Grey Boy. He
didn't deserve that. He was only little. And poor Violet, she had
him for less than an hour. If only I hadn't brought my car over.
This is all my fault. You were trying to make things better and I've
spoilt it all. "

"Listen, it was my idea to bring your car here," said Theo,
"and it wasn't your fault the kitten bolted. If anyone's at fault, it's
Aquila. As usual, he was driving too fast."

"I still feel responsible."

"Emily," said Theo, tenderly, "Trust me. Things will be all
right. I promise."

And he kissed me gently on the lips.

16. Surveillance II

The large black bird skimmed through the night sky, riding the thermals and surveying the village below. Its wingtips were outstretched and flight feathers spread, smaller contour feathers overlapping to smooth the flow of air and ensure optimum performance. Its beak curved downwards in a cruel arc, ready to tear apart any fresh meat, while its sharp black eyes scoured the air and fields looking for prey.

The nearly new moon was momentarily hidden behind a lone cloud, briefly concealing its light, so that fields, woodland and village were cloaked in darkness. The air was crisp and cold, and a light frost had already begun to coat grassland and trees, pavements and road surfaces, creating a sugared finish that twinkled faintly under the misty glow of the street lamps.

The bird was hungry and needed to eat, and flew high over the fields to the south of the village. Spying the white bobtails of a rabbit family below, as the moon emerged, it swooped on its unsuspecting prey, silent and deadly, gathering speed as it neared the ground, talons outstretched and ready for the kill. Attacked from behind, the rabbit knew nothing and death came quickly, the bird rapidly gaining height with its bloodied meal suspended below. Carrying its prey to the safety of a large old oak tree, it quickly tore away the flesh with its large, hooked beak, forcing huge pieces of fresh meat down its throat until all was consumed.

Then, satiated and re-energised, the bird took once more to the skies, flying upward with fresh intent, focused on its mission ahead. Like a dark shadow, it flew over the honeyed walls, slated roofs and turreted towers of the sleeping hall, circling twice as it scanned all below, then flying to the east for a short distance until it spied its target.

Gliding through the night air on silent wings, it came to rest on the slim branches of an ornamental cherry tree that stood in the garden of a village house. The bird manoeuvred itself precariously, almost too heavy for the willowy branch on which it perched. Still bare after winter, with small brown buds only just appearing, the tree provided little camouflage or cover, but the bird seemed unaware, its attention rapt as it gazed through an upper window of the house. The curtains fortunately remained open, giving the bird a perfect view of the room within, where a girl lay sleeping on the bed. The bird's eyes narrowed, and curling its beak down unwittingly, it gazed with dislike at the sleeping form.

Inside, the girl tossed and turned in the throes of a disturbing dream, peace of mind destroyed by dark terrors within. As she threw her head back on the pillow, arms flailing backwards, the bird saw with a jolt the necklace that came to rest on her breastbone. It was a necklace the bird instantly recognised and had seen before many times; a silver chain bearing a pale blue crystal...

In the dark grey, pre-dawn light, the crystal began to glow intensely, until its clear blue light was shining brightly. Nightmare over, the girl slept calmly, a serene expression on her face. The bird eyed the crystal with anger and loathing, only too aware of the protection it afforded the wearer. Gathering its wings closer to its body, it tightened its grip on the branch, sunk its head into its neck and prepared to watch. For the moment, intervention was prevented, but surveillance and patience would soon provide a chink in the armour, of that it was sure.

17. A Beast in the Fields

Watching from an upper window, which afforded the best view of the sheep and the field in which they grazed, Grace Wisterley took a sip from her hip flask and looked at her watch. 12 midnight. By her side lay her husband's 12-bore shotgun, unused for the last five years, but with a full chamber should the need arise.

"Just try it one more time, you horror, and I'll have ya, see if I don't," she muttered into the night. "That's the last of my sheep you'll be taking. X-ray vision that's what I've got, see better in the night than I do in the day."

She pulled on an old red woollen hat, making sure her ears were well-covered and tucked back straggling grey hairs with hands that were protected with fingerless black knitted gloves. Her ancient Drizabone coat covered her like a huge brown autumn leaf, making her look like a vast, overgrown toad, and her Hunter wellingtons left fragments of dried soil on the threadbare landing carpet. Picking up the shotgun and checking the hipflask was in her pocket, she walked down the stairs, along the hallway and into the old farmhouse kitchen. The ancient Aga kept things nice and warm, and for a second, she hesitated, unwilling to exchange the cosy warmth for the cold darkness. Then with sudden resolve, she quietly opened the back door and let herself out. The night around her was silent and dark, shrubs and bushes creating strange, eerie shapes, like tortured souls that raised their misshapen limbs in silent supplication to the sky. She shuddered involuntarily and tightened her grip around the shotgun. Purposefully, she strode down through the garden, out of the rear gate and into the field that adjoined her house. As the moon emerged from behind a cloud, she could see the silent shapes of the sheep, like small blocks of wood, dotted around the field.

"It's alright, my beauties," she said under her breath. "Don't take any notice of me. I'm here to protect ya. Nothin'll attack ya while I'm in the field. An' if they do, they won't last long."

She sat down on an old upturned milk crate that lay in a corner of the field and settled herself in, pulling her hat down and her coat around her. This was going to be a long night, but she had to be ready. Slowly, she scoured the field, looking for any sign of movement, but all appeared still. Perhaps the creature wouldn't come tonight. In a way, she hoped not. But if it didn't come tonight, it might come tomorrow, and sooner or later she had to take action. She couldn't go on losing sheep, that was for sure. How many of her prize Jacobs had she lost now? Too many. Four in the last week, three the week before. The flock was diminishing in front of her eyes and so far, she'd done nothing to stop it. The council had assured her that putting up posters would solve the problem, advising dog owners to keep their animals on a lead or pay the consequences.

"I've seen sheep that've been attacked by dogs," she'd told them, "and this ain't the work of any dog. This is somat much more powerful, with far bigger jaws. Them sheep weren't just savaged, they were torn apart, like somat 'ad picked 'em up in its mouth, shook 'em around and ripped 'em open. They were partially eaten… the remains were tossed around the field like old rubbish. That's not the work of a dog, that's a major predator."

But they'd refused to listen and now, rather than lose any more of her prize beauties, she was taking the matter into her own hands. Let the beast attack now and she'd blast it to kingdom come. She stroked the barrel of the shotgun, comforted by the cold, dark metal. "Don't let me down, old friend," she said quietly. "I'm relying on you." Once again, she surveyed the field, her eyes straining in the moonlit darkness to see the slightest movement. But all remained still and quiet.

Out in the fields two yellow eyes watched her, saw her come into the field, muttering to herself, and sit down in one corner, holding the old gun. Two wide nostrils inhaled deeply, taking in the scents of the night, the damp hedgerow, the stench of the cowpats, the fresh blood of the sheep, pulsing through their veins, waiting to be taken. Saliva dripped from its mouth in anticipation, the lips pulled back revealing jagged white teeth, and a low growl emitting from its throat.

Sensing an alien presence approaching, and their instincts warning them of impending danger, the sheep reacted, calling loudly to one another, legs stumbling in their panic to escape, desperately trying to form a group. Grace Wisterley moved quickly, raising her gun and looking across the field. She could see nothing, hear nothing except for the sheep's noisy commotion.

"Come on, show yersel, yer coward, get out in the open," she muttered into the night. This was going to be harder than she thought, and possibly more dangerous. Old Tim Mastock from down the road had offered to help her but she'd turned him down, telling him she could manage quite well on her own. Now she began to wonder if her confidence had been a little misplaced. She knew something big was out there and had heard the low growl, but whatever it was, the beast was keeping a very low profile.

Hidden by the hedge surrounding Grace's field, the creature slunk along on its belly, its black fur rendering it virtually invisible. Slowly and silently it crept, circling the field until it was positioned alongside her. It watched her walk into the centre of the field, the sheep bleating and cowering to her left, and saw her raise the gun. Keeping low, the creature continued around her, until it had Grace's back clearly in sight. Slowly it crept, dropping to its haunches and getting ready for the kill, its yellow eyes never leaving its prey, every muscle in its sleek black body taut and tight, its concentration absolute. Then, at the crucial moment, just as it prepared to pounce, it lifted its ears, detecting an almost inaudible sound. The animal cautiously raised its head and looked up, ears pricked, hearing once again the summoning call. With a regretful glance towards the field of crazed sheep and the woman in the centre, it turned round and bounded silently across the fields, intent now on one thing only, getting back to the voice that called it.

Standing stock still, every cell in her body on high alert, Grace Wisterley sensed movement behind her and turning rapidly, swore she saw something large and dark moving speedily across the fields and she knew she'd missed her chance.

"Yer'll be back," she muttered under her breath. "I might have scared y'off this time, but yer'll be back. And I'll be waiting for yer, whatever y'are."

She stomped back into the house, pulling off her old red woollen hat and kicking off her wellington boots. She carefully placed the shotgun in the cupboard and warmed her hands against the old Aga. She felt chilled through, and it wasn't just the temperature of the night air.

18. Party preparation

"I won't be able to see you for a few days," said Theo, sitting opposite me in the cafeteria, gauging my face for a reaction.

"Why not? Are you going away?" I asked, a little surprised.

"No, it's not that. We have a big function coming up at Hartswell Hall, and it's all hands on deck. I need to be there to help my mother and father." He spoke in the matter of fact voice that I'd come to recognise. There would be no changing his mind, although I decided to have a go anyway.

"What kind of function? Can I come and help you?"

"Sorry, Emily, not allowed," he said firmly. "It's a private party for friends, colleagues and acquaintances of my parents, before we open to the public. ... All very boring, but Violet, Joseph and I need to be there to help. Believe me, I'd much rather not be involved, but I've promised. Sorry." He laughed nervously, and I knew he hadn't been looking forward to telling me.

"When is it?" I asked.

"Two days' time. We need to prepare the house."

"Must be some party if you need to spend the next two days getting ready."

"It's important to my parents. They have friends coming from all over the world. Some are well known and expect total privacy. We can't let it be known that famous people will be visiting, otherwise we'll have the media swarming all over the place. So, I'm afraid it's strictly no visitors until it's over."

"Famous people?" I questioned him. "Like who?"

"I can't say, sorry. I've already told you too much."

"Can't I even come and peek from the sidelines? Hide in the shrubbery?" I joked.

"No," he said sharply, "absolutely not."

"It's okay, I was only pulling your leg. If you say you need privacy, I'll respect that. I'm just intrigued, that's all." I smiled at him, surprised at his reaction, "No doubt you'll be offering an exclusive to Hello magazine and I can read about it later."

He looked at me quizzically, not sure if I was still joking.

"I can assure you, Emily, Hello magazine will most certainly not be there. These are very important people and it's vital we assure them of total privacy."

"Is it like a Secret Ball?" I pushed him.

"Sort of, now please don't ask me any more questions. I can't tell you any more."

That was as much information as I could get out of him and, for the moment, I had to be satisfied with that.

Theo and Violet rode with me on the bus on the way home. Aquila was busy on family business and had no time to collect them, so for once they had to do what the ordinary folk did. Violet seemed to have made a full recovery from Grey Boy's death and told me not to feel responsible.

"It was a lovely gesture, Emily," she'd said. "That's what's important. Sometimes accidents happen…."

"Are you sure you can lower yourself to ride on public transport?" I teased Theo, as we climbed on board.

"It'll do me good to see how the other half lives," he countered. "And anyway, it'll be good to get away from Aquila's ugly mug for once."

"I'll second that," I said. "I've never known anyone who scowls so much or is totally incapable of a pleasant word. Has he always been that bitter and twisted?"

Theo laughed. "As long as I can remember," he admitted. "He's not one for pleasantries or smiling."

We sat near the back of the bus. Tash had gone home early for a dental appointment, and so Violet sat with Seth on the seat in front.

"The thing about Aquila," said Violet, turning round, "is that he is a very loyal servant. Wouldn't you agree, Theo?" I noticed an edge to her voice and wondered if she was warning Theo not to say so much.

"Yes, it's true," he answered, "Aquila has been with our family for many years and has always been there for us 100%. He looks out for us and we all feel safer for him being there. So, I really shouldn't say anything against him."

"Except he looks like he's continually sucking a lemon," I said, "You can't deny it."

"No," agreed Violet, laughing, "but there again, we didn't employ him for his personality. He's there to do a job."

"That job being?" asked Seth, who had no idea who we were talking about.

"Sorry, Seth," answered Violet, "Aquila is our chauffeur. Emily's met him a couple of times. He's very efficient but not terribly amenable."

"That's an understatement," I said under my breath.

"No, we had that problem with our chauffeur too," said Seth with a straight face, "You just can't get chauffeurs with good personalities, can you?"

It took Violet a second to realise he was teasing her.

"Ha ha, very funny," she said, pretending to look offended, but I could see she secretly liked it.

"And as for our house-keeper..." began Seth.

She cut him off.

"Don't even go there. We have one of those as well."

"But of course," said Seth. "Silly me. I should have guessed."

Violet pretended to tell him off. "You may mock. But it's quite normal in Egypt to have staff, you know. And before you say any more, she's every bit as uncommunicative and surly as our chauffeur."

"Isn't that how servants are meant to be?" said Seth. "Not that I'd know.... Not living in a twenty-bedroom mansion..."

"Thirty-bedroom mansion that's about to become a leading conference venue," corrected Violet.

I listened closely to their conversation. If I wasn't mistaken, they were flirting with one another. I smiled to myself, thinking about future possibilities.

"What are you smiling about?" asked Theo, putting his hand over mine.

Sparks of energy flew into my system and I tingled all over.

"Oh, nothing," I said, "Just thinking that life's become very interesting since you and your family moved into Hartswell Hall."

His hand tightened over mine.

"It's the best thing we've ever done," he said. "We're all excited about the future, especially me. I'm only sorry I won't be seeing you for a few days."

"Well, you do have a big celebrity party to host," I said. "I'm sure you'll be far too busy to miss me."

"Of course I'll miss you," he turned and looked into my eyes, "I'd much prefer to be with you, but this… 'party' …needs to happen. It's very important to us, to my parents…."

"Hey, it's only two days, I'm sure I'll survive," I said brightly. "I've got an English Literature project to do. …the metaphysical poetry of George Herbert…I can get on with that. At least you won't distract me."

The bus stop by Hartswell Hall appeared ahead, and Violet and Theo prepared to get off the bus.

"Why don't you pop in now, just for a few minutes?" asked Theo.

"I thought you were in the middle of party preparations," I said. "You don't want me in the way."

"It'll be fine today," answered Theo. "Come on, why don't you?"

The bus stopped and I made a last minute decision.

"Okay, I'll come with you."

"How about you, Seth?" asked Violet. "D'you want to come?"

Seth looked very surprised and more than a little pleased to be asked.

"Thanks for asking," he said, his fringe flopping forward, "but I've gotta get back. It's my mum's birthday. I need to get home. Another time?" He raised his eyebrows hopefully.

"Sure. Another time," said Violet, "See you."

The three of us walked up the driveway and soon the hall came into view. Maybe it was the afternoon sunshine on the honeyed Cotswold stone, I don't know, but it seemed to shine and pulse with energy. The thought went through my head: 'It's alive, it's excited at the prospect of the party', as Theo opened the front door. We walked into the reception area and everything had a freshness and sparkle about it.

"Looks like Pantera has been busy cleaning," laughed Violet.

Viyesha walked into the reception area, calling instructions over her shoulder.

"I want lilies on the big table …." She stopped short when she saw me, and a flash of confusion crossed her features before she smiled charmingly.

"Emily, what a surprise, I didn't expect to see you today."

"It's alright, mother," said Theo, quickly. "I won't be seeing Emily for the next two days, so she's just popped in for a few minutes."

"Sorry, Viyesha, if it's inconvenient…" I began, feeling in the way, but she held up her hand.

"Nonsense, of course it's convenient. I'll get Pantera to make some tea." She spoke quickly and efficiently, and I began to realise what a force majeure she could be where organisation was concerned. Disappearing down the corridor, she called, "Violet, could you come with me and help me sort out the room plans, please?"

"Yes, mother," said Violet. She looked at me quickly. "I'd better go. See you in a few days, Emily."

I glanced at Theo.

"I shouldn't have come. You obviously have a lot of things to get ready."

"It's fine, Emily. Don't worry. Come on, come into the ballroom."

We walked through the double doors on our right and, once again, a large fire was burning brightly in the huge fireplace. I followed Theo to the large purple sofas and sat where he indicated.

"I'll go and get the tea," he said, when I'd sat down. "It'll save Pantera a job."

"It's okay, Theo," I protested, "I don't want tea. I'm fine."

"It's no trouble, honestly."

He left the room quickly and I sat, feeling glad I wouldn't have to encounter the housekeeper again. She gave me the creeps and was the last person I wanted to see, apart from Aquila, that is.

Theo had only been gone for a few minutes, when the French windows leading to the rear gardens opened and Joseph walked in, carrying an armful of roses.

"Emily," he said, his face lighting up. "I didn't expect to see you here. Come to check up on your car? It's not quite ready yet."

"No, of course not, take as long as you want. It's just a quick visit. Theo invited me back," I explained, looking at the roses he was carrying and feeling more in the way than ever. "I know you have a party to organise and loads to do."

The scent of the roses assailed my nostrils and I breathed in deeply, adding, "They smell glorious, your guests will love them."

"I hope so. We're really pulling out the stops. It's not every day you have a Blue Moon Ball."

"A Blue Moon Ball," I said, opening my eyes wide, "that's sounds…"

"I probably shouldn't have told you that," said Joseph, grinning but looking rather awkward, "It's a …"

"Private party. I know," I said.

"No, you shouldn't have said that, should you Joseph?" said Theo, pushing open the double doors and carrying in a tea tray. He looked at Joseph, "I think those roses need putting in water, don't you?"

"Yes," said Joseph, taking the hint, "Yes, I must go and sort out the roses." He looked at me briefly. "See you Emily. Bye."

He left the room through the double doors and Theo closed them firmly behind him.

"So, the Blue Moon Ball," I said, knowing that I shouldn't push the point, but unable to help myself, "That sounds exciting."

Theo placed the tea tray on a side table and sat down next to me, choosing his words carefully.

"Yes it is exciting. And it's also very secret. As Joseph has unwittingly told you what's happening, I'll give you a little more detail, on the understanding you tell no one. Is that clear?"

"Yes," I said. At least I would find out what was happening.

"The Blue Moon Ball happens every three years or so and has done so for many, many years. It's like a family tradition, although it obviously extends beyond our family. We hold the ball in honour of the Blue Moon – I take it you've heard the phrase 'Once in a blue moon'?"

I nodded.

"To put it in its simplest terms, a Blue Moon happens approximately every three years when two full moons appear within a single calendar month. Normally, you get one full moon in a month, but it just works out that every so often, there are two. The first of these is very powerful and is known as a Blue Moon."

"Yes, I think I've grasped the concept," I said. "I have heard of this before."

"Okay," continued Theo, "We belong to a kind of secret society, for want of a better description, that attributes certain powers to the appearance of the Blue Moon…"

"Yes?" I breathed, leaning forward, hanging on his every word. I half wondered if he was making it up and at any moment would start laughing at me. But he remained serious and I continued to listen avidly.

"At the time of the Blue Moon, we follow certain rituals that we believe harness its power. It's not just family and friends, we have people coming from all over the world: famous sports people, film stars, pop stars, TV personalities, wealthy industrialists...."

"Wow," I said.

"It will be the most incredible evening, particularly now we're in Hartswell Hall," Theo said. "This could be the biggest and best ball we've ever had. But you can see the need for total secrecy and privacy. And why you can't come. If this ever got out, it would be disastrous."

This was bigger and far more serious than I could ever have imagined.

I had to ask: "When you say rituals, Theo, it's not devil worship, is it?"

He laughed. "No, nothing like that..."

He didn't have a chance to say any more because the double doors were suddenly

flung open and Aquila rushed in, looking angrier than I had ever seen him before.

"Stop, you fool," he spat his words at Theo, who sat white-faced and shocked. "What are you doing? You are breaking every code you have sworn to uphold. Do you want to destroy everything? Say no more. You have already said too much and will answer for your indiscretion."

"It's okay," I started to say, "he's hardly told me anything..."

"Silence," shouted Aquila. "You are nothing. Nothing but an irritation that needs removing."

"How dare you speak to her like that," commanded Theo, standing up and facing Aquila. "You know who she is, and yet you choose to deny it. She is far more important than you will ever be."

"You are wrong," Aquila hurled out his words like firecrackers. "She is no-one. You are mistaken and your mistake could cost us everything. How can we trust her now you have chosen to divulge secrets you had sworn to protect? Does it all mean so little to you, that you would risk everything? You know I cannot allow her to leave now."

"She knows nothing of importance, Aquila. And if you lay a finger on her, you have me to answer to." Theo positioned himself protectively in front of me, his anger vibrating and pulsing like an energy field, sparks appearing to fly from his body.

They stood facing each other like two unexploded bombs about to detonate and I hardly dared move, at once fascinated and horrified by their words.

"Move out of the way," Aquila instructed Theo. "You leave me no choice but to act. You should have considered the consequences of your actions before you betrayed us."

He went to push Theo out of the way and I shrank as far back into the corner of the sofa as I could, feeling suddenly very afraid. Fortunately, salvation was at hand, as Viyesha burst into the room, the double doors crashing with the impact of her entrance.

"Enough," she said in an icy cold voice. "You have both said too much." She addressed me, her voice quivering with urgency. "Emily, leave. Leave now, while you can. Run and don't look back." She held the door open for me and I needed no further bidding, I ran for the door. As I passed her, Viyesha put her hand on my arm, stopping me momentarily, as if suddenly realising the need to defuse the situation. "We can trust you not to say anything, can't we, Emily?"

As her hand touched my arm, my fear left me and feelings of calmness and serenity flooded my being. I looked into her beautiful face and big blue eyes, radiating kindness and concern.

"Of course, Viyesha," I found myself saying. "My first loyalty is to you. It always has been."

"Good. Tell no one what has occurred here this afternoon. Neither friends nor family. If you remain loyal to us, I can protect you. Do you understand?"

"Yes," I whispered, "I'll tell no-one."

She smiled at me, and as she did, I noticed tiny wrinkles at the corners of her eyes that I hadn't seen before, and furrows in her brow that had once been smooth.

"Now go," she said, taking her hand off my arm. I glanced down and was surprised to see her hand looking claw-like and frail, the veins lifted, the skin puckered and dry. She quickly crossed her arms, placing each hand within the wide sleeves of her gown, nun-like, so I was unable to see anything more. "Go," she repeated and I needed no further bidding.

I ran through the reception area, nearly tripping over something that darted from an open doorway. Stepping wide in an effort not to stand on it, I looked down to see what I had so nearly trodden on. There was no mistaking the fluffy grey bundle that sat on the black and white tiles looking up at me. It was the kitten, as alive and playful as it had ever been.

"Grey Boy," called Violet's voice from the open door. "Come here, you naughty thing."

I didn't look back. Reaching for the latch of the oak door, I lifted it quickly, opened it and ran as fast as I could through the courtyard and down the gravelled driveway. I didn't stop. I ran until I had no breath left. One thing I knew above all else, I had to get away from that house of horrors while I still could.

19. Family pow wow

The family gathered once again in the library. Theo and Violet sat on one Chesterfield, Joseph on another. Pantera and Aquila stood behind, and facing them all were Viyesha and Leon. They all looked ill at ease and nervous.

Viyesha began by addressing them all.

"As you now know, a situation has arisen which is extremely worrying. And it is all the more urgent, given its timing. We have just two days until the Blue Moon Ball, and just a day until our guests start arriving. Nothing can be compromised at this late stage. As you are only too well aware, our existence depends on the Blue Moon Ball taking place."

She paused for breath, looking stooped and tired, her usually luminous skin heavy and pale. Taking advantage of the break in her words, Aquila spoke in rasping, venomous tones. "You should have let me take care of the girl while I could. That would have guaranteed our safety, now we have a loose cannon out there. What if she brings others here? What happens then?" His dark skin creased into lines of worry, like deeply engraved grooves etched across his sour features.

"She won't," said Viyesha, "I am confident that we have her loyalty."

"I'm sorry, Viyesha," said Joseph, his usually curly hair flat and straight, streaks of grey intermingled with the lustreless blonde tresses. "This is all my fault. If only I hadn't mentioned the Blue Moon Ball, none of this would have arisen."

"That was bad enough, idiot," exploded Aquila, "but it was this moron who did all the damage." He poked his bony finger into Theo's back as he spoke. "You had to tell her, didn't you?"

Theo turned as if touched by an electric cattle prodder.

"Don't touch me, you filthy scavenger," he said through clenched teeth. His face looked haggard and tired, jowls beginning to appear at either side of his mouth. "If you lay a finger on her, I swear I'll kill you."

"You'll have to get past me first," hissed Pantera, still tall and majestic, but now looking thin and careworn.

"This is getting us nowhere," thundered Leon in a loud, commanding voice that shook them all. "We have no time for recriminations or threats. The question is what do we do now? We have such little time." He paused, the exertion causing him to stop and catch his breath, his film star looks appearing tired and worn.

"He's right, mother," said Violet, looking small and hunched. "I'm frightened. What if we don't make it this time? What if Emily brings people here?"

"D'you really think she would, Violet?" asked Theo. "You're forgetting one very important factor. Her feelings for me. If she tells anyone or brings anybody here, she jeopardises her relationship with me. Do you really think she'd do that?"

"Can we risk it?" rasped Aquila. "You should have let me take care of things while I could. Before you gave her the necklace."

"I gave her the necklace to protect her from creatures like you," said Theo in disgust. "How do you know about it, anyway? Nobody else did."

"You forget I have eagle eyes," said Aquila triumphantly. "You can hide nothing from me."

"Please, everyone, be quiet," said Viyesha, sounding tired and old. "Theo, what is this necklace of which Aquila speaks?"

"I gave Emily my Celestite crystal necklace," said Theo. "It was the only thing I could think of to keep her safe."

"I see," said Viyesha slowly, "I suppose we gave you no choice, but you should have consulted me first. I need to know what you're doing."

She addressed the rest of the assembled family. "Listen closely. We cannot waste what remaining strength we have on argument and dissent. This is what I propose. We must carry on preparing for the ball. We have only two days, and limited resources left within us. I am confident Emily will not compromise our safety. If, as Theo believes, she is one of us, we truly have nothing to fear. If we find out otherwise, we may have no choice but to eliminate her. And Pantera, that task will fall to you. Not you, Aquila. I find your propensity towards violence disturbing and abhorrent. We are peaceful, we do not seek to destroy. That comes as a last resort only when all other avenues are closed to us and we are faced with a kill or be killed situation. Do I make myself clear?"

She looked from one to the other, all around the group.

"Yes, Viyesha," said Joseph.

"Yes, mother," said Theo, sounding weary and hollow.

"Yes, mother," echoed Violet.

"Pantera and Aquila, do I have your agreement?" asked Viyesha, looking at them with tired, watery eyes.

"Yes, Viyesha," said Pantera, quietly, not meeting her gaze.

"As you wish," said Aquila arrogantly, tossing his head back. "But I hope you're not making a huge mistake. For all our sakes."

Viyesha looked at Theo.

"There is one more thing to discuss. Theo, if you truly believe Emily is who you think she is, if you are convinced she is 'the one', she has no other choice but to join us."

"But, mother, it's too dangerous," said Theo, looking anguished. "I can't put her through that."

"You must, Theo, surely you see that?" said Viyesha quietly.

"No!" he exclaimed, "I cannot inflict that upon her. It must be her choice. If she joins us it's because she wants to, because she understands the risks. She may not survive. She has to understand the dangers involved and that the odds are against her."

He sat back, looking hunched and old, his brow creased, his problems weighing heavily on his shoulders.

"Theo," said his mother, kindly, "for now we must concentrate on the Blue Moon Ball. There is time enough to consider Emily's fate after that."

Slowly, they filed out of the library, seven world-weary figures, their posture stooped, their faces tired and drawn, their energy levels all but extinguished.

20. Arrivals

Once more, the mist had descended on Hartswell-on-the-Hill, its tendrils curling around vegetation and trees alike, clothing them in a dark grey mantle. It was 2am and the mist combined with a cloudy night to reduce visibility to almost zero. The cloying heaviness pressed against windowpanes and doors and, had the sleeping residents attempted to look out, they would have seen nothing more than a thick grey wall encompassing and entombing them.

While the village slept, tormented by wild dreams and fevered imaginings, strange things were occurring at Hartswell Hall. Aquila drove the sleek black Jaguar up the driveway, seemingly oblivious to the fog. The wheels crunched on the pebbled courtyard as he parked the car, then opened the doors for the occupants to disembark,

A slim leg in a silk stocking appeared first, the sheer denier failing to hide the varicose veins, and an elderly, veined hand grasped the rear doorframe. Slowly, the old woman pulled herself out of the car, standing precariously for a moment. She was followed by an elderly gentleman with silver white hair and deep jowls, who slowly got out of the front passenger seat, leaning heavily on a silver-topped cane. Two further old ladies eased themselves out of the rear seat, one with the bobbed hairstyle of a much younger woman, contrasting incongruously with her heavily lined face; the other with grey-streaked auburn tresses and a tight red dress revealing a once stunning physique that was now hunched and stooped. Both wore large framed sunglasses, concealing most of their faces.

A welcoming committee stood on the front step.

"Viyesha," said the woman with auburn hair, slowly walking towards her. "My dear, so pleased to see you again."

She went forward and they embraced with an air kiss, Viyesha murmuring "Chevron, as always, you are most welcome."

One by one, the guests climbed the front steps, embracing Viyesha and shaking hands with Leon.

"Rachael, lovely to see you. Sugar, welcome…. Roberto… do come in."

Viyesha indicated for Pantera and Aquila to collect the guests' luggage and carry it into the house. Then she ushered her guests into the main entrance hall and reception area.

"You are the first to arrive, which means you have plenty of time to make yourself at home. Your bedrooms are all prepared and may I suggest you rest as much as possible for the next two days, conserving your energy for what lies ahead. And on that score, please be assured everything is in place and all will happen as it should." She cupped her hands in a circle in front of her solar plexus and crossed her thumbs, saying softly, *"We hold eternity in our hands."*

On cue, her guests each gave the well-practiced signal, cupping their hands and crossing their thumbs in a similar fashion, and echoing her words. *"We hold eternity in our hands."*

"Please," instructed Leon, "follow Pantera up the main stairs and she will show you to your rooms."

The party began to ascend the huge, carved central stairway, each holding on to the polished mahogany bannister and moving slowly, pulling up their old bones step by step.

Viyesha watched them go, murmuring to herself, "Perhaps an elevator for future years…?" She turned to Leon and smiled. "It's begun, my love. We've made it and this time nothing can go wrong."

He put his arm round her shoulders and holding her close, said into her hair, "As always, you have led us to safety, Viyesha. We owe our existence to you, not one of us is in doubt of that."

She turned up to him, her eyes shining amidst her tired, lined face. "Soon we will party again with the vigour of youth, Leon. Not long now."

* * *

Outside, in the fields beyond Hartswell-on-the-Hill, where the mist petered out and the world was near normal, strange amorphous shapes moved through the grass. Black shadowy nostrils inhaled the breeze, searching for familiar scents. Finding none, they dropped back to the earth, hissing and clicking in their frustration. Time and again, they approached the outer boundaries of the mist, trying to penetrate its wall-like intensity. Time and again, they were beaten back, unable to get any closer to the object they sought, unable to glean even the faintest whiff of its existence.

21. The Blue Moon Ball

I crouched in the undergrowth alongside the main driveway of Hartswell Hall, feeling rather than seeing a vehicle cruise slowly by on its way up to the house. Everywhere around me the mist clung, heavy and oppressive, swallowing any light, and preventing me from seeing even a few inches ahead. High up, above the mist, the moon shone brightly, but had no impact on the ground below.

It had taken me a long time to get here, walking as if I were a blind person, feeling the way, running my fingers along neighbours' front walls, carefully putting one foot in front of the other, stumbling as the pavement gave way to the road. Luckily, I had a good sense of direction and knew exactly where I was headed, but the lack of vision disorientated me. I was sure I had plenty of time. I'd left the house just before 10.30pm. Mum and Granddad had each gone to bed, both complaining of a headache, which I attributed to the unusual weather and abnormal air pressure. Ever since I'd been wearing the blue crystal necklace, I'd felt amazingly vibrant and energetic. Some nights I'd needed only a few hours' sleep, arising in the early hours to do my homework and excelling at college to the amazement of my tutors.

Now, I gazed ahead in the direction of Hartswell Hall, wondering how to get in without anyone seeing me. I was determined to find out what was going on at the Blue Moon Ball. Once again, the phrase 'like a moth to a flame' kept going through my head and that's how I felt, like a small, vulnerable creature drawn to the light, not caring whether or not it heralded destruction. Instinct had taken over from rationality, like an ancient response deep within me, and I was simply doing what I felt I must.

Slowly, I crept closer to the hall, sometimes going on my hands and knees to feel where the edge of the driveway met the grass verge. Occasionally, the blue crystal swung forth, shining brightly in the dense mist, and I hastily tucked it back beneath my sweater in case it drew attention to me. At last I reached the courtyard, and narrowly missed being spotted, as Aquila drove away from the hall, nearly catching me in the Jaguar's headlights. Pressing myself to the old stonework, I shrank into the mist and remained out of sight.

Walking in through the main entrance wasn't an option, as I would most certainly have been seen. I had to find another way. Slowly I edged round the side of the hall, feeling the old stone walls beneath my fingers. I continued round the building until I was at the rear of the hall, the lawns and ha-ha falling away behind me. Now I was close to the ballroom, where all the action would be taking place. My excitement stirred as my fingers touched the framework of the large French windows. There was no way the doors would be open, I reasoned, but tried nonetheless. To my amazement, the door swung inwards. I quickly pulled it back and slipped inside.

Holding my breath, I closed the door behind me, thankful to leave the cloying mist outside. Fortunately, long heavy velvet drapes concealed me, enabling me to look into the ballroom without being seen. I heard a band playing a slow jazz number and, over the top of the music, the sound of people laughing and talking, and the chink of glasses. I glanced at my watch. It was 11.30pm. Determined to take a quick snapshot of the Blue Moon Ball, I took out my cell phone, remembering to turn off the flash and set it to silent. No point drawing attention to myself.

Peering through the curtains, I looked into the room and gasped. What I saw was all the more shocking for being so unexpected. If I'd thought the ballroom would be full of fashionable men and women, dancing, mingling and enjoying themselves, while musicians played contemporary music, I was wrong. Perhaps I'd seen too many period dramas, but the sight in front of me was so far removed from this, it was almost laughable. This was more like the communal lounge of an old folks' home.

The room was candlelit and atmospheric, with a fire burning brightly in the huge ornate fireplace. The large purple sofas had been pulled back against the far walls, and pretty chairs with blue backs and tables with delicate blue coverings placed along the sides of the room. A small group of elderly musicians were seated at the far end, playing a low-key jazz number, but no one danced and the central area remained empty. Sitting and standing around the edges of the room, some on their own and others in small groups, talking quietly, were around fifty people of greatly advanced age. I stared, not comprehending what I was seeing. Where were the rich, glamorous sophisticates who'd travelled from across the globe to be here? I'd expected to see beautiful people on a par with the de Lucis family, not a collection of stooped old folk, with wizened skin and thinning hair, who'd left their best years firmly behind them. True, the ladies were dressed for a ball, but mottled parchment skin and hunched backs did nothing for the exquisite ball gowns I saw before me, while the abundance of beautiful jewels hardly drew my attention from their owners' shrivelled faces and scrawny arms. Talk about mutton dressed as lamb, I thought, these people had serious style issues. Someone should have told them to dress their age, not hang on with desperation to the last vestiges of a youth that had well and truly disappeared.

A woman in a stunning emerald green ballgown came to stand close to me, with emeralds and diamonds at her throat and in her hair, but I could hardly bear to look at the folds of creased, papery skin covered with lesions and blemishes that the plunging back of her dress revealed. I took her photo and shuddered with revulsion.

It was obvious why Theo hadn't wanted me around, I thought. This was just plain horrible. It wasn't a glamorous, star-studded event, it was a geriatric get together. These people may be wealthy and famous, but their stars had most definitely faded. It was not a pretty sight and I was hugely disappointed. I didn't recognise a single one. I took a couple more photos just for the record, and had just decided to creep back out of the French windows and beat a hasty retreat home, when I heard a commotion at the ballroom's double doors. The band stopped playing and I clearly heard Viyesha's voice saying, "Friends, it is time. The heavens have aligned, the moon is full, and it is time for us to renew and re-energise. Please follow me… It's time to be re-born….. We hold eternity in our hands."

I peered through the curtains and saw an old woman in a royal blue gown cupping her hands in front of her, with crossed thumbs, giving some kind of sign. In unison, the guests echoed her: "*We hold eternity in our hands*", each cupping their hands in a similar way. I stared aghast. Surely it couldn't be Viyesha? The woman was ancient, with a stooped back, snow-white hair and marked, mottled skin. She certainly resembled Viyesha and was possibly her mother or grandmother even.

Then I remembered the clawed, shrunken hand I'd seen last time I was at the hall, and how Viyesha had hastily concealed her hands beneath her sleeves. Could it be possible this hunched, old creature was she?

I continued to watch from behind the curtains as the old folk began to form a queue. As they passed through the double doors, the ancient Viyesha-woman handed each a midnight-blue hooded cloak, which they hung around their shoulders, pulling the hoods up over their heads. On the back of each cloak was a strange symbol: a circle, crossed by an infinity sign. It was the same sign I'd seen hewn into the stonework at the top of the Clock Tower. Suddenly, the sound of whispered chanting filled the air. The old folk seemed to be saying: "Lunari... Lunari .... Lunari..." over and over, filling me with a dread I couldn't explain.

I waited until the last one had exited the ballroom, then cautiously stepped out from behind the curtains, looking nervously around the empty room and wondering what to do next. Half empty glasses stood upon tables and the band's instruments were laid carefully on their seats. I felt the blue crystal on my breastbone tingling and vibrating, and knew I had to follow them. As quickly as I could, I crossed the ballroom and looked through the double doors. The reception area was empty and I saw the last hooded figure disappearing up the main central staircase. Still they chanted, adding a demonic feel to an evening that was already weirder than anything I could have imagined. I shivered, but never once considered leaving, committed to seeing this through, whatever the outcome.

Seeing a spare cloak lying on the floor, I picked it up and put it on, admiring its deep, soft velvet. I pulled the hood tightly around my face and breathed a sigh of relief. Now, at least I blended in and wouldn't be noticed.

I crossed the reception area stealthily, walking on tiptoes, and ascended the large carved staircase, my heart beating against my ribs, my breathing fast and shallow. In front of me, I saw the last person gliding along the corridor to the left, the sound of chanting filling the air. I crouched low on the stairs and peered over the top step. The old folk were queuing on the landing and I gasped as I realised where they were going. One by one, they filed up the old servants' staircase. 'Structurally unsound, my foot!' I muttered to myself, "I knew there was something up there they didn't want me to see." I waited as they climbed up the stairway, then crept along the corridor, keeping as close to the walls as I could, hiding in the shadows. I was so close to uncovering their secret, it wouldn't do to be discovered at this stage.

When they'd all disappeared into the upper reaches of the hall, I crept forward and followed them. The old gas lamps had been cleaned and lit, I noticed, casting a dim glow. The cobwebs had all been swept away and a thick, dark blue carpet had been laid on the stairs. Good, that made it easier to follow without being heard. Up I climbed, the air feeling chill as I reached the upper landing. I looked around. A long corridor stretched in front of me, various doors leading off it. Towards the end of the corridor, I saw the hooded figures shuffling forward, silent now and queuing once again, and I quickly took another photo. I had to know where they were going and where this corridor led. At regular intervals, square pillars jutted out from the walls, acting as plinths for decorative arches that spanned the corridor, and creating dark recesses that were perfect for concealment. Quickly, I moved to the first pair of pillars, pressing myself into the recess and peering round. No one had seen me, and the queue of stooped, elderly people was getting noticeably smaller. I risked moving forward to the next pair of pillars. Now, I was afforded a better view and strained to see, through the dim light, where the old folk were going. At first glance, it seemed that the corridor reached a dead end, but as I crept forward, I realised there was a small spiral stairway that

could lead nowhere else but up into the Clock Tower. A number of
figures were congregated on the corridor, awaiting their turn. A
dim blue light shone down the stairs and I realised that a door
leading to the upper tower rooms must have been opened. As I
watched, the blue light became stronger and I was aware of people
coming back down the stairs. Panicking that I was about to be
discovered, I looked around for somewhere to hide. Seeing a
doorway immediately opposite, I darted across the passageway,
opened the door and flung myself inside, closing the door silently
behind me. For a second I stood, leaning against the doorframe,
calming my breathing as I realised what a near miss I'd just had. If
I'd stayed on the corridor a second longer, my cover would most
certainly have been blown.

I knew, now, where they were going, but I still didn't know
their secret. What was in the room at the top of the Clock Tower?
Why was a blue light shining out? And why were the old people
queuing to go up there? I had to find out what was going on.

I took a brief look around the room in which I stood. It was
probably once a servant's bedroom, but there was nothing in it
now, except for an old wardrobe on the far wall covered in dusty
cobwebs. I turned back to the door and opened it slightly, peering
through the gap. This gave me a perfect view of stairs
disappearing upwards and I could clearly see the last few old folk
queuing to go up, while others came down and started to file back
down the corridor. The sight that met my eyes as they passed my
doorway made my blood run cold. It was surely impossible …

A procession of the most beautiful beings walked slowly by,
their heads held high, their backs straight and their posture perfect,
each one looking radiant, glamorous and young, and each holding
a blue cloak over their arm. I realised one woman had been
standing near me in the ballroom, wearing the emerald green ball
gown. Gone was her sagging, creased flesh: it had been replaced
by firm, well-toned, ivory skin with the translucence of alabaster.
Her chestnut hair gleamed, her eyes sparkled and she dazzled with
the radiance of a beautiful jewel. Her lips were full and pink, her
features perfectly formed and her figure like a Vogue model. On
her shoulder, etched into her skin like a glowing blue, translucent

tattoo, was the same circular symbol crossed by an infinity sign. With a jolt, I realised she was a well-known TV star, who had recently made a comeback, looking younger and more glamorous than anyone would have thought possible.

She paused and waited for the man behind her to catch up, linking arms with him and laughing. Her laugh was high pitched and clear, with the resonance of tinkling bells, and her teeth were dazzlingly white. Her partner was equally spellbinding and I gasped anew, as I recognised one of Hollywood's leading men. His skin, too, was ivory-toned and unlined, and he glowed with the radiance of youth. His eyes were clear blue, dancing and bright, his features chiselled and angular, and his shoulders broad and muscular. Quickly, without thinking of the danger, I pulled out my phone and, placing it right up against the gap in the door, took a picture. I simply had to have a souvenir of this amazing evening.

More beautiful people followed. I saw a well-known pop star, who by rights should have been in her sixties, looking no more than twenty-five; a famous actress, with a perfect, air-brushed face, immaculate teeth and hair, and the most beautiful slender body; and a famous footballer, who had just made the headlines for signing a multi-million pound deal. Other people filed past me, laughing and chatting animatedly, each looking young, vibrant and glamorous. The women were stunning in their haute couture ballgowns, the men debonair and sophisticated in their black dinner suits and dress shirts. I watched for maybe half an hour, until I figured nearly fifty people had emerged from the Clock Tower's upper room. Some looked very young, others slightly older, but none of them appeared to be above mid-thirties, and I knew without doubt these were the same people that I'd seen in the ballroom looking frail and old. Now they were rejuvenated, heading back downstairs to have the kind of party I'd expected to see when I first looked in. Some I recognised, famous movies stars, models and moguls; others I didn't know, but could tell by their demeanour, they were powerful, dynamic people, exuding the charisma and vitality of youth and beauty. Whenever I had the opportunity, I took photos, my hands shaking, my mind unable to compute what I was seeing, but knowing I needed proof that I hadn't imagined any of this.

Finally, the last few stragglers filed past the doorway, their laughter and gaiety filling the corridor. Then my hand froze and my heart felt as if it had stopped. There, coming down the spiral stairway, was Violet and Joseph, each looking as if they'd been through a fabulous makeover. They glistened, they glowed and they glittered with a blinding radiance, their skin so perfect I wanted to reach out and touch it, their beauty so mesmerising it literally took my breath away. Violet was wearing a stunning purple off-the-shoulder, slinky chiffon gown that showed her amazing physique off to perfection, Joseph looking impossibly handsome in his dark dinner jacket and white starched shirt.

Viyesha and Leon followed, holding hands, more beautiful and more attractive than I'd ever seen them, their blonde hair immaculate, their faces tranquil and serene, Viyesha sublime in shimmering royal blue silk. With horror, I realised it was the same blue gown I'd seen the old woman wearing who had handed out the cloaks. I stared, transfixed, as they passed by, my brain hardly able to compute what I was seeing before me. This couldn't be happening, surely? And yet the proof was there in front of my eyes.

One person remained that I longed to see. Where was Theo? Surely, I hadn't missed him amidst the earlier throng of guests that had passed down the corridor. I looked again, but the spiral stairway was empty, a faint blue glow still just about visible. Was he still up there? Dare I go and have a look? As I was contemplating my choices, the light suddenly became stronger, and there he was, my Theo, bathed in blue, walking down the stairs, the most beautiful creature of all, so exquisite I had to fight back the tears. I gazed at him enraptured. Never had he looked so amazing, so alluring or quite simply divine. The attraction I felt for him possessed my whole body and I knew I had to be with him, whatever the consequences. Quickly, I opened the door and stepped into the corridor, pulling back the hood from my face. As he saw me, an expression of joy then horror passed over his face.

"Emily," he whispered, "What are you doing here? Don't you know how dangerous this is for you? If they find you, they'll kill you."

He pushed me back into the room that had been my hiding place, closing the door silently and quickly behind us.

"Theo, I'm sorry," I started to say, but his lips were upon mine, kissing me with a passion and ferocity that touched my soul. I responded with equal passion, feeling his energy and radiance fill my being, consuming me, possessing me. I was lost in his kiss, lost in the strange existence of Theo's world, love and desire burning within me. The moth had reached the flame and I didn't care if it destroyed me. Suddenly, he broke away. "Emily, no," he spoke breathlessly. "We can't do this. You have no idea what you're getting into, how high the stakes are..." His piercing blue eyes stared into mine and I saw an eternity of suffering, torment and pain within him.

"I can't let this happen..." he began to say, when voices outside the door stopped him. We listened in horror as Aquila's rasping voice spoke: "Pantera, I heard voices, I tell you..."

"It was probably our guests," came Pantera's reply.

"May be," answered Aquila, "but we can't leave anything to chance."

Theo indicated the wardrobe at the side of the room and silently pulled open one of its heavy wooden doors. Just in time, we concealed ourselves within, pulling the door to, as Aquila flung open the door to the room. For a few seconds, time stood still as he looked around and I held my breath, praying he wouldn't detect our presence or hear my heart beating with the ferocity of an express train. Eventually, he went out and we could hear him moving down the corridor, opening other doors and looking into rooms. We heard Pantera call out, "Aquila, did you find anything?" and from down the corridor, his answer: "No, I think you were right. It must have been guests."

Then we heard her say, "Come Aquila, we need to secure the casket and the room. Then I'll take a look outside." There was a muffled sound of another door closing and then it was quiet.

"Quickly," said Theo, opening the door of the wardrobe, "We don't have much time. I have to get you out of here."

"I'm sorry, Theo," I started to say, but he cut me short.

"Not now, Emily, I need to think."

He walked over to the doorway, opened it cautiously and peered out.

"Okay," he whispered to me, "come quickly before they return."

I followed him out, and the next minute we were walking rapidly along the corridor, our feet sinking into the plush dark blue carpet, down the old servants' stairway and onto the main landing. My blue cloak billowed behind me and I gathered it close, pulling the hood down over my face. Theo led the way past the top of the main stairway and onto the other corridor that lead to the right. He indicated a doorway.

"In here, Emily, you'll be safe for a while. This is just a store room."

Looking around to make sure we were alone, he quickly opened the door and we crept in, breathless and tense. Theo closed the door and turned towards me.

"Now perhaps you'll tell me what you are doing here, despite my warnings?"

I threw back the hood. "I'm sorry, Theo," I whispered, "I had to come and find out what was going on."

"And what did you see?" he asked urgently.

I bit my lip. "I saw a lot of old people, all stooped and grey. I saw them going up the old servants' stairway and along the corridor, up the spiral stairway that I assume leads to the Clock Tower. I saw a bright blue light shining down and then I saw the old folk emerging, rejuvenated. They were glowing, Theo. How did that happen?"

He thought for a second, then asked me, "What do you think? Do you have any idea?"

"Well, I don't think you're vampires..." I began.

"Vampires?" He laughed dismissively, "Who wants to be a vampire and drink blood for eternity? What we have discovered is far more seductive and a great deal more dangerous."

"Then what is it, Theo? What have you discovered? You have to tell me ...."

He put both hands around my face and looked into my eyes. "Not tonight, Emily," he said, "I will tell you, I promise, but not tonight. There's no time. I have to get you out of here, before you're discovered."

He looked so beautiful and so vulnerable, it was all I could do not to kiss him again.

"Keep the cloak on," he advised, "But keep your head down and don't speak to anyone. I'll let you out of one of the side doors. Don't go down the main driveway. Go past the Clock Tower to the circular fountain. There, you'll find the newly cleared pathway to the church. Take that pathway. If you feel anyone is following you, get to the church and stay there until daylight comes. You'll be safe in there."

"Theo, you're frightening me," I said. "Can't you come with me?"

"Emily, I want to come with you," he took my hands in his, "but I can't. I'd be missed. And it's not safe for you to stay. You cannot be discovered. It would mean certain death."

I swallowed. "Okay, I'll go."

I drew the thick velvet cloak around me, and Theo carefully pulled up the hood. For a second, he gazed into my eyes, then his lips were upon mine kissing me hungrily and passionately. Despite, or because of, the danger, I responded with an intensity I had never known before, and as our lips fused together, I felt our souls touch and unite. If I didn't make it, this might be my last encounter with Theo, the love of my life, my reason for being, and my future, if destiny allowed. I could feel Theo's energy, his life force, filling my body with a spiritual consummation that possessed every fibre of my being. But time was against us and he broke away, pain and anxiety etched across his beautiful face.

"You must go, Emily, before it's too late." Silently, he arranged the hood so that it hung over my face, concealing my features.

"Say nothing to anyone," he cautioned, "Walk slowly and purposefully. Don't draw attention to yourself."

He opened the door and looked out.

"All clear," he said, "Let's go." He led the way along the corridor to the head of the main stairway and slowly, we started to walk down. Fortunately, there was some kind of commotion going on in the reception area that was claiming the attention of all present. A male guest appeared to have collapsed on the floor and others were tending to him. I could see a figure in a black dinner suit lying on the black and white tiles, his legs splayed out awkwardly, with others leaning over him.

I saw a beautiful woman in a red ball gown, with blonde hair piled high and long red gloves, say tearfully to Viyesha: "He arrived too late. There was a delay in his travel arrangements and he arrived too late. This is our worst nightmare. Is there nothing we can do for him?"

Viyesha put a protective arm around her shoulders and I heard her saying softy: "No. I'm sorry. The power of the Blue Moon has passed. There is nothing more that can be done."

The red gowned woman stifled a sob, and there was a collective gasp from all those who attended the man. I felt Theo's hand on my waist, guiding me past the assembled guests and projecting me forward. As I walked around the edge of the crowd, a sudden gap presented itself between the guests and I was able to see the man. It was all I could do not to cry out in horror. I saw a wizened, shrunken face, surrounded by wispy white hair. His mouth was open as if gasping for air, his claw-like hands were up round his throat as if he'd been trying to open his shirt. That he was dead was bad enough, but in the brief glimpse I had of him, I saw him decay before my eyes. I saw the flesh disintegrate on his face, falling into his cheekbones, I saw his eyeballs dry out and shrink, leaving two cavernous eye sockets, and I saw his lips draw back to reveal yellowed, blackened teeth in a hideous grin. The man was turning into a skeleton before my eyes. For a second I was frozen with fear, unable to move another step, then once again I felt Theo's firm hand behind me, guiding me forward. I moved on autopilot, incapable of rational thought. The next thing I knew we were in a small passageway and Theo was opening a door. I felt the cold night air on my face and heard Theo say: "Go left past the Clock Tower, keep going until you reach the fountain, then take the pathway through the woods to the church. Go quickly." Then the door was closed behind me and I was on my own.

Instinctively, I kept close to the walls of Hartswell Hall, bearing to the left until I reached the Clock Tower. The mist had lifted and a magnificent full moon filled the night sky, providing all the illumination I could ask for. Looking up at the turreted upper windows of the Tower, I could see a faint blue light and I knew that was where the guests had been. There was no time to linger and I ran on, reaching the circular feature in just a few minutes. Amazingly, it had been transformed into a beautiful fountain, the water spraying upwards to a height of about two metres, glinting seductively in the moonlight before falling back into the dark waters below, where I saw the silver moon clearly reflected, shimmering in the rippling water. Fleetingly aware that it was impossible to have renovated the fountain in such a short time, I kept moving. Behind the fountain was the pathway, leading through the woodland, the undergrowth cleared away and fresh bark laid down to create a good walking surface. I knew it wasn't far to the church, no more than a few hundred metres, but it seemed to take an eternity, my breath shallow and harsh, my heart beating fast, the blood rushing in my ears. The woodland was alive around me, every rustle, every sound making me jump. Then suddenly, the church was in front of me and I ran as if possessed through the graveyard, along the ancient path that led past the vestry, until I reached its main doors, praying silently that they would be open. I turned the old metal door ring and thanked all the angels in heaven when the huge old studded door opened before me. Quickly, I pushed it wide and fell into the church. As I turned to close the door, I glanced into the graveyard, where the gravestones glinted spookily in the moonlight. There, in the undergrowth, I saw two huge yellow eyes watching me. With a cry, I slammed the church door shut, dropped the latch and fell sobbing to the floor.

PART THREE – KNOWLEDGE

22. Kimberley Chartreuse

In her Leicestershire mansion, Kimberley Chartreuse (aka Wendy Tubbs) lay back amidst her white silk sheets on her monster-sized waterbed and looked contemptuously at husband number four. He was obedient and biddable, but boring as hell, as she'd found out too late, just after they'd got married. It had seemed a huge laugh at first. Queen of Glamour gets hitched to Prince of the Reality World. He'd been a big hit on his reality TV show and everybody wanted a piece of Jakey-Boy. Including her. But once all the hype had been stripped back and his physical charms had started to fade, she'd found he was just a handsome husk with nothing between the ears. He'd served a purpose, she supposed. Her ratings had been dropping slowly but surely, not catastrophically, but enough to get her agent worried.

"We need a big event, Kimberley," he'd said, in his flat Black Country accent. "I don't care what it is. Well, not another breast enlargement. Perhaps husband number four? Someone that's current you can ride on the back of, as it were."

"Who d'you have in mind, Danny?" she'd asked, and he'd twiddled his cigar and said: "Jakey-Boy, of course. He's hot, he's single and he's gagging for you."

She'd grinned, liking the sound of it and after that it had been easy. Leave it to the agents. They'd sorted everything: the first date, the declaration of love, the disagreement, the reconciliation, the proposal, the engagement and the wedding. The media had been alerted at every stage and it had worked a treat. Her ratings had soared and she was back on top. Even the national news had given her coverage. She was an icon, a national treasure, the darling of young girls everywhere.

For a time, it had been enough. She'd had more modelling assignments than ever, a new TV show, her own brand of Forever Youthful make-up and perfume and enough product endorsements to last a lifetime. Whatever she touched became gold. The money poured in and her coffers were overflowing. She skied in Saint

Moritz, sunbathed in Saint Tropez, cruised on a yacht, had a hair stylist in London, a botox technician in LA and a costumier in Paris. All the usual clichés you needed to buy into the jet set.

But just recently, things had started to slip. What had once been effortless, now seemed tiring. What had once been easy, was now hard work. Upward and onward had always been her motto. Now she felt gravity pulling her downward. It was Jakey-Boy who'd first lit the blue touch-paper, which was when she realised just how much she despised him. They'd been invited to yet another celebrity function, some party or dinner or opening or first night, she really couldn't remember. She'd been getting ready to go out, preening in front of the mirror, admiring her long, shapely legs, tight ass, flat stomach and voluptuous chest. Jakey-Boy had watched, fascinated: Kimberley Chartreuse, the living Barbie Doll, everything fake, everything false, from the sprayed on tan to the enormous, double 'F' bazoomers. Then, horror of horrors, he'd leant forward, looked closely and said, "You're getting lines! You're showing your age." She'd frozen him with an icy stare, walked out without speaking and had hated him ever since. That night, when she got back, she'd sat in front of her dressing room mirror for an hour and studied her face. She had a permanent trout pout thanks to too many collagen injections, she'd been under the knife more times than she could remember and it seemed every few weeks she was rushing off for a bit of 'bo'.

"God, how I hate getting old," she moaned to the mirror. "If he's noticed it, others will, and I know what the press are like. They'll seize on every little wrinkle."

She picked up her cell phone and brought up an app that showed how you'd look as you got older. With trembling fingers, she selected a photograph of herself and, at the press of a button, watched her face transform into that of an old witch, creased and lined, hanging and drooping, everything going south. With a cry, she threw the phone across the room.

The thought of having to hide her aging face made her feel physically sick.

"I was made for the limelight," she declared. "I need people, I need fans, I need to be adored."

She retrieved her phone and dialled her agent's number. "Danny? It's Kimberley. I need you to do something. It's urgent and it's top secret…"

Danny listened silently as Kimberley outlined her requirements, then he puffed on his cigar and smiled.

"I know just the person. Leave it to me."

23. **Truth**

At seven in the morning, I figured it was safe to open the church door. It was going to be a gorgeous day. The sun had already risen, streaking the few clouds that drifted across the sky with golden light, and all seemed fresh and clean and new. I breathed in deeply, and looked around. The gravestones were serene and peaceful in the morning light, dew lay on the grass and birds sang in the trees. It was the kind of morning that made you glad to be alive, all the more so for looking out over a graveyard. I peered at the bushes, but could see nothing ominous or threatening. No evil yellow eyes stared back at me and I began to wonder if I'd imagined it. I daren't even start to process what I'd experienced, I needed to get home and surround myself with the routine of everyday life. I needed time to sit and think, and decide what to do. I didn't know when I'd next see Theo and I had to be prepared when I did.

I was still wearing the long blue velvet cloak and now I took it off and folded it carefully. Carrying it under my arm, I stepped out of the church and closed the heavy oak door behind me.

Ten minutes later I was back at home, creeping up the stairs and into my room. I hid the velvet cloak at the bottom of my wardrobe, pulled off my clothes and took a long, hot shower. I luxuriated in the hot water, feeling it wash the excitement, the fear and the passion of last night out of my system, and emerged feeling calmer, cleansed and able to think more clearly. I realised I was famished and, donning my dressing gown, went downstairs to have some breakfast. I made myself a large bowl of porridge, followed by a boiled egg on toast.

'Now I feel more human,' I said to myself, then shuddered at the thought. Those people last night, surely they weren't human? But if they weren't, then what were they exactly? Theo had scoffed at the idea of vampires. So were they some kind of aliens? Let's face it, I'd witnessed some very old people being transformed into young, beautiful beings, without blemish or imperfection. And Theo was one of them. As were all the members of his family. I loved Theo to distraction and had never experienced such feelings of intensity and love as I had last night. But what had I fallen in love with? And where did that leave me? Theo had been most insistent I leave the hall as quickly as possible. He said I was in terrible danger. Was I still in danger? Or could Theo keep my presence last night a secret? Surely, if no one knew I'd been there, I was safe, wasn't I? Or did I really see two yellow eyes watching me in the graveyard? And if I did, who was it? And did they know I'd been at the Blue Moon Ball? I didn't have any answers. The only person who did was Theo and I had to wait until I saw him again before I knew what they were.

My mum came into the breakfast room. "Hi, Emily, you're up early," she said, in surprise.

"Hi Mum, I couldn't sleep." That was the truth, I didn't mention I'd never been to bed.

She examined her face in the mirror on the breakfast room wall and exclaimed: "God, I'm looking old. I'm going to need a facelift soon." She stretched the skin upwards with her fingers. "There, that looks better, doesn't it?"

I stared at her in alarm. "Old is good, mum, don't worry about aging naturally. Take it from me, you're fine the way you are."

She stared at me in amazement. "Well, thanks, Emily, I didn't know you felt so strongly on the subject."

"I don't," I back-tracked, "it's just there's nothing wrong with getting old gracefully. Anyway, if you're worried, I've got this really good facial stuff Tash gave me. Made from beer. Makes your skin feel amazing. Allegedly."

"So, you haven't actually used it?"

"No, but look at Tash's face. Her skin is amazing, you have to agree."

"Alright, I'll give it a go. Leave it out in the bathroom for me."

"Okay. Always remember, mum, natural is best."

"Er, haven't I been saying that for years? Every time you attempted to go out plastered in make-up?" she said, looking at me strangely.

"That was in my Goth phase last year," I informed her. "I am so over that now. Can't you tell?"

"Yes, I think I might have spotted that. I must say, your current look is a huge improvement. In fact, just recently, you've been positively glowing. Must be love...."

It was definitely time to change the subject. This was getting into cringe territory.

"Is Granddad up yet?" I asked.

"No," answered my mum, pouring a cup of tea and looking concerned, "he's not too good. He says he's going to stay in bed today."

"It could be the virus I had," I suggested. "We need to build him up with home-made chicken broth."

"Yes, let's do that," my mother smiled at me. "I'm sure he'll be fine. He's made of strong stuff."

"I'll take him a cup of tea," I offered, jumping up and going into the kitchen. I needed to stay occupied, I felt jittery and on edge. I made the tea, dark and strong, just how he liked it, and carried it upstairs, knocking on his door.

"Come in," said a weak voice inside.

It was dark in the bedroom, so I opened the curtains just enough to let in a little light.

"How are you Gramps?" I asked, looking down at him.

I was quite shocked by his appearance. He seemed to have aged since I'd last seen him, which had only been the day before. He lay back on his pillows, looking frail and ill. His eyes were watery and bloodshot, his face thinner with an unnatural flush to his cheeks, and his forehead was shiny with perspiration.

"I've felt better, Emily," he said, smiling feebly and struggling to sit up. "It's this old body. Can't fight off the germs as well as I used to. It's probably nothing more than a cold, a few days in bed will see me right."

I looked at him with concern. He seemed to be breathless and struggled to get out his words.

"Do you want me to ring for the doctor?" I asked, feeling somewhat inept.

"No," he said sharply, "I've no need of the quack. You know what he'd say: 'Rest, drink lots of liquids, take paracetemol. 'Can't treat a virus, your body has to fight it off.' It's always the same."

There was no telling my Granddad. He was one of that generation who had no faith in the medical profession and certainly not the village doctor. In Granddad's book, there was no better medicine than fresh air, good food and a whisky nightcap. It had seen him in good stead so far, and he wasn't going to change the pattern of a lifetime.

"Okay. Shall I bring you up some breakfast?" I asked.

"Not just yet," he answered wearily. "Let me come round a bit first. I'll be down for breakfast when I'm ready."

"Alright," I said, walking to the door, "but if you want anything, just shout. I'll bring you a nice bowl of porridge, a bacon sandwich, whatever you want."

"Maybe," he said, looking exhausted.

I closed the door to his bedroom and went back downstairs.

"Gramps doesn't look too good," I informed my mother. "He says he doesn't want the doctor, so what d'you think we should do?"

"You know what he's like," answered my mother. "Don't worry, I'll look after him. I can work from home today, and you need to get to college."

College! I'd completely forgotten about it. Somehow, with everything that had happened, it seemed more like a weekend. Now, I realised it was Friday and I had just ten minutes to catch the bus. I tore upstairs, ripped off my dressing gown and flung on my clothes, and got to the stop with just a minute to spare.

"You look like you've been up all night," observed Tash, which didn't make me feel any better.

How I wished I could have told her what I'd experienced the night before. Never had I needed a friend to confide in more than now. But how could I? For a start, it sounded incredible. Old people going into a room with a blue light and coming out young… What would I think if someone told me that? Either they were winding me up or had been drinking. Then, there was the danger element, which was a great deal more worrying. If I really wasn't safe, then I couldn't drag Tash or Seth into this. I'd chosen to go to the Blue Moon Ball, despite all the warnings. I'd seen more than a few things that didn't add up at Hartswell Hall, and yet I'd still gone back, aware that something strange was going on. I simply couldn't involve my friends. Tash had been right to be suspicious of Theo, but she had no idea what was really going on. I had to wait until I'd spoken with Theo, then decide whether to tell them.

The day passed uneventfully and I had great difficult staying awake, particularly in the Modern History lecture. Mr Greaves' monotone voice droned on soporifically, citing battles and dates and theory and stratagem until everything blended together and I couldn't stop myself dozing off, prompting his sarcastic comment: "Are we keeping you up Miss Morgan? Please don't let my lecture interfere with your need to nap."

The end of the day couldn't come soon enough and I gratefully climbed onto the bus, feeling worn out and drained. Never had I been happier to get home and I slumped against the front door once it was closed, hanging my head and staring at the carpet.

"Are you alright, Emily?" asked my mother, walking into the hall. "You look done in. I hope you're not coming down with that virus again. They do say viruses come back if you do too much."

"No, I'm fine, mum," I answered, "Just tired. How's Granddad? Is he any better? Can I go up and see him?"

"Leave him be for the moment," she advised. "He's sleeping and I think it's better not to wake him. He's had a reasonable day... came down this afternoon for a couple of hours and had a bowl of soup. I'm sure he'll feel better tomorrow."

She put her coat on. "I have to pop out for a while. I need to return my library books and pop in to the vicarage. Can you listen out for Granddad waking up and, if he does, see if he needs anything?"

"Yes, of course," I said, stifling a yawn. "I'll see you later." "Bye, love," she kissed the top of my head and was walking out of the front door, when she turned to me and called back: "Oh, by the way, I forgot to tell you, Theo called."
A bolt of adrenalin shot through my system. "What?" I asked, suddenly wide awake, "What did he say? Why didn't he call my cell phone?"

"He says he tried, but you weren't answering, so he called the landline instead. He said not to call him, he'll call back. Now, I must go. See you later."

She walked up the front pathway and I shut the door behind her. I searched frantically for my cell phone but couldn't find it anywhere. In a panic, I remembered photographing the beautiful people the night before. That was the last time I'd used it. I'd been so tired today, I hadn't even missed it. I couldn't lose my phone. In desperation, I searched my pockets and my backpack, then ran upstairs and searched my bedroom, pulling out the clothes I'd worn the previous evening, looking under the bed and in the bathroom. But it was nowhere to be seen.

I sat on my bed with my head in my hands, various scenarios racing through my mind. Could I have dropped it at Hartswell Hall? That was worst-case scenario, particularly if it fell into the wrong hands and they saw the pictures I'd taken. Could I have dropped it while running through the woods, or while I was in the church? There was nothing for it, I would have to go back and search. But I couldn't leave Granddad. I paced across my bedroom, feeling powerless and afraid, willing my mother to come back. I had to find my phone. Then just as I heard my mother's key in the lock, the landline rang downstairs. I heard her pick up and answer as she walked in to the hallway. Jumping down the stairs, two at a time, I nearly collided with her as she handed me the receiver.

"It's for you," she said, "It's Theo."

"Hello," I said, walking quickly into the lounge and shutting the door behind me. This was one conversation I didn't want my mother overhearing. "Theo?"

"Hi Emily," he said, "Where've you been? I've been trying to call you all day."

"Sorry," I said, "I've lost my phone. I can't find it anywhere." I couldn't bring myself to tell him I'd taken pictures of his guests with it the night before. It seemed too voyeuristic, somehow.

"How are you?" he asked. "You obviously made it back to the church okay."

"Yes," I answered, unable also to tell him about the two yellow eyes I thought I'd seen in the undergrowth watching me. Now it just seemed ridiculous.

"Emily, I need to see you..."

My heart was thumping in my chest. "Okay," I said, wanting to say so much, but hardly able to speak. I didn't know where to start, so I let him take the lead.

"Are you alright?" he asked again.

"I don't know, Theo, I'm very confused."

There was a silence before he said: "Can you meet me tonight? In the church?"

"Yes," I said breathlessly, "What time?"

"11 o'clock. Our guests are in the process of leaving. I should be able to get away by then."

"Is it safe?" I asked.

"Emily," he sighed, "Nothing is safe." And the line went dead.

At ten minutes to eleven, I started out for the church. It was the second time this evening. Earlier on, I'd searched inside the church and along the pathway, looking for my phone, but it was nowhere to be found. I'd encountered Father James, just finishing evening prayer, who was somewhat confused at the likelihood of my phone being in the church, given my lack of attendance at church services, but said he'd look out for it. Now, I told my mum I was going to bed, and guiltily putting a pillow under the blankets to resemble my sleeping form, crept quietly down the stairs. Granddad was sleeping peacefully in his room and my mother sat watching a comedy show on TV in the lounge, the canned laughter so loud she didn't hear me open the front door and close it carefully behind me. I walked on tiptoes up the front pathway, then started to run down the road and didn't stop until I reached the old Lych Gate leading to the church. I looked around furtively, feeling suddenly scared I'd see yellow eyes watching me. It was a cloudy night and the moon was obliterated, so there was very little natural light. I stepped through the Lych Gate and into the graveyard. The undergrowth that surrounded the graveyard was black and impenetrable, which only increased my fear. Why had Theo suggested we meet here? Of all places, it was the scariest. But also the safest, a little voice in my head reminded me. Forcing myself to breathe slowly and walking with my head high, I made my way towards the church, passing the vestry and along the church's east wall, before reaching the entrance. Quickly, I turned the heavy iron door ring and pushed open the door, just as the clock was striking eleven o'clock in the bell tower. The church was in darkness and I faltered as I closed the door behind me, dropping the iron latch into place. What if it was a trap? Almost immediately, I heard a voice to my left. 'Emily, I'm here. Don't turn on the lights. Come this way.'

I felt Theo's hand reach for mine and lead me into the church. We seemed to be going down the central aisle and into the nave, past the choir stall and organ pipes, and up to the high altar. As my eyes grew accustomed to the dark, I could just make out Theo's blonde hair ahead of me. He led me to the wall on the right hand side of the nave, where a large tapestry hung. He lifted it up, revealing an arched recess and door concealed behind it, and placed a key in the lock. He turned it and the door swung inwards. He stepped in, pulling me with him and I heard the door close behind us. It was pitch black and smelled dry and dusty. I guessed we were in a passageway, but didn't feel brave enough to put out a hand and feel the walls. Almost immediately, Theo said, "There are spiral steps leading down. Put your right hand on the wall and you'll find a handrail. Keep hold of it as you go down, it's quite steep."

I let go of his hand and did as he said. My hand touched an old stone wall, with large, uneven bricks. I ran my fingers down until they touched a handrail. It felt like polished wood and I guessed it had been worn smooth by generations of hands holding on to it as they descended.

"Where are we going, Theo?" I whispered.

"To the vault," he whispered back to me. "It was the safest place I could think of."

For the next couple of minutes, I concentrated on holding the handrail tightly and putting one foot in front of another as the spiral steps led down and round. It was not a pleasant experience in the pitch darkness and I was glad when my feet touched a flat, even surface. I heard Theo say, "That's it. We're at the bottom of the steps." Then there was the sound of a door being opened in front of us, the hinges creaking loudly, and I felt Theo's hand reach for mine and pull me forward. The air smelt dry and stale, as if untouched for many years, but it was still pitch black and I could see nothing until Theo struck a match. In the faint glow, I could see a small room, maybe three metres square. He lit two candles, placed in a recess hewn into the thick stone walls, and I was able to make out an arched ceiling above us, and two more recesses containing old books, candlesticks and some ancient tools. An empty shelving system stood against one wall and apart from that, there was little else of interest. I was very relieved to see an absence of coffins. I didn't think I would have been able to stay for a chat if I was sharing the room with mouldering old skeletons.

"Where are the coffins?" I asked Theo, whispering in the gloom, "I thought this was a vault."

"They were removed a long time ago," he whispered back, "This room isn't used for anything now. I don't think many people know it exists."

"Except you," I pointed out.

"Yes. And Joseph. He discovered it when he was looking at some old plans. It links to the hall."

"You mean there's a secret passage way?" I asked, incredulously. This was like an Enid Blyton story, or it would have been if it weren't so scary.

"Yes," said Theo, "there's another door over there, under that tapestry, leading to the hall."

"Is that how you got here?" I asked, walking to the ancient tapestry covering the wall and lifting a corner. Sure enough, there was a door behind it.

"Yes, it seemed the easiest way. I didn't want anybody to see me leaving."

"Are your guests still there?" I asked, pulling the tapestry back into place.

"They're getting ready to go, so I won't be missed for a while. But I don't have long."

I turned to him. "Theo, what I saw last night…"

"I know," he said, "you need an explanation. And I'll do my best to tell you everything, but I must be back before midnight."

As yet, apart from holding hands, we'd kept our distance from one another. Now, I yearned to be held by him, to kiss him, for things to be normal, to say last night had all been a misunderstanding, and they'd been playing a strange kind of party game. I looked at him closely, so ethereally beautiful in the flickering candlelight, his skin smooth and white, his hair golden and his eyes large and dark. I felt the energy around him, almost crackling in its intensity and experienced the most intense desire within me, heightened by the darkness, the mystery and the danger surrounding us. But there was no time for embracing. I had questions that needed answering and the clock was against us.

"Go on," I demanded. "Tell me what's going on… Who you are? What are you?"

He hesitated for a moment, then started to speak.

"What you saw last night really happened. You saw old people being rejuvenated, their youth, vitality and beauty restored. You also saw what happened to the one that didn't make it. You saw him decay before your eyes, and that is the danger facing us all, unless we bathe in the light given out by the crystal of eternal youth."

I couldn't help it. I laughed. "What? Are having me on? This sounds more like some kind of weird science fiction story."

"Emily, believe me. It's true." Theo's voice became more urgent. "You need to know, so you can understand the danger you're in."

"Carry on," I said, hardly able to believe what I was hearing.

"It began many thousands of years ago, in the time of the Ancient Egyptians. It was 1350 BC and Viyesha was a High Priestess in the reign of the heretical king, Amenophis IV-Akhenaten."

I cut in, my voice scathing: "You mean Viyesha is thousands of years old?" Now I really was having difficulty suspending my disbelief.

"Emily, you have to listen," said Theo patiently, "I don't have long." He took a deep breath and continued: "Viyesha was the daughter of a slave girl and, amidst a nation of dark-skinned people, was revered for her white-blonde hair, blue eyes and pale skin. She grew up in the palace of Queen Nefertiti at Amarna, and when she was thirteen, she became a High Priestess in the temple at Akhenaten, known today as Tell el-Amarna. The temple was dedicated to the worship of Amun-Ra, the Hidden One, God of Eternal Life, and it was said that a powerful crystal, kept within the temple's inner sanctum, was a gift from the God himself and had the power of bestowing eternal life. As High Priestess, Viyesha had made a sacred vow with Amun-Ra to keep the crystal safe and protect it with her life. All was well until the king, also known as Akhenaten, prohibited the worship of Amun-Ra and insisted, on pain of death, that his people worshipped Aten, the Solar Globe. Viyesha fled from the temple, in fear of her life, taking with her the precious blue crystal and escaping into the mountains. For a number of years, she lived alone in a cave, guarding the crystal. Every so often, she would take it out and run her fingers over its hard, smooth facets, and every time she did so, she experienced the most exquisite feelings of energy, well-being and power. When she looked at her reflection in a nearby pool, her skin was glowing, her eyes bright and her hair shining. She had never felt or looked so amazing. Occasionally, followers of Amun-Ra would visit her secretly and ask after the crystal, but fearing spies from the king, she could trust no one and always denied its existence. Over time, it fell into the realms of myth. Still she guarded it, touching it only once a year, to renew the feelings of well-being and vitality that it promoted within her. The revelation of the crystal's true power came in the year 1332 BC, when Viyesha was 30 years old. It was the night of a Blue Moon, an important and mystical event in the ancient calendar. As she brought out the crystal to touch it, the moon's rays fell upon it, activating its hidden properties. Blue flames leapt from the crystal and Viyesha was bathed in their brilliant blue light. She felt like never before. Renewed, restored, rejuvenated. After this, she stopped aging. As all around her began to show signs of the passing years, she maintained her youth and beauty. Now, at last she understood the meaning of the strange hieroglyphic in the temple's inner sanctum: a circle crossed through by an infinity sign."

"The same sign on the back of the cloaks and on the Clock Tower," I declared, "And I saw it again on the shoulder of one of your guests."

"We all bear the mark of the crystal," said Theo. "I, too, have such a symbol on my shoulder. It glows brightly or grows dim, depending on the lunar cycle. But let me finish my story, Emily. I don't have much time. Two years after Viyesha had discovered the crystal's power, the king died under mysterious circumstances and was succeeded by Tutankhamun, who proceeded to reinstate the cult of Amun-Ra."

"D'you mean the famous Tutankhamun? The one whose tomb was found by Howard Carter in 1922?" I asked, remembering amazing pictures of the golden and blue death mask.

"The same," replied Theo. "Viyesha shared her knowledge of the crystal's power with Tutankhamun. He told her he would start using the crystal's power in his eighteenth year, but before he could do so, he fell ill and died, some say murdered. Fearing for her life once again, Viyesha took the crystal and disappeared."

At this point, I interrupted. "It's a brilliant story, Theo, but do you really expect me to believe Viyesha is over three thousand years old? Even 'vampires' is a more believable story than that. And if she's three thousand, how old are you?"

"My story is for another time," he said, hurriedly "I must get back, but there are things I still need to say."

"Go on, then," I said, my mind reeling. I still thought it was some kind of elaborate joke.

"To maintain our youth," he continued, "we must bathe in the light that emanates from the blue crystal when it is at its most powerful, at the time of the Blue Moon...." he paused, "...an event that happens once every three years or so, in a year which has thirteen full moons."

"And if you don't, you age rapidly and die," I said, thinking of the unfortunate guest.

"Exactly," said Theo. "Aging and death occurs within minutes."

"So your guests..." I said slowly, "all those famous people that I recognised last night....those distinguished men and women..."

He finished my sentence: ".... have all been rejuvenated using the blue crystal. Each one of them enjoys eternal youth... more accomplished, more beautiful and more charismatic than ever before, all blemishes, imperfections and irregularities removed."

"But why them?" I had to ask. "Why were they selected?"

Theo smiled ruefully. "Some because we chose them, others because they can afford it. Eternal youth doesn't come cheap, Emily. Privilege and opportunity has always been the domain of the super-rich."

"And you can trust them to keep the secret?" I asked. "Surely they could sell the information and make millions?"

He laughed. "Money has no meaning to them. They have all the wealth they need. They count currency in something far more valuable: longevity. Besides, each one has sworn never to reveal the secret of the crystal, or be cast out and face annihilation."

"Cast out by whom?"

He looked down and considered his words before replying. "The Lunari," he replied, "The order that was formed many years ago to protect the crystal."

"Lunari?" I echoed, remembering the strange chanting from the previous night.

"You must understand," said Theo, "this is a secret that can never get out. If it fell into the wrong hands, its power could be abused and employed as a destructive force. Nations have fought wars for less. The Lunari exists to ensure this never happens. And if they find that anyone has gained knowledge of the crystal whom they have not initiated, they take immediate steps to eradicate the threat."

"Eradicate is a strong word," I said. "These Lunari people… do they know about me? Were they at the Blue Moon Ball?"

"No, they weren't at the Ball. They have their own means of ensuring their immortality and have no need of a blue moon. For the moment, I believe they don't know of your existence. We have contained the information, but the Guardians are unhappy."

"And they are?" I asked, although I suspected I already knew the answer.

"Aquila and Pantera," he answered. "You may not know it but you have been under surveillance for some time. They are shape shifters appointed by The Lunari to safeguard the crystal and advise of any threat they detect. The Lunari have given them absolute power to destroy where necessary."

"Shape shifters," I repeated. "You mean people who can assume other forms?"

"Yes, Aquila becomes a black Eastern eagle who sees everything, and Pantera a black panther, with exceptional speed and strength…"

"And large yellow eyes?" I asked.

"Why yes," said Theo, puzzled. "You've seen her?"

"I think so," I swallowed, "I think she may have seen me entering the church last night, although the hood was pulled around my face, so she may not have identified me. There again, if they have the authority to kill and I'm such a threat, why am I still here?"

"Because you have protection," said Theo, reaching over and hooking the silver chain that hung around my neck with his finger. The blue crystal shone in the candlelight, its many facets sparkling and twinkling.

"Is that…?" I started to say and Theo smiled.

"Yes, it's a tiny fragment of the big crystal. We all wear them. They give us protection. As long as you wear this, Aquila and Pantera cannot touch you."

"And you wear one as well," I said, "but yours has a white cameo placed at its centre… bearing the picture of the girl who looks like me…"

Theo looked into my eyes. "Emily, the girl doesn't just look like you. I believe it is you."

"What do you mean?" I cried, "I've never met you before."

"It's a long story and one I don't have time to tell now," he said. "But many, many years ago, I met a girl who was the very image of you. I loved her more than life itself, but something happened and I lost her. I thought I would never see her again, until the day I went to Hartsdown College and there you were. We shook hands and the connection was there, do you remember?"

"How could I forget?" I murmured. "You gave me an electric shock."

"The energy is there between us, the same energy that existed before. Believe me, I fought against it. I didn't want to endanger you and risk losing you again. But the pull was too great. I had to be with you."

"How did you lose this girl? What happened?"

"That is something I will tell you another time. I cannot speak of it now."

This was all getting too much to take in. I needed time and space to digest what he was saying. But there was more…

"Emily, you're not just at risk from The Lunari."

"Great, this gets better and better. Who else wants to get rid of me?"

"We have enemies," he said flatly, "There are those that know of the crystal's existence and would steal it from us. We call them the Dark Ones, shadow beings who live by dark means, who crave the crystal's light to assume human form. Some, known as The Reptilia, have achieved a low evolutionary form; others remain dark creatures of anti-matter, parasites who leach the life-force out of living beings to stay alive: Feeders, as we call them. All are malignant and deadly, and would stop at nothing to possess the crystal."

"But how are they a danger to me?" I asked. "They know nothing about me."

"These creatures are waiting and watching all the time. They are constantly looking for the crystal. That's why we had to leave Egypt. It was getting too risky. They will search for any way to gain leverage over us and compel us to hand it over." He dropped his voice: "Emily, they will exploit any weak link in our armour."

"And that weak link is me," I said faintly. "I'm not just in danger from The Lunari and the Guardians, but some kind of weird reptilian shadow creatures who drink human energy and crave human form, who would use me as leverage to get to you."

I looked into his eyes.

"Theo, please tell me this is some kind of elaborate wind up."

"I can't, Emily. I'm sorry. These threats exist. And there may be more: scientists searching for the elixir of life; powerful individuals looking to cheat death; others who would stop at nothing to possess the crystal. That's why we must protect it at any cost."

"At any cost," I repeated after him, "That doesn't sound good for me. According to what you've just said, you'd be better off getting rid of me."

I looked at him wide-eyed, the enormity of the threat facing me just beginning to dawn. "It would appear I don't stand a chance. Especially not now you've told me everything. At least an hour ago I still had ignorance protecting me." I glared at him angrily, "Why have you told me all this? Now I have this knowledge, my life really could be in danger."

He looked at me sadly. "Your life was in danger the first time I brought you back to Hartswell Hall. I should never have done it. But don't you see? You've come back to me. I thought we could be together again."

I took a deep breath and exhaled slowly. "For a start, I'm still having difficulty in believing all this. But just supposing it's true.... I can see only one solution to the problem." I paused and bit my lip, then looked him straight in the eye and said, "I have to join you. I have to bathe in the light of the crystal and become one of you. That's the only way we can be together."

"No," he cried, "it's too risky. The crystal is too powerful and not everyone survives. And if they do, well...... It's a blessing and a curse. Eternal youth, beauty and special powers are yours, but your whole life is governed by the crystal and the necessity to bathe in its light every Blue Moon. Should you survive the initiation, and many people don't, how can I put that burden on you?" he broke off, looking desolate.

"Is there any other way?" I asked.

Just as I spoke, we heard the distant chimes of the church clock striking midnight.

"I must go," he declared anxiously. Placing his hands around my face and looking deeply into my eyes, he said in a broken voice: "Emily, forgive me. I love you. I never wanted to do this to you. I only ever wanted to be with you."

My mind reeled and a thousand thoughts crowded in at once.

"I need time to think, Theo. This is all too much to take in."

"I must go," he said again, "every second I spend here puts you at greater risk. If The Lunari find out about you…"

I stopped him. "They may already know," I said. "I've lost my cell phone. I think I may have dropped in at Hartswell Hall last night. I've looked everywhere, but I can't find it. "

"You could have left it there on an earlier occasion," he said. "It doesn't prove you were at The Blue Moon Ball."

"I'm afraid it does," I said miserably. "I took photos of the beautiful people as they came out of the light and walked down the corridor. It's irrefutable proof I was there and I know what is happening."

I couldn't mistake the panic in Theo's eyes.

After he'd left, I spent a cold, sleepless night in the church for the second night running, once again too afraid to leave. This time I understood the threat that existed out there, and the four old stone walls of the church seemed my only sanctuary.

24. Under threat

Kimberley Chartreuse drummed her perfectly manicured fingers impatiently on the table. She wasn't used to being kept waiting. She was the one who made people wait. Now she was sitting here in this grotty little office in a back street in Digbeth, in down town Birmingham, waiting for some slimy little nobody, who had the temerity to be late. Didn't he know who she was? She had vaguely toyed with the idea of bringing the cameras with her. It would have made a great storyline for her reality show, but some things she knew had to remain private and, given her reasons for employing this man, this was better handled in the shadows. Pulling out her phone, she impatiently called her agent.

"Danny," she drawled, in her flat, pseudo transatlantic tones, "I'm still waiting for this joker to turn up. If you've made a mistake, you're fired, d'you hear me?"

He was prevented from answering by a shuffling and snuffling outside the door. Kimberley clicked off her phone and turned her head, a look of disgust flitting across her features. A middle-aged man in a brown raincoat had opened the door and was blowing his nose loudly on a handkerchief that had clearly seen better days.

"Ms Chartreuse?" he asked, in a down-at-heel, flat Brummie voice. He extended his hand. "I'm the joker you're waiting to see."

She made a show of refusing his hand, saying to him coldly, "Mr Nelson? You're late. I've been waiting for over five minutes."

He grinned at her cheerfully, revealing a row of black and yellow-stained teeth. "Sorry," he said, making it quite plain he wasn't, "Bit of business to attend to."

She noted the bottle that stuck out of his pocket, the florid cheeks and the alcohol fumes that wafted across the room. He leered at her appreciatively. "Won't you sit down? Ah, I see you've already made yourself at home."

She regarded him disdainfully. The man was a fool, a grubby, drunken idiot. She'd made a huge mistake coming here. He sat at the desk opposite her and proceeded to rummage around in a drawer.

"Mr Nelson, I really don't..." she began, but he interrupted her. "Aha, here it is" and pulled out a gnarled old pipe which he stuck between his teeth and proceeded to suck on with great vigour. She shuddered and looked at the wall over his head, where an old tattered picture of Columbo was pasted. He saw her glance upwards and said, "Columbo, greatest living detective. I model myself on him. Genius, pure genius."

"Mr Nelson," she said icily, "Columbo was a TV detective. He wasn't real. Everyone knows that."

"Ya don't say?" he said in his best Columbo voice, raising one eyebrow at her. "Ya learn somethin' new everyday." She looked at him coldly and he sat back, eyeing her with interest.

"Mr Nelson, unless you have anything to tell me, I'm wasting my time."

He said nothing, just carried on watching her.

Leaning forward over the desk, she whispered through clenched teeth, "I thought you had something for me."

"All in good time," he said, enjoying her discomfort. And he grinned at her, until she began to wonder if he was mentally deficient. Suddenly, his grin vanished and he pulled a small, torn notepad out of his pocket and carefully leafed through it.

"Aha," he declared, "Here it is."

"Yes?" she demanded, trying to see.

He looked up at her and grinned again. "Fee first, information second. Do you have the cash?"

"Yes, I do," she said, patting her handbag, "but it's 'no information, no fee'."

Two could play at that game. If he wanted to play hardball, he'd get it.

He regarded her for a second, then said, "Compromise. Half up front, the remainder when you've verified the information."

"Deal", she said, satisfied, reaching into her large red Jimmy Choo hand haversack and pulled out a thick brown envelope. She tossed it over the table to him. "£25k. Now, what have you got for me?"

At the sight of the money, he snapped into professional mode.

"As I understand it, you were looking to acquire trade secrets of up and coming new health and beauty products; new recipes, latest formulations, herbs, plants, vitamins, minerals, anything, I believe, to help you push back the aging process?"

"Carry on," she demanded.

"Oh, we have it all here. Amino acids, Alpha Hydroxy acids, Omega fatty acids, Hyaluronic acid, Glycolic acid, Beta-Glycyrrhetic acid … Green Mussel, Brown Algae, Black Cohosh, alfalfa, allantoin, horsechestnut, calendula, ginseng… Locust Bean Gum seeds, yeast extracts, Grape polyphenols, anthocyanidins, ubiquinol, pycnogenol, bisabobol, silicon ….. There are creams and peels, serums and scrapes, masques, milks and moisturisers, treatments, toners, cleansers, concentrates, lotions and gels …"

He paused to draw breath.

"There's ultrasonic cavitation, micro-dermabrasion, radio frequency, … mesotherapy, thermotherapy, LED light therapy… micro current therapy, 24 carat gold therapy… not forgetting Far Infra Red therapy for increasing atomic activity, and Cryolipolysis Fat Freezing, with anti-freeze to stop you getting frost bite. Jesus, do you women really go for all this stuff? They used less than this to create Frankenstein."

He fixed her with a world-weary expression.

"Need I go on?" he asked. "There are a million different products out there, and a million more being researched, each claiming to keep you young, reduce wrinkles, tighten skin, boost collagen, plump you out, firm you up, improve pigmentation, increase density, enhance elasticity, fight aging… nurture, nourish, soothe, oxidise, repair, replenish, support… and so on and so on and so on."

"Is that all you've got for me?" she asked scornfully. "I know all this. You've told me nothing."

"Precisely, my dear," he said, making a revolting popping noise with his pipe. "I could have brought you any manner of new formulations from the latest laboratories in LA, claiming this, that and the other. Industrial espionage is my second name. But d'you really think it's going to do anything for you? D'you really think a cream or a potion or a lotion is going to halt the aging process? My dear, you are subject to the laws of physics, as are we all. There is no magical potion that's going to stop you getting old, other than the surgeon's knife. And that's only superficial. Won't stop your organs aging." He leered at her triumphantly.

She smashed her fist down on the table.

"Then what am I paying you for, idiot? To sit there and tell me the bleedin' obvious? I wanted something new."

He watched her closely with rheumy, bloodshot eyes. He might go under the guise of an idiot, but he had the survival instincts of a sewer rat and the morals of an alley cat.

"You want something new, Wendy Tubbs," he rolled the name around on his tongue, "or should I say Kimberley Chartreuse, Queen of the Falsies?" he leered at her suggestively.

"How dare you…" she began, but he cut her short once again.

"I'll give you something new, lady. Something so unbelievable, it'll blow your mind, let alone stop you aging."

"Really?" she snarled at him. "I doubt that."

"What if I told you I'd found something that would stop the aging process altogether, give you eternal youth and beauty so you never need think about using one of these potions ever again?" He had a glint of satisfaction in his eyes.

"I probably wouldn't believe you," she admitted. "It sounds too good to be true."

He smiled. "I've had my spies out and about, on the ground, underground, looking, listening, learning… And word has it there's a cult of people who have found the secret of eternal youth."

"Really," said Kimberley in a sceptical voice, "Do you have any proof?"

Mr Nelson didn't answer. Instead, he took a large brown envelope from his desk and opened it.

"Viyesha and Leon de Lucis," he said, pulling out a photocopy of a yellowed old press cutting and placing it on the desk, "Tel el Amarna, Egypt, 1955."

He placed a photocopy of a more recent press cutting next to it. "The same couple. Tel el Amarna, Egypt, 1995."

Then he placed two colour photographs alongside the press cuttings: "Viyesha and Leon, taken a week ago in the UK." Looking at Kimberley, he said, "Notice anything strange about these photographs, Wendy Tubbs?"

She gasped and said in a whisper: "They haven't changed."

The colour drained from her face and she felt a tremor of excitement in the pit of her stomach.

"Exactly," said Mr Nelson, triumphantly.

"What more do you know about them?" she demanded.

Mr Nelson sat back and plumped out his chest. "They are wealthy hoteliers. Recently renovated a large country house in the village of Hartswell-on-the-Hill, set to open as a luxury hotel and conference centre in two weeks time. They have two children, Violet 17 years old, and Theo two years older, plus a nephew staying with them, Joseph, early twenties." He threw down photos of each on the desk as he spoke. "These photos were taken last week using a telephoto lens. But this picture," he threw down a third photocopy of another old press cutting, showing a family group, "was taken twenty-five years ago."

Kimberley looked at them, then raised her eyes to meet Mr Nelson's. "Even their children haven't aged," she said excitedly, "How do they do it?"

Mr Nelson leant forward and said conspiratorially: "Something to do with crystals. I'm still working on it."

"Sounds like new age gobbledegook," said Kimberley disdainfully.

"Oh, this is the real thing, I quite assure you," he said seriously.

She sat and thought for a moment, letting her brain compute the information, then turned back to the private detective.

"Mr Nelson, I'm no fool. Images can be manipulated. These pictures are not proof. I'm going to need something more than this."

He looked at her without smiling. "Dear lady, one thing I would never take you for is a fool. You have been more successful in turning base metal into gold than any living creature. Perhaps you'll let me continue?"

"Go ahead."

"I've taken the liberty of booking you in to Hartswell Hall as soon as it opens. Second week in May. Giving you the opportunity to see the de Lucis family for yourself. The proof you seek will be in front of your very eyes."

"Then what?" she asked. "If they truly have discovered the secret of eternal youth, they're not just going to hand it over to me, crystal or otherwise. What we need is leverage. Some means of forcing them to share their secret."

"All in hand, dear lady," smirked Mr Nelson, and threw his last photograph on to the desk. "Emily Morgan, 17 years old. Lives in the village. An ordinary college student…"

"Hm. Pretty, I suppose. But what's she got to do with anything?" snapped Kimberley.

Mr Nelson smiled horribly. "A few weeks ago, Theo started a relationship with Emily. They are, by all accounts 'in lurve'. It would seem that Theo would do anything for Emily." He paused, letting his words hang in the air.

"You mean trading the family secret to ensure her safety …." said Kimberley softy.

"Dear lady, you read my mind," he said.

"Mr Nelson, you are brilliant. I could kiss you." She thought for a moment, and said, "But I won't."

Mr Nelson sat back in his chair, popping on his pipe and feeling pleased with himself. He'd found the proverbial goldmine and could see large rewards coming his way.

* * *

As the last of the guests left Hartswell Hall just after midnight, dark shapes and figures could be seen gathering in the fields around the mansion and a strange hissing filled the air. To the uninitiated it sounded like a hundred airbeds were being deflated. To those who were attuned, words could clearly be heard, carried on the breeze:

"Crysssssssstal….crysssssssssstal….crysssssssssstal. Give usss the crysssssssstal ….."

A large black panther with yellow saucer-eyes bounded down Hartswell Hall steps and made its way speedily through the grounds, dropping to its belly as it approached the fields, every sinew and every muscle tensed in anticipation. Overhead an eagle flew, wings outstretched and talons at the ready. Together they struck: silent, ferocious and deadly. For a few seconds, the air was rent with screaming and thrashing as teeth and claws, beak and talons did their worst. The black figures were torn to pieces without discrimination or mercy, fronds and shards of dark matter littering the grass or picked up by the breeze and dispersed into the hedgerows and trees, where they snagged on branches like flimsy black rags, flapping in the cold night air. Such was the ferocity of the attack, it was over in minutes.

Surveying the massacre and ensuring all were destroyed, the predators retreated as speedily and silently as they had attacked. One to the air, the other back into the undergrowth.

Slowly but surely, the pieces of dark matter were absorbed into the atmosphere, each becoming gradually more transparent before disappearing entirely, leaving not a shred of evidence that minutes earlier the field had resembled a battlefield.

Only one small shadow remained, hidden in the undergrowth, wounded and flailing but not destroyed. Once the predators were gone, it cautiously broke cover, looking around for other survivors. Finding none, it crawled to the edge of the field and lay waiting, weak and wounded, silently watching for some life form to appear. A sheep or dog would do, but a human was preferable. The battle had seriously depleted its strength, and its energy was all but gone. It needed to feed quickly if it were to survive. As if in answer to its prayer, old Grace Wisterley stepped obligingly into the field, shot gun at the ready, eyes peering through the darkness. She'd heard noises and was determined none of her sheep would die that night.

"Come out, yer blighter," she said into the night, "show your face. I'll make short work o' thee." She shone a torch around the field but could see nothing out of place. "Just as well I penned the sheep up las' night," she muttered to herself.

The shadow crept up silently behind her, and in an instant it attached itself to her back like a limpet, feeding off her energy field. Grace walked on, unaware of the parasite she'd picked up, flashing her torch and peering through the dark for any sign of the predator she knew was out there. She checked the pen and finding all her sheep accounted for, walked back to her house, feeling suddenly heavy and tired and old.

"Crikey, Grace Wisterley, yer age is catchin' up wi' thee," she muttered to herself.

The shadow continued to feed, getting stronger with every mouthful of energy it consumed.

* * *

Back at Hartswell Hall, in a small underground room beneath the Clock Tower, a door opened and Theo stepped over the threshold, cautiously looking around him. Fortunately for him, he had not been missed.

25. Granddad

At 6.30am, I opened the church door and once again ran down the hill towards my house. I'd spent a cold, difficult night in the church, trying to sleep on one of the pews. It had been a futile exercise. The heating was switched off over night and I was freezing. On the few occasions I managed to drop off, my fevered imagination created such horrors, I woke within minutes, heart beating rapidly and bathed in a cold sweat. In one nightmare, a blue crystal hovered before me, but when I reached out to touch it my hand turned black, and stumbling backwards I felt a black beast sink its teeth into my shoulder. When I turned round, I was faced with three luminous beings firing bolts of lightning from their fingers, each one searing and burning my skin. In another, I saw Theo ahead of me in a dark passageway and ran to keep up with him, but always he was one step ahead and I just couldn't reach him. I called his name again and again, and when finally he turned round, his face looked different. Blood-red eyes shone through the darkness and when he smiled at me, he revealed huge white vampire teeth stained with blood. At one point when I woke, I could swear I heard screaming and crying somewhere outside, but as I strained to hear more, all was quiet and still, and I decided it was yet another nightmare. Eventually, not wanting to risk sleep any more, I sat in the cold until I saw the first rays of dawn break in the sky.

Arriving back at home, I let myself in through the front door and attempted to climb the stairs and creep into bed. But my mother surprised me by coming through the lounge doorway fully dressed.

"Oh, there you are. Where d'you think you've been all night?" her voice had an edge to it I didn't like.

"It's not how it seems, mum, I wasn't with Theo."

My reply seemed to surprise her. It was obviously not what she'd expected to hear.

"Well, if you weren't with Theo, where were you? This had better be good. I've been sitting up worrying half the night. Every time I phoned you I got voicemail."

I thought quickly, I had to find some excuse that sounded plausible. Secret passageways, blue crystals and eternal youth would not go down well.

"For a start, I've lost my phone," I said, "I can't find it anywhere. That's why you couldn't reach me. I was in the church." I decided honesty was the best policy, well up to a point.

"The church? What were you doing there?" This was a curved ball and took her by surprise.

"I, er, went to pray," I said, failing to convince even myself.

"To pray? You're not even religious. Since when did you go to the church to pray on a Friday night? Please credit me with a little more intelligence and at least come up with a more plausible excuse."

This was not going well. I tried one more time.

"I've been studying George Herbert's religious poetry for English, and I decided I wanted to look in the church. While I was there, I decided to say a prayer for Granddad, then when I came to go out, the door was locked and I was stuck overnight. I couldn't call because I didn't have my phone. Believe me, it's not an experience I want to repeat. It was freezing and I didn't sleep. I only got out when someone unlocked the door." It was as close to the truth as I dared tell, just a couple of small white lies in there.

My mother looked at me as if I'd totally lost my marbles.

"I guess you'd better go to bed for a while. Just as well it's Saturday."

I climbed the stairs to the landing, then called softly back: "How's Granddad?"

My mum looked up worried. "He's okay, but he's not getting any better. I may ring for the doctor this afternoon. We need to keep an eye on him."

"He won't like that," I commented. "Once I've had a sleep, I'll sit with him."

"Thanks, Emily, he'll like that."

I went into my bedroom and crawled into bed fully clothed. Worn out by the events of the last two nights, I fell immediately into a deep, dreamless sleep and didn't wake until two in the afternoon. I showered and pulled on fresh clothes, then went downstairs. My mother was sitting in the breakfast room, drinking tea.

"Would you like a cup? There's tea in the pot," she said.

I poured myself a cup and proceeded to make myself cheese on toast.

"You had a good sleep," she commented, coming into the kitchen. "Do you feel a bit better now? I can't believe you spent the night in the church."

"Neither can I," I said, and that was most definitely the truth. "How's Granddad?"

"Still not good, I'm wondering whether to call for the doctor. Have you seen him?"

I shook my head. "I'll pop in when I've eaten."

As soon as I saw Granddad, I knew something was wrong. The room felt hot and airless, and the curtains were partially drawn, keeping out the daylight. Granddad lay back on the pillows, his eyes closed, face pale and his lips a blue colour. He seemed to be having difficulty breathing.

"Granddad?" I called, trying to rouse him, "Granddad, can you hear me?

His eyes flickered open, trying to focus on me.

"Emily?" he said faintly.

"Don't try to speak," I instructed him, "I'll get mum. You don't look well."

His eyes flickered shut again and his breath sounded ragged and shallow. I ran to the top of the stairs and called down to my mother.

"Mum, mum, I think you'd better call an ambulance. Granddad really isn't well. I don't know if he's had a heart attack."

My mother appeared downstairs carrying the portable phone.

"Let me see," she said and ran up the stairs into Granddad's room. She took one look at him and said, "Right, I'm dialling 999. Hang on in there, Dad, we need to get help."

Ten minutes later, the paramedics arrived and my Granddad was on oxygen. It seemed to revive him a little and he gave me a weak smile. They placed him on a wheelchair, wrapped him in blankets and carried him carefully downstairs.

"Can I come with you?" I asked, as they wheeled him into the back of the ambulance.

"Yes, that's fine," answered the young male paramedic who was tending him. "He may have had a mild heart attack, we need to get him to hospital as soon as possible."

"I'll drive behind in the car," said my mother, her face white and drained.

In no time we were at the hospital and Granddad was placed in an Assessment Bay. A young male doctor came to see him immediately.

"We need to get him up to the Assessment Ward straight away and ensure he's stabilised." Seeing our distraught expressions, he added kindly, " Please don't worry, he's in the best possible hands. Wait in the Relatives' Room and we'll let you know as soon as you can see him."

My mother and I waited, barely speaking, for what seemed an age.

"He can't die," I said tearfully, "he's the only Granddad I've got."

Eventually, a dark-skinned nurse in a starched white uniform, with a jolly Caribbean accent informed us that we could see Granddad.

"We don't think he's had a heart attack," she informed us. "It's more likely he has bronchitis and needs antibiotics. We've booked a chest x-ray and will know more then."

Granddad sat up in bed with a clear oxygen mask around his face, attached by a tube to a large oxygen canister. He looked much better than I was expecting and even managed to smile.

I put my arms round Granddad and gave him a big hug.

"Gramps, you had us worried," I said. "I thought you were at death's door."
"Glad to see you're looking better, Dad," said my mum. "Sorry to get the ambulance, but I didn't have any choice."

"I know," he said through the mask, "don't worry, I'll be back at home in no time."

He wasn't though. While the x-ray showed no evidence of a heart attack, it did reveal that he had emphysema of the lungs, which was not good news. We were told it was too risky for him to go home while he had a chest infection and that he needed to stay on oxygen until he'd stabilised. There was no cure for emphysema, it was a chronic lung condition probably brought about by many years smoking Woodbine cigarettes when he was younger, and in latter years a pipe. We sat with Granddad until early evening when it was obvious he needed to sleep. The sister suggested we go home.

"I'll call you if anything changes," she told us, "but the best thing you can do is get some rest and come back in the morning. I'll take care of him, don't worry."

My mother drove home slowly, both of us shell-shocked. Granddad was the lynchpin that held us together. We simply couldn't comprehend a world without him. At home, we drank sweet tea to give us energy, but neither of us had much appetite. My mother sat in the lounge watching Saturday night trivia shows on television, but taking nothing in. I went upstairs and lay on my bed, feeling empty and strange. I thought about the last few days and all that had happened. It seemed dreamlike and remote, as if it had happened to someone else, and I could hardly focus on any of the detail. The reality was Granddad lying gravely ill in hospital, suffering from a condition that would never get better and which would eventually kill him. If only there was a magic potion, I thought, that would heal his lungs and make him better. Then I remembered the kitten. Violet's kitten that I'd seen run over and killed in that terrible accident, then miraculously brought back to life with no apparent injuries or after-effects. And what about the old people at the Blue Moon Ball? Those gnarled old fossils who'd been restored to youth. Would it be possible....? I hardly dared hope... I knew the de Lucis family had the power to heal and restore. All I had to do was ask Theo. They had the blue crystal. If it could keep them young for centuries and bring a kitten back to life, then it could surely heal Granddad's lungs. I went downstairs to find the portable phone and took it back up to my bedroom. With trembling hands I dialled Theo's number.

As I waited for him to pick up, one hand went subconsciously to the crystal hanging round my neck and squeezed it tightly. Then Theo was speaking on the phone. "Emily, are you alright? What's happening? Are you in danger?"

"No, no," I'm fine," I said, unsure what to say next. Then suddenly my words came out so fast they were falling over one another. "It's not me, it's Granddad. He's in hospital. It's serious.

We thought he'd had a heart attack, but it's bronchitis. They've done a chest x-ray and discovered emphysema. Theo, he could die."

"Emily, I'm so sorry," he said gently. "It must have been an awful shock for you and your mother. Do you want me to come over?"

"Yes. No. I don't know." How could I ask him? I had to. He was the only person who could help me. "Theo, I need your help."

"Yes, anything, just say."

"Anything?"

"Anything within reason, Emily." I think he was beginning to see where this was going.

"Can you make him better, Theo? Like the kitten and those old people at the Blue Moon Ball? Can you use the blue crystal?"

There was a silence on the other end of the phone. Then he said, "It's not quite as simple as that, Emily. We can't make an old person young and well again. It's not possible."

"But you brought the kitten back to life."

"That was different," said Theo. "The kitten had a faint pulse when we picked him up. He was badly injured but his life force was strong. We were able to heal him. Your Granddad no longer has that life force. We can't make him young or healthy again."

"But you made all those old people at the Blue Moon Ball young again?" I persisted.

Theo sighed. "Emily, they were young when they first used the crystal. That's the way it works. It restores you to the age you were when you first used it. The only reason they were aging is that it was time for them to renew their energy. At your Granddad's age, he'd never survive the crystal's power. He's not strong enough. And even if he did, would he want to stay at that age forever? For all kinds of reasons, it's not possible."

"So you won't do it?" I asked.

"Not won't, Emily, can't."

"You mean we're not rich enough," I said coldly. "I remember what you told me. 'Eternal youth doesn't come cheap.' What you really mean is my Granddad isn't wealthy enough."

"No," protested Theo, "it's got nothing to do with money. I would do anything for you, Emily, anything within my power. Surely you know that?"

"I thought I could count on you, Theo."

"You can, Emily, just not for this. I'm sorry."

"So am I, Theo. Well, at least I know where your loyalties lie. And they're not with me."

"Emily, it's not like that," he started to say, but I interrupted him.

"I'd like to say it's been nice knowing you, Theo, but I can't. Goodbye."

Tears choked my voice and I hung up, throwing the phone onto the bed. My hands went to the silver chain hanging round my neck and, pulling it sharply, I attempted to hurl it across the room. But it wouldn't break no matter how hard I pulled, and when I tried to find the fastener, it wasn't there. It was just one continuous chain. And now I had a sore neck where it had cut into me. I lay on the bed and sobbed. Only a few weeks ago I had a normal life, with good friends and everything ahead of me. Now, my life was in danger from all kinds of enemies, supernatural and otherwise, I'd met a boy who wasn't human, I had to decide whether I wanted eternal youth or not, and if I did I might die in the process. On top of that, my Granddad was ill in hospital, I'd alienated myself from my friends and I'd just split up from my boyfriend. Could things really get any worse? Hearing me sobbing, my mother quietly opened the door and came in to sit by me. She gently stroked my hair, like she did when I was little. I put my arms out and pulled her close to me.

"Oh mum," I sobbed, "Why is life so difficult? Why can't it all stay simple and easy?"

"Because life isn't simple and easy," she said, holding me tight. "You're growing up and finding out how painful it can be. When you're a child, you're sheltered from all this, but I can't protect you forever."

I buried my head into her shoulder and said through my tears, "I've just split up with Theo."

"Oh, Emily, I'm sorry. He seemed so nice. Do you want to talk about it?"

Where would I start? That my beautiful ex-boyfriend was actually thousands of years old, that he bathed in the light of a powerful blue crystal to stay young forever, that he'd placed me in mortal danger and even as I spoke strange creatures could be outside our house planning my demise. How could I tell my mum any of that? It was ridiculous beyond belief and so I just said 'no' and cried some more.

"You're worried about Granddad, as well, aren't you?" asked my mum, gently.

How could I say that I'd split up with Theo because he wouldn't use his super powers to save Granddad? It was all too complicated.

"Is Granddad going to die?" I asked my mum tearfully.

"He's very poorly," said my mum, "and he's not going to get better, you have to understand that. Until we talk to the consultant I don't know what the prognosis is. It's going to be tough, Emily, but we have to be strong. For his sake."

And that only made me cry all the harder. Because I had a solution within my grasp and I couldn't use it.

The next morning, we went back to the hospital. Granddad was sitting up in bed and had eaten breakfast. He'd had a good night and was on antibiotics. He still had on the oxygen mask, but seemed much brighter.

"Hi Granddad," I said, kissing his forehead. "You gave us all a scare last night."

"I told you, Emily," he said with a smile, "I'm made of strong stuff. Tough as old boots me. I'll go on forever."

But it was obvious his breathing was unnaturally shallow and fast, and when we saw the consultant, he spelled it out for us. The prognosis wasn't good. My Granddad couldn't go on for much longer. In the consultant's words, he could go out like a light bulb at any time. There would come a point when his lungs wouldn't take in enough oxygen and he would quickly lose consciousness. At that point, there wasn't much anybody could do.

"But some light bulbs go on for years," I pointed out hopefully.

"Not this one, I'm afraid," he said, which was when I knew it wouldn't be long.

I left my mum sitting with Granddad and on the pretext of finding a drinks machine, went for a walk in the hospital grounds. They weren't particularly pretty, just a few sparse areas of grass and some planted beds here and there, in between the car parks, with the odd tree dotted around. But at least I could get some fresh air and try to come to terms with the car crash my life had become. I found a seat overlooking a small courtyard and sat contemplating the world. I hated Theo with a vengeance and was glad I'd lost my cell phone. At least he couldn't contact me and I couldn't see if he was trying to. Why wouldn't he help? He knew how much this meant to me. He had the means. He had the power. He just didn't have the inclination. He wanted me but he didn't want my Granddad. Well, I was clear about one thing. I didn't want him. Or his strange world. Or eternal youth. I just wanted plain, simple normality back in my life. And what was that story about The Lunari? Surely by now they would have found my phone, discovered the evidence against me and closed in for the kill. That is, if Theo could be believed. I seriously doubted there was any truth to his stories. He was probably the ultimate fantasist and I'd been the gullible fool that just happened to come along. Proof of that was the fact I was still alive. I hadn't seen a single Lunari, Reptilia or any other creature he'd said was stalking me. I'd had enough of fantasy. Stark, cold reality was staring me in the face in the form of my Granddad's illness, and that was all I was capable of focusing on.

I went back in and sat with Granddad for a while and I couldn't help it, I had to ask.

"Gramps, if a magical power existed to make you well, but you had to stay this age for ever, would you use it?"

"Where did that come from?" he asked. "Have you been watching too many science fiction films?"

"No," I laughed, "I just wondered, that's all."

He thought for a moment before speaking. "Emily, I've had a good life and a long life, and as much as I don't want to leave you and your mum, I don't want to go on forever. Can you imagine being stuck in this old body for eternity? Why would I want that? It would be purgatory. There's a natural order, a time for birth and a time for death. When my time comes, I will accept it with grace. You know why? Because I'm going to see your grandma again. I want you to remember that. Will you do that?"

I stared at him with tears running down my cheeks.

"I'll try, Gramps, but you always said 'when you're dead, you're dead'. I thought you didn't believe in an after-life."

"Truth is, Emily, I don't know. I only know I'm coming to the end of my allotted time, and I feel very strongly your Grandma calling for me. That's all I can tell you." He smiled at me. "I'm not frightened. This is how things are meant to be. The natural order. I want you to look after your mum for me, make sure she's all right. And Emily?"

"Yes, Granddad."

"I like Theo. You go together well."

"Oh Gramps," I sobbed, my voice choking, my cheeks wet with tears. "Don't go, please don't go. Don't leave me."

Later that evening, my Granddad died. The infection had taken too strong a hold and he couldn't fight it. He went out like a light. No struggle, no breathlessness, no pain. One minute he was talking to us, for a second he seemed to have difficulty catching his breath and then he slumped forward unconscious. They tried long and hard to resuscitate him but to no avail. He'd gone.

The next few days were spent sorting out details. I had no idea there were so many things to do when someone died. We had to get the death certificate from the registry office, tell friends and relatives, notify banks and building societies, talk to the tax office, appoint a solicitor and, of course, arrange a funeral. Theo called the house a couple of times and spoke to my mum, but I refused to talk to him. He knew now that my Granddad had died and I hoped he was feeling guilty. I still felt he should have interceded.

On the day of the funeral, a cold wind blew and small white clouds scuttled across the sky. The sun shone, but the easterly wind was strong and my lasting impression, once we'd endured the church service, was of a cold, bright graveyard and a small crowd of people standing round the grave side, holding their coats around them, looking pinched and frozen. I watched the pallbearers carry Granddad's coffin out of the church, the wind tugging at their black suits. A large hole had already been dug in the ground and I watched as the coffin was lowered slowly down. I'd thought the words 'ashes to ashes' and 'dust to dust' were only used in films, but the Father James spoke them, picking up some earth and letting it fall through his fingers onto the coffin. I threw a red rose in after it. There weren't many mourners, just my mum and me, a few relatives that I didn't see very often, some neighbours and others from the village that Granddad had known. It was a small, low-key affair, which is just what he would have wanted. A big, grand affair would have been wrong. My Granddad had been a quiet, private person, with a small circle of friends, and I was glad his funeral reflected that. We'd played jazz music in the church, Stranger on the Shore by Acker Bilk, and I could still hear the beautiful, lilting melody in my head. The cold weather and dazzling sun suited my mood perfectly, a biting reminder of the harshness of reality. This was what happened. You were born, you aged and you died. It was the natural order and there was no other way. I'd been a fool to think otherwise and let my head be turned, albeit momentarily, by fantasist nonsense.

After I'd thrown my rose onto the coffin and the vicar had finished his words, I looked over to the far side of the churchyard, where the pathway led to Hartswell Hall, remembering my flight of the other night. How ridiculous it all seemed now. How juvenile and meaningless. I felt I'd aged a million years in the last few days. I'd looked through the doorway of death and seen the truth for myself. And the truth was not a blue crystal, eternal youth or a long lost love, it was an open grave in a cold, windswept graveyard, where decaying flowers marked the passing of others who had gone before. My eyes scanned the trees and the pathway beneath, the wind teasing the branches pale green with new growth, and then I saw him. I saw Theo standing on the newly cleared pathway, watching me closely. For a second our eyes met and such a yearning passed through my body, I felt as if I'd been riven apart. I hadn't thought the pain could get any worse, but I was wrong. It hit me afresh. As I looked at his beautiful face, with his clear blue eyes and translucent skin, utter desolation and emptiness struck me with the force of cold concrete. If I'd experienced love just a few days earlier, now I felt jagged, twisted agony tearing me apart.

I turned away, unable to look at him any longer, and slowly walked back down the ancient church pathway to the Lych Gate, tears in my eyes and the words of John Donne forming in my mind.

"He ruin'd mee, and I am re-begot of absence, darkness, death; things which are not."
Never had I felt more alone or unhappy.

26. Reconciliation

The next day I decided I might as well go to college as stay at home. It all seemed pretty meaningless, but I needed to see my friends. I'd hardly been out since my Granddad died, there'd been so much to do and I hadn't felt up to it. I'd sat in my room night after night, crying and listening to Lenka singing 'Like a Song', until I had no more tears left. Granddad was gone and I couldn't bring him back. Theo had broken my heart and filled my head with mumbo jumbo. What I really needed was to see Tash and Seth, to laugh and joke with them, talk about last night's TV programmes, compare assignments, hang out in the café and do all the stuff we always used to do.

I took my new Hollister sweatshirt, skinny jeans and wedge boots out of the wardrobe, feeling strangely comforted by the routine and safety they represented. I didn't want to make adult decisions, I just wanted to focus on the trivial side of life: what outfit to wear, which eye-shadow to choose, latest music, designer labels, fad diets, college gossip, all the commonplace strands that held my life together. Once I was back at college, others could take responsibility. All I had to do was attend lectures, go to tutorials, write essays and catch the bus every day, things I felt capable of achieving. Suddenly, I was back in my comfort zone and it felt all the more secure for having stepped out of it for a while. This was where I belonged and the big wide world could go take a hike.

I sat at my dressing table and decided for once I'd follow a beauty routine. Using my mum's Forever Youthful cleanser and toner, I cleansed and toned, then liberally applied her Forever Youthful Day-Glow Moisturiser. For a moment, I looked into the mirror, staring at my sad expression and thinking about all that had happened. I'd seen enough of the aging process to last a lifetime. My eyes had been opened to the inevitability of aging and death and I knew that I had to enjoy youth while it was still mine. My clear, smooth skin would be gone all too soon, as life and experience left their indelible mark and the passing years took their toll. I wondered how long it would be before tiny wrinkles started to criss-cross around my eyes and lines began to etch themselves into my face.

Unless ....

I hardly dared let the thought form in my mind. There was an alternative if I chose to believe Theo. I thought about his flawless skin, translucent glow, mesmerising eyes and effortless beauty, then smiled ruefully. Whether I believed him or not, it was all academic. The opportunity had gone. As had my future with Theo. What faced me now was a long, slow decline into old age. Alone. Whoever else I met could never match up to Theo and would always be a poor imitation of love. I'd encountered perfection and lost it. There would be no one else.

I forced myself to concentrate on the here and now. What Theo had offered was an illusion, not based on reality. Had he really found a means of cheating death? And was my life really in such terrible danger? Now I saw it in the cold light of day, I realised how ridiculous it all was and berated myself for believing him.

I picked up my new Hollister top, wondering if life would ever get back to what it had been. I might not look old, but I felt it. Naivety and innocence were things of the past and I realised there was no way back to the world I'd once known. I'd walked through the doorway of awareness and it had slammed shut behind me. Like it or not, I was in unchartered territory, and I had to face it on my own.

As I pulled on my top, I noticed the blue velvet cloak I'd borrowed from Hartswell Hall, lying folded at the bottom of my wardrobe. I'd pushed it to the back, trying to hide all proof of its existence, but now my eyes were drawn to it and I pulled it out, letting my fingers run across its smooth velvety surface. As I did, I felt a hard object concealed within its folds. Intrigued, I shook out the cloak and realised something was in one of the deep pockets. Putting my hand inside, my fingers closed around a hard, oblong shape. I pulled it out. It was my cell phone. I gasped. I'd been so sure I'd dropped it at Hartswell Hall on the night of the Blue Moon Ball, its presence in my hand was something of a shock.

"So The Lunari didn't have it," I found myself saying. "That's why they haven't come looking for me. They didn't know I was there."

As soon as I uttered the words, I realised I'd crossed another line. I'd just acknowledged that the reason I was safe was not that they didn't exist, but rather that they didn't know about me. As I looked at the cloak, a flicker of doubt went through my mind. Could Theo have been telling the truth? I'd certainly witnessed a very strange phenomenon that night when dozens of very old people had apparently been rejuvenated. But were they even the same people who came back out of the room? I'd assumed they were the same because they were wearing similar clothes. But what if the old people had gone out by a one door and a different set of young people had come in via another? I knew there was another entrance at the bottom of the Clock Tower. Joseph had said the wood was too warped for it to open, but he'd said he was going to replace it. If he had, it would be easy for people to get in and out of the upper Clock Tower room without having to go through the house. But why pull off such an elaborate hoax? And for whose benefit? Then I thought about Theo and his family. They'd been looking old and tired, yet when they came out of the Clock Tower room they were radiant and youthful. I realised I was going round in circles. Just as I had formulated a rational explanation, doubt crept in again. And what about the kitten? "Ah, but was it the same kitten?" my rational self demanded. "They could have easily bought another one."

My head was starting to spin, so I bundled the blue cloak back into my wardrobe and concentrated on getting ready for college. I placed the phone in my backpack, not yet ready to look at the pictures I'd taken at the Blue Moon Ball.

At the bus stop, I met up with Tash and Seth.

"Sorry to hear about your Granddad," said Tash.

"Yeah, sorry, must have been a shock," said Seth.

I smiled at them. "Thanks guys, it's good to know I have you."

Seth put his arm round my shoulders and hung over me, his long black fringe flopping forward. "You always have us Emily, we're like a bad rash that won't go away."

"Nice analogy, Seth," said Tash, poking him in the back.

I laughed. It was good to be back with my friends.

"How's lover boy?" asked Seth as we got on the school bus.

"He's not lover boy any more," I answered. "I'm not seeing Theo. It's finished."

"You're kidding," exclaimed Tash, sliding into the seat next to me. "What happened? I thought you were love's young dream."

"That's just the problem, Tash, the dream was turning into a nightmare. It was all getting out of hand."

"Tell me!" she commanded, turning to face me.

"Let's just say, I think Theo may be a bit of a fantasist," I said, trying to choose my words carefully. Some of the things that had happened seemed so incredible, I didn't think I could even begin to speak of them without sounding like a gullible fool.

"This is getting interesting," said Seth from the seat behind, waiting for more.

"Believe me, it's more than interesting, Seth," I said. "Some of it's completely unbelievable, and I don't know what's true and what's not. Theo told me my life was in danger and he was so convincing I believed him."

"Your life was in danger?" echoed Tash. "You know I always had a funny feeling about them, especially after that incident with the wall."

I thought about the phone in my pocket. Perhaps now was the time to look at the photos I'd taken. I took my cell phone out of my pocket and clicked on the camera icon. I could see there were around a dozen pictures taken on the night of the Blue Moon Ball.

"What have you got there?" asked Tash.

"Some photos I took at the hall. They had a private function, the Blue Moon Ball. Theo said I wasn't invited. So I crept in and took some pictures of it."

"Sounds glamorous," said Tash. "How come you weren't invited?"

"It was some kind of secret society, all very hush hush."

"Secret society? Why didn't you tell us?" asked Tash, looking enthralled. "We'd have come with you."

"Well, it was a sort of last minute decision. Sorry, guys. I needed to do it on my own."

"Let's see the photos," said Seth, hanging over the back of our seat.

I clicked on the images, nervous to see what they'd reveal.

"These were the pictures I took when I first arrived," I explained. "I was hiding behind the curtains."

"What's this?" said Tash, laughing. "An old folks' reunion?"

"Exactly, they're all ancient," said Seth. "What was it? A Saga knees-up?"

"Just keep looking," I advised. "See here, they're queuing to get out of the ballroom, and here, you can see them putting on these strange blue cloaks with this weird symbol on the back. They were chanting as well."

"Getting slightly weird," commented Seth.

"Yes, well it gets a whole lot weirder in a minute," I warned him. "I put on one of the blue cloaks and followed them to see where they were going."

Seth and Tash both looked at me incredulously, unsure whether I was winding them up or not.

"OMG, that was brave. What did you see?" asked Tash.

"They went to the top of the house, into the old servants' quarters, and then up into the Clock Tower, where this strange blue light was shining out. I hid in one of the old servants' rooms and took photos as they came back out again."

The next few shots weren't brilliant, as they'd all been taken through a small gap in the door. The first showed a glamorous woman walking towards me, laughing, arm in arm with a handsome man. Despite the photo's poor composition, they looked fabulous, sparkling with excitement and energy.

"Isn't that Chevron d'Ego, the game show hostess?" asked Tash.

"Yes," I answered, "That's her. Just made a TV come-back, looking fabulous and young, as if she's defied old age...."

"And, OMG, she's with Christian Hart, the Hollywood heart-throb," shrieked Tash, "Hang on, I thought the party was full of old people. Where have they gone?"

"They haven't gone anywhere," I said enigmatically. "Keep looking at the pictures. See who else you recognise."

They looked at the second photo.

"This is Sugar, the famous singer," said Tash. "She looks amazing, you'd never know she was in her late 60's."

The third showed a close-up of a woman's face. She was young and stunningly beautiful.

"Coola boola!" said Seth. "She is fit."

"Hang on," said Tash, "She's that actress from the 60s. Rachael Ravel. My mum was watching a film she starred in the other day. She's got to be in her 70s now. It can't be her."

I showed them the next photo.

"Half-man-amazing!" exclaimed Seth. "That looks like Sergio Brioche, the footballer. Just signed for Barcelona for £95 million. What's he doing there?"

"What was this, some kind of celebrity lookalike party?" asked Tash, "And what's happened to all the old folk?"

"These are the old folk," I informed her. "What I showed you first were the 'before' shots, when they were old. And these are the 'after' shots, when they became young again."

I could see from my friends' faces that they weren't keeping up with me.

"Sorry, you've lost me," said Tash. "You're saying these shots were all taken on the same evening and are the same people? I don't understand."

"You mean they went through some kind of rejuvenation process," said Seth, "Sounds spooky."

"It's more than spooky, Seth," I told him. "This is like a horror film. Even your theory about vampires was easier to get your head around than this."

I had their full and undivided attention.

"Hit us with it," said Seth.

"Look again at this photo of the old folk," I said, showing them the first photo I'd taken. "See this woman in the stunning green ballgown...."

They both looked closely.

"Now, look at this photo taken around fifteen minutes later. See anything similar?"

"It's the same dress," said Tash in a whisper.

"Exactly," I said, "I believe the old folk and the beautiful people are one and the same. They started the evening old and they ended it young and beautiful."

Tash looked at me as if I'd lost leave of my senses.

"Impossible," she said.

Seth whistled through his teeth. "Weirdo, schmeirdo. I knew it," he said, "I knew there was something going on." He balled his fist in a victory gesture. "Yes! Seth's sixth sense strikes again. Try saying that quickly!"

"Seth, this is no joking matter," I said sharply. "I don't know what's going on at Hartswell Hall. Theo's told me this story and I don't know whether to believe him."

"What's he told you?" asked Tash.

"This may take a while," I warned them.

"That's okay," said Seth, "we've at least another twenty minutes before the bus gets to college."

And so I told them all about the party, about seeing the dying guest who arrived too late, about escaping through the woods and spending the night in the church... I told them about meeting Theo in the church the following evening and going down into the vault, and how he'd explained about the blue crystal, kept securely in the Clock Tower, with its amazing youth bestowing properties, and the Blue Moon Ball, attended by the rich and famous who'd paid a fortune for eternal youth, but were sworn to secrecy on pain of death. I told them about Viyesha's life in Egypt three thousand years ago and how she'd discovered the crystal's power, how Theo believed we'd been together many years ago, about The Lunari, Aquila and Pantera, and the other so-called dark forces... how my life was in danger and how he'd given me a blue crystal pendant to wear for protection. I told them about Violet's kitten and its miraculous recovery, how I'd asked Theo to help my Granddad and how he had refused. When I'd finished there was silence. My friends looked at me incredulously.

Then Seth grinned widely and said: "Cool bananas! An ancient blue crystal with the power of giving eternal youth... guarded by shape-shifters and a secret society... with a soupçon of celebrities thrown in ... This is great! And to think I thought it was vampires. How wrong can you get? This is a million times better."

"Or a million times worse, depending on your perspective," I pointed out. "If it's true, it's not looking good for me."

"Talk about The Beautiful and Damned," said Tash.

"Very good," said Seth, "F. Scott Fitzgerald. An apt analogy, Tash. Although personally I think it's more like Faustus, you know, selling your soul to the devil. That's on the A-level English Lit syllabus for next year, by the way, I've just been reading about it. Christopher Marlowe."

"Forget Faustus and Scott Fitzgerald," I said. "What about me? I appear to have a choice of becoming Beautiful and Damned or finished off by dark forces. Neither option is great. And that's supposing the crystal doesn't finish me off first."

"That's if you believe what Theo has told you," said Tash. "The only bit that stacks up for me is rich and famous people paying a fortune to try and stay young. There's nothing new in that. The rest sounds like something out of a fairy story."

"I agree," said Seth. "Some of these looks-obsessed celebs wouldn't give a toss about selling their soul for smooth skin, firm buttocks and a flat stomach. They'd buy into anything to keep their careers going, the adulation flowing and the cash rolling in. Maybe it was all just an elaborate illusion to relieve rich punters of their money."

"Exactly," said Tash. "The guests' transformation could have been done with masks and prosthetics, or simply different people. There are plenty of celebrity lookalikes around. That would be easy enough to do. Perhaps the ones you saw going up the tower weren't the ones who came down."

"A scam to draw rich people in…" I said. "The ultimate con trick. Could be, I suppose. But what about the guest who aged and died? I saw him decay in front of my eyes? That was like something out of a horror movie. If it was a scam, why let that happen? That would only alienate potential new clients. And where were these rich potential punters? I only saw old people. And then there's the estate agent. She aged and died prematurely, just like the guest at the party. I'm sure she was somehow drawn into this. And you didn't see the de Lucis family when they came down the spiral staircase. They looked amazing. More beautiful, more vibrant, more radiant than I've ever seen them."

I paused and looked at my friends.

"Believe me, guys, I've been through every scenario, ranging from illusion through to Theo being some kind of fantasist control freak and the more chilling alternative that it's true."

They stared at me, not knowing what to say.

I sighed unhappily. "Other people just have to deal with a break up. I have to deal with eternal youth, a secret society, rejuvenated celebrities and enemies all around. I don't know what to believe. I haven't seen any sign of The Lunari or Dark Forces, so maybe it is all fantasy. Perhaps it will all go away now Theo and I have split up."

Seth looked doubtful. "If there's any truth in this, do you think the family will let you walk away, knowing what you do?"

"Thanks, Seth, that's really put my mind at rest," I said.

"Can we see your necklace?" asked Tash.

"That's another strange thing," I said, showing them the pale blue crystal. "I tried to take it off the other day and the clasp has vanished. It's a continuous chain that I can't take it off."

"It's beautiful," said Tash, attempting to hold the crystal. As her fingers touched it, she leapt backwards. "Ow, it's burnt me."

"Don't put it near me," said Seth, retreating to the back of his seat.

Tash rubbed her fingers, looking worried. "D'you think the family will be happy that Seth and I know what's going on?" she asked.

"Don't tell me you really believe it, Tash?" I said. "If it's true, then I've just placed your lives at risk too!"

"Chillax, Emily," said Seth. "How could they know? You've told us at the back of a noisy bus. Nobody can hear us. The point is what are we going to do now?"

"We?" I asked.

"Absolutely," said Seth. "If it's your problem, it's our problem. We can't have our best friend taken out by some secret society or supernatural force."

"And I can't bear the thought of you becoming unbelievably beautiful for eternity," said Tash, making us all laugh.

"So, it's one for all and all for one!" said Seth, dramatically, raising his fist, "Brotherzone!"

"Except for one thing, Seth," added Tash, drily. "We're not the three Musketeers. And for God's sake stop reading the urban dictionary. It's driving me loopy. "

* * *

If I thought it was over with Theo, I was wrong. He found me at break time, when I was putting some books into my locker.

"Emily," he said, standing behind me and I froze. I'd forgotten the effect his voice and his presence had on me.

"What?" I said, afraid to turn round and look into his eyes. If I gazed into those deep pools of blue, I wasn't sure I could control my emotions. Mentally, I put a force field around my body, trying to ward his energy away from me.

"Emily, don't close me out," he begged. "We need to talk. Please turn round."

He sounded so sad and forlorn, I wavered. "Turn around," he pleaded again.

I strengthened my resolve and spoke without turning. "I've got nothing to say to you, Theo. You told me an elaborate story and expected me to believe it, then when the chance came for you to prove it, you wouldn't do it. So what am I supposed to believe? I don't want to look at you and I don't want to see you any more."

"Emily, I tried to tell you...' he began, but I interrupted him.

"Theo, my Granddad is dead. If you and your family have the powers you say you do, you could have saved him. But you didn't."

"Couldn't, Emily, couldn't. I tried to explain."

"So you couldn't help my Granddad, but you could help all those old folk at the Blue Moon Ball?" I turned suddenly, my anger getting too much.

If anything, he looked more beautiful than ever. I yearned to touch his smooth, perfect skin, gaze into his troubled blue eyes and feel his soft, sensuous lips on mine. The attraction between us was almost too great. I steeled myself and resisted the temptation to fall into his arms.

"The Blue Moon Ball was different," he said. "Look, we can't discuss this here. There are too many people. And it's all too complicated. Meet me later? Give me a chance to explain properly?"

I stared at him, trying desperately to control my emotions.

"You're not listening to me, Theo. It's over. I don't want to see you any more. Please leave me alone." I turned back to my locker and continued taking out my books.

I felt his face close to the back of my head and heard him say, "For now, Emily, but it's not over. You know it."

At lunchtime, he found me again. Seth was at rugby practice and Tash had a dental appointment, so I sat in the far corner of the cafeteria feeling alone and vulnerable. It was inevitable he would seek me out. As I sat, pushing the food around my plate, without any appetite, he slid on to the chair opposite me before I realised it.

"Theo, I've told you….." I started to say, but he interrupted.

"Emily, listen to me. You have to let me explain properly. You owe me that at least."

"You're not going to let this go, are you?" I said wearily.

"No, I'm not, so you might as well let me have my say."

"Okay, go on then."

"Not here, it's too public."

"I'm not going anywhere, Theo. It's here or nowhere, take your pick."

He grinned at me. "You can be very forceful when you want, Emily, your energy is very strong."

"I thought you were going to give me an explanation," I said coldly.

"I am." He looked at me earnestly. "Emily, what were the last words your Granddad said to you? Think clearly."

His words took me by surprise and I faltered. "That's none of your business."

"Did he say he wanted to live forever?" persisted Theo.

"No," I had to admit, "he didn't."

"What did he say? Emily, this is important."

I remembered back to that afternoon in the hospital. "He said he'd had a good, long life and although he hated to leave us behind, he didn't want to go on for eternity. He said there was a time for birth and a time for death. The natural order. That's how things were meant to be." The tears were starting to stream down my cheeks. "He said he was going to see my Grandma." My voice was little more than a whisper. "He told me to remember that."

"You see, Emily, your Granddad didn't want saving. He understood the natural order. He knew it was his time to go." Theo spoke kindly.

"No," I said, through my tears, "it was too soon. I didn't want him to go."

"I know," said Theo. "Death is never easy to accept, but sometimes we have to."

"What do you know about death?" I asked him angrily. "Haven't you and your family managed to cheat it for thousands of years? How could you possibly know what I'm going through?"

"Death is a constant fear for us, Emily, and it doesn't happen naturally," he replied. "Ours is one of rapid aging and decay, as you saw with our unfortunate guest. Can you imagine how it feels for your skin, your organs and your senses to shrivel to nothing within minutes? For your hair to thin, your teeth to fall out and your body to fail in less time than it takes to walk across a room? There's no slowing up, no gradual descent into old age for us. It hits us full in the face, like being hurled off a precipice." He laughed scornfully. "That's the threat hanging over us and that's the price we have to pay for eternal youth. Which is why I don't want it for you."

"But what about your guests at the Blue Moon Ball?" I asked, "They were old and yet you made them young."

"I know that's how it looked, Emily, but the truth is, they were young when they were first initiated, and that's the age they'll remain, frozen in time for eternity."

"But they were old when I saw them," I persisted.

"That's because every three years, their life force begins to ebb away and the accelerated aging process kicks in. The only way to reverse it is to bathe in the light of the crystal at the time of the Blue Moon. It's the only way we can recharge our energy and rejuvenate. If we don't," he faltered, "well, you saw what happens."

"You say 'we', Theo," my voice was a whisper, "That means you as well."

As much as I didn't want to hear it, I had to know the truth.

"Yes," he said reluctantly, "yes, I had started to age, which was one of the reasons I couldn't see you. I couldn't bear for you to see me looking like that."

"Oh, Theo," I said softly.

"Now, perhaps you can see why I'm so confused about everything," he said sadly. His eyes were full of pain and love and emotions I could barely understand. "This is not the life I want for you. I love you, Emily, and I want to be with you, but, more than anything, I want you to have an ordinary, happy, normal life."

I stared at him, not knowing what to say.

"And you have to believe me, Emily, there was truly nothing I could do to save your Granddad. Sometimes, you just have to let go."

I looked down. "It hurts, Theo, more than I ever imagined. I've never lost anyone before. Well, my dad, perhaps, but that's different. I lost him to another country and another family, not to death. It's just so final. And I feel so alone."

"But you're not, Emily, you have your mum, you have your friends, and you have me."

"Do I?" I asked, "You come from a strange world, Theo, one that you don't want me to belong to. What future could we possibly have?"

"I don't know, Emily," he said sadly. "I only know that I need to be with you. I don't want to lose you. I love you, Emily, so much. If you only knew…."

I put my hand on his and squeezed it.

"I do," I said. "My granddad said we went well together. But can't you see how much I've had to take in over the past few weeks? I still don't know if I believe all you've told me, it sounds so far-fetched. And, by the way, I found my phone. I hadn't dropped it at Hartswell Hall. It was in the pocket of the blue cloak you lent me. So, there's no way The Lunari can know about me. There's nothing to link me to the Blue Moon Ball. That is, supposing The Lunari actually exist. Don't you see, Theo?"

"It doesn't matter, Emily," he said slowly. "I'm glad you didn't drop your phone at the Hall. It makes life marginally simpler. But don't you see? Pantera and Aquila know about you. At the moment, two things stand in your favour. Firstly, they don't know that I've told you the truth, and, secondly, for the moment, they're obeying Viyesha and not telling The Lunari about you. But that could change at any moment."

"What do you mean?" I asked.

"I mean, the hotel opens for business this weekend, and The Lunari are coming to visit. They'll be here in Hartswell-on-the-Hill and The Guardians will have no option but to tell them about you."

I looked at him wildly.

"So, I have less than a week," I said in horror. "Everything changes in days?"

"Yes," said Theo sadly. "Just days for us to decide what to do."

27. Attack 1

Grace Wisterley took her evening constitutional as usual, walking through the fields where her sheep stood grazing, then cutting back through Hartswell Hall grounds, and on to the gravelled driveway that led to the High Street. She intended to call in on Tom Mastock for a nightcap, as she often did, finding a drop of his Jamieson's whisky sent her off to sleep a treat when she returned home. But on this occasion, she never made it beyond Hartswell Hall's driveway. She'd been feeling out of sorts for a few days now and wondered if she was sickening for something. Her head ached permanently, her mouth was dry and her back was playing up something rotten. She'd even developed a stoop in the last few days.

"Don't know what's up wi' me," she'd said to her daughter on the phone, "I've no energy to do 'owt. All I want to do is sleep or eat."

"You can't be feeling too bad if your appetite is good," her daughter had pointed out.

"It's better than good, it's insatiable," she'd laughed.

And indeed it was. Whatever she ate, she simply couldn't get enough of it. The shepherd's pie that would normally last for three days was gone within minutes, shovelled down as if it were her last meal. She'd eaten a whole roast chicken, too hungry to wait until she'd carved it, tearing off great chunks of meat with her teeth and not stopping until it was all gone, bones and all. Then she'd gone to the butchers' and bought as much red meat as she could carry, staggering home with a variety of steaks, minced meat, cutlets, liver and kidneys, not even waiting until she arrived home before she started to eat it raw, the blood dripping down her chin.

But no matter how much she ate and how much she slept – and she found herself dozing off all the time – she couldn't shake this feeling of bone-weary tiredness. Her limbs felt heavy and cumbersome, her energy levels were at an all time low, and her back had hunched alarmingly.

"It's almost as if I'm carrying a huge weight on my back," she'd told Tom Mastock. "Something's draining my energy, and

no matter how much I eat, I'm permanently exhausted. I don't think much o' this getting old malarkey."

"Pop in for a night cap on your way back home," he'd suggested. "That'll make you feel better."

And that's what she was about to do, except she never made it.

One minute, she was walking past Hartswell Hall, her feet crunching on the gravel, the next she hit the deck, landing flat on her face, dead as a doornail, her eyes staring straight ahead.

Silently, the black shadow on her back disengaged itself, sliding on to the pathway, replenished and recuperated. As it did so, the dead woman's bent spine slowly began to straighten as if the cares of the world were finally leaving her now she was unable to carry them any longer.

The black shadow stretched up into the air, blacker and more substantial than it had been for a long time. Quickly, it assessed its bearings, realising it could not have asked for a more convenient drop-off. Without a sound, it glided towards Hartswell Hall, aiming for the great oak front door, and flowing beneath it like a dark, deadly gas.

No one was in reception and it continued on its way unheeded, flowing quickly and unnoticed up the main stairway. The object of its desire was getting ever closer and freedom was at last within its grasp.

28. Martha

Tash and Seth weren't too pleased when I told them I was back with Theo.

"I thought you said he was a fantasist weirdo," said Seth, "or is that what you're into nowadays?"

"Be careful, Emily," said Tash. "There's something strange going on and even if you're not in danger, you could get hurt."

"I'm okay, guys," I said. "Just forget all that stuff I told you. I was going through a funny phase after Granddad died. I wasn't thinking straight. Theo told me this story to take my mind off things. I got muddled up and ended up thinking he was telling me the truth. Turns out he was just trying to make me feel better."

"But what about the photos on your phone?" persisted Tash. "What was all that about?"

"Oh, they were two separate events," I lied, "One was a celebrity look alike party and the other was an old folks reunion, both held at Hartswell Hall. Sorry, guys. I didn't have a very good grip on reality after losing Granddad. I didn't know what was fantasy and what was fact."

"Loony toony!" said Seth, "People go on medication for less than that, Emily."

"I know. I fine now. I'm over it. Theo and I are good."

It sounded odd and I knew it. I could tell they weren't convinced, but they kept their distance and were coolly polite whenever they saw Theo. For the moment, an odd sort of status quo existed. I knew Tash and Seth were watching and waiting, and in a strange way I welcomed it, like having a safety net in place. In truth, I was just glad to have Theo back in my life, to be able to slip my hand into his, see his magical smile and feel my energies levels rise whenever I was with him. He made me feel good. Very good. But I also knew it couldn't stay that way, that something would have to change and the days were ticking past.

On a lighter note, Joseph finished working on my car and one evening he and Theo delivered it to my driveway. I could hardly believe what I saw.

"It's fantastic, Joseph," I said, giving him a hug. "Are you sure it's the same car?"

Martha indeed looked completely different: her paintwork, her hub caps and her chrome work shone with an intensity that was blinding, and inside she smelled as if she'd come straight from the showroom.

"She has new spark plugs, new brake pads, a new battery and new tyres, and I've given her a spring clean inside and out," Joseph informed me.

"It looks more like a complete overhaul," I said in amazement. "Thank you so much, Joseph, you don't know what this means to me. Tell me how much I owe you."

Joseph put up his hand. "Nothing, Emily, it was a pleasure. I love bringing things back to life."

"Come on, let's take her out for a spin," suggested Theo. "You can drive, Emily."

I sat in the driving seat, Theo by my side and Joseph in the back. As I turned the ignition, she roared into life and shot forward the moment my foot touched the accelerator. I braked quickly.

"Whoa! What have you done to her, Joseph?" I squealed. "She was never this powerful."

"I might have modified her engine slightly," admitted Joseph. "Sorry, couldn't resist it. I should have told you."

I looked in my rear view mirror. "Modified it how, exactly?"

"On a par with a V8 engine," he said gingerly.

"OMG, you're kidding! Did you know about this, Theo?"

"Nothing to do with me," he said, grinning. "Just take it slowly, okay."

"I don't think that's possible in this car," I laughed.

This time I eased forward tentatively, aware of the power beneath my feet. Martha moved effortlessly up the lane and slowly I began to get accustomed to her new levels of responsiveness. She went like a dream, a deep throaty roar emanating from her bonnet, and I headed for the motorway. It was 7pm and the rush hour traffic had dispersed, giving me the open road to play with. Theo turned on the sound system and Jon Bon Jovi's 'Livin' on a Prayer' filled the cabin.

"These acoustics are amazing," I shouted back to Joseph. "Don't tell me she's got a new sound system too?"

"Latest Fender soundpack. Just wanted to check it out," he grinned.

Once on the motorway, I put my foot down and Martha surged forward, burning rubber and blasting rock music. It felt fantastic and for a short time I was lost in the moment, oblivious to everything but the pounding beat, the roaring engine and the rapidly disappearing tarmac. And, of course, the two beautiful creatures with me in the car.

All too soon, it was over and we were back on my driveway. I turned to Joseph. "Wow. That was unexpected. You are full of surprises."

He gave a mock bow. "We aim to please, madam."

How I loved this family. If only they'd been ordinary people. If only they'd been human.

29. **Viyesha**

After my trip out in Martha, I couldn't take the grin off my face, but next day came the news I'd been dreading. I was summoned to have a 'chat' with Viyesha.

It was now the second weekend in May and Hartswell Hall was open for business. As yet, there was no sign of The Lunari, but I knew their arrival was imminent and there was no doubt in my mind as to why Viyesha wanted to talk with me. Just over two weeks had passed since Granddad died and although I still felt raw and out of kilter with the world, I had begun to accept he wasn't coming back and that Theo had been powerless to alter the course of events. Without Granddad's guiding hand in my life, I found myself relying on Theo more and more. My mum seemed glad I had a boyfriend to lean on, especially such a good-looking, reliable, sensible boy as Theo. I had to suppress a rueful smile when she said that. If only. She admitted that she'd met someone, too.

"It's not serious, just someone from work," she told me, "We've only been on a couple of dates, so I won't introduce him yet. But he makes me laugh and that's what I need right now."

It was a glorious summer afternoon, the bright sun giving everything a lazy, hazy feel, as Theo and I walked up the gravelled drive to Hartswell Hall. I was going to drive over in the new rejuvenated Martha, but decided against it at the last minute as I didn't want to advertise my presence. I preferred to stay as low key as possible.

Violet stood on the steps waiting for us, watching us approach.

"Hi, Emily, how are you?" she asked sweetly, embracing me and giving me one of her most engaging smiles. "Mother's in the library. Come and say hello."

She led the way past the reception area, decorated with beautiful flower arrangements of red and pink roses, blue irises and white lilies. The windows were open, letting in the fresh air and sunshine, and it felt warm, welcoming and normal.

"We have our first guests," announced Violet.

"That's great," I said, feigning interest. I felt too nervous of what lay ahead to take much interest in their new business venture.

"We're hosting the annual conference of the National Institute of Plastic Surgeons," said Violet, "and Kimberley Chartreuse, the famous glamour model, has booked in for a couple of nights."

"That's really exciting," I said flatly. "I've seen her reality TV show. She looks amazing, but I suspect she's had a lot of work done. Just as well you've got plastic surgeons on hand in case she needs anything else fixing."

"Take it from me, there's nothing natural about her," said Violet. "And what a prima donna. She arrived last night, all airs and graces. Changed rooms three times, insisted on having a full tour, broom cupboards and all, and gave mother a real grilling, asking her where she'd come from, how long she'd been here and how old she was. I don't know how mother stayed so polite. I'd have told her to take a running jump."

"Probably jealousy," I said, "because Viyesha's more beautiful than she is."

By now we were standing outside the library and Theo opened the oak panelled door.

"Good luck," he whispered, as I walked in.

In the library, Viyesha sat on one of the leather Chesterfields, turning the pages of a fashion magazine with beautifully manicured, slender fingers. She was dressed immaculately, as always, this time in a pale blue Chanel-style jacket and matching pencil skirt, with a soft white cashmere rollneck. Her lips were painted pale pink, her blonde hair was loose around her shoulders, and her blue eyes sparkled and twinkled. A CD of Liszt's Liebestraum played softly in the background.

"Emily," she purred, placing the magazine on the coffee table in front of her. "Come and sit with me. It's delightful to see you."

She patted the place next to her and, like an obedient pet, I walked over and sat down. At once, I experienced the most wonderful sensation of wellbeing.

"Hello, Viyesha," I purred back, "It's good to see you, too."

I heard the door close behind us.

"Can I get you anything?" asked Viyesha. "A cup of tea, a drink?"

"No, I'm fine, thank you," I said politely.

"I won't beat about the bush," said Viyesha, sitting back in the Chesterfield and turning to face me. "There are things of which I need to speak, Emily."

"I know," I said, feeling nervous. This was it. The conversation I didn't want to have.

"I understand Theo has told you certain things?"

"Yes," I said, looking down. I didn't want to look into her large blue eyes.

"Tell me what you know, Emily," said Viyesha softly.

I swallowed, unsure what to say, then looked Viyesha square in the face.

"I know about the blue crystal and its powers of conveying eternal youth on those who bathe in its rays," I began, feeling self-conscious. "And I know you have to wait for a Blue Moon to activate the crystal. I also know you brought the crystal from Egypt…" I faltered, then said, "The truth is, Viyesha, I don't know what to believe, it all sounds so incredible. Theo said I would be at risk from The Lunari, but I've seen no evidence of them. He also said Aquila and Pantera consider me a threat, but apart from them being generally unpleasant to me, there's hardly been an attempt on my life. Well, apart from the wall collapsing on me," again I faltered, "but that could have been an accident."

I dared not mention the Blue Moon Ball, or that I had secretly observed her guests and taken photos.

Viyesha stood up and walked to the window. She looked out over the grounds and seemed to be thinking what to say. Then she turned to face me. "Emily," she said in a matter-of-fact voice, "be under no illusion what is going on here. Believe me, The Lunari exist and they would eliminate you like that if they so wished," she snapped her fingers, "Be under no illusion about Aquila and Pantera, either. They are Guardians of the crystal and have killed many times to protect it. While you wear Theo's crystal necklace you have protection, but should you remove it, I cannot guarantee your safety."

My hand went involuntarily to the crystal hanging round my neck, my fingers touching its smooth, faceted surface. Viyesha looked at me a little more kindly.

"I'm sorry, Emily. It was not my choosing to bring you into the family or place you in danger. That was Theo's doing, which leads me to a further complication. Theo believes you to be the reincarnation of the woman he loved and lost many years ago. There certainly appears to be a connection between you, and you bear an uncanny resemblance to the woman he once loved as you saw on the necklace he wears."

She smiled softly, "He believes it is you. But he wants to protect you from the crystal, in case its power should prove too great and he loses you again."

She returned to the sofa, taking her time before speaking again.

"Emily, my son has been unhappy for many years and I would do anything within my power to change that. The obvious solution would be for you to join us, but you are young, with your life ahead of you and it is not for me to force you into a course of action you will regret for the rest of your days. You need to think through the options carefully before making your decision. It may still be possible for you to walk away and for me to appease Pantera and Aquila and The Lunari, but you would never see Theo again."

My mind filled with dread. The thought of losing Theo was more than I could bear.

"The alternative is for you to bathe in the crystal's light and enjoy the gift of eternal youth….and Theo's love for eternity."

"As long as I survive the crystal's power," I said.

"It is true, many do not survive the initiation," she said, "The crystal is immensely powerful and its rejuvenating powers can work in reverse, speeding up the aging process. We have no way of knowing how you would react. The risks are great."

She looked at me anxiously. "There again, should you rejuvenate successfully, the rewards are infinite. Time cannot touch you, the world is your playground and you would be with Theo forever, enjoying eternal youth together. You would step beyond the confines of the mortal body and experience supernatural power and beauty."

I stared at her in dismay. It was like being faced with a proposal of marriage, but too early on in the relationship to know if it was the right thing to do. What she was saying was so far beyond my powers of comprehension, I simply couldn't apply reason and common sense. My future hung in the balance, my life was at a pivotal stage, and I had no way of knowing which choice to make.

"I don't know what to do, Viyesha," I admitted. "Half of me wants to have an ordinary life and enjoy all the things other people of my age are doing." My voice dropped to a whisper. "But the other half wants to be with Theo and stay young forever, to bathe in the crystal's light. I couldn't face a future without him."

"It is a blessing and a curse, Emily," said Viyesha, "to live through history and experience it first hand as time rolls through the centuries.... to enjoy youth and beauty others can only dream about... to live a life of magic and mystery, with untold wealth and power...to live as an immortal and hold eternity in the palm of your hand."

Her eyes shone as she spoke and I knew she was seeing things in her mind that I couldn't even contemplate: events, people and places that had shaped history; experiences, opportunities and possibilities that were limitless, ageless and timeless.

"But the bad almost outweighs the good," she said, in a whisper. Now her eyes clouded over and she was seeing a different picture. "Imagine, Emily, having your very existence dictated by an event that occurs every three years; having to bathe in the light of a crystal to restore your failing youth or endure an unimaginable death: the agony of rapid aging as your organs cease to function, your bones grow brittle and your skin dries out... to cease being, all in a matter of minutes..."

She stopped and took a deep breath.

"Forgive me Emily, I don't wish to frighten you, but your eyes need to be opened if you are to make the right decision. Now, ask me anything and I will try to answer."

"Okay," I said, the issues before me so huge and incomprehensible as to render my mind blank, "What do you eat? I've never seen Theo or Violet eat."

Viyesha threw back her head and laughed. "Oh, Emily. So many metaphysical and esoteric issues, and you pick the mundane." She smiled at me. "I'm sorry, I truly forget how young you are and how many moons I have seen pass. It is a relevant question. The answer is that we eat sparingly and discerningly. We are highly evolved Light Beings, which means our bodily systems are extremely sensitive and can digest only that which comes directly from light: vegetarian food as you call it, plants, vegetables, seeds and nuts, which we produce ourselves. The Lunari are so refined, they metabolise the sun's rays into energy and live on light alone."

"Light Beings," I repeated, trying to understand what she was saying. "I see. And your symbol is the circle crossed by an infinity sign. I saw it on the Clock Tower and on Theo's arm. "

I dared not admit I'd seen it on the backs of the cloaks at the Blue Moon Ball or on the shoulder of a guest.

"Yes, that is The Lunari's symbol," said Viyesha, "The circle represents the full moon, and the infinity sign, eternity. We greet each other thus." She cupped her hands in a circle in front of her, crossing her thumbs, replicating the symbol.

"Is there anything else you wish to know?"

"Theo told me how you discovered the crystal's power and kept it in Egypt, but why bring it to Hartswell-on-the-Hill?"

"This site has long been known to us as an energy centre of great power, a natural meridian where ley lines cross," answered Viyesha. "It was for this reason that one of The Lunari built Hartswell Hall back in Victorian times. He had intended to live here with his wife, but she took her life before it was completed and he closed up the house, preferring to travel the world alone. He returned in recent times to live as a recluse, but ultimately chose to end his life. Without his wife, he saw eternal youth as a curse. We keep the crystal in the Clock Tower, where the energy is strongest."

She paused for a moment before continuing.

"We stayed in Egypt for many years, but we have enemies and it was getting too dangerous. It was agreed we would come first to prepare the hall, and that Joseph would follow, bringing the crystal. We believed he journeyed in secrecy, but it would appear that old enemies of ours, The Reptilia or Dark Ones, desperate for the life form that the crystal would grant them, have discovered our location. Believe me, Emily, it is they rather than you, who presents the real threat. So far, we have protected the location of the crystal with our mist shroud, which the Dark Ones find impossible to penetrate, and Aquila and Pantera were able to destroy all those who congregated beyond the mist. But more will come, of that we are sure."

"I see," I said again, not seeing at all, but aware of other questions I needed to ask.

"What about your family, Viyesha? Is Leon as old as you? And are Violet and Theo your natural children?" That was a key question. I had to know whether I would be able to have my own children if I chose to join them.

"Leon and I have been together since the early days," she answered. "I was a High Priestess and he was a Priest during the reigns of Akhenaten and Tutankhamun. After the murder of Tutankhamun, I renounced my religious vocation and went into hiding. Leon joined me later. Violet and Theo are our natural children. Light from light. Although they were not ready to bathe in the crystal's rays until their teenage years."

"And what about the others around the world who bathe in its light? The rich and famous people who've paid for the privilege? Where do they fit in?"

"Not all have paid, Emily. Some are family, some friends of many years' duration. In recent years, The Lunari have allowed elite individuals to pay for the crystal's services… those with a need for eternal youth, and the funds to buy it."

"The mega-rich, you mean," I said, disparagingly. Viyesha shrugged.

"It is The Lunari's decision. They will only allow those whom they trust to join us. Any who compromise our safety are eliminated immediately."

Her words were cold and an involuntary shudder ran down my spine.

"You must understand, Emily, The Lunari have one loyalty only, and that is to the crystal. Our survival is dependent upon it." She paused. "Something else you should understand. Only the young can bathe in the crystal's rays. Anyone older than mid thirties would not survive the process, their body chemistry is simply too compromised. I know you wanted us to save your grandfather, Theo pleaded with us, but believe me, it wasn't possible."

"I understand that now," I said sadly. "But what about me, Viyesha? I'm not wealthy. I can't pay. Why should The Lunari accept me?"

"I will intercede on your behalf, you can rest assured. My word carries much weight and these are exceptional circumstances."

In other words, my chances were good, but there were no guarantees. Neither was there any guarantee I would survive the initiation process.

"Do you have any more questions?" she asked gently.

I paused. "What happened to the estate agent who arranged the sale? Did she touch the crystal?"

Viyesha looked troubled. "No, she didn't. The whole incident was unintentional and most regrettable. When we walked in that first time, the house came alive and our energy levels were activated. As she shook Leon's hand, she absorbed some of the energy. It rejuvenated her for a few weeks, then proved too much for her."

"But I had that same energy transference when I shook Theo's hand," I pointed out, "and I didn't shrivel up and die."

"I cannot explain what you experienced," she admitted, "It is most unusual. Certainly Theo's energy would not have been as powerful as Leon's on the day we arrived here. But if you are truly Theo's lost love, your energies will be in tune and there will always be a powerful connection between you."

"How did Theo lose me, Viyesha? I have to know."

She looked into the distance, deep in thought and I knew she was remembering. At last she spoke: "I cannot speak of it, Emily. You must not ask me. Theo will tell you when the time is right. And there is only one way to find out if you truly are his lost love…"

"…bathe in the crystal's light," I finished for her. "And if I survive, what are these supernatural powers you mentioned?"

"Heightened sensitivity, a greater appreciation of sight, sound, smell and touch, possibly special powers. No one knows until they have been through the process. Theo has the gift of speed, as you may have seen. I have the gift of serenity, Leon strength, and Joseph abundance. Violet has the gift of musicality and seeing auras."

"I'd choose invisibility. Or flying."

She smiled. "This isn't Harry Potter, Emily. Who knows what your power may be? Now, time is getting on and you have much to think about."

"One last question, Viyesha," I said, plucking up courage. "Can I see the crystal?"

She gave a sharp intake of breath. "The crystal is very powerful, Emily, and the Clock Tower room has been attuned. It might not be safe for you. Should you decide to join us, we would have to dissipate the power of the crystal and the energy field."

"So I wouldn't have to wait for a Blue Moon?" I asked.

"Absolutely not," Viyesha assured me. "The crystal's power would be far too strong for a new initiate. A full moon is all you require."

She sat in silence for a moment, considering her options, then made a decision.

"Come, I will take you to the Clock Tower and let you see the crystal. But I cannot allow you to enter the room. It is too risky."

She led the way out of the library, and I followed, knowing I was closing forever the option of living a normal life.

29. The blue crystal

Guests were beginning to arrive in the reception area. A group of tanned, good looking men, all dressed in varying shades of beige, stood in a group, their Louis Vuitton luggage stacked to one side. Violet sat at the reception desk, welcoming them to Hartswell Hall and requesting that they fill in the necessary forms.

"Mother," she called, as we appeared from the doorway, "the plastic surgeons are here."

They all turned as one and stared at Viyesha, as well they might. She was the living embodiment of the perfection they sought through the surgeon's knife.

"Excuse me for one minute," she said to me softly and moved forward to greet them.

"Gentlemen, welcome to Hartswell Hall. I am Viyesha. You are most welcome and I hope your stay here is satisfactory. My daughter, Violet, will take care of you."

One of the coiffed, manicured beige men stepped forward and introduced himself.

"Good afternoon, madam, I am Michael Malfit, Chairman of the Institute. I am very pleased to make your acquaintance."

He proffered his hand and Viyesha shook it gently, smiling. He stared at her face intently, as if looking for evidence of surgery and she gazed back coolly, her blue eyes glittering.

"Is everything alright, Mr Malfit?"

"Absolutely," he breathed, "I am transfixed by your beauty. May I say, what an excellent job somebody has done. You must tell me the name of your surgeon. Is it one of ours?"

He glanced back at the other beige men waiting at the reception desk.

Viyesha laughed.

"Gentlemen, I assure you I have never succumbed to the surgeon's knife and never will. What you see is entirely natural. Now, if you will excuse me. My daughter, Violet, will show you to your rooms and I shall see you later. A champagne reception has been prepared for you in the old Billiards Room. Please feel free to come down as soon as you have refreshed yourselves."

"We look forward to it," said Michael Malfit, smiling smoothly. "Can I say what a beautiful establishment you have here? A real gem in the heart of the English countryside. Just like yourself."

I dared not look at Violet in case we started laughing. This man was nauseous: plastic and pretentious, just like his trade.

Viyesha smiled, graciously.

"Thank you. Now, I really must go. I have business to attend to. Come, Emily."

She turned majestically and I followed her up the main stairway, aware of his eyes on my back.

"He's creepy, Viyesha," I whispered, as we reached the top of the stairs, "Did you see the way he was looking at you?"

"Men such as he will always be in awe of physical beauty, especially given the nature of his work," she said dismissively, "It is something to which I've grown accustomed. Now, come, before I change my mind."

She continued along the corridor leading to the old servants' quarters and I followed, part of me burning with excitement, the other more than a little afraid. Was I safe? Was this an elaborate ploy on Viyesha's part to lure me to my death? Would Aquila and Pantera be waiting for me in the upper room to finish me off quickly and silently? Would the crystal be the cause of my demise? It was too late to go back, I was committed to this course of action, whatever the consequences. And I had to know what the crystal looked like and what the process involved.

Silently we climbed up the old servants' stairway and onto the upper landing, and once again, I felt my feet sinking into the deep blue carpet. I looked along the corridor, remembering my previous visit, wondering if Viyesha had any idea I'd been present at the Blue Moon Ball. If she did, she said nothing, and continued walking ahead. Then we were at the foot of the stone spiral stairway leading up into the Clock Tower. Viyesha turned.

"Are you sure, Emily? With knowledge comes power, but also danger. You are stepping over a threshold from which there is no return."

"What do you mean?" I faltered.

"Once you have seen the crystal and know of its power, you will become a real and tangible threat to The Lunari. At this moment in time, if you choose to walk away, there is still a chance

I can save you. But once you have looked upon the crystal, you will have no choice. You must join us or The Lunari will destroy you. I will not be able to save you."

I swallowed. "I understand, Viyesha, but I have to see it. I have to know."

"Very well," she said, and turned to climb the stone stairs. Then she stopped, turned to me and said, "Emily, I have to ask. Have you told anybody what is going on here. Your school friends, your mother?"

"No," I said instinctively, "of course not." I laughed nervously. "I don't think they'd believe me anyway, the whole thing is so......." I was going to say preposterous, but realised how insulting that would sound. "So unbelievable," I said.

I thought back to what I'd told Seth and Tash. Although I'd told them what was going on, I'd recanted and made a joke of it. The question was whether they believed me. They had their suspicions, I knew, but would they come looking for answers, just as I had, or would I be able to convince them that all was well and I'd just been paranoid?

"Please, Viyesha, you have nothing to fear."

"I hope so, because The Lunari would not think twice about eliminating extraneous threats. It would look like an accident, of course. They never leave a trail."

For a second, I wavered. If I thought for a moment I was placing my friends or family in danger, I could not go on. But what did they know? Nothing tangible. Just a silly hocus-pocus story.

"Lead on, Viyesha, I need to see the crystal." I spoke clearly and confidently, my words providing a cover for my beating heart and dry mouth.

We carried on climbing the spiral stairway, higher and higher, up into the Clock Tower, until an ornately carved, heavy oak door, with a huge iron keyhole, blocked our way. Viyesha removed a loose brick to one side of the doorway and took out a large iron key. She placed it in the lock, slowly turned it and pushed the door open.

I don't know what I was expecting, but I was disappointed. It was an empty, hexagonal room, with long thin windows on every alternate wall. The walls were made from the same honey-coloured Cotswold stone as the rest of Hartswell Hall and a vaulted ceiling rose above us, creating light and space. Sunshine flooded in, giving the room a warm, bright, welcoming feel and the only thing of any interest that I could see was a series of strange blue and green markings etched into the smooth, worn floorboards in the centre of the room.

"Oh," I said, taken aback, "Is this it?"

"This is it," said Viyesha, laughing at my confusion. "What were you expecting, Emily?"

"Well, the flames of eternal youth, a big blue fire, I suppose."

"It looks very different at the time of the Blue Moon, I assure you, but for now, there isn't a great deal to see."

"But the crystal, where is it?" I asked.

"All in good time," said Viyesha. "Wait here." She walked to one side of the hexagonal room, and loosened another brick in the wall, which she placed on the floor. Behind it was a lever, which she turned. As she did so, a portion of the wall slid to one side, revealing a small stone alcove in which stood a silver casket, less than a foot long and decorated with ancient symbols. She carefully took it out, warning me as she did so, "Remember not to step over the threshold, Emily. The power in this room is still great and I cannot vouch for its effects. Stay where you are and observe. If the light becomes too bright for your eyes, look away and I will place the crystal back in the casket."

My heart was in my mouth as I watched Viyesha place the casket on the floor to one side of the hieroglyphics and open the lid. Immediately, the most brilliant blue light filled the room. I leaned forward to see better and there, nestling inside the casket was a large blue crystal, its many facets glinting and shining so brightly, I could hardly look at it.

"Avert your gaze if the light is too strong," advise Viyesha. "People have been blinded by looking at the crystal too long."

I did as she bid, looking to one side of the casket, but still mesmerised by the blue dancing light that shone around the room.

"It's beautiful," I gasped. "I've never seen anything like it." I felt the crystal around my neck glowing, giving off warmth, as if in tune with the larger crystal.

I watched Viyesha through half lidded eyes, as she picked the crystal up. Brilliant blue light engulfed her hands and her arms, running in rivulets of energy up to her shoulders. She closed her eyes and breathed in deeply, absorbing the crystal's energy into her being.

"Its power is waning," said Viyesha. "A residual energy remains, but not enough to reenergise and rejuvenate us, although enough to do you serious harm, Emily. You wouldn't last two minutes."

Gently, she placed the crystal back into the casket and closed the lid.

"That's enough, Emily, I cannot risk you seeing more."

At once the room seemed dark and flat and I felt the most intense disappointment, as my body were being denied an essential nutrient, making me feel negative and irritable.

"Once you've experienced the power, you want more," explained Viyesha, "but more would kill you. It's like the most powerful drug, overcoming rational thought and possessing you with desire. What you are experiencing now are withdrawal symptoms, which will fade as your etheric body stabilises. Perhaps now you understand a little of the crystal's power. In the wrong hands, it would be destructive force, which is why we guard it with our lives."

"Thank you, Viyesha," I whispered, "thank you for showing me. Tell me, what are the markings on the floor? Are they to do with the crystal?"

"They are the coordinates that unlock the crystal's power," she said. "Ancient Egyptian hieroglyphs aligned with the natural magnetic lines of the earth. When the crystal is placed within their circle, at the time of the Blue moon, they act like a nuclear reactor releasing the crystal's full power. Its light becomes intense, filling the entire room, enabling us to bathe in it and absorb its energy."

She picked up the casket and placed it in the alcove, then moved the lever back into the upright position, triggering the wall panel to slide into place. She replaced the loose brick, then walked back around the room to where I stood.

"Now do you understand why you would not survive the crystal at the time of the Blue Moon?" she asked. "An ordinary full moon would be sufficient, and even that may be too much for you. That is the gamble we are asking you to take, and to which Theo is so violently opposed."

"Yes, I understand," I said, thinking of Theo and longing to be with him, imagining occasions in the future when we could bathe together in the crystal's light, feeling its power simultaneously. It was a powerful image and I quickly pushed it from my mind.

"Surely the crystal needs protecting, Viyesha," I said, "Couldn't anyone come in and take it?"

"Oh believe me, if anyone other than us were to touch the crystal, the guardians would know about it," she replied, "They'd be here in an instant."

Viyesha tensed suddenly, her senses on high alert. "We must go," she said urgently, "things are happening."

"What things?" I asked, confused, "How do you know?"

"The Lunari are coming," she said, closing her eyes. "I feel their presence drawing close. Come, we must hurry."

She quickly stepped over the threshold of the hexagonal room, closed the oak door and turned the key in the lock. I watched her place it behind the loose brick, then followed her down the spiral staircase, hardly daring to think what lay ahead.

30. Attack 2

As we came down the central stairway, we found Theo, Violet and Joseph in the reception area, waiting for Viyesha. They looked tense and ill at ease.

Aquila stood in the background, surly and menacing as ever, and I carefully avoided his gaze. Pantera stood by his side, her face impassive and impossible to read.

"They've arrived," said Theo in a flat voice. "Flew in to Birmingham Airport in a private jet just minutes ago. We should go to meet them."

"Agreed," said Viyesha. "we'll take the limousine. We need to talk to them, appraise them of the situation before they arrive at Hartswell Hall. It's too bad Leon isn't here."

"Where is he?" I asked.

"He had a business meeting," said Viyesha. "He should be back by now, but we can't delay. I'll call him from the car and ask him to meet us at the airport."

She paused, then quietly gave her orders.

"Aquila, bring the limousine to the front door. Joseph and Theo, come with me. Violet, stay on reception, it's business as usual for our guests. Pantera, continue to organise the champagne reception for the Plastic Surgeons."

She addressed me: "Emily, soon it will be time for you to meet The Lunari. Please, wait in the ballroom and don't come out until I summon you. That is most important. Do you understand?"

I nodded, not trusting my voice to speak.

"Let me stay with Emily, mother," pleaded Theo. "I can't leave her alone. She needs me with her."

"No, Theo." Viyesha was firm. "I need you with me. We have to face The Lunari together. Come, we have delayed long enough. We must go."

I hadn't seen Aquila leave, but already the limousine was drawing up outside the front door. Viyesha hurried out, followed by Joseph, who turned and winked at me as he went. For a split second, Theo held me in his arms, speaking to me softly. "Do as my mother says, Emily. Go into the ballroom and wait there. Don't come out until she tells you. Whatever happens, remember I love you."

Then he was gone and the limousine was speeding down the drive, wheels spinning and gravel flying.

I turned to Violet.

"This is it," I said, shakily.

She smiled. "It'll be fine, Emily, don't worry. My mother's in control. You have nothing to fear from The Lunari."

There was a snort from Pantera, who still stood at one side of the reception area, observing me closely.

"You have everything to fear from The Lunari," she spat at me. "They can extinguish you like a flame on a candle if they so wish. Enjoy what remaining time you have."

With a look of scorn and derision, she brushed past me and disappeared down the corridor, leaving the air churning behind her.

I looked in panic at Violet.

"Ignore her. Just do as my mother says, Emily," she said quickly, "Go into the ballroom, and stay there until she returns."

Needing no further prompting, I let myself in to the ballroom. I shut the double doors firmly behind me, and leant against the doorframe, trying to calm my rising panic. Inside, all appeared normal. The large purple sofas were soft and inviting, sunlight streamed in through the windows and sunbeams played games on the glass facets of the chandelier. The pleated drapes, modern art and contemporary colour scheme was as fashionable and chic as you could wish for, creating an air of luxury that was a million years away from a world of secret societies, age-old beings and eternal youth. I moved quickly to one of the sofas and sat down, pulling a large cushion on to my lap and holding it tightly. Instinct told me to get out of Hartswell Hall while I still could and run to the safety of my home, but I knew that would only give me temporary respite. I had helped to create this situation. There had been enough opportunities to walk away, and every time I'd forged ahead, all too aware of doors closing irrevocably behind me. Now I had to face the strange world that had become my reality and hope I was strong enough to survive it.

My cell phone pinged suddenly, making me jump, and I saw that a text message had come through. Quickly, I scrolled down. It was from Tash:

Seth & I worried bout u. Ur mum says u r @ Hall.
On the way. One 4 all, etc. xxxx

This was not what I needed right now. I appreciated their concern and they obviously thought they were helping, but this was a misplaced rescue mission. They were out of their depth and this could have serious repercussions if they arrived at the wrong time. More than anything, I didn't want to place my friends in danger. If they rushed in just as The Lunari were arriving, who knows what might happen? Like it or not, I was on my own and I had to put them off. I quickly texted Tash, trying to sound as normal as possible:

Thnx 4 ur concern, all ok. Having quiet afternoon with Theo.
Get my drift? I need space, dudes. c u Monday. xxx

I pressed SEND, then stared aghast, as my message refused to send. What was going on? My phone pinged again and the 'low battery' message filled the screen. No, I screamed silently. Not now. This was the worst possible timing. I pressed SEND again, but it refused to go. Now I had a real situation on my hands. All I could hope was that Seth and Tash turned up before The Lunari arrived and I could persuade them to go.

I went to the ballroom door, opened it and looked out. Violet was still there, manning reception.

"Violet," I whispered.

She looked up, eyes wide with anxiety. "What?"

"We have a situation. Seth and Tash are on their way. I have to head them off but I can't get in touch with them. My phone has a flat battery. I can't let them arrive at the same time as The Lunari. And I can't let Pantera see them. Heaven knows what she would do."

"Do you want to use this phone?" she asked, indicating the reception system.

"Yes, good thinking." I started to cross the reception area, then froze in my tracks, as I saw two familiar figures walking up the driveway.

"It's too late, they're coming. They must have texted from the driveway. What can I do?" My mind raced and went blank.

Violet took control.

"They have no idea of the danger they're walking into. We have to get them out of here before the Lunari arrive. Go back into the ballroom and I'll send them into you. Persuade them everything is okay and get them to leave as quickly as possible, preferably by the French windows. While you do that, I'll divert Pantera's attention."

"Okay, good plan," I said, trying to calm the panic rising within me.

I stepped back into the ballroom, closed the door and went to sit once again on one of the large sofas.

"Just the person I want to see, Emily Morgan," said a voice from the far side of the room.

Startled, I turned to find a glamorous young woman, wearing a body-hugging cat suit that emphasised her impressive curves, emerging from behind the long aubergine drapes. I recognised her from television. It was the glamour model, Kimberley Chartreuse, and she held a gun in her hand.

"What are you doing?" I asked, not understanding how she knew my name and why she was in the ballroom, let alone pointing a gun at me.

"That's a pretty crystal you're wearing," she said, moving forward.

"What do you mean?" I asked.

Instinctively, my hand went to the crystal around my neck. Even if I tried to summon Theo, I knew he couldn't come, and I was all too aware that Seth and Tash could walk into the ballroom at any moment. This was not good timing.

Kimberley fixed her gaze on me disparagingly, opening wide her huge kohled eyes with their bat wing eyelash extensions, and let out a deep sigh of exasperation through her overly large shiny red lips.

"Quit the dippy chick routine, Emily," she said in exasperation, "Let's cut to the chase. I know about the crystals the de Lucis family wear around their necks... how they have youth-giving properties that have kept them young for years. What I didn't realise was that you wore one as well, which makes my life so much easier. I thought I was going to have to take you hostage and trade you for a crystal. But here you are, alone and unprotected, wearing a crystal necklace. What was the family thinking of? Now, take it off and give it to me."

My mind began working overtime. She obviously didn't know about the large blue crystal in the Clock Tower. That was good.

But if she took my crystal, I'd be unprotected, and that was dangerous. On the other hand, I needed to get rid of her as quickly as possible.

As I considered my options, I heard voices outside the ballroom door and saw the handle turn. Quick as a flash, Kimberley slid back behind the curtains, hissing at me: "Act normal. Remember, I have a gun pointing at you."

The door opened, and Violet showed Seth and Tash into the room.

"Here's Emily," she said in a bright voice, "You see, everything's fine. She's just waiting for Theo."

"Hi guys," I waved at them, trying to sound normal, willing Violet to see the panic in my eyes. She didn't.

"I'll go and see if Pantera needs any help with the conference," she said in the same bright voice, and left the ballroom, closing the door behind her.

"Are you alright, Emily?" asked Tash, stepping forward.

"We were worried," explained Seth.

"Yeah, I'm fine, I tried to text you, but the battery in my phone was flat…" I started to say, but a voice from behind the curtain interrupted me.

"Shut up, Emily, and take off your necklace." Kimberley Chartreuse emerged from behind the curtain, moving forward and pointing her gun at my head.

"OMG, you're Kimberley Chartreuse. I've seen your reality show on TV," said Tash in an awestruck voice.

"Cool," said Seth, eyeing her up and down.

This was clearly not what they were expecting.

"Shut it, both of you," said Kimberley, "Can't you see I have a gun pointing at your friend's head?"

"It's okay, guys, don't panic," I said, sounding more cheerful than I felt.

"Who's panicking? I'm not," said Seth.

"Typical," said Tash, rolling her eyes.

"Cheers, guys," I said, disdainfully, "So much for rescuing me."

"Why d'you want the necklace anyway?" Seth addressed Kimberley, "Oh, I get it, you think the crystal has magical properties or something like that. "

"Be quiet, all of you. Take off the necklace, Emily, and give it to me," demanded Kimberley.

"I can't," I said truthfully.

"I don't think you understand how serious I am, Emily," said Kimberley, "I want that crystal."

"No, I mean, really I can't. It has no clasp. The chain is sealed around my neck. See?" I held up my hair to show her.

Kimberley laughed. "Removing a necklace is simple when you come prepared."

As she spoke, she took a small pair of stainless steel wire cutters from her pocket and cut through the silver chain. My necklace fell into her open palm and she wrapped her fingers around it. Immediately, I felt depleted and empty, and an intense weariness filled my being. In the same split second, Kimberley shrieked and threw down the crystal.

"What is this?" she cried out, "It's just burnt me." She looked at her hand and there on her palm was a red, raw burn mark.

Tash watched horrified, but Seth was enjoying himself immensely.

"I don't think it likes you, Kimberley," he said, grinning widely.

"Seth," I said in a warning voice, but he was on a roll.

"If that's what the small crystal does to you, I don't rate your chances with the big one." Kimberley stared at him, taking in the implication of his words.

"So, this isn't the one I want," she said, picking up my crystal necklace with a small silk handkerchief and holding it up, "Turns out there's a big crystal."

"It's only make believe…" began Seth, then saw my expression. His eyes widened.

"OMG, it's true," said Tash, "that story you told us…"

"I think you'd better take me to the big crystal, Emily," said Kimberley, placing my necklace in her pocket and moving swiftly across the room. She pointed the gun at Tash.

"Emily," said Tash in a shrill voice, "Tell her where the big crystal is, for heaven's sake."

"I can't," I said, feeling faint and cold, "It's too dangerous."

And not just for you, I thought silently. If The Lunari find us with the crystal, they'll kill us all. Unless Pantera gets there first. I stared, not knowing what to do. The situation had suddenly become critical. Now my friends were in real danger.

"Take me to the crystal or Ginger gets it," said Kimberley, raising the gun to Tash's head.

"I am so not ginger," said Tash faintly, "I'm a redhead."

"She hates the word ginger even more than being held at gunpoint," said Seth.

"Shut up, both of you," said Kimberley in a low voice, "this is no joke." She clicked the safety catch off the gun, "I will use this if I have to."

"Emily, do something," said Tash, her voice trembling.

"Okay. Let them go and I'll show you the crystal," I bargained.

"D'you think I'm a fool?" asked Kimberley, in a steely voice, "They're my collateral. They're coming with us. Now, show me where the crystal is, Emily."

A vague plan formed in my mind. It was crazy and dangerous, but it was all I had. "Alright. I'll show you where the crystal is, Kimberley, but we have to hurry. The family will be back soon."

Kimberley gestured to Seth to move in front of Tash.

"Let's go," she instructed, "And don't try anything stupid."

Slowly, I opened the ballroom double doors, praying that Violet would be standing at the reception desk, but the area was empty and she was nowhere to be seen. If only I had my necklace. I felt horribly vulnerable without it.

"Up the stairs," I informed Kimberley.

"Good girl," she said patronisingly, "Just keep going and your friends won't get hurt."

We climbed the stairs and reached the central landing, Seth following me, and Kimberley bringing up the rear, jabbing the gun into Tash's back.

"Now where?" asked Kimberley.

"To the left."

"Come on, Emily, move it. I need to find this crystal quickly. I don't want your precious family spoiling my plans." She jabbed the gun into Tash's head to make her point.

"Please don't screw up, Emily," said Tash, tears in her eyes, "I don't want to die."

"You won't," I assured her, "Everything will be fine."

"What plans are they, Kimberley?" asked Seth, conversationally, as if they were talking over coffee. I had to admire him, he was very cool.

She laughed. "To be young and beautiful for ever, of course. Have you any idea what I go through to look like this? Botox, collagen, hair extensions, nail extensions, teeth veneers…. It's a full time bloody job. I've been snipped, tucked, lifted, stretched, trimmed and filled, but I can't hold back time. I need a more permanent solution."

"Crikey," said Seth, "and I thought my life was tough."

By now we'd reached the stairway leading to the old servants' quarters. We climbed the steps and then we were walking along the upper passageway, our feet sinking into the deep blue carpet. Then the spiral staircase was ahead of us. I began to climb, my heart racing, with Seth, Tash and Kimberley following. Would my plan work? Would the family stay away long enough for Seth and Tash to escape? Would Pantera sense someone entering the Clock Tower room? I prayed I wasn't leading us all to a violet death. I just needed a few more minutes. We reached the old oak door with its carved symbols and huge iron keyhole.

"We're here, Kimberley," I said, "This is where you let me and my friends go. I'll show you where the crystal is, but I'm not going into the room. It's too risky."

"Open the door," she instructed, "I want to see what's inside."

Quickly, I pulled back the loose brick and took out the key, placing it in the keyhole. It turned smoothly and then the door was opening and we were on the threshold of the Clock Tower room.

"Where's the crystal?" demanded Kimberly, unable to hide her disappointment at finding an empty room.

"Over there," I pointed to the far wall. "There's a secret panel with a casket behind it."

"Get it out," she instructed.

I hovered on the threshold, Viyesha's words fresh in my head. Seth and Tash watched, wide-eyed.

"This is as far as I come, Kimberley. The room has been attuned and isn't safe. I'm not stepping over the threshold. If you want the crystal, it's over there. Now, let us go."

"I don't think so, Emily. Get the casket out. Now!" She held the gun against Tash's temple. "If you value your friend's life, you'll step into the room."

"Please, Emily," said Tash faintly.

This wasn't part of my plan, but I had no choice. Closing my eyes, I stepped into the room. Nothing happened. No strange feelings and no sudden aging. I was okay. Slowly, I walked over to the loose brick and pulled it out, revealing the lever. As Viyesha had done, I moved it to the right, and, as before, a panel in the wall opened, revealing the secret alcove containing the silver casket.

"Wow," whistled Seth, "That is cool."

"So much for the room not being safe, Emily," scoffed Kimberley, "A nice ruse but I'm not buying it. Now pick up the casket and place it in the centre of the room."

With shaking hands, I lifted it out, and placed it amidst the hieroglyphics. Kimberley watched as the ancient symbols started to glow, and the faint, inky blue and green became bright and effervescent. I was in unchartered territory now. Viyesha had kept the crystal away from the hieroglyphics, so I had no idea what would happen. She'd said they would act like a nuclear reactor, triggering its power, so I assumed I was about to see the crystal in all its post-Blue Moon glory, and was all too horribly aware what that signified for me.

"Open the casket," said Kimberley, standing in the doorway, her eyes full of anticipation and wonder. This was what she'd been searching for, the answer to her prayers, eternal youth within her grasp. She had no idea of the crystal's destructive power.

"I can't," I said, "The crystal is too powerful. I don't know what it will do."

"If you won't, Ginger will," said Kimberley, pushing Tash into the room.

"Emily, don't make me do this," sobbed Tash, "I don't want to go near the crystal. I just want to go home."

I looked at Tash and at Kimberley. If I opened the casket, this could be the end for me. But what choice did I have?

While I procrastinated, Seth grabbed the opportunity.

"I'll do it," he said, stepping forward, in a misplaced attempt to play the hero.

While I admired his bravery, I couldn't let him. He had no idea of the consequences and, as he went to open the casket, I snatched it out of his reach.

"No, Seth, you can't. Get back! You don't know the stakes you're playing with. I'll do it. Everyone get out of the room."

Looking surprised at my tone of voice, Seth backed away.

"I mean it," I said, "Every one, step back over the threshold. I don't know what's going to happen."

Kimberley gestured for Seth and Tash to fall back, and they all stood in the doorway, watching me silently.

I said a prayer, placed the casket on the floor and slowly lifted the lid. Immediately, the room was filled with a brilliant blue light. The crystal sparkled and shone, bright blue veins of pulsing energy running along its facets, spilling out of the casket and onto the floorboards.

"Oh my God," whispered Kimberly, completely awestruck. "It's beautiful. I had no idea. I can feel the energy. It's already making me feel young."

"OMG, that is amazing," said Tash.

"Yowza wowza," said Seth, "Look at that!"

Blue light filled the room and, despite the danger, I felt an overwhelming sense of wellbeing and love as I looked at the crystal.

"Pick it up," instructed Kimberley.

Aware that this really could be the last thing I did, I placed my fingers around the crystal's cold, hard surface and felt its warm light travelling up my arm, energising and rejuvenating. Slowly, I picked it up and held it in the palm of my hand, blue shards of energy pulsing around me. I felt amazing, invincible and strong, as though a powerful drug was pulsing through my veins.

"Dangerous my foot!" exclaimed Kimberley. "You just want eternal youth for yourself. Let me have it."

She dropped the gun and, pushing Seth and Tash out of the way, darted towards the crystal, her eyes glinting with desire, the blue light flickering in her face. She smiled at me as her fingers closed around the crystal and then it was in her hand, and the blue flames were running up her arm, pulsing all round her body, consuming her in a living blue light.

I turned to Seth and Tash.

"For God's sake, get out of here now! Before the family gets back or Pantera comes. She can't know you've seen the crystal."

"Not without you, Emily," said Tash, firmly.

"We're not leaving unless you come with us," said Seth.

I could see they were determined, but they had no idea of the danger they were in. I had to act quickly if I were to save my friends.

"Okay," I said, thinking fast, "There's a door at the bottom of the Clock Tower leading to the gardens. We'll use that. Let's go."

I just hoped Joseph had replaced the warped, swollen door. If not, we were dead, because by now, I knew Pantera would be on her way. Quickly, we ran down the spiral steps, Seth and Tash leading the way.

"Don't take the corridor," I instructed, "Keep going down."

It seemed to take forever, going round and round, down and down the spiral staircase, until finally we reached the ground floor. I looked around. We were in a small dark empty chamber and there to one side was the door, thankfully replaced with new timber, a metal key in the keyhole.

"This way," I said, running to the door and turning the key. The door swung outwards, sunlight pouring in, and I opened it wide for Seth and Tash. I let them believe I was coming with them, following them outside and saying: "Over there to the circular fountain, there's a pathway that leads to the church." Then, at the last minute, I stepped back in, closed the door behind me and turned the key.

"Emily, what are you doing?" cried Seth, turning and hammering on the door.

"Come out, Emily, don't be stupid," called Tash.

"Sorry guys," I called from behind the door, "I have to go back. I can't come with you. Take the path to the church and you'll be safe. I have to see Theo. I'll see you in college on Monday and I'll explain everything."

I left them calling and hammering on the door, and prayed I was doing the right thing.

As fast as I could, I ran back up the spiral staircase, up to the Clock Tower room, not knowing what I would find. Breathless, I arrived and stared at the sight before me. Kimberley was standing in the centre of the room, bathed in blue light, the crystal still in her hand, rivulets of blue energy covering her body in a criss-cross network. She looked radiant, her skin glowing and translucent, her eyes shining and bright. I knew what she was feeling. That over-powering sensation of wellbeing and euphoria, as if you could do anything, take on the world. Then, slowly her face began to change and I saw a startled, uncomprehending look pass over her features. Before she could speak, there was a popping sound as her lips burst and collagen oozed down her chin. The veneers in her mouth dropped like peas from a pod, revealing blackened stumps beneath, and her hair became wispy and grey, the long extensions dropping to the floor like freshly cut corn. Her skin began to droop and sag, hanging on her bones like rags on a tree, and her body began to stoop and shrink, her catsuit too large for her wizened frame. With a horrible smacking sound, her breast implants fell to the floor, simply too large for the shrunken creature she'd become.

"No," she screamed, in a harsh, rasping voice, looking at the wrinkled, mottled skin on her arms. "What's happening? I want to stay young." She threw the crystal onto the floor and backed towards the wall.

"Stop it happening," she croaked at me, "reverse the process."

I stared at her aghast. "I can't. I'm sorry. I tried to warn you. The crystal's just too powerful."

Her back was up against the window and I could hardly bear to look at the grotesque creature she'd become. She seemed to crumple and shrink before my eyes, her skin drying out like old parchment, shrinking and splitting to reveal the skeleton beneath. I turned away, unable to watch this premature death and decomposition. It was horrible but at least the demise of Kimberly Chartreuse was quick. Within seconds, she was nothing more than a heap of bones, and then even the bones began to disintegrate, turning into a pile of fine grey dust. What normally took thousands of years had occurred in less than a minute.

I slumped back against the cold stone wall of the Clock Tower, stunned and shocked, the thought running through my head: "That could have been me". If I thought the ordeal was over, however, I was wrong.

The crystal lay in the centre of the room, blue and pulsing, the energy radiating outwards. Although I didn't hear anything, I was aware of something above my head and slowly looked up. There above me, nestled into the wooden struts that formed the room's arched roof was a malevolent black entity. It hung, like an ominous black bat, two glistening eyes watching all that had happened. I tried to scream, but the sound died in my throat and I was aware of a terrible chill emanating from the creature. I pushed myself closer into the wall, wondering if I could make it to the door or whether I should try to put the crystal back in the casket. This, I knew, was one of the Dark Ones that Theo had mentioned, dark matter that sought human form, its only means of achieving its goal the crystal that lay before me. What was it Theo had said? This was the threat the Guardians took seriously, the dark force they thought they'd destroyed that night in the fields. Clearly, they hadn't been successful, and a stray had somehow found its way to the crystal. When I opened the door, I must have inadvertently let it in.

Instinctively, I put my hand to my neck, expecting to find my crystal there. Then I remembered. Kimberley had taken it. So where was it now? I looked over to the pile of dust at the far side of the room, and there, twinkling and shining amidst the remains of Kimberley Chartreuse, lay my crystal with its silver chain. With a gasp, I dived for it, my fingers delving into the dust and clasping the crystal for all I was worth. At the same time, the entity dropped and I had the sensation of a black octopus landing over me, cold and clammy, fastening on to me and sucking out any positive thought. Never had I felt so negative, weak and utterly exposed. I tried to scream, but the blackness filled my mouth, suffocating and smothering, and as I fought to breathe, I realised the monster was sucking the breath out of me, pulling out my life force with deadly speed and precision. Just as I felt I was slipping into unconsciousness, a blood-chilling, deep-throated roar filled the Clock Tower room, its reverberations echoing around me, and I felt the hideous black entity being ripped from my body. I was thrown to one side like a rag doll and lay, spent and exhausted, watching as another black shape, all sinewy muscle and gleaming fur, fell upon my attacker. For what seemed like an age, but was in reality no more than a few seconds, the two forces did battle: one an amorphous black shadow, the other a magnificent black panther, with gleaming white teeth and savage yellow eyes. I cowered as I watched the panther sink its hooked claws into the black matter, tearing it apart with power and fury. A horrible screaming rent the air and within seconds the black entity was dead, ripped to shreds that fell to the floor like pieces of blackened, burnt rubber. Instantly, they began to disintegrate, evaporating into the air until nothing remained.

Silently, the huge black cat watched, making sure no portion remained, then in front of my eyes, its sleek black form began to change. The fur retracted, its shape elongated upwards, and it began to take on human form. Suddenly, I was looking at Pantera, haughty, ruthless and condescending as ever.

"Pantera," I gasped, "Thank you…"

"Thank you for what?" she spat at me, "You think I did this for you? My job is to protect the crystal. Not you. If you didn't have your protective necklace in your hand, I would have destroyed you as well. " Her voice was full of hatred and dislike. She indicated the pile of dust on the floor that had once been Kimberley Chartreuse. "You and that harlot let this damned creature in. You had no right coming to this room. It is hallowed territory and you betrayed us."

I gasped at her words. "No, Pantera. I would never betray you…."

"Silence! You should have gone the same way as her. Done us all a favour."

"What kind of creature are you?" I asked her. "Do you have no compassion or feeling?"

"I am older and more powerful than you will ever be," she hissed back at me.

Quickly, she picked up the pulsing blue crystal and placed it back inside the casket, closing the lid firmly. At once, the room became drab and monotone, as if we were in an old black and white movie, and I felt a chill descend around me. She placed the casket into the alcove and moved the lever into the upright position, so the panel slid back into place. Then placing the loose brick into the wall, she turned to me and said in a cold, matter of fact voice: "Your death would be a blessing. You place the crystal at risk, which we cannot allow. Whatever the family's wishes, your days are numbered. I personally will see to it."

She turned to walk out of the room and nearly collided with Theo, moving rapidly up the stairs.

"Emily," he shouted, running in to the room and seeing the dusty heap that had once been Kimberley. "What are you doing in here? Are you all right? Thank goodness Pantera was here to protect you." He pulled me to him and for a split second my eyes met Pantera's over his shoulder. Her enmity and hatred sliced into me, then she was gone, disappearing down the spiral stairs. I clung to Theo, feeling his strong arms around me, providing a haven of safety and security. He saw Kimberley's small black pistol, lying on the floor where she had thrown it, and held me tighter. "Emily, what happened here today? I should never have left you."

"I'm okay," I said quietly, "Now you're here, Theo, everything's alright."

But his next words brought a fresh chill to my heart and my newfound feeling of wellbeing was short lived.

"I'm sorry, Emily, we have no time," he said gently, "The Lunari are downstairs and they want to meet you."

31. The Lunari

Theo and I walked into the library. The curtains had been drawn and the light was dim. The family sat at one side of the large polished mahogany table, and I noticed Leon was back. As usual, Aquila and Pantera stood to one side, surly and aggressive. I made sure not to make eye contact with either of them. I needed my wits about me and would not let them intimidate me. Two empty chairs were placed at the table, between Violet and Joseph, and Theo and I sat in them. Opposite were three more empty places and I looked at Theo questioningly, but he shook his head, telling me not to speak. We waited in silence for no more than a minute, then the library doors were flung open and three individuals, wearing long blue cloaks, entered the room. Each had the smooth even features of the de Lucis family and long blonde hair. I guessed they were male, but their beauty was so intense, they could have passed for either gender. In a split second, my eyes took in the details: the dark glasses giving an air of intrigue and mystery, the ivory skin and cruel mouths, the exquisitely manicured hands, large jewelled rings and long fingernails tapering to sinister points. They were sleek and deadly, like beautiful vipers.

As they moved into the room, everything began to ripple and change around me, as if in a dream sequence. The walls extended outwards and the wooden panelling became rough, dark stone, while the ceiling rose upwards into an inky blackness. Beneath my feet the floor became smooth and cold, and torch lanterns, placed at regular intervals along the walls, created sombre, dancing shadows, their flickering light revealing strange markings carved into the stone. Yet again, I noticed a circle crossed by an infinity symbol. An eerie chill filled the air, making me shiver, and I realised we were in a stone chamber of cavernous proportions. The table at which we sat had also altered, changing into a huge oval of smooth black granite, lit from above by a large, wrought iron lantern, bearing hundreds of small burning candles, and suspended from the cavern roof by a heavy black chain. Our seats were immovable stone thrones, placed at regular intervals around the table, each made comfortable by cushions in thick, blue woven fabric.

The three creatures took their seats at the head of the table and the one in the centre began to speak, making my skin prickle and the hairs on the back of my neck stand up.

"Good evening, every one. Good evening, Emily. Please forgive our indulgence, we do so prefer to be in familiar surroundings. As it was not possible for you to come to us, so we have come to you, bringing our world with us."

He spoke in soft, sibilant tones, his voice smooth and caressing, but with the hypnotic power of a snake about to strike. A hint of menace hung in the air and I felt I'd entered a deep pool where hidden underwater currents swirled ominously below the surface, threatening to pull me under.

Once again, I looked at Theo, questioningly, and again he shook his head.

"Emily, I must apologise," the creature continued, "I have the advantage. I know you, yet you know nothing of me. Let me introduce myself. I am Badru, head of the Lunari, and these are my elders, Atsu and Ata, the twins."

The two men either side of him raised their fingers off the table in greeting, but neither spoke or altered their expression.

Badru held his arms aloft, gesturing at the chamber around him.

"A little dimensional trickery, Emily, nothing more. Our world exists alongside yours, as real and tangible as your reality. We have simply created a bridge from one to the other, for the purposes of our 'discussion'. A word of caution, though, do not leave the table. You run the risk of becoming lost in our reality and there may be no way back."

He smiled, but there was no warmth in his face, just an icy composure.

"Let's cut to the chase, Emily. We are most impressed with what Viyesha has achieved. " He nodded his head slightly towards Viyesha in acknowledgement. "Hartswell Hall has become a living entity, reborn and renewed. Its energy field is powerful and its protective powers are strong. So far, so good, but then the story changes… as you step into the picture."

He paused and seemed to choose his words carefully.

"It seems to me that you compromise all we have established over the centuries, the stability, the safety, the security of our world and our people. I know of the events that have taken place today, Emily... Pantera has regaled me how you led a would-be thief straight to our crystal and allowed one of the Dark Ones to enter our most hallowed of places..."

I opened my mouth, but he put up his hand to silence me.

"You shall have your opportunity to speak, Emily, but hear me out first. Perhaps you do not realise the danger in which you inadvertently placed us... The woman was nothing, an expendable frivolity, who would never have survived the crystal's power. It is doubtful she will even be missed in her own superficial world. But the Feeder was different... To allow a creature such as that to get so close to the crystal is unforgiveable and a situation that must never be replicated. Thanks to Pantera's quick action, the threat was removed," he bowed briefly in her direction, "but we can rest assured that others will follow. And eventually, the Reptilia themselves will come, desperate for the crystal's energy to give them human form. We cannot allow anyone or anything to place us in that level of danger."

Badru still wore his dark glasses, so I was unable to see his eyes, but his voice was icy and I felt panic rising within me. This was real. This was happening.

He continued: "How can I put it, Emily? You are a chink in our armour. You bring with you nothing but weakness and immaturity, impetuousness and naivety. Plus, your human ties are too strong. Quite simply, you do not fit the criteria for joining our order and I can see no reason to extend an invitation to you, despite Viyesha's intercession on your behalf."

Theo's hand closed over mine on the table.

"Very commendable, Theo," said Badru, disparagingly. "You will of course defend her. But what of your family? Where do your loyalties lie? You know we cannot allow outsiders in, unless they become one of us. Must we destroy you as well?"

The anger in his voice was palpable and I began to feel afraid. I had no doubt these creatures could kill me without thinking twice.

"I know the rules," said Theo tightly. "Emily does not present a threat."

"On the contrary," said Badru, "I think she does. Today's events prove that. She knows too much and others can use her against us. Do I have to spell it out, Theo? She threatens our very existence. And by association, you are complicit."

"No, Badru, I cannot accept that," interjected Viyesha.

"Silence, Viyesha," he commanded. "You should have let the Guardians deal with this. Instead of which, you allow an outsider to see the very thing that is our life force and place us in great danger. You have been lax and the time has come for action."

"Don't I get a say in this?" I said, pulling my hand away from Theo and glaring at Badru. I'd heard enough, the time had come for me to speak and defend myself.

He regarded me curiously. "Very well, speak if you must," he said, disparagingly. "This is a fair trial, I suppose."

"I would never compromise the crystal's safety, Badru. Kimberley Chartreuse had a gun and gave me no choice, but I knew she wouldn't survive. It seemed a watertight plan."

"Commendable, my dear," he said sarcastically.

"And to prove my loyalty, if you will extend the invitation, I am ready to join you…"

"No," said Theo faintly, "it's too risky. I can't lose you again."

"Ah, of course, Theo, you believe Emily to be your long lost love," said Badru, with a chilling smile. "How sweet. What a lovely story. The woman you've waited for through the centuries has come to you once again. But what proof do you have of this, Theo? A face on a necklace? Circumstantial. You have nothing concrete to place before me."

"Badru, you have to give her the benefit of the doubt," interrupted Viyesha. "At least give us some time. It could be her. We have to find out."

"Wait," I said, "I don't know if I've been reincarnated or not. I have no memories of a past life. But I do know that Theo and I have an amazing connection. There is a bond between us I can't explain. We belong together."

"Yes, yes, love's young dream, very romantic," said Badru in a bored voice, 'if that's your defence, I'd give up now. It is really neither here nor there whether you are Theo's lost love. All I want to know is whether you have anything to offer us. And at the moment I see nothing. In fact, I see less than nothing. I see threat and danger."

"There is something," I said. "Viyesha told me I wouldn't survive holding the crystal. It was too powerful. But look at me, Badru. I'm still here. I should have aged and died like Kimberley, but I didn't. I held the crystal and survived. Does that not tell you something?"

He leant forward and regarded me closely.

"It is true the crystal is still powerful and should have had an effect on you, and yet you appear to be untouched. That is unusual. " He paused for a moment, as if thinking.

"Violet, what aura do you see around Emily?"

"Blue," she answered, surprised to be consulted, "Emily's aura has always been bright blue, the same as ours."

Badru continued to stare at me.

"I must admit, that is unprecedented. Maybe you do have something, Emily."

He stroked his chin thoughtfully.

"Very well, here's my proposition. I find you interesting, Emily, and that has bought you some time. You have until the next full moon. Theo, it would seem the love of your life is not quite as fragile as you think. She has a strength that could be of use to us. If she withstands the initiation, she may join us. Of course, if the crystal destroys her, then our problem is solved. Viyesha, you know what needs to be done?"

"Yes, Badru," she bowed her head.

"For now, I will call my dogs off." He leaned back and smiled at me. "The Twin Assassins, that's how Atsu and Ata are known in the order. Although I warn you, Emily, any step out of line, and I will not be so generous second time around."

"Thank you, Badru." I stared back at him, disliking him intensely, yet all too aware of the power he held.

"Now, one other small matter," said Badru, "How did this woman come to know of our crystal and its youth-bestowing properties? It is a closely guarded secret and I do not know of any lapses in our security. "

Leon, who up to this point had remained silent, now spoke. "We believe we know the source, Badru. Two weeks ago, Joseph disturbed someone in the grounds taking pictures with a telephoto lens. He saw the same individual speaking to Kimberley Chartreuse in the gardens late last night. Turns out he is a private detective known as Mr Nelson, a grubby, two-faced opportunist, who would sell his own grandmother if the price were right. I paid him a visit this morning. He passed on photographs and information to Kimberley Chartreuse, a woman paranoid about aging, in exchange for money."

"I see," said Badru, thoughtfully. "And where is this Mr Nelson now?"

"Disappeared," admitted Leon. "For all his dishevelled appearance, he is clever, with the survival instincts of a cockroach. He simply blended into the background and vanished. But Aquila will find him and silence him."

"Very well," said Badru, "Aquila, your priority is to find this scum before he does further damage. Destroy him."

"Consider it done," said Aquila, in his rasping voice.

Badru looked around the table and smiled pleasantly, as if he'd just chaired the parish council AGM.

"I believe that concludes our business," he said briskly. He turned to me: "Remember, Emily, if you haven't become one of us by the next full moon, you know the consequences. And I won't delegate the task to my twins. I will come for you myself."

He smiled sweetly and, to make his point, removed his dark glasses. I had assumed he would have clear blue eyes, but I was mistaken. I stifled a scream. Instead of beautiful eyes, Badru had red rimmed, empty eye sockets. It was like looking into the face of an angelic demon and an involuntary shudder ran through my body. He spoke in a whisper: "You may think I see nothing, Emily, but I see everything. The mind's eye is so much more powerful." He replaced his dark glasses and rose from the table, then as afterthought, turned and said: "Your friends, Seth and Tash..."

The blood drained from my face. "Yes?" I asked, fearing the worst.

"They were at the hall earlier this afternoon. I've let them go for now. But I shall be watching. If I find out they know anything...." He drew his finger across his throat in a slicing movement.

"Do you understand?"

I nodded, unable to speak.

Badru clicked his fingers and his henchmen rose too. Then, before my eyes, all three disappeared. I stared in disbelief. One minute, they were there, the next they were gone, and simultaneously, the dark emptiness of the torch-lit cavern vanished and I was looking once more at the familiar wood panelling of the library.

32. Family

As before, the de Lucis family sat around the table and the three seats opposite me were empty. The only difference was that Aquila and Pantera were gone.

I turned to Theo, sitting beside me. "Did that happen or did I have a really weird dream?"

He said nothing, but smiled sadly and squeezed my hand. He looked shell-shocked.

Leon spoke: "It happened, Emily. And bravo for defending yourself. There aren't many who could remain so composed under such circumstances."

"Honestly, talk about mind games," said Joseph, in disgust. "Why do they do that?"

"You have to admit, it is kind of cool," answered Violet.

"There was nothing cool about that," said Theo, angrily.

"Okay, everyone, quiet," said Viyesha, holding up her hands. "Emily, I'm sorry you had to go through that, but you should never have taken that woman into the Clock Tower or handled the crystal yourself. It was a dangerous strategy and, but for Pantera's quick action, could have had disastrous consequences."

"It's our fault, mother," said Theo bitterly, "It would never have happened if we hadn't left Emily on her own. The blame lies with us for leaving her exposed and vulnerable."

"True, Theo," answered Viyesha, "but in a strange way, it saved Emily. I have seen Badru destroy people for less, but he's intrigued to know why the crystal had no effect."

She turned to me: "You had a close call, Emily, but you've come through it. Now you've seen The Lunari and know their capabilities. They have conquered death and time, and live according to their own rules. Never underestimate their power."

"Where are they now?" I asked.

"Aquila is taking them to the airport," answered Violet.

"If they've conquered time, can't they just teleport?" I suggested.

"Excellent idea, Emily," laughed Joseph.

"Transference of matter is beyond even their capabilities," said Viyesha, calmly. "What you just experienced, Emily, was a trick of the mind, a powerful form of hypnosis that they have mastered."

"But no less real for existing only in the mind," added Leon. "In fact, all the more dangerous, because imagination is limitless, and in The Lunari's reality you create your own nightmares."

I shivered and felt for Theo's hand. He closed it around mine and I felt his energy flow into my body.

"Well, look on the bright side, at least I've bought myself some time," I said in a cheerful voice that masked my fear.

"Time is all you have, Emily," said Joseph, solemnly. "Your other options have run out. You have no choice but to join our family now."

"Assuming she survives the crystal," Violet reminded him.

I looked around the table and realised how fond I'd become of Theo's family.

"Oh, I'll survive it alright, Violet," I said purposefully. "I survived it earlier on tonight when the crystal was much more powerful. All I have to do is wait for the next full moon. You just watch me."

Theo looked at me angrily, his face white and strained, but he was powerless to argue.

I stared back at him, looking eternity in the face and wondering if I had just made the biggest mistake of my life.

More great books from Hashtag Books
'Demonica' By Will Davis
'Stilts' By Tim O'Rourke
'Gentleman Traitor' Alan Williams
'Barbouze' Alan Williams
'The Beria Papers' Alan Williams

www.hastagbooks.co.uk

Printed in Great Britain
by Amazon.co.uk, Ltd.,
Marston Gate.